Slave Catcher's Woman

A tale of love, intrigue, death and awakening in the Antebellum South

James N. Littlefield

Husky Trail Press LLC

ISBN 978-1-935258-15-5

Library of Congress Cataloging in Publication Data

Cover Illustration: Erin Doherty
Cover Design: Ray Campbell
Illustrations: Erin Doherty
Editor: John Geida
Original Content Editor: Mark Hogan

Husky Trail Press LLC
PO Box 705, East Lyme, CT 06333
www.HuskyTrailPress.com
info@huskytrailpress.com
www.JimLittlefield.com

Manufactured in the United States of America

10 9 8 7 6 5 4 3 2 1

DEDICATION

to Georgia Lee,
my Cynthia,
who shares my name and my life.

CONTENTS

INTRODUCTION

With a barely audible whisper, 301 South Liberty Street gave up its last secret, one it had held within its walls for a hundred and forty-four years. This once stately and proud antebellum home, located in the college town of Milledgeville, Georgia had earlier in the spring of 2008 suffered a bout with fire which had left it uninhabitable in its most recent role as a school dormitory. Roofless, with an open invitation for further decay, it soon became a shadow of its former self and helplessly awaited the inevitable arrival of the wrecking ball. Just days before it was to be demolished, however, a somewhat tattered manuscript was recovered on April 19, 2011 in the basement amidst a pile of old newspapers from the Civil War era. The still legible hand-written pages were crudely held together with what was left of some decaying fabric. Printed boldly on the outer cover was the following inscription:

Coswell Elias Tims

Milledgeville, Georgia

1867

Carefully opening the cover, the first entry appeared written in quite legible, albeit heavily slanted script.

"Well the fact of the matter is…I never expected to be settin my life down on any written-up page. I do suspect the trackin of desperate fugitives may offer more than a passin interest for some folks, but as a general rule I've always believed most of it to have been a private affair. A family or business matter, might be a proper way to think on it. How the Tims brothers raised up their fetch hounds and took to the trail, folks that hired the job done, the money that was made, those that ran…why, many was the things we just sorta kept all to ourselves. And then, course, there's them secrets I suspect others may have kept as well, that are so dark they could barely be whispered, let alone be splashed all over some page where more than our own eyes could get a proper look-see."

"Nevertheless and notwithstandin, I fully admit to takin pen in hand, maybe so's to make a clean breast of things or maybe it would be to profit a man who might be comin up the trail behind me and lookin in my direction for a helpful word or two. I do believe it fair to say that slave catcher Coswell Tims has had more than his share of cuts and bruises over the years, but I would also tell you true that all the pain added in together don't amount to a half pint of humbug when I look to the many blessins life has seen fit to send my way."

"My greatest blessin, so called, come sometime back in the form of a woman by the name of Cynthia. She brought many changes into my life, she did. It may even be fair to say that she lies at the center of this little missive, hard to say for sure. One thing I know for certain is that life ain't been easy for the two of us, but I do believe it is possible for folks to manage their way through the whole of it even though it might take a little doin on their part. Maybe some advice from someone who's been down life's hard trail before might just be the very thing that gets a man on the strain over the hump. In our line of work sometimes me and my brother Jesse often say what is needed is an old dog for a hard trail. Well, I reckon maybe it's time for this ol dog to tell his tale and let the devil take the hindmost."

"I do realize full well the dangers involved here. It is my hope that this slave catcher's tale remains unread well into the foreseeable future. 'A man don't need to dangle from his own hook,' as my daddy, Obadiah Tims, used to say on frequent occasions. I feel sure there will come a time, however, when this here story will see the light of day once more and if it don't, well made me feel good just to write it and I reckon whatever way it turns out, it will suit the likes of Coswell Tims just fine."C.E.T.

Note from Jim Littlefield: The story that follows is drawn from the recollections of a man named Coswell Elias Tims of Milledgeville, Georgia penned shortly after the War Between the States. I could have never imagined for one moment my good fortune when visiting that historic area of the state in the spring of 2011 that I would stumble across such a man who would willingly share with me his personal and private story. In passing this account along to others I have entitled it: "*The Slave Catcher's Woman*" and have added chapter headings and illustrated sketches suggested by his descriptions. Beyond that I have taken few liberties with the manuscript other than transcribing it from the man's original handwriting into modern printed form. It would be my hope that if this individual could somehow miraculously be spotted still walking behind his trusty scent hounds in the backwoods of rural Georgia, he might just pause long enough to tip that wide-brimmed hat of his and nod approval of these efforts made on his behalf.

Chapter 1

ALL NESTLED IN

The life of a slave catcher's woman can be a lonely one indeed. Lookin back I remember it to have been most daylight when I stood with that very woman in the doorway of our small farmhouse on the outskirts of town. Many's the time the two of us stood in just this fashion...maybe on just this spot, both high contractin parties as still as a statue and as quiet as the grave. An observer might offer up the opinion that these two forms was fixed forever in timeless embrace, but as much as my heart may have caught the spirit, I knew there really weren't nothin in this world that could be set in stone and forever is never most like as not. I knew only too well them two forms that was wrapped so tight round one nother at this very moment would soon take their leave...one takin to the trail while the other would take up yet another lonely vigil. I do believe this little scene would like to repeat itself many times over durin our years together. But it is hard on a trackin man as well, to be gone from the place and the one he loves, specially when he knows somewhere deep down his goozle that the runaway he seeks might very well cost him all he leaves behind. Why even a fool a few bricks shy of a full load don't need to be told there's always a cost for doin business.

I could feel strength in my arms as I held the woman tight to me. I guess our many struggles over the years had seen to that. I could feel great strength comin from her as well. I know for a fact that any hound that's let into the house and allowed to sleep away the better part of the day ain't gonna amount to much as a trackin dog when the road gets hard. Cynthia and me, why, we had been down many a hard road together and that's certain-sure to tightin the bond twinxt folks. It was them experiences, bad as some may have been, that I believe may have caused the cheese to bind here.

As I held her to me, my mind began to wander off to other things as I found it was often inclined to do. I reckon this may come natural to a man, as early on in history our forefathers had to always be on the lookout for danger and such and could never afford to think on any one thing for too long a time. Now a woman, she's of a different persuasion. She will notice everythin and anythin and tend to all the important details of life that a man's sure to miss. I am of the opinion that when properly joined up together, a man and a woman can be a powerful machine indeed, maybe just what Mother Nature or the Good Lord had intended when things was first drawed up way yonder.

I found this restless mind of mine to soon settle on the early mornin air and what I might come to expect of the new day. My first inklin was that it had the smell and the feel of a dark and overcast affair with the sun by my reckonin declinin to make an appearance for maybe the better part of the day. It really made no nevermind to me. Fact of the matter is, I believe I have been partial to days like these all my life. Never could figure out why that was so and it remains a puzzlement to me to this very day. Might be as simple as the thrill and excitement of a sudden storm, somethin out of the ordinary you could say, or maybe a day like this puts me in mind of some of the more soberin messages of life, that there's often more in store for folks than just sunshine and happy days.

Like an old friend whose familiar and welcome footsteps you

could hear come cross your porch fore you ever laid an eye on him, an old memory suddenly dropped in for a little visit, replacin any thoughts I had as to the weather. Why I could suddenly see it, just as plain as day, right there in my mind's eye. It was a day very much like this one, but I couldn't have been more than half a leg high at the time, maybe eight or nine years old. It was a good day as I remember, as my daddy had let me take leave of my regular chores and was takin me to a nearby farm to pick out my first hound dog. "Life's bout choices and responsibility," I could still hear Obadiah Tims a-sayin as we braved the threatnin weather together and trudged the several miles over to the Miller place. I seem to recollect that he took his old shotgun and I took that new rifle he and Mamma give me for my birthday, just in case we spied somethin the Tims family might fancy on their dinner table that evenin. I guess it ain't much of an exaggeration to say that young boys in the south learn to shoot and hunt most as early as they learn to walk. We never shot nothin that dark, dreary day, but I remember it bein one of the best days of my life.Yes sir, I loved bein with Daddy. God, I surely did love that hound dog…first one I ever had. I also learned to love the trail and the thrill of the hunt, but the woman, this woman I count myself fortunate nough to now be holdin in my arms, why she come to mean more to me than anythin ever took in a breath.

"I will miss you, darlin," I said finally to Cynthia as I reached back for my wide-brimmed hat that sat by its lonesome on the corner of an otherwise empty table near the open door.

"Oh, Coswell, you hold me close now," she instructed. "You know how I worry when you're gone. It's lonely here with Sanford livin in town and the dogs, well, they really ain't much company."

I give her a good-bye hug, squeezin a might harder than I would if I was just goin off to town or headin out to mend a fence or feed the chickens..

"Now don't you get yourself all in a pucker, sweetheart," I replied. "I only rented out Sanford for a week and I could be back as early as nightfall, maybe tomorrow noon at the latest. All depends on how much of a headstart that big negro over at the Jarratt place got on us. If he runs like most of em do, I figure I'll be back right quick. More like as not he just took to the woods to think things out or cool down some. Often happens when they change owners, get a whippin or loved ones get sold off. When it comes right down to it darkies ain't that hard to figure out and the good thing is when they run they usually don't run far. I'll be takin Beauregard, he's got the best nose of the bunch. Why I will tell ya that dog will have the trail, my brother will be watchin my backside and, my God, woman, the more I think on it now, if things was any better I would have to start in believin I weren't totin fair and maybe start to feel a might guilty bout even bein in this here trackin business."

Tellin her how easy it was all gonna be brought a little smile to her still beautiful face as I tried to reassure her, knowin full well that the manhuntin business did have its fair share of dangers. But as I've often said to her and anyone else over the years that was fool enough to stop and listen, if a fella was to keep his wits bout him and done things right and proper, why he could make a right fair livin at slave catchin and that's a fact.

"You know I wish you would try your hand at another line of work, Coswell. Not just cause of the danger, mind ya. Remember, without you there is no me and you know just what I mean there," Cynthia added, somewhat profoundly as I was bout to turn to leave.

"Let's not talk on this right now," I replied, as I give a quick nod in the direction of two rockin chairs cozied up side by each on our front porch. "There be plenty of time when we be settin right out here with our feet up on them railins and we can give this whole affair all the ruminatin it needs."

I had noticed that Cynthia had been bringin up this subject more regular of late, but she don't know how hard it is for a man to give up a job he is good at, one he's done for some time and one that pays good as it does. Yes sir, returnin two-legged property to their rightful owners, a fella could do quite well. As a general rule he could figure to collect maybe 5% of that slave's total value.To do some quick cipherin here, a slave worth one thousand dollars would generally fetch maybe a fifty dollar bounty, but of course more valuable slaves, missin for long periods of time or runnin long distances could drive the price up considerable. Some slavetakers might realize a two or three hunded dollar reward for the return of a bondsman or woman when all was said and done. I reckon if I was to tally it all up, I would have to admit to makin a more than a respectable livin in this here family business.

Now I knew Cynthia's concerns. Knew em well. Her fear for my safety was heartfelt, but that pleadin tone, well, I never could quite get my arms round the whole of that. Make no mistake bout it, this woman was strong, been through a lot and "come out on the perpendicular," as Daddy liked to say. Sometimes I wondered if she really depended on me all that much or she just kinda knew how much a man needed to feel important and needed in the eyes of a woman. Leastways, I freely admit to lovin her with all that's in me and any time apart I would certainly have to count it up as a loss to my side. Four-legged or two-legged, though, when you strip life down to the barest of essentials...why, it's all bout huntin up food for the table, ain't it? A slave catcher, like any other individual in this life, is obliged to make a livin.

"I'll be fine," I repeated, as I let her hand drop from mine and headed out towards the pen to rouse the sleepin manhunters.

As I closed the door and tried to get my mind right, I set my eyes straight ahead and took to walkin down them wooden front porch steps, musterin all the stength and purpose of an eager young Georgia preacher on his way to deliver up his Sunday sermon. I may have lost a parcel of my resolve, however, when I felt the need to turn back slightly, hopin to catch one last look at this wife of mine. She might just be smilin and restin both her hands on the porch railin or maybe inside wavin and lookin out one of them front porch windows. Could be she had taken to posin with all her feminine charms, big as life back there in the open doorway. Cynthia would often do them things when I come home or when I was leavin to go out on the trail...sometimes make a big production out of the whole of it, she would. I would have to say there weren't a time that happened, when I didn't think back to the very first moment I saw her, walkin regal-like, back and forth on the upper deck of that old steamboat. Maybe more than a few years ago it was now, but it sometimes seems like it was only yesterday. First impressions, I have come to believe, are often the slowest to fade from a man's memory.

But all I could lay claim to seein at that moment was the

house. Smoke risin up from the chimney stack give off a most invitin smell—like to finally draw me full round just like a wind-blown scent will often turn an eager trackin dog. I soon found myself starin blankly at that building, puttin me in mind of a fella I once saw mesmerized at a circus. I remember his eyes was wide open but his head appeared bout as empty as an old deserted barn.

I couldn't help but think back to how hard Cynthia, Sanford and me had worked on this place. Ten acres and an old run-down log house with a few outbuildins, originally built at the turn of the century when the Creeks was leavin and whites was a-movin in, certainly weren't much to brag on when we handed our hard-earned cash money over to the Central Bank. But it sure did look invitin now, makin me wish I was returnin with the fugitive in tow rather than facin the uncertainty of the trail ahead.

Now I would have to say that this house of ours weren't nothin special, raised up on stones as it was with no foundation like many houses in central Georgia.We had put wooden sideboards over the original logs, fixed up the roof where it was all stove in and got that chimney back in fine workin order. Maybe someone from town would chuckle at them hayseed crackers that mixed in the fieldstone with bricks here and there in the old chimney, but we used what we had and only bought what we didn't. If a man were to press me on it, I would have to offer up the opinion that the red in the new bricks blended tolerable with the earthlike colors of the old stones. Guess it only goes to show how things so different can sometime come together to become a family of sorts. Why even the wood on the sides of the place was weatherin nice too, blendin with the landscape the whole of it was nestled in. It was home, it was our home, and I guess Sanford, Cynthia, the dogs and me, we was all pretty much blended in together as well. My guess is that, cept for one experience that still pains me to remember and even has the power to haunt me from time to time, we've been just bout as happy there as is possible in this very difficult and subloonary world.

Shakin myself some, I tried again to get my mind right and tend to what I set out to do. As I walked by the barn I caught sight of the pen Sanford and me had built up for the hounds. It had a roof over the back part of it to protect em from the weather, but it also had a fairly large open area so's they could frolic about. Daddy used to say a pen or a fence should be "mule high, bull strong and pig tight," but these here dogs weren't much on runnin off. They did like to wrassle round some but often slept away the better part of the day. Guess the worst thing they ever done outside of eatin us out of house and home was make the place look like a batttlefield with all the large holes they's always partial to diggin.

My eyes soon come to rest on a confused jumble of five furry faces hangin out over the sides of the pen, all with full complement of oversized noses, tongues and floppy ears. They appeared to be writhin bout like a basket of large furry snakes in eager anticipation of my arrival.

Them big, tough paws that rested atop the wall had much to say bout the critters themselves. Here was an animal born to run, not fast, but steady over any type of ground, born to follow anyone, anywhere and for whatever time might be deemed both fittin and proper. Paws was large, for sure, which kept em from sinkin into the mud of the swamps, yet the pads was tough for when the ground got hard. Long, strong nails to the forefront give em more than a fair chance at a firm purchase on the ground if they were to take a notion to climb a hill or two.

These trackin dogs was large and muscular as well...oversized in general I would have to say. Why they was most as tall as a man when standin full up on their hind legs. They was all glad to see ol Coswell and crowded round when I opened up the pen door. Daisy Mae, the smallest of the bunch, she stood back apiece like she often done, but soon joined in after addin a little tongue to the still mornin air.

Now it is a fact that some slavetakers will use most any kind of dog for their work, (cept'n a white one, of course, as even a sorry fool knows a white dog can't smell worth a lick) but these here dogs, all presently beggin for my attention, was all cut from the same piece of cloth. The bloodhound weren't called the "the nigger dog" round these parts for nothin, as they proved time and time agin their ability to return those of em that took a notion to run. It is my understandin that this critter gets its name from its pure-blooded lines that can be traced back a thousand years or so, not on account of it sniffs or is partial to any smell or taste of blood. It was the only dog the Tims brothers fancied. We have had more than our fair share over the years and we knowed from experience they was the finest trackers in the world. There was no doubt in our minds that they, probably more than anythin else, was responsible for Jesse's and my success in this family trackin business. "COSWELL AND JESSE TIMS—MASTERS OF HOUNDS," just like our advertisement in the *Southern Recorder* and *Federal Union* newspapers read. Why we had no trouble believin we was the best in the business and I come to figure most people round the central part of Georgia would either agree with that statement, or would be hard pressed to name anyone better. Folks that hired us knew the reputation of our ketchhounds and knew full well the reputation of the Tims boys that owned and trained em up. I believe it fair to say a slaveowner would be as certain-sure as a man can be in this uncertain life that when they hired it done with the Tims boys, they knew they now had the best chance possible of gettin back lost two-legged property that had somehow strayed from their care.

Beauregard needed no wakenin when he set his eyes on me. All the dogs knew that saddlebags slung over the shoulder with a faint rattle of chains inside and the presence of a trackin harness in one hand and a sawed-off shotgun in the other weren't just a daily visit for feedin or tendin the pen. No sir, they knew it was a sure sign that the fun was to soon start in commencin. Their movements told me all of em was up for the task, but Beauregard, why he didn't seem the least bit surprised when I singled him out for the job. Like Jesse and me, that dog had no trouble believin he was the best in the business.

Now the two of us needed to meet up with my brother Jesse over at his place, which was bout a mile to the south. From there we would take our horse and the dog down to the Jarratt plantation just a short distance away where this little adventure would have its beginnin. It would be there that if past times be any guide, things just might start in a-hoppin like peas on a hot shovel.

Walkin with the dog on the lead beside me, I breathed in the early mornin air and got to thinkin bout Cynthia's last words to me. They was heartfelt and somewhat hauntin. "Without you, there is no me," I repeated under my breath as I shut my eyes briefly and remembered squeezin her small, white, somewhat calloused hands in mine as I took my leave.

The day hadn't got much brighter when the dog and me finally come on Jesse's place. The sun would normally be peekin through the piney woods over to the east at this time, but even without the sun, Jesse's house was still a welcome sight. Made me think again on how I fancied a day such as this one here.

Actually, the more I thought on it, maybe takin to days of this nature was just a practical matter. You see, I knew as a long time trackin man that the scent a fugitive would leave behind under these here conditions would be heavy and drawed down to the ground, with the dog generally makin short work of its responsibilities. Maybe it was all just as simple as that. You see a bloodhound will track on a balmy day with its head up, nose all a-quiver, lookin to the bushes and the air for clues, but on a day like this one, why they will just drop their nose to the trail and follow up behind. I reckoned that if things went the way they do most times, in short order ol Beauregard would be down on that scent and have no trouble deliverin up its rightful owner. Why then me and Jesse could return the fugitive to its rightful owner, so that rightful owner could then rightfully pay us for our services. Ain't it grand the way nature just sorta rightfully sorts itself out and follows along on its own natural course?

Arrivin at Jesse's house, I walked up the worn, wooden stairs to a rather run-down porch. The whole house showed the neglect that can come when a man loses a woman. I banged on the door rather forcefully. "Jesse, you up yet?"

"I'm right here and I'm ready to go," come an immediate reply from within. Jesse opened the door and throwed his worn frock coat over that old striped shirt of his that come to have more holes in it than trackin jobs the Tims brothers have taken on over the years. His tall, slender frame and weatherbeaten appearance always brought a smile to my face and today weren't no exception. Although five years older than me, Jesse Tims probably looked a darn site older than that in the eyes of most folks, maybe due to all he had been through. He has his own ways bout him, maybe even borderin on the peculiar, but then I've been knowin Jesse all my life and can willingly raise my right hand and testify fore God and my fellow man that there ain't a finer individual a-livin here today in the state of Georgia.

"Got a need to make some money and uphold the law at the same time," Jesse announced. "Real pillars of the community we are there, little brother."

I always hated it when Jesse poked fun at our callin. As sure as God made little chickens, trackin people that was runnin from the law was a benefit to the public good. It's true that some folks looked down on slavecatchers, but it was both legal and necessary. Me and Jesse was upstandin, lawbidin citizens, for sure, not like them peckerwoods who was landless individuals, unable to read or write a lick and took to trackin just cause they could do nothin else. I guess more trackers than not did fit this general description, but my brother and me, why I come to believe some time back that we was more than a cut above them boys. We got ourselves some good book-learnin from Mr. Denison thanks to Daddy and the money he made down in his blacksmith shop. With very little free-schoolin in Georgia at the time, my brother and me have always figured our education to have set us apart and been a true benefit and blessin.

Thinkin back, I remember the plantation owner, Mr. Jarratt, had been quite clear that this would be no ordinary fugitive we'd be a-trackin this day. Big Sandy had run off three or four times in the last couple of years and had been whipped repeatedly all to no good end. Even the threat of castration and constant reminders that he could be sold down the river where he was assured conditions was much worse than the Jarratt place, did nothing to change Big Sandy's disposition. He remained as ornery and uncooperative as ever.

He was a big strappin fella, well over six feet tall and the weight of maybe two men. Big Sandy still had value for studdin even if he refused the regular field work assigned to him. Many slaves resented this contrived matin arrangement, but just as a slave master could terminate a relationship if he took a mind to, he also had the power to encourage one, specially if it was to profit him in some way. Just like one of my neighbors says regardin his farm stock: "they should all be multiplyin and replenishin accordin to scripture." And make no mistake bout it, slaves was plantation stock, property that needed careful tendin if'n they was to turn a profit.

Jarratt told my brother Jesse and me that Big Sandy needed to be caught if for no other reason than to serve as an example to others. Defyin the master was not to be tolerated in plantation society as that small, closed-in community operated under the direction of its white master and white or black overseer and any challenge to that arrangement could have contagious consequences. Whatever Jarratt had in mind when we brought the big fella back, me and Jesse both figured it was probably the end of the line for Big Sandy. The punishment would most likely be very severe and very public.

Jarratt met us down at the slave quarters where Big Sandy had slept the night before and after exchangin a few pleasantries, we asked him if he had a scent item that the dog could lock on to. It was real important that the dog be given a little clue at this time as to the identity of the fugitive in question, somethin he could take up his nose and hold there for future review on the trail ahead. Jarratt disappeared directly into one of the slave cabins that flanked the dirt road out behind the Big House. I noticed the windows and doors of them cabins all faced the Big House and not each other. A curious arrangement someone might think till they realized it give certain folks in high places the best possible chance to keep an eye on the comins and goins of all who lived there. Beauregard sat patiently by my side unaware and unconcerned bout such architectural matters.

I could feel a slight tremble of anticipation comin from the large hound dog as I reached down and stroked his soft, furry head. I could feel the bony ridge to the back of the skull, which many believed was these talented dogs "knowin knot," the imagined source of their strange and almost mystical powers.

Now this bloodhound, Beauregard, was a fine trackin dog to be sure, weighin maybe 130 pounds. Very strong and with great endurance, I couldn't remember a time when this flop-eared critter didn't do his job proper-like and make his masters both proud and maybe a little more prosperous as well. He reminded both Jesse and me of his daddy, Cooper, who was also a big red and had been our finest tracker right up to the day when he got hisself gator-bit trackin down in the swamp. Out of nowhere this infernal reptile rose to the surface and snatched the dog from me, takin him under with a pull and a twist, leather lead and all. Why, the thing liked to have dragged me along for the ride if my hand hadn't shook lose of the leather grip, leavin me muddy, wet and on my knees, sorrowful but thankful there weren't two casualties to be tallied up that day.

Dogs of this quality are very expensive, not only in the buyin but in the investment in their trainin and care. I seem to recall a fella up in Moore County, South Carolina, who paid some $1500 for a pack of ten bloodhounds at auction, but I think the most I ever heard a man give for one bloodhound trackin dog was $300.00. This weren't no barnyard mutt, mind ya, that every farmer's got ten of and needs but one. The loss of a bloodhound, any bloodhound, would be a serious business expense for any individual in this line of work.

"This should do just fine," Jarratt said, returnin from the cabin and wavin a piece of slave cotton in the air that our runaway had slept on the night before. Beauregard began to stir a bit, but continued to sit, bidin his time.

Before I took the item, I turned to Jesse as I always done and asked him if the horse and all the supplies was in good workin order. "Whenever you're ready, Coswell," he reported, as I made Beauregard sit quietly once more to complete the last of this little ritual. As the dog sat next to me I slipped the heavy leather trackin harness over his head and as it come to rest on his back, I reached to the sides and fastened up the buckles, lastly attatchin a twenty-foot leather lead to the iron ring atop the whole affair. It has been our experience that once the scent item was presented to the dog it was bout all the quiet an animal of this general persuation could stand, so everythin needed to be readied-up beforehand. Jarratt handed me that piece of slave cotton and I put it to the dog's nose, givin that big red hound all the sniffin he thought necessary.

"Find!" I yelled at last, grippin down hard on the end of the lead which I held tightly in my hand, anticipatin the violent shock soon to come. Sure nough, with a mighty tug in a direction of his choosin, the eager manhunter pulled me forward.

I knew a black fugitive somewhere out there led the way. A large and determined trackin hound now followed an unknown distance behind. Coswell Tims, well, he was to be found exactly twenty feet to the rear of that big red dog and brother Jesse and his horse, they was less than a stone's throw back, bringin up the last of this little caravan. We was now all on our way. I believe every heart to have been beatin fast, as the thrill of the hunt worked its way through both man and beast. "God, I love this job!" I remembered sayin to myself, but later on this day I would recall makin that very statement, and I believe I shook my head in disbelief at the time and vowed never to offer up a premature judgement like that one ever again as long as there was a breath of air to be had inside me.

Chapter 2

ON THE TRAIL

"Good luck, fellas," the plantation master shouted as we headed out into the field.

"We'll bring em home, Mr. Jarratt, if'n we have to go through hell and half of Georgia to do it," I yelled back, tryin to keep both my feet under me and keep pace with the big hound dog all at the same time.

I think the one thing that needs sayin from the get-go here is that the pull of a bloodhound ain't nothin a man should take on lightly. Ol Jeremy Prigg, who done his fair share of trackin in his younger days, used to say a man ownin a bloodhound trackin dog always stood out from other dog owners cause the poor fella, upon close examination, would be found to have one arm considerable longer than the other. Now I always figured that to have been somewhat of an exaggeration, maybe even a bold-faced lie, but without givin the whole idea too much extra thought, I did, after a spell, find myself switchin that lead to my other hand.

Now there is one other thing I need to say bout this here trackin business. It is near impossible to do the job proper-like all by your lonesome, it's at least a two-man undertakin. One individual ain't gonna keep up with a bloodhound on foot over a long period of time if'n he's let loose, so the dog needs to be on a lead. On account he often goes into the underbrush and such, it makes it near impossible to track from a horse. A man does need a horse for supplies... food and water for trackers and dogs, shackles and bindin rope for restrainin the prisoners. Scattergun, whip and various other items also needed to be figured into the general mix. One fella on a horse and another leadin the way behind the dog, separated by just a thin, twenty foot leather lead. The man on the ground and the dog, of course, they was the most important part of this here machine. They had to be trustin in each other's skills to have any chance of makin the hunt successful.

Jesse and me had spent so much time with our animals over the years, it was most like we knew the workins inside them droopy, wrinkled-skinned heads. There was some invisible world of scent and images a-workin there for sure, hard for most folks to understand, but somehow, most mysterious-like, these dogs seemed to be able to link up the scent item with the individual that left it behind. It was for this that the bloodhound was bred and made him prized over all other dogs by any serious tracker. Jesse often says when I start in philosophizin on the subject as I am often inclined to do, that a fella don't need to understand the whole process, he just needs to appreciate the results.

"Where in tarnation's this boy goin?" Jesse yelled from the horse as the dog took to followin the trail east towards the river.

"I wouldn't be surprised if he weren't headed for water, Jesse," I replied. "Probably thinks takin a bath might just improve his chances of gettin away."

Well, it become obvious to us after the first half mile or so just what Big Sandy had on his mind. He had gone east to the Oconee River for a little swim fore continuin on to the south. Instead of headin for freedom in the north like many black runners done, he was runnin south, towards the swamps of southern Georgia and Florida. There was more than a few of his kind that had tried that escape route over the years, specially when Spain had owned that territory earlier in the century. Them Spanish devils, maybe the cruelest of slave owners, was all for settin American slaves free, not out of any humanitarian sense mind ya, but in an effort to weaken the southern economy. Also, the difficulty of the terrain favored the fugitive over the tracker. The Great Dismal Swamp up there on the North Carolina-Virginia border was another place black fugitives often sought safe haven. In the Okefenokee as well, them snakes, mosquitoes, red bugs and yellow flies, along with the swampy terrain made the slavetaker's job near impossible. Big Sandy weren't no fool. He must have heard the stories on the plantation and figured this to be his last best chance.

Well, the big negro's plan didn't work worth a cent, leastways the first piece of it. I have often said that a man runnin from a bloodhound who tries to lose his scent by walkin round in water will succeed in one thing only...gettin his feet wet! Why I have seen bloodhounds track right in the water, even track in a boat and go right to the very spot where a man has drowned up. I have witnessed first hand bloodhounds take to swimmin right behind their black quarry who figured to outsmart or outswim their four-legged pursuers. Scent will hang on the water just like it clings to the land and a bloodhound trackin dog ain't gonna be fooled by this kind of shecoonery any more than he would be if a runaway were to stop and add a touch of kiam pepper mixed up with lard to the bottoms of their feet as they often foolishly attempt to do.

Just as we figured, Beauregard picked up the trail where Big Sandy come out of the river. That fella might have been a might cleaner, but he still had that dog and the Tims boys on his trail, makin the whole thing somewhat of an exercise in futility. An occasional human footprint in the red clay or the sandy soil along the way told us our hound was doin a respectable job followin up behind his nose.

We had been trailin Big Sandy for several hours when I heard Jesse yell over from the horse. "Coswell, you want to switch up and I take the trail for awhile?"

"Nah, Jesse," I said, turnin round. "You bein older and all, I don't want you to strain yourself cause of your advanced age," I added, tryin to get a little smile to replace that serious expression most people come to expect of the likes of Jesse Tims. "Sides, I think we're startin to close in. We've been trackin steady and Big Sandy is gonna go cautious in the daylight."

"Alright there Little Brother, but leastways let's stop and water the animals fore too long," Jesse countered. "Can't say as I want that dog's nose dryin up any time soon."

It's a certain-sure fact that a dog with a dry nose will no longer be able to track a man. It's also often the case that after a bloodhound locks on to a scent that food, water and sometimes even relievin themselves is often put on hold. Some dogs will piss up a storm, but I remember ol Cooper, Beauregard's daddy, would wait till he spotted the fugitive fore he'd finally lift up his back leg and tend to any personal business.

Bloodhounds ain't stupid but they can sometimes appear to take leave of their senses when they head out on the trail. I remember a friend of mine over in Macon lost a bloodhound on the railroad tracks. Let him run free, he did. That dog never paid no never-mind to that oncomin train as he was too busy sniffin up a storm. I would tell you firsthand that a locomotive is large, smells God-awful like fire and brimstone, and often whistles well in advance of it ever comin into view. It don't go that fast neither, but that train made short work of that hound, it surely did, and as I remember ol Joe Harris found very little left of his prize trackin dog to take home and bury on the family farm.

Jesse's suggestion, though, was a good one. We had been trackin steady for bout four hours and it was approachin mid-day when we stopped for the first time. The day looked to clear some and I knew the dog would have his nose off the ground soon, sniffin bushes, trees and air for those last few last clues he needed to finish up the job.

"Hand that water over here, Jesse," I said. "I think my nose is dryin up."

That got a little chuckle out of my older brother, but the fact is that trackin in the late summer Georgia heat even on a cloudy day like this one was pretty drainin business. My wide-brimmed straw hat was more than a might wet on the inside and my clothes, trousers, shirt, vest, coat, well, they all took to lookin like I just jumped off one of them small steamboats that come by Milledgeville on their way up and down the shallow Oconee River. The pistol that hung at my side felt like it weighed a site more than it did a few hours ago when we had first left the Jarratt place. Lookin over at my brother I could tell he weren't farin much better even though he was ridin. The heat of midday was wearin on him as well.

"Let's get goin," Jesse finally said after a short rest. I handed him the water jug. The dog moved anxiously about and shook his head violently from side to side, a trait common to the breed. Bloodhounds do that, and, course, slobber flies off every which- a-way, but me and Jesse think that this is just the natural way this animal clears out past images and memories and readies up that ol sluethin nose for some new delights headed in their direction. After all, a dog can't just blow his nose into a comfortable old handkerchief like a fella can, can he?

We was on the trail, oh, maybe nother half hour or so, when we began to sense a change in the way Beauregard was goin bout his business. His movements had quickened for sure, as he would lift up his head with the end of his nose all a-quiver, only to quickly return it to the ground and begin rootin round, remindin me of one of them unwelcome critters that might come into the family garden from time to time to try to quick help hisself to some stolen delight. This agitated sort of behavior told Jesse and me we was gettin mighty close.

Despite the excitement, my mind got to wanderin some as it often does, back to a poem about bloodhound tracking dogs, our teacher Mr. Denison had shared with Jesse and me many years ago. I believe the poem was written in Scotland way back in the Middle Ages or some time akin to that.

"Hark, hark the deep-mouthed bark
Nigher, still and nigher.
Burst on the trail the dark bloodhound,
Tawny muzzle sniffs the ground,
And red eyes shoot fire!"

Why, it weren't more than two ticks of the clock later when ol Beauregard give out a hoarse, ringin, bloodcurdling bay, the kind that folks come to associate with that particular animal. The dog began to pull me with all his might towards a large grove of scaly-bark hickory. With that tawny muzzle fully commited to the ground before him, I knew the heavy and abundant skin from Beauregard's head, neck and shoulders had fallen forward, droopin his eyes considerable and exposin the red that lay beneath. I'll be bound if that poet didn't have it just right, but I'll bet he never had the foggiest notion when he penned them words that when this happens, it makes a bloodhound most full blind, forcin the dog to rely more and more on that large sensitive nose of his. Mother Nature must have had big plans for this critter to have made double-certain-sure its nose would be leadin the way.

The dog's tawny muzzle was, indeed, sniffin at the ground and I found myself directed rather forcefully over towards that grove of trees. Jesse followed up close behind.

It seemed like all three of us must have looked up at the same time and caught sight of a large black form, maybe 20 or 30 feet off the ground, doin his level best to flatten out a large, muscular body gainst the trunk of that tree. Beauregard threw his head back and issued a long, drawn-out howl. I looked over to Jessse and Jesse returned the glance. I noticed we both come to have matchin smiles painted up on our faces. We had him for sure, and my guess was that Big Sandy, seein all this from his lofty perch, also had to be of like mind. This black man had run from his white master for the last time.

The dog's nose was all a-twitchin and he had taken to lookin skyward as we reached the base of the tree. I craned my neck upward also but took a little time so's to clear my throat and mind and think on the proper message I needed to send up to our dark-skinned fugitive.

"Big Sandy," I finally announced, "I am here to tell ya that your runnin days are at an end. You come down and I promise not to let the dog have at ya or whip your black hide. You have my word on that. Now you come down out of that tree right now, you hear?"

An instant reply: "No sir, no way dis nigger comin down!"

I waited just a minute to digest his remarks fore sendin back a response of my own, but then did so this time a little louder so's to make my point. "I'm gonna make a strong suggestion that you rethink your position up there. Time is money and the longer you sit up in this tree, the more money you are costin us and the more you cost us, the less friendly we are gonna be. Do you take my meanin?" I asked.

After a short pause, I thought I heard a somewhat muffled response, most like the fella was talkin out loud to hisself. "I not gwine back, not on yaw life. I die fust!"

"I heard that," I shot back, "and I can certainly arrange for that very thing to be the case!" Now hearin nothin from up in the tree, I turned to my brother who had just dismounted from our horse and presently stood, as he did on frequent occasions, right by my side.

"Jesse, I would appreciate it very much if you would fetch me that shotgun off the horse and…and if you would be so kind, maybe you could put a little rock salt down one of them barrels." We had often used this technique before to get uncooperatives out of the trees. That double-barrelled shotgun was a sawed-off affair, mind ya, that spreads the shot out pretty good and that rock salt could be pretty persuadin without bein lethal.

With powder and salt tamped down the barrel and a cap applied to the nipple, Jesse handed me the shotgun as I repeated my request.

"Big Sandy...it ain't no use resistin now. This be your last chance. You get your black ass down on this ground this very minute or there is gonna be hell to pay," I said, as I began to draw a bead on the dark form barely visible through the lower branches of the tree.

As soon as he got the word "no" out of his mouth, I fired at the backside of his trousers and like many times over the years (maybe thanks to Daddy) I hit just the spot where I was aimin. I knew that it shocked and stung the big negro, musta felt like a nest of hornets had just taken up residence somewhere inside his britches. It was downright amazin to Jesse and me how fast this individual chose to come down out of that tree. I admit to bein of the general opinion that sometimes a person just needs a little gentle persuasion to come round to the proper way of thinkin.

I do have to say that it was at this time that I thought I saw somethin…somethin gleamin out the backside of Big Sandy's trousers. Didn't know for sure, maybe the sun that had now started to riz up had caught a reflection or maybe the speed at which the negro dropped played tricks with my eyes, but for whatever reason I did not react. I guess that was probably cause I was unsure of what I had seed. Now I knew for a fact that indecision has taken its fair share of casualties with folks over the years, but ain't it also true that we all hope to be an exception if there was to be any general rule?

I had let go of Beauregard's lead when I took the shotgun from my brother and that dog was right there by his own account at the bottom of the tree when Big Sandy reached the ground. As I remember, that dog did what was often right and proper for many bloodhounds to do when they completed a chase and that was to attempt to put his front paws right up there on the fugitive's shoulders and get ready to deliver a big old sloppy hound dog tongue full on the face. This was sort of the official endin of the game of hide and seek the dog was playin in his mind. It's true that there are trackin dogs that will tear a runner to pieces, but these nigger bloodhounds are a lot gentler than their reputation makes em out to be. In all the years we worked with these dogs, we only had one I recall ever bit a man and lookin back on it, I think I would have bit the man myself had not the dog had the good sense to beat me to it.

I would like to disremember what happened next, cause it was at this very point in time when Big Sandy took out from the back of his britches the biggest Bowie knife I'd ever laid my eyes on. Why the thing had to have had a blade more than a foot long. I watched helplessly in horror as he plunged that knife hard into the side of my fine, fine hound dog. Beauregard dropped to the ground with a whimper. There weren't no doubt in my mind it was a mortal wound for sure.

My brother was close, too close to Big Sandy to give a good account of hisself. He had been holdin the shackles and bindin rope in his hands and had been countin on the dog to steady the runaway and make it possible to ready him up for the trip back to the plantation. I heard myself yell out most like one would do in a dream.

"J e s s e . . . J e s s e . . . t h e k n i f e!"

After stabbin the dog, Big Sandy had quick drawed back his arm, ready to strike once again. I could see the big knife full well, now covered with the blood of my hound, and as I shouted to Jesse, the big negro lunged in his direction. Jesse turned to avoid bein stabbed in the chest, but the desperate fugitive did succeed in drivin a good part of that steel blade right into my brother's left shoulder. Jesse first dropped to one knee, screamin in pain, but shortly fell silently in a heap just like Beauregard had done previous. Fearin the fugitive would strike the mortal blow if he hadn't done so already, I throwed myself full at the attacker, grabbin at the knife in his hand, just hopin for the best.

Now a knife fight can be a terrible experience, that's a fact, and I hate to admit the misfortune of bein party to two others in the course of my lifetime. Never took to that type of engagement, not like that famous slave dealer Jim Bowie fella who seemed to fancy it. But to tell the truth and maybe shame the devil here, I need to say straight out that I also never had the misfortune to have been the bottom dog in a fight and I full well didn't intend on changin that fact any time soon.

As I fell upon Big Sandy we both struck the ground hard and the long, sharp object in his hand flew harmlessly off to the side. Feet, arms, hands and legs all got swung round and then got joined in together as we rolled in the dirt, each man tryin to gain some advantage over the other. Some early blows was struck from both quarters, but I must confess that I lost all track of time, and don't remember entirely all that happened. I do remember we both got tuckered out pretty quick and soon found ourselves quietly locked in each other's embrace. It was a moment I will never forget. We looked each other square in the eye, we did, and for one brief instant it most seemed like I could see right into this black man's soul and seen all he had been through in his life. All the runnin, the whippin, all the pain and humiliation that come with his enslaved condition. His skin, I noticed for the first time, was darker than most of his kind and the white arms and hands that clung tightly to him was all the whiter for the contrast. Suddenly, Big Sandy, recognizin this slave catcher for the adversary he always knew him to be, crashed his black forehead directly into the middle of my face, endin any thoughts I had on quiet reflection.

"Son-of-a-bitch!" I yelled out, knowin full well he had broke my nose. We continued to wrassle round on the ground with the blood from my nose findin itself generously distributed over the both of us, makin anythin either one of us tried to grab hold of both sticky and slippery all at the same time.

Big Sandy was as strong as he was desperate, but I was more than a might wrathy myself. Fear, anger and desperation was all workin on me pretty good. Finally, I pushed him away best I could, and brought my knee up quick, luckin up by catchin the big fella full in the crotch. He give out a grunt and released me momentarily, just long enough to free up my right hand and reach into the holster which was positioned backwards on my left side. If there had been an eye-witness to the whole sorry affair, why I suspect he would have said I should have shot Big Sandy straightaway, but I reckon my instincts to protect my brother must have outweighed the intelligent thing to do. Seizin the advantage, I drawed back the hammer of my Colt and come to stick the muzzle hard up under Big Sandy's left cheekbone. The runaway's eyes growed wider and wider, "cotton-eyed" as folks like to say and the wider them eyes got, for some reason the more excited I become. I was most out of breath at this time, but I remember shoutin somethin bout how I was now in a position to oblige that earlier request for freedom. "You...you are now free to meet your Maker, Big Sandy," I fairly screamed in his face. My trigger finger twitched just slightly, maybe out of nervousness or excitement it was, but damn if it weren't just enough to bring this fugitive's earthly life to a loud and screechin halt.

The roar of that pistol goin off inches from my face most deafened me. When I opened up my eyes, I looked through the powder smoke still comin from the gun barrel and I couldn't believe the damage that had been done. Gore, that had once been the back of Big Sandy's head, was spread out over the ground and over much of me as well. It was a sickenin sight to behold. I got up half expectin to find Jesse dead. My brother lay there moanin but alive, a huge gash in his shoulder. He was holdin on to his arm.

"Jesse, you alright?" I asked excitedly, wipin one brain-stained hand on my trousers and wipin my bloody nose on the sleeve of my coat.

"That black bastard took me by surprise," Jesse managed to say as he winced in pain. "I guess it's a good thing I got me a little brother to watch my backside."

I bandaged up Jesse best I could, usin some pieces of cloth I ripped from the back of the dead negro's shirt. I buried my dog in a shallow grave usin a cookin pan we had brought along and usin some of the bindin rope that had fallen to the ground during the scuffle (and usin that very tree the fugitive had once selected for refuge) I managed to hoist the dead man's body up onto the back of the horse. We knew full well we would probably get no reward for bringin him back, but at least Jarratt would have proof to show the others down in the quarters that for their kind, escape was near impossible and the sooner these folks made peace with that fact, the better it would go for the lot of em.

I looked again at the form now draped over the back of the horse as Jesse, with some difficulty, got up into the saddle for the long and painful ride home. My mind got to thinkin that just a short time ago Big Sandy had been full of strength, hope and life, a far cry from the busted institution I now saw before me. Jesse caught me starin at the mutilated corpse and I could tell he was wonderin what was on his younger brother's mind.

"I guess this is just the cost of doin business," I offered, hunchin up my shoulders some. Jesse cringed in pain as his shoulder begged a little more of his attention, but he give me a knowin nod nonetheless, fore returnin to the uncomfortable task of tryin to set up a might straighter in the saddle.

I felt for my pocketwatch to check the time of day. After all, time is money to a businessman. The chain had been tore clear off the vest pocket. I thought back to Cynthia and I knew full well I had some explainin to do bout this whole unfortunate affair if there was to be any mendin done.

The journey home was a long and quiet one. I missed Beauregard already, but the anger that I felt towards his killer soon began to subside. With the horse, the rider, and the dead passenger in full view before me, I took notice of the black man's empty hands which hung down limp-like on one side of the horse, reachin most as close to the ground as did his bare feet on the other side. The loose limbs of the dead body swayed slightly from side to side, in rhythm with the horse's steady gait. A fair-sized openin, courtesy of Coswell Tims, could be seen on the back side of Big Sandy's nappy head.

I began to get an uneasy feelin that maybe I had not seen the last of the likes of Big Sandy. He might just be returnin…if not in my thoughts, then maybe in my dreams, maybe long after this day was over. I could feel a dark cloud start to come right over me, despite the appearance of the sun which, after great effort, had finally rizzed up by mid-afternoon only to now hang a little lower in the west in anticipation of yet another day come and gone.

I found myself at this moment wishin I had chosen some other line of work, just like my lovin wife had offered up earlier this very mornin. This weren't the way things was supposed to be. This weren't the way a chase ended. Of course experience told me runaways had been kilt or brought back unfit for work before, but I knew that I just didn't feel quite right bout what had happened here and the part Coswell Tims had played in it. I don't know why, but I soon found myself lookin down at my hands, maybe to see if any trace of today was upon em. I could see nothin and then remembered earlier wipin em pretty clean. I know my eyes must have growed bout as wide as Big Sandy's, however, when I spotted a small white sliver of bone on the lower part of my soiled coat sleeve. I pulled it from the fabric. I believed it to be a piece of Big Sandy's skull! A shiver went through the whole of me and I noticed my hand shakin slightly as I held that small piece of evidence up to the light of day.

"Oh Coswell," I heard a voice from somewhere say, "maybe it ain't for your eyes to see, but you have got blood on your hands for sure and make no mistake now, that blood ain't gonna be washed away no matter how many times you make light of the matter by tellin yourself this here is just the cost of doin business."

I shot a quick look up at my business partner to see if it was him that had spoke up, but Jesse was a-settin straight up on that horse with his mouth and eyes closed tight shut. I did notice, however, that his head was slowly noddin up and down with every step the horse took, and I suppose a good lawyer fella might just make the case that he looked to be in full agreement with any voice I thought I just heard.

I looked away, lookin down again at hands that most often as not will do a mind's biddin. I looked once more down the road before me. Did I really need to kill that nigger, I thought to myself. Did I really need to take his life as the man lay helpless before me? Jarret would have probably killed him anyway, I reasoned in, so the result would most likely be the same now wouldn't it? Maybe the whole thing was just an accident, as I didn't think I really squeezed that trigger hard enough for the gun to go off even though somehow it did.

I wondered what lurked round the next bend. My mind was heavy with pieces that seemed to be all in place a short time ago but somehow now seemed either missin or now moved from their comfortable and familiar location. It was right then and there, I come to figure, that them hauntin words crept in again, maybe to fill up the empty space. "This is just the cost of doin business. This here is all just the cost of doin business. You knew all long that there was a cost for doin business, didn't you Mr. Tims?" Them words echoed round and round inside my head and I began to feel I would go bout as crazy as a betsy bug if I didn't soon take to screamin out loud.

Shakin hisself full awake, Jesse Tims suddenly blurted out from high atop his horse: "Uh, uh...Coswell did I hear you say somethin?"

Now I knew full well there was no one in this world that knew me better than my brother. Tryin to get my mind right I took care to form up my words in proper fashion as I took off my hat and wiped away the little beads of sweat that had took up residence there on my forehead.

"Don't know what you heard, Jesse, but I do believe I said nothin t'all," I managed to finally say. I saw my brother nod without a word and close his eyes once more but for some reason I felt the need to add under my breath: "Less you can read my mind or Coswell Tims here has suddenly taken to doin all his thinkin out loud for the whole God damn world to take notice!"

Chapter 3

HOME, SWEET, HOME

It was most nightfall when we spotted the familiar stately brick buildings, broad sandy streets and the well laid out public squares befittin the capital of our fair state of Georgia. Milledgeville had been home to the Tims family for all of my lifetime. My daddy, Obadiah, and my mamma, Hattie Tims, settled here back in '03 (two years fore I was born) after the land was declared open by the federal government. They got the land in a lottery system where tickets was printed up that equaled the number of people in the state eligible for the draw. Each ticket had a district and lot number written on it and folks drew from a large box after a proper shuffle. I reckon them Creek Indians had run up more than a few tradin debts with whites and had to settle up with the loss of much of their land. It weren't long after that plans was set in motion to make this centrally-located place on the west bank of the Oconee River the state's capital. Of course that was many decades ago and Milledgeville has changed considerable from the sleepy log cabin farms of the early

Tims family.

"How you doin, Jesse?" I asked after a rather long period of silence. Jesse continued to stare down the trail ahead, still astride his horse. It most seemed like we had said very little to each other since the events of midday. I knew for a fact I was feelin my share of regret over what had happened back there on the trail and the profanity I had offered up in its aftermath. I reckoned the two of us each had our own kind of pain and felt the need to keep to ourselves for a spell, but after a fashion Jesse did speak up.

"I've been better," was his simple answer, still lookin straight ahead. "But I'm sure this ain't nothin ol Doc Fort can't handle."

Jesse had great faith in Dr. Tomlinson Fort despite the fact that the man was unable to save Jesse's wife Becky from the pox back in '41. Over the years Milledgeville has had more than its fair share of health problems, with summer generally seein the worst of it. Tuberculosis, typhus, scarlet fever, the bloody flux, typhoid, bilious fever, all pretty common, specially in them early days when folks was first settlin in.

Becky, she got the spots on the tongue and mouth, then the rash and raised bumps all over the whole of her durin the summer of that very year. It was smallpox, for sure. Poor woman was in pretty bad shape when we called for the doc, but I never knowed a man to work more tirelessly on another's behalf than did Dr. Tomlinson Fort.

We all remembered that it had been the doc's stated intention to stay with Becky throughout her quarantine. She had been placed in the old pesthouse on the outskirts of town which was generally considered right and proper at the time for people who had fallen victim to contagious diseases. Many of the townsfolk, however, fearin for their own safety, had held an emergency town meetin and were crammed in down at the local saloon tryin to stop the doc from treatin Jessie's wife altogether for fear of spreadin the disease to others. Dr. Fort and Jesse had to use a ladder to get up to the window of her padlocked sick house and the fact that both men carried a firearm at their side, why, that testified to their firm intention to stay with this woman till she either got better or took a turn for the worse.

Becky soon come to know she weren't gonna make it and just bout told Jesse as much. It was hard to mistake her meanin when she said she suspected that she weren't never gonna see the home they both loved again. My brother never cried till that very day (that I know of) and I don't believe the man has squeezed out a single tear since. Two days later Becky was dead and in the ground, but Jesse never blamed the doc, no sir. Fact of the matter was, he never soured on the man, not by a jugful. Jesse admired his courage and knew he had risked life, limb and livelihood tryin to save his patient, a woman who just happened to be the one love of my brother's life.

We crossed over Fishin Creek and headed up Liberty Street to Doctor Fort's place. It stood right there at the corner of Liberty and Greene, not a fancy house like the Ormes or Rockwell places nearby, but kind of a proud, two-story affair with an odd, wavy two-gabled roof atop it. There was only a few people out on the streets at the time and our little group of two white men and a horse with a dead nigger draped over its back seemed to attract very little attention.

By all accounts the bleedin in Jesse's shoulder had stopped, or leastways the bandages I had fashioned up from Big Sandy's shirt like to soak up enough blood so's nothin new appeared to be comin from the wound. Jesse reported that the shoulder had tightened up considerable but he did say he had some movement in it and the pain weren't nothin he would wish for out of hand, but he figured the whole thing to be "tolerable," as he often said. After tyin the horse to the hitchin post out front, I helped Jesse dismount and together the Tims boys, with my arm firmly round my brother's waist, slowly made their way round to the back of the house where the doc had his office.

Knockin on the thick wooden door, we was greeted by a "quiet, grave man of great sobriety and learnin," as the good doctor was once described by an admirin reporter. Tomlinson Fort was really quite famous in these parts as a former militiaman and captain of the Baldwin Volunteers back in the War of 1812 or the "Creek War" as local folks often called it. The man had written books on medicine and had been politically active in state and local politics. He was well-liked and respected by anyone who had the good fortune to have ever crossed his path.

Physically he was rather angular and although he towered above most other men in life, this weren't the case when strictly confined to the perpendicular. He had a prominent nose and ears that stood out maybe a might more than most. He walked with a limp but even that had a certain dignity bout it. Why I remember when the good Doc Fort died in '59, there weren't a soul in Milledgeville who didn't feel the loss and the pain of his passin. It was a sad day for sure.

"What's the problem here boys?" he said as he opened the door and saw the two of us standin there before him.

"Well, Doc…seems as though Mr. Jarratt's runaway done run a Bowie knife right through my left shoulder here." Jesse offered.

"Well, come on in and let's have us a look," he said as we both stepped inside.

"If I could hazard a guess as to the attacker, might it be that it was Big Sandy did the damage?" he asked, lookin out over the undersized spectacles that sat out upon the end of his nose. Not waitin for a response, he began to unwrap the bandages. "We heard tell he was on the loose again and figured maybe you boys might just be the ones called in."

"Well Doc, Big Sandy is wrapped pretty tight round the backside of our horse right at this very moment, and truth to tell, we don't figure him to be doin any runnin anywhere, anytime soon," Jesse answered.

Doc give a nod, not for one minute takin his eyes off the medical condition that had gained his full attention.

Tomlinson Fort was, indeed, a knowledgeable man. His book on doctorin was kinda like a textbook for other doctors and even common folk if they knew how to read. His skilled hands quickly cleaned up the wound much better than I had done out on the trail. Goin over to the shelf he took out a bottle with a special concoction of red bark solution he had ground up usin his own secret ingredients which he had skillfully added to the mix. He was always comin up with new ideas and new recipes for helpin the sick or injured. It was applied liberally.

"This has astringent properties and promotes the healin process," he announced.

Sewin up the gaping wound with cotton thread and dabbin at the stitches to keep the blood under control as he went, the doc bandaged the whole thing up and told us "For God's sake, stay out of the way of Bowie knives and such." As he placed Jesse's left arm in a made-up sling, we both give him thanks and told him that we'd be settlin up with him sometime soon. He didn't seem much concerned bout such matters and just kinda give us a knowin grunt and waved us out the door.

Outside the office evenin was now findin itself and Jesse and me both found ourselves wishin for the comforts of home. Even though it was gettin late, we knew we needed to stop by the Jarratt place first and finish up our business with the wealthy plantation owner.

All of the field hands had finished their work when we come on to the Jarratt plantation. It was now full dark but lights comin from fires inside the slave cabins attested to their whereabouts. The slave quarters at the Jarratt place were orderly and neat. Maybe as many as a dozen small, single story buildins lined both sides of a dirt road out behind the Big House. They was all pine-boarded on the outside with shingle roofs and brick chimneys. Each had a couple of windows. Inside was a planked floor and small loft. I have seen slave quarters a site worse than these, with many darkies crowded into small, windowless, rundown log shanties; but Jarratt, he was a wealthy man and took great pride in his place. He took good care of his human property too, that is, less they misbehaved.

The Big House was lit up pillar to post. Center to the whole plantation, the master's house was a white two-story affair with large pillars on the front porch.

Several servants come out of the house to greet us and took charge of our horse, shootin a quick glance over in the direction of Big Sandy's corpse that was draped over its backside. Master Jarratt suddenly appeared in the doorway. Kinda majestic like, he placed his hands upon his hips and announced:

"Well, I see you boys done brought me a present!"

"Sorry bout this Mr. Jarratt," I replied. "We tried to take him peaceable but he just weren't goin back without a fight. He kilt my dog and Jesse here just got back from seein ol Doc Fort."

"Well, I guess I would expect as much from the likes of Big Sandy." Pausin for a moment Jarratt added "I tell you what I'm gonna do, boys. I know legally I don't have to give you a damn thing, but you've always done right by me before…and you lost your dog, maybe an arm for all we know, and a day's work, besides. I'm gonna give you one hundred dollars for your time and effort. Hell, you could have dumped the nigger's body back at the site and returned home both ridin instead of walkin!"

The plantation master turned to one of his house servants. "Caesar, you and Amos go take Big Sandy off that horse and string him up outside the barn." Pausin briefly he added, "and make sure you hang him upside down for good measure. That's right! I want him to be lookin down on the place he run from. He had it pretty good here…ungrateful nigger! Certain folks need to be reminded what the consequences can be for fuzzy-headed thinkin. Oh, and then I want you to put that horse there in a stall as we are gonna have us some company for the night," he said, now lookin over in Jesse's and my direction.

"What do you say, boys?" Jarratt offered. "You both look exhausted and I don't think Jesse here could make it another hour back to his place. How bout somethin to eat and a soft place to bed down for the evenin?"

The logic of Jarratt's offer was hard to argue. As much as I wanted to return to Cynthia quick as I could like I promised, Jesse's condition was probably a more important consideration. Sides, any suggestion from a plantation master was not somethin a person, black or white, would tend to think on lightly.

As soon as the guests was announced, Jarratt's wife began to bustle bout, instructin her black staff on all the particulars. Plantation mistresses were supposed to be second in command of this whole machine but from what I have seen over the years their authority was often questioned. Servants would come to realize that the wife, just like the slaves on the plantation, also come under the authority of the master and often found they could use her insecurity to their advantage. When the master was away on business, slaves often tested the limits of that authority. I'd seen and heard tell of that very thing happenin many times over. Of course that weren't the case here with Master Jarratt, just as big as life, givin out all the orders and overseein the whole affair.

"While we wait on all the fixins, what say we tend to the misfortunes of the day with a little ol orchard, boys," Jarratt offered, as we walked into his large study where books seemed to be found on most every wall. Standin before his desk he pointed down to a bottle and several empty containers that stood like glass soldiers on a tray before us. "This will free up a man's mind and get him back on the right path, I'll make book on it," he said.

The glasses were then quickly filled by one of the house servants. As I looked down at the golden brown contents, I couldn't help but remember Mamma's warnin bout that stuff early on. "It don't profit a man, Coswell, if he takes to anti-fogmatics, julips and other combustables," she liked to say. I know Daddy used to sneak a little shine down at the blacksmith shop on occasion and Jesse and me done our fair share of experimentin as we growed up. "Giggle soup" is what some folks liked to call it. I looked to Jesse and saw he downed his straightaway, which earned him a quick refill. I took to followin my older brother's example and after several glasses I found myself "back on the right path" just as Jarratt had predicted, but also more than a might swimmy-headed.

The food was soon brought out to the table with the speed and efficiency of the black staff easy for all to see. These vittles was most certain better than what we had taken with us on the trail, but Jesse weren't too hungry and I guess that affected my appetite as well. I noticed him wincin once or twice as he moved restlessly in his chair, tryin to be sociable and eat what was given. Jarratt was pleasant nough and certainly accommodatin, but he did press us for more information on the loss of his substantial investment in the big negro.

"Well boys," Jarratt asked between bites of his sweet pork and taters, "Big Sandy done give you a good run for your money, is that a fact?"

Even though I really did not want to relive this story at the present time and wasn't even sure from the whisky I had consumed if my mouth would be sayin what was intended, I knew Jesse had little left in him for a proper answer, so I spoke up.

"Guess he did Mr. Jarratt. He run maybe twenty or so miles, ran south he did, fore he took a notion to climb that hickory tree. I reckon he was of a mind that he would end his days at that very spot," I answered.

"Did you have to shoot and kill him like a coon to get him to the ground?" Jarratt asked.

"No sir, I didn't," I replied. "Used a little rock salt in the shotgun, that's all. Fired it off in his general direction and he saw the wisdom of comin down."

"Well if that don't beat all. When he got to the ground did the dog have at him and wear him out some?"

I paused. "No, Mr. Jarratt, it weren't the dog that took him, it was me," I answered, with the tail end of my answer trailin off into the silence of the room.

I found myself suddenly dumbfounded and confused and hung my head down with really nothin left to say. It was then and there I took notice of the plate of food directly in front of me. The plate was oval in shape and put me in mind of an old oval picture frame that once hung in the Tims' family home when I was a boy. It held memories it did, for inside that frame, as I remember, was a picture of some colorful flowers that Grandma Tims had growed up in her garden and painted so's folks would always remember how beautiful they was. She said she figured folks would probably not remember her when she was gone, but thought it was a downright pity if the beauty of them flowers could not remain for all time, so she painted em up, puttin em inside that oval frame. Good memories are important, I suppose, but the trouble here was, at this very moment them flowers seemed to be givin way to a more recent memory, a memory darker and not so beautiful. Maybe it was the alcohol, but I must have jumped clear out of my chair when Big Sandy's face suddenly appeared in the picture frame before me! He was on my plate! That big nigger was on my plate for sure! Why I could see him just as clear as day. His eyes was open wide and they got wider and wider the more I stared back at him as if he knew full well my grim intentions. I felt my stomach fairly twist and turn and what little food I had eaten started to make its way back up to the table. I started to gag, and puttin my hand over my mouth, rose up quick-like from my chair, turned and run towards the door. Relief come moments later out on the front porch of the Big House.

Jesse told me later when we was a-bed that night that everyone at the table was at a loss for words after I had suddenly took sick and run for the door. I guess they really didn't know what to make of it. Ain't like that sort of thing happened at every meal or if it did, I reckon Jarratt would soon be lookin to find hisself a new cook!

Jesse told me that Jarratt tried to put a good face on the whole of it, though, announcin to everyone that he thought the Tims boys had a pretty tryin day and that maybe it was somethin Coswell ate on the trail that didn't agree with him or maybe it was things that happened that just didn't set too well. He told Jesse he thought the both of us had a lot on our plate right now and that probably the best thing to do was to head off to bed, as he was sure everyone would feel better come mornin.

A lot on my plate indeed! When Jesse shared this last remark later that night, I thought I would laugh out loud till I near busted my guts. The man's eyes shoulda seed what my eyes seed!

Black servants began to scurry bout, one helpin Jesse out of his chair, one comin outside to fetch me, and others headin for the bedroom to make sure everythin was all readied-up. It weren't too long fore the two of us was bedded down in one of the upstairs rooms where this day would mercifully come to an end.

I don't figure Jesse slept too well as he tossed and turned, occasionally groanin when some movement he made ran afoul of his recent injury. As for me, I remember lyin there most of the night, thinkin back on the events of the day. Some days, I guess, are just different than others and I wondered bout that.

When I did fall asleep, Big Sandy walked right up to greet me just like I suspected he might. In that dream he was restored to his full vigor but said nothin at all to his killer. He just wagged his black finger at me like I was a child, a little ankle-biter who had done somethin very wrong and was bout to get a lickin. I'll tell you for sure, Big Sandy is alive and well and is still runnin just like he always done, but this time he's runnin right through my thoughts and dreams, he is.

Jesse and me both heard the bell ring over at Patrick Kane, the overseer's place, at four o'clock in the mornin. We knew the field hands had one-half hour to eat and get readied-up and standin in the fields by four-thirty, to commence in workin. We also knew that anyone late would start their day with ten lashes from the overseer's whip.

Jarratt had about fifty field hands and probably another twenty or so that tended the house and did other work on the plantation. His was one of maybe fifteen or so plantations in Baldwin County that had fifty or more slaves. Maybe only about a quarter of white families in the south actually owned any slaves t'all and of those of em that did, why I would be bound to say maybe they had ten or less. Large rice plantations long the Georgia coast or large cotton plantations like this one here needed that large labor force. Cotton was king in Georgia and bein as it was late summer, pickin cotton was the number one priority here at the Jarratt place and would be probably right on through to late November.

As I lay there in the early mornin hours, I could full well imagine a scene that was all too familiar. Each slave would soon be grabbin two long coarse cotton sacks from the field wagon which they would suspend from their shoulders or waist. They had to know the day would be long and their backs and bodies would feel the strain of their labor. I'm sure they all hoped that they would not also wear the marks of the overseer's displeasure on their backs as well. A 200-pound day was the minimum. You had to work fast and keep dirt and stems out of the bag. Clean cotton was what was needed and maybe with the exception of Big Sandy who had refused the work and had run off, the slaves in the fields were for the most part, competent and compliant. Why they often times even sang songs as they went bout their business, although I never really come to understand why that was. Some say it's cause they are a musical people by nature and just given to that sorta thing. Some say it's cause they are happy and thankful that so much of their life is tended to by white folks. After my run in with Big Sandy, I guess I began to wonder if maybe they did it so's to hide their pain.

At full light when me and Jesse finally got ourselves out of bed, we could see clearly the fugitive we had returned to the plantation the night before. He was a-hangin there outside the barn with the flies already startin to take notice. His world was upside down for sure just as Jarratt had commanded. It was a pitiful sight to behold! I was certain-sure that image weren't lost on the bondsmen who had walked by earlier to take their places out in the fields. Maybe their world weren't that much different than his, I thought silently to myself. But after all is said and done, I concluded…it didn't matter a lick what Coswell Tims thought on the matter. If things went the way they did most times, why this new day would be just like any other summer day under the hot Georgia sun.

Chapter 4

"PECULIAR INDEED"

Slavery is a peculiar institution, yes indeed. Now I have seen slaves treated as well as any white member of the family and yet I've seen black men and women tore apart by the whip. Hard to figure, I guess. I fully admit I never questioned the rightness of the thing, after all, it's bigger than the likes of Coswell Tims and been here a lot longer than me. I do think it is fair to say that as long as there has been a white America, there has been the institution of slavery here in the "land of the free" as folks like to call it, and I can't think of any part of this country able to claim an honest exception. I have heard the most learned of men speak on the many virtues of the institution, how all great civilizations in the past was based on it and how it come to produce an educated group of folks that could direct and oversee things without wearin out from the work themselves.

The negro, I was raised to believe, was made by God like all His creatures just for the roles they played. Their dark skin, strong bodies and weaker minds made em well suited for hard labor under the hot Georgia sun. Besides, folks say they was given the benefit of Christian learnin and had all their basic needs of food, clothin and shelter met by their white masters, no small or inexpensive matter, that's sure. Saved from cannibalism and savagery in their native lands, why there was little doubt these darkies was in a better place despite their bonded condition. No one, however, would be fool enough to offer up the opinion that their lives was completely free from trouble. No sir, no one ever born of this earth was, is, or ever will be free from trouble and care.

Now the Tims family, like most families in the south, never owned a slave outright although I will say Daddy did sort of rent a black man from Mr. Johnson on occasion to help him down in his blacksmith shop. It's a funny thing but Jesse and me never really took to smithin despite the fact that our daddy was held in high esteem and believed to be the best out of the two or three smiths workin in Milledgeville at the time. I remember that slave's name to be Sampson and he looked every bit what I imagined the biblical character to look like, cept'n, of course his hair was not long and flowin but thick and nappy and he was bout the same color as the coal that Daddy burned in the forge. To this day I can still see the big fella standin at the anvil, wearin a full leather apron with no shirt. He had arms big as tree trunks, he did, and when he would strike that hot iron with a hammer, the power of it would just set them sparks to flyin off in all directions. I also remember that man weren't just strong in body, but often offered up an idea or two bout workin iron that he shared with Daddy. No one could ever quite figure how all them ideas come to get into that nigger's head, but I do believe one day when I offered up the opinion that maybe he was just smarter than most folks, that idea was met with considerable resistance. It was labeled as so much bullfeathers and I remember being told that I hadn't ought to be expressin thoughts at my age on subjects I knew so little bout.

Obadiah Tims weren't no small man neither. He was a few inches shorter than Sampson and I would have to say more than a few shades lighter in color. He had broad shoulders and dark wavy hair…had a black mustache too. He and Mama was well suited for each other, both fine lookin people, but not a trace of arrogance in either one of em. Why me and Jesse always respected and held em both in the highest regard and said "yes sir" and "no ma'am" right up to the very day we put their earthly remains in a grave box and laid em both to rest in Memory Hill.

"Coswell what are you thinkin on?" Cynthia said, breakin the silence as she had slipped unnoticed into the parlor of our three-room farmhouse where I had been settin quietly, starin out one of the front porch windows. She had just finished puttin clothes away in our bedroom and I reckon she felt the need to have us a little conversation fore finishin up her business back in Sanford's room.

"I saw you lookin out that window and figured maybe you were standin in need of somethin to quiet that restless mind of yours."

Now a woman has a way of talkin and bein that is different from a man. They will often try to get right at the heart of the matter and try to draw the most sense out of life. Daddy used to say that Mamma was like oil on the axle of a wagon. She made everythin run smooth, includin him. Why I might have just stared out that window for hours, piddle-didlin round with nothin substantial to show for the effort if it weren't for my Cynthia. I gathered up my thoughts best I could and tried puttin em into words as I reached out for her hand.

"Well, I guess I was thinkin bout a lot of things, darlin. Course the Jarratt job a few weeks back with Jesse gettin hurt, losin ol Beauregard and, course, what happened with Big Sandy. That's weighed my mind down considerable, it has. Haven't slept too well neither, but I guess things will improve with time." I continued to ramble on.

"Found myself thinkin back to when Mamma and Daddy was still livin and then how they took down with the fever. I was thinkin on Jesse when he lost Becky to the pox and even back to some of the terrible things happened to you early on...sure appears that life brings with it its fair share of troubles, don't it? To tally it all up, I guess I was just thinkin bout how difficult life can be," I concluded, droppin both my head and voice somewhat with the last few words.

Cynthia dropped her hand from mine and set it upon my shoulder, knowin there was more in me that needed to come out. I found the last of it burst forth like a dose of ipecac.

"Well, the funny thing is I took to rememberin way back when me and Jesse was younguns and Mamma bought us a little book from that feller Parson Weems who come through town with his "Flyin Library," so called. The man said his mission in life was to preach the importance of book learnin. Now I don't recollect the name of this little missive, but it was small and black in color (looked most like a Bible) had no pictures inside, but I do remember it talked bout the importance of thinkin long and hard on things. It even got me thinkin that this Parson Weems fella sure was makin hisself a lot of money at other people's expense, but it was true that folks round these parts needed to be reminded that, as a general rule, they never questioned things much. Doin and sayin what others was doin and sayin was bout as common as pig tracks when it come to home folk. Mamma said the Tims family was different and reminded Jesse and me to always think for ourselves, addin in it would be "a downright cryin shame if them pretty heads of yours were really nothin more than fancy hat-hangers."

Cynthia waited to see if I had anythin else to add fore she finally tossed in her thoughts to the matter. "I think your mamma would be right proud of you and your brother and the way you have used your heads and gone about the business of life. As far as all these great difficulties that Mr. Coswell Tims feels so free to talk about, I would say what folks have to do more than anythin else is to think more on the good they see, or maybe the good that they are a-hopin for, and not always be lookin round for the fly in the biscuit," she offered. "We do need to think hard on things and I figure if a body does that the trouble you mentioned gets balanced off pretty good in this life after all is said and done. There is much to be thankful for when a person takes the time to look around."

I looked up at the woman standin by my side and took her hand once more. These words were comin from an individual who had seen and been through much in her lifetime, I thought to myself. Her long, light colored hair I noticed was folded up careful atop her head as often was the case when she was takin care of house business. Her blue-green eyes I could see were alive with both intelligence and concern. She had on that old familiar red plaid cotton work dress and that brought a smile to my face. I remember it had seen its finer days early on as a day dress with much the frills and fancy. Of course that brought to mind an even earlier day down New Orleans way when this same woman boarded a yellow coach in the most fashionable blue travelin dress a person would ever want to see, all smarted up with plumed hat, parasol and high topped shoes. What a fetchin picture of pure feminine elegance she did make that day!(But then I am gettin a little ahead of myself in this here story.)

It's true that most earthly things fade with time, but the latest edition I now saw standin before me, (complete with a brown mustard color apron that was pinned to the front), still showed her for the handsome woman she was. Beauty may be skin deep in some cases, but I reckon I had me an exception if there was to be any general rule.

Cynthia spoke again. "As a matter of fact, Coswell, today when you was out somethin good did happen. Mr. Lamar sent one of the field hands over here from the Cobb place to tell you that the litter of hounds they have over there is ready for the pickin. I know you been lookin forward to gettin and trainin up a new ketchhound to replace Beauregard."

"My God, woman, I swear time sure is a-flyin. I really can't believe that it has been seven weeks already," I replied. I started in thinkin bout the young bloodhound pups I had observed over the years and how much fun they was to watch. Just a pile of fur and fury, they would all be in a jumble, some sleepin and others would be tuggin away on each other's long ears. Maybe one or two would be lookin out the pen for what lay in store for em outside that small world. The curious one, just like Parson Weems said with people, might be the best bet and be just the critter I was lookin for.

Now most folks don't bother with a young pup for another couple of weeks but me and Jesse have found that any longer than seven weeks with a bloodhound pup and you risk gettin one that is litter bound and no good for trackin. They tend to lose their independent spirit and natural curiosity if they start payin too much attention to one another in the pen. No, seven weeks we have found, is just bout right. With maybe as many as twelve pups in a typical litter to choose from, I was sure there was a good replacement for Beauregard to be had somewhere in the bunch. I knew that I wanted one that stood out from the others, one with strong physical attributes and one with a curious nature. I would know it when I saw it. Male or female, didn't matter a lick. Some trackers say that females are more loyal and are easier to handle while others prefer the male's strength and stamina. It really made no nevermind to Jesse and me as we have had em both and if trained up right, they always served us well.

"I'll know the right dog when I see it," I finally said to Cynthia as I give her that all-too-familiar goodbye hug as I made ready to leave. "I knew you was the right one when I first saw you, didn't I?"

"Coswell, you likenin me to a dog now?" Cynthia said in sort of mocked anger.

"I'm sayin some things come to a person straightaway with no thinkin or questionin necessary. Now you hand me that hat over there and be sure to miss me while I'm gone, you hear?"

As I walked out the door, the excitement I felt for the new dog got overtopped some by a feelin that seemed to always come on me whenever I would take my leave. I guess I just felt somewhere down deep inside that one day the two of us would part and Cynthia, well, she wouldn't be there when I returned. Don't know why I come to have that feelin…maybe seein Jesse lose Becky. She had been the love of his life, somethin good and then, why the Good Lord saw fit to up and take her just like that. I have seen the pain of the thing and seen Jesse struggle with it. Sometimes, even nowadays many years later when we be trackin and busy like, I get the feelin that my brother is sorta holler inside and maybe a good stiff breeze might blow right through the whole of him and start in to makin a kinda whistlin noise if a man had the ears keen enough to hear it. I felt the need to look back over my shoulder once more for reassurance that my Cynthia was right in the same place I had left her.

Seein her wavin through the glass of the front porch window and feelin a might better for the look-see, I saddled up our horse for the ride over to the Lamar place. I did have one thing that needed tendin first. I knew Sanford was workin out in the garden in a small field out behind the barn, so I headed over to see our young negro fore leavin for the Lamar plantation.

Bendin over with hoe in hand, Sanford's familiar form and his smilin face soon greeted me. I swear, seein that boy was always like seein the sun rise up in the mornin. That full head of black, nappy hair tucked under his ragged straw hat and all them pearly white teeth with the familiar space up tween the front two, the whole of it wrapped up in a smile, why Sanford could make a person feel good on a bad day. I believe I have known this boy as long as I had been knowin my wife…fact is, I guess you could say they come into my life as a package, a present or a blessin to be more clear on the matter. Although everyone in town thought of him as our slave, we was more inclined to think of him as a friend or family member. He slept right in the back bedroom of our home, ate at our table, and sat as an equal round the fire for evenin conversation. I will admit that we would rent him out from time to time, but what was also true was that we always let him keep the money he earned. Keepin up the formal appearance of a slave, didn't draw no unnecessary suspicion on the part of the townsfolk. People hereabouts always got real nervous if a darkey was given too much freedom, specially after the Nat Turner affair back in '31. It was always about the "contagion," don't you know.

"Sanford, I'll be headin over to the Lamar place for probably the better part of the day," I announced from my horse. "You keep an eye on your mistress, now, and I should have somethin to show you when I return."

"You know you can count on Sanford, Massa Tims. Won't let nothin happen to Miss Cynthia, the dogs, or dis place here."

"You know Sanford, I probably trust you more that any person alive, ceptin my brother, of course. I can well imagine that a man who don't trust no one has more than a few sleepless nights and probably some anxious days to boot," I added.

"Spectso, Massa, spectso. Friends and fambly most impotant in dis here life. Thank ya kindly," he replied, tippin his hat in respect as I spurred my horse in the direction of the Lamar place.

Now that plantation was an interestin affair. It was actually owned by Howell Cobb but was managed by his brother-in-law, a fella named Lamar. It was a large cotton growin plantation with over 150 slaves, one of the largest in the area. The problem with the place and many others round here like it was that neither Cobb nor Lamar actually come to live on the premises. They both lived in town so's they could tend to their business affairs, creatin sort of an absentee-landowner type arrangement on the plantation itself. Even though Mr. Cobb did stop by most days, its whole operation was really under the direction of an overseer and that could really be a problem sometimes with the way folks was treated. Plantation owners that lived on the place with their darkies often had a paternal attitude towards em and often lacked the stomach for whippin em direct or maybe even whippin em t'all. Overseers, as a general rule, operated under no such constraints. Hard men of business who got their money from what the slaves produced, why they'd generally drive em hard so's to yield the most profit. As I thought on it, I suspected that it was the overseer, not Lamar who had sent the message over bout the pups.

Now they say a trackin man who is on foot can cover about three miles in an hour behind a good hound dog. On horseback without the dog, however, I reached the plantation in less than half the time.

"Your horse, sir," was the first words out of the mouth of a rather well-dressed black man who had the appearance of some sort of coachman. He wore high boots, with coat and tie and his mannerisms showed good breedin and refinement. You could tell straightaway that this here fella was at the top of the peckin order in slave society.

"Thank you," I said. "My name is Coswell Tims and I was informed earlier in the day bout the dogs..."

"Joshua, you come over here and take Master Tims down to the barn," he instructed, motionin to a young slave boy who stood nearby. "You let him get a good look-see at those dogs down there."

I walked with Joshua to the barn but no sooner had we arrived than I heard a commotion of some sort directly out in back. Both Joshua and me was drawn to the old barn wall where several holes in the planks provided a tolerable view. We could see two white men standin over a black man who was down on his knees. His hands was tied and offered up in a pleadin manner.

"Oh, Massa, please Lord God don't hit me again!" the black man begged.

"I told you never to use the name of the Lord in vain," said a man I knew to be the overseer, as he laid on another lash from the whip he held tightly in his hand.

"Pray, Massa, pray," was the response, but the beatin continued unabated.

At one point the overseer told the petitioner that he was goin to turn the whip over to a friend of his who, he felt, could better instruct the negro on proper deportment.

The beatin continued with equal if not surpassed relish, this time from another quarter. I knew I must be witnessin what slaves feared most…a "whippin frolic." This would be where one of their number was singled out for whatever reason for a beatin that would last the better part of the day. It might be that the white men was competin to see who could lay on the most pain, or sometimes maybe it would be caused by excessive drinkin or just plain orneriness on the owner or overseers part. One thing for sure, it generally ended out pretty much the same way with the nigger's dead body bein throwed into the slave cemetery to lay there for a spell and be buried the next day by fellow slaves when their work in the fields was done. There were laws in Georgia and most other slave states that prohibited the murder or mutilation of slaves, but seein as them laws was written by whites for whites, black rights didn't count for much. It would probably be fair to say that the laws regardin slaves and the institution of slavery depended more on the disposition of the slave master hisself rather than any legal code the government had worked up. After all, the master of a plantation was like a little king and his kingdom would be run accordin to the way he was so inclined.

Now I never really could understand the reason for many or maybe even most of the slave whippins I witnessed durin my lifetime. I remember that Master Billy Boone over at the Boone plantation nearby liked to freshen up his slaves on a regular basis by chainin em naked over a barrel and hittin em with a wooden cobbin paddle which had forty or so holes in it. Everywhere there was a hole it would draw up a good size blister and the whippin Reverend Boone would then lay on afterwards was sure to break them blisters and produce a very bloody affair. I reckon that was done more for effect when added to the painful salt bath that was sure to follow. Lots of screamin and hollerin there was, but I don't remember anyone dyin or bein hurt so bad they was unfit for work.

"My black family needs to be frequently reminded to have a healthy attitude concernin discipline and proper behavior," I remember him sayin one day when I visited the plantation to discuss some important business. Reverend Boone would often be heard quotin St. Peter from scripture: "Servants, in all things obey your masters, for it is the will of God." I also remember this same man quotin a fellow Georgian minister on frequent occasion, a fella named Reverend Holmes, who wrote for the local newspaper. "Christian master, enter the dark cabin of thy servant, and with the lamp of truth in thy hand, light up his yet darker soul," he would say with all the conviction of a true believer.

Many owners, however, was never given to whippin their slaves t'all and what's more, sometimes instructed their overseers never to beat em either. I've even knowed overseers that was let go during a busy plantin season for not carryin out the masters' wishes regardin fair treatment of the work force. Yes sir, seems to me some slave owners treated their slaves right well. It really don't make much sense to me to damage valuable property. Now a little healthy fear might be a good thing cause a darkey can get lazy like most folks, but what I just saw out behind the barn caused my stomach to feel uneasy and just made no sense to my way of thinkin.

Joshua continued to stare wide-eyed at the whole sorry affair, but I soon felt the need to look away and try to get my mind right as to why I had come here in the first place. Lookin down finally at the ten or so bloodhound pups that was put up in a little makeshift pen, I paused only a moment fore makin my decision. With Joshua finally freein himself up from the fascination of the frolic, I announced: "I'll take that one over there," as I pointed to the red male with a dark muzzle that stood apart from the others who was either sleepin or wrastlin round with each other. The young pup I had pointed to had been starin most intently at a bird that had flown into the barn and had perched hisself high up on one of the rafters. Here was a dog that has a strong need to notice and investigate things, I thought to myself.

I could still hear the commotion out behind the barn, the crack of the whip and the screams of pain sure to follow, as the young slave boy and I began to walk back to the hitchin post where I had left the horse. I counted out one hundred dollars cash money for the "coachman" to give his master for the dog. I got up in the saddle and motioned for Joshua to hand me that little bundle of fur. I knew it was the first time the little fella had ever been away from his family and he was all a-quiver and looked like he could use a good friend. I decided it was best to bundle him tight up inside my coat so's the heat comin from my body might relax and reassure him that things was gonna work out just fine.

I looked down at him. "I think I'll call you Moses," I said. "Yes sir, Moses just like in the Bible. Who knows…maybe someday you will lead your people to the promised land," I added, kinda amusin myself at the thought. Yes sir, I would have been willin at that moment to wager that someday this little bloodhound pup just might prove worthy of that famous name. For some reason I just had that feelin inside as I checked one last time to make sure the little critter was tucked in good and tight and with that, I spurred my horse for home.

Chapter 5

ONLY DOIN WHAT IS RIGHT AND PROPER

Moses, he took to trackin straightaway, which I suppose weren't nothin more than someone would come to expect from a creature of his general persuasion. Nevertheless and notwithstandin, it seemed to me (and Jesse will have my back on this) that this new hound was just a might more anxious than most of his kind to get out of that pen and try his hand at sniffin out the new world around him.

We started him off like we done all our dogs at eight months or so with sight trainin. Now what I mean by that is pretty simple. The pup would use only his eyes in trailin a fugitive. The whole thing would start off with me puttin on the trackin harness and gettin him cozied up to the idea of that leather contraption. It was lighter than the one he would wear when he was full growed, but it was important that the dog make his peace with the routine and what to expect whenever that harness made an appearance. As a general rule the dogs never seemed to mind it much, maybe cause the leather is spread out over the critter's chest, back and shoulders and don't restrict em, like somethin that takes em hard around the neck. After gettin the dog to sit and slippin the harness on, I would fasten the lead I held in my hand to the ring atop. The dog needed to understand that he weren't alone in this process and there was someone else he needed to be mindful of at the other end. A fetch hound will pull mightily at first, but with time and constant remindin, the two high contractin parties generally can come to agreement on proper spacin and the amount of pull that is both necessary and acceptable.

With the dog all readied-up, Jesse would then come into the picture, callin the dog by name and encouragin him to follow as he run off towards the woods. I would let my young canine friend know that I was excited too and that there was some sport to be had here. I would yell "find" and off we'd go, lightin out after Jesse for all we was worth. The dog would narrow the gap till my brother would finally stop, then we'd all waller round in the grass so's to increase the fun of it all. It really weren't much of a feat when you boil it all down …just chasin somebody that was runnin, but that's where this whole trackin notion gets put into the dog's head.

Bloodhounds are by nature gentle and fun-lovin critters and do love a frolic that a good trainer will provide. They don't even bear the fugitive any grudge and like him to join right in with the festivities. Jesse and me think it kind of amusin that the dog enjoys such a fierce reputation when it really don't fit their true nature. One thing is true here and I can testify to it…a man should have a healthy fear of a bloodhound, but only if he is on the run and deathly afraid of gettin hisself caught!

After a couple of weeks of this sight trainin business, we would add a little more to the mix by gettin Jesse to disappear completely from view fore we took up the chase. The dog could sense somethin had changed here. With no fugitive in sight, Moses would now have to use his nose for the chase to continue. Jesse might have helped things long some by jumpin up and down fore he disappeared, droppin off a little more scent than might normal fall from a man. It's often hard for folks to believe cause their eyes is so bad and their noses so poor, how much scent (flakes of skin, "skerf", so-called) actually falls off a runner and comes to rest on the ground.

Bloodhounds learn this right quick when they no longer can see the runaway. It's downright amazin how fast these dogs will swap up their eyes for their nose at this point and begin to enjoy the smell of the chase.

After sniffin out my brother, the reward was again praise, maybe some wraslin round or maybe we would just give em a good scratchin as these wrinkle-skinned critters seem to be quite partial to havin all their loose skin tended to. Sometimes we would let em jump up and put their paws on Jesse's chest just like Beauregard done back with Big Sandy. I'm sure that dog never thought for the life of him that his reward for findin the big negro would be paid out at the sharp end of a Bowie knife. I have to admit that whole sorry affair still puts a knot in my tail to this very day.

Now the last and most important step in teachin this trackin process was always the introduction of a scent item. The dog would be harnessed up and knew a chase was in order, but there would be no fugitive anywhere in sight. Only an article of clothin or some such item containin the scent of a runner would be offered. The dog would then be allowed a good sniff with familiar instructions to "Find!" That would get him all riled up and he would most like as not, start in sniffin the ground for all he's worth to find that same scent down there to match the one he had been given. We have found over the years that it was best in the beginnin to take an item that had a scent the dog was familiar with, maybe even partial to, so's this invisible person was someone the hound really wanted to find.

"Cynthia?" I asked one mornin as I made short work of the barefoot bread that had just come my way from the fireplace (they was drippin with butter and sorghum syrup…that woman truly does love ol Coswell, for sure.) "I'm standin in need of you givin me a hand with Moses' trainin today. He's ready for the last little parcel and you are the perfect person for him to hunt down and find."

"That is not the least bit funny, Coswell," she replied. "Don't need no trackin dog lightin out after me like I was some white master's property. Have you taken leave of your senses?"

"Now darlin, I wouldn't be askin if the young dog didn't regard ya so highly. If we are goin to make a livin at this here trackin business, we need to train up our hounds right and proper," I concluded.

"Well, you know how I feel about this line of work anyway… guess I explained it away till I was most blue in the face. I thought that set-to with Big Sandy might have finally convinced Mr. Coswell Tims that the next time might be worse than a broken nose, a dead hound dog and a torn vest pocket."

"Now Cynthia, you know how much that whole thing wore on me, it truly did, and I really have been thinkin more and more bout some changes in our future, but then there's Jesse to consider as well as how we are regarded by townsfolk hereabouts. Most slave catchers are no-accounts, maybe even fair to say their juice ain't worth the squeeze, but me and Jesse, why we're near the top of the pile and highly thought on. Sides, don't you think people might start in askin questions on why we would up and quit a successful business like this one here," I added, hopin this last point might just turn the corner in favor of my position.

"Oh, I suppose you are right," she relented. "Maybe this just ain't the right time to be discussin this. What needs doin with the dog?"

I told Cynthia that she needed to lay track fore the whole thing commenced by walkin previous in a deliberate straight line, scuffin the ground and sorta draggin her feet some, lettin the scent fall off good and heavy. After the dog would get a sniff of one of her cookin aprons or the like (without havin seen her) I would give the command "Find!" and take the object away so's the dog would then have to drop its head to the ground to sniff round some in an effort to locate her trail to continue on.

Now most any dog can be taught to do this. Trackers down our way might use coonhounds, staghounds, bulldogs, or maybe even barnyard mutts, but they are all overtopped by the blooded hound. Bloodhound's noses ain't only long but quite wide and all them wrinkles everywhere are designed to hold scent. Even the long ears of this particular animal are intended to sweep scent forward toward the nose. The loose skin or cape around the neck holds the scent to the front end of the dog. Dame Nature knew exactly what she was doin when she designed this animal for trailin those people who were runnin from the law. It was the "Law of Moses" as hardshelled Bible-thumpers like to say, and this dog here, why I figure with a name like his, he might just continue on with that proud tradition. Me and Jesse was both quite happy bout the progress our Moses was makin in the field with his early schoolin.

Well now, as I remember it was late in the year, somewhere round October, when Moses got his first chance at some serious trackin. Milledgeville had been the home to the state penitentiary since 1817. That buildin shared a large square with the court house and the local jail. It was one of four such public squares in Milledgeville which was laid out in checkerboard fashion with streets some 100 feet wide. What made this town different from many others laid out in this same manner in Georgia was the number of private homes built most right up to the streets and even at intersections with no front yards to speak of—really a nice blendin of public and private. I guess it made people more sociable and yet folks still had their privacy in the back where stables, poultry houses, gardens and orchards, johnnyhouses and maybe even a burial lot or two were often found. Sometimes people did complain bout the prison and the riffraff it attracted causin problems for the neighbors, but for the most part, I guess folks was generally tolerant of its more-than-ample presence down on Penitentiary Square.

Over the years many interestin folks, both men and women, had found themselves locked inside those brick walls. Jesse and me had been called in several times to track down some of the more adventurous, resourceful or desperate of their number who decided to up and leave fore their proper time. Seein as though Baldwin County had no trackin dogs of their own, private contractors like the Tims boys were an absolute necessity in keepin things quiet and serene. A message had recently been sent askin once again for our assistance.

Upon arrivin at the prison, the Principal Keeper (as he was called), one C.H. Nelson, greeted Jesse and me with an amusin story of a prisoner who had just escaped no more than four or five hours previous. The man's name was James Hunter and he had been awaitin execution for killin a fella by the name of Lovejoy. Some said he had killed the man in an attempt to protect his wife from Lovejoy's insults and slander, but the Superior Court over in Chattooga County failed to cozy up to that particular defense. "Murder," it was and "death by hangin" was the verdict. The sentence was to be carried out on the first day of December, but I guess this Hunter fella had other ideas.

This prisoner had the good fortune to have a loyal wife who the guards said had visited him every single day since his arrival… never missed a one. Those same guards said she was a good-looker, too. Now I don't know if 'n it's good or bad, but I have noticed that there are men in this world who have demonstrated a heap of devilment inside em and yet some fine woman will come along and take up their cause and love em like no tomorrow. I'm of the humble opinion that every person in this world needs love, but maybe this kind of love prevents a man from gettin his just comins and that can't be a good thing as I figure it interferes with the larger laws of nature. Anyways, when visitin time was over and it was time for the woman to leave, the wrong person up and walked out the door. That's right! Mr. James Hunter had exchanged clothes with his loyal wife and had left the prison dressed in colors somewhat more fashionable than the striped prison issue of black and white.

Now this weren't the first time somethin like this had happened. Jesse and me both remember a few years back when four women prisoners dressed themselves up as men by sewin their blankets and bed sheets into some pretty convincin male clothin. They broke a hole through the floor near the kitchen and descended down into the courtyard where they walked out of the prison without so much as a question or howdy-do from the deputies or the turnkey.

As I remember, trackin those women didn't amount to much as they jumped a train to Augusta and quickly slipped our grasp. Ol Jeremy Prigg used to say "You can't track an iron horse," and although I have found through experience that ain't entirely true, most trackers do recognize the difficulty and generally give up a train-car chase. The women were captured several days later, no thanks to the two of us, and returned to the penitentiary where they were to serve out the rest of their sentences.

This time, however, we was determined to bring back the escaped prisoner, despite the fact that the dog we had chosen for the job had the least experience of the lot. There was no question that Moses had shown great promise in his trainin, but this was now the real thing. Sometimes that can be a different bucket of possums. We was hopeful, though (me in particular) that this dog's name would soon come to match his ability.

"How long you say he's been gone?" Jesse asked Mr. Nelson.

"Well, we have nine deputies here, one for every ten prisoners. The last time one of em checked this particular cell was about five hours ago," he answered.

"Maybe you folks ought to be checkin in on these people a little more often," I added.

"Now wait just a minute, Tims," Nelson replied. "We take what the Board of Inspectors gives us. You boys ain't got no call tellin me my business, specially seein as you stand to make thirty dollars on this deal. I don't tell you how to track a man, do I?" Nelson added.

"Is that where Hunter slept last night?" I asked, tryin to change the subject some to prevent antagonizin the warden any further. Nelson nodded his agreement.

"We'll use that bed sheet as a scent item," Jesse offered. "Forget bout them clothes that the missus be wearin, and don't have any fear that the dog will be followin her scent. The scent he be leavin will be his own, I will assure you that."

Mrs. Hunter had been detained up on the second floor where women prisoners were held and we were told she would be charged with accessory to a prison break and would assuredly find herself behind these walls for some time to come.

We brought in Moses, sat him down and put on the leather trackin harness. Moses' legs was shakin more than a little in anticipation of the chase, makin his youth and inexperience all the more obvious.

"That dog gonna track or is he gonna piss hisself all over the floor of my prison?" Nelson asked, mockingly, seein an opportunity to get even for my earlier remark.

"Now, look-a-hear, Mr. Nelson, there ain't no call to sour on this hound. When you hire it done with the Tims boys, it gets done and that's all there is to it. This young dog will get your man and you can make book on that," I replied, with maybe a little more enthusiasm than I was actually startin to feel inside.

I held the bed sheet up to the young manhunter's nose. "Find!" I yelled loudly.

The cell door was flung open and out we went, into the courtyard and over to the gate which "Mrs." Hunter had walked out only hours before. Down Hancock Street we went, towards Fishin Creek and over the bridge leadin south out of town.

Now I am absolutely sure that bloodhounds can see what they are a-smellin cause they never seem surprised when the chase ends. "I knowed it was you all long," they seem to almost say when they meet the person in question and howdy for the first time. I was doin my share of imagining, thinkin bout what this fugitive must look like at this very moment. Chucklin a little to myself, I could just see this dangerous escaped murderer runnin for his life all dressed up in women's clothin. Why, it had to be a fine sight indeed. "Hope this fella don't trip over his hemline," I said to Jesse as the dog led us up into the woods. Jesse let out a little snicker.

We tracked James Hunter for bout an hour's time, findin occasional articles of woman's clothin discarded long the way. The dog would stop to examine those items fore he continued on. I was more and more convinced we had us a fine trackin hound here, but Jesse said he would reserve final judgment.

As we reached a thick grove of trees on a slightly elevated piece of land, the dog began to show signs of confusion. He started pacin back and forth with nose to the ground, tail waggin and blowin scent off the ground, then sniffin it in for further review. It was obvious to us that the fugitive had stopped here and must have been ponderin somethin as he had walked back and forth.

Suddenly Moses up and took to headin west, but after a spell, headed north back in the direction we had come.

"What the hell is this damn fool dog doin now?" Jesse asked. "He's so fogged-up he's goin backwards! Mark my words, Coswell, that dog you're so high on is all vine and no taters. I knew we should have brought one of the older dogs, this one's gonna cost us thirty dollars for sure."

For all Jesse's protestins, Moses did seem to believe he was headed in the right direction. I told my brother I did not think the dog was just callyhootin round with no purpose, and besides, we had no other choice at the moment but to follow and trust in the young dog's lead.

Eventually the trail led back to the bridge, up Hancock Street and, don't it beat all, over to Penitentiary Square and right up to the prison gate where we started.

There was more than a few smiles greeted us when we come inside.

"Well I guess that young dog of yours scared this fella right back into my prison!" Mr. Charles Nelson announced, as he and his deputies broke out into fits of laughter.

After everyone got over enjoyin the moment at our expense, we found out the truth of the matter. Seems as though Mr. Hunter had a change of heart out there on the trail and could not bear the thought of his wife bein in jail for somethin he himself had done. He had come back to turn hisself in and face the gallows rather that have his wife be imprisoned for helpin him escape, certainly a noble and unselfish gesture on his part.

What I found out later on added even more to this interestin story. The state legislature happened to be in session in Milledgeville at the time and caught wind of what had happened and I'll be black-dogged if they didn't issue a full pardon for the man. They were so taken with his honorable decision that they proclaimed: "Mr. James Hunter is hereby declared to be fully, freely and entirely pardoned as if the conviction and the sentence had never taken place or the offence committed."

Of course the local paper was eager to pick up the story and announced in their headlines "MR. JAMES HUNTER: HERE IS A HUSBAND WHO WAS INDEED WORTHY OF HIS WIFE!"

Now somethin else that come out of all this, despite all the laughter, was that this young trackin hound named Moses had definitely proved hisself. That contaminated scent and the double direction could have throwed a lesser dog, maybe even one with a great deal more experience. Yes sir, even Jesse was on board with the notion that this new dog of ours looked to have a bright and promisin future.

Chapter 6

NO ONE EVER BORN OF THIS WORLD IS FREE FROM TROUBLE

To backtrack some in this story here, Jesse and me ain't always been in the slave catchin business. My brother worked over at the saw mill for years and I knocked bout with little purpose in life, workin on occasion for Daddy in his blacksmith shop, sellin paints, dyes and medicines for Doc Wilson down at the apothecary and even tendin to things over at the Big Indian Saloon on the north side of Green Street. Mamma and Daddy never did like me workin in that place, said I could take on some bad habits, even though it was popular with the legislators and highbrow folk as well as locals who could afford the inflated rate of ten cents a drink ("be it plain or fancy" was their motto). I figured Gus Randolph to be a fair man, though, maybe chargin a little more than most saloon owners, but providin better service and comforts for his payin customers. I always had a suspicion the thing Mamma hated most bout the place was the large, carved wooden Indian that stood out front…said it scared the puddin right out of her as it held a savage scalpin knife in one hand and had an evil lookin tomahawk danglin from its belt. Had a frightful look in his eyes, too, all painted up the way he was. Mamma said Indians was terrifyin things to behold and she said if she never saw another live one in her lifetime that would suit her just fine. I never knowed much bout the red man myself, but admit to listenin intently whenever the ol timers would start in tellin tales of their run-ins with em. At the time I couldn't have known that one day I would have my own stories to tell on the matter.

Well, it was back in the spring of '35, as I recall, when ol man Parker come runnin into Daddy's blacksmith shop, an old rundown lookin affair set back off South Wayne Street near Eagle Tavern. I remember I was workin there with him that day, repairin some farm equipment for a neighbor by the name of Ezra Johnson. As was often the case there was a number of folks gossipin bout the forge when we all heard the news.

"Hey, you boys hear what happened down in Columbus the other day?" Parker announced, almost out of breath.

Nobody seemed to pay him much nevermind as Daddy was still hammerin away at the anvil and a couple of folks was still carryin on a conversation over by the slack tub. Parker, he raised up his voice some and started in again over the din of the shop. "Seems as though them murderin red savages left their reservation over in Alabama, crossed over the Chattahoochee and killed quite a few of our neighbors down in Muscogee County!"

All conversation come to a halt. Daddy put down his hammer and tossed the piece he had been workin on into the slack tub. It give off a loud hiss as it hit the water, most like someone had put a finger to their lips to quiet a disrespectful congregation just as the preacher had stepped to the pulpit to deliver up his Sunday mornin sermon.

The Creeks had been put on that reservation back in '29 and were required by law to have a written pass to leave or cross the river into the state of Georgia. These Indians had proved themselves formidable adversaries early on in the century and white fear that still lingered had resigned em to reservation life, "for safe keepin," it was said. White folks, as a general rule, hated and feared the red man, knowin firsthand the devilment they was capable of. Now there was Indians who owned travelers' taverns and had taken on farmin and other white ways, but even them folks were looked on with more than a little suspicion.

Several people started in askin questions all at the same time but Jesse overrode the lot of em, voicin a loud concern bout the casualties. "Anyone we know?" he asked.

"Actually," Mr. Parker began excitedly, "that fella Flournoy who killed the man in the whorehouse down there on Franklin Street a few years back, why I guess them murderin redtails beat on his skull so bad you could barely recognize the corpse! Guess they skinned him up to boot."

It took me by surprise when I looked over at Daddy for his reaction and thought I saw a slight smile come to his smoke-stained face. In all my life I had never knowed Obadiah Tims to take delight in another man's misfortune. I felt the need to ask for an explanation.

"Well, son, I'll tell ya straight out," he replied. "We all knew William Flournoy was guilty even when he walked out of that court a free man. It was that prosecution lawyer fella who put the notion in his head...said he got away with murder and would be haunted so bad the rest of his days that he'd never have one more restful night's sleep. Appears to me that's just bout what happened here. Folks say he's been wantin to die ever since, so I guess the man finally got his wish."

Daddy spit out a pretty tight stream of brown tobaccer juice onto the dirt floor of the shop as he continued on. "Of course we all have to be very careful of what we are a-wishin for in this life, as it has been my observation that it just might come our way. Can't imagine that Bill Flournoy wanted to go out like that, though," Daddy said, droppin his head slightly, I figured as a sign of respect.

"Anybody else from these here parts?" Mr. Johnson interrupted, now more concerned with the welfare of his neighbors than the repair of his farm equipment.

"Well, as a matter of fact," Parker added as if he were hangin on to his prized information as long as he could without sharin so's to raise up its value. "Mrs. Clark who lives up the road apiece had the misfortune to be visitin relatives down there just at this very time and got herself scalped for her trouble. Heard tell they got hide, hair and all. She's still among the livin, however."

My mamma's concerns bout that carved Indian with his raised up scalpin knife held for all to see come to my mind with Parker's announcement. I felt right sorry for Mrs. Clark. She was a good woman by all accounts and certainly did not deserve to get her hair lifted. I couldn't see how it was possible that she could still be alive, knowin full well how damagin that procedure could be. Grabbin hair to raise up the scalp some, a sharp knife could quickly be brought to bear from front to back (or back to front dependin on the way the attacker was standin) and the whole affair would come off in pretty short order. I figured it would be just a matter of time fore the exposed skull would turn black from contact with the air and Mrs. Clark would be joinin Bill Flournoy on the south side of the grass.

Scalpin was certainly nasty business, been round probably as long as fightin has been goin on in this part of the world. Of course the white man weren't innocent of this activity either. The whole thing I figure probably started out as a fair way of countin up the dead, better than fingers, toes, ears or anything else the body can boast more than one of. After all, a person ain't got more than one head of hair that I know of.

Tryin to take in the whole of it, it is fittin to say problems with the Indians was nothin really new in these parts. The old deserted fort in Milledgeville on the Oconee River, Fort Wilkinson, still silently bore witness to the fear and danger them savages caused over the years. I remember Daddy tellin me a story when I was a young boy bout an Indian named Red Eagle who had his mind set on wipin out all the white folks in the area. His warriors (they was called Red Sticks cause of the red war clubs they carried) massacred upwards of maybe a thousand of the settlers hereabouts in the early part of the century. White children was left with no heads, white women ravaged and white men tore apart in sport. Why if it hadn't been for that fella Andy Jackson (may God forever bless his name) people say there would be no tellin what this place would be like today. Now here they are, at it again. People, just like all critters born of nature, are inclined to certain ways, I come to figure.

"Did you hear anything else?" I asked Mr. Parker.

"Well, I did hear that there were about five hundred of these varmints under some chief named Jim Henry that were cavortin round and doin all the damage. Heard tell several plantations was burned, slaves stolen, livestock killed and even steamboats attacked and destroyed. Guess it's a real mess down there and we could be next!" Parker added to drive home his point.

Everyone in the shop got real quiet after that, chewin on the new information and offerin up their best guess as to the future. There was some general mumblin and movin bout in the shop as folks soon began to take their leave.

That night Jesse and Becky come over to the house and the Tims family all sat down at the supper table to discuss the news and what should be done. All the Tims men was in the local militia and served on alarm duty, as all males fifteen to sixty years of age in Georgia was legally required to do. I can't say we was much of a fightin force, though. Once a month we met for drills, marchin round, shootin at targets and such…more of a social event than anythin else might be a fair statement to make.

All three of us was eligible to volunteer for this set-to, but seein as though Daddy was needed to run the blacksmith shop and Jesse was recently married to Becky and workin over at the mill, the only one that really wouldn't be missed was me. I would have to say I was proud to volunteer and so I joined up with some fifty seven others from our county under a fella named Hamilton Gaither who we elected captain. We come to name this fine fightin force the "Baldwin Hussars."

It couldn't have been more than two days later after we rounded up all our fightin gear and supplies that we had a nice little parade right through the streets of Milledgeville. Folks cheered us and give us encouragement, knowin full well some of us would most likely have our collars unbuttoned and never see home again. One woman give me a cake in a sack in appreciation as we walked by. We had the well-wishes from a grateful community as we marched south out of town, some ridin and others like myself, walkin on two legs, off to engage the likes of Jim Henry and his red marauders.

We vowed we was goin to give them savages an ass-whoppin they would never forget.

Well, it weren't but two weeks later when the glory of the thing began to fade some as these same Baldwin Hussars that had marched off so piss proud just a short time earlier, found themselves all lyin faces to the ground, pinned down in an open field somewhere in the south of Georgia. I remember seein some sport in this desperate situation, however, and managed a little chuckle when Wiley Tompkins, a good friend and private like myself, yelled over to me under a hail of arrows and bullets that he thought this here heroic and glorious fightin business might be somewhat overrated.

I remember also that just as Wiley had finished his commentary, a ball naked man, covered in mud from head to toe, come runnin by us screamin and carryin on like a person who just escaped from the Milledgeville Lunatic Asylum. He was holdin on to his musket for dear life, as it appeared to be the last possession the man had left in this world. I almost mistook him for a savage and might have dropped him dead on the spot had we not all taken to highsterics and laughter and, to a man, been unable to pull the trigger. Let me be a little more clear on the matter.

Them Creek Indians were nothin if not resourceful and I got to admit earlier in the day they had cleverly lured a group of Georgia militia from Gwinnett County into a trap. Seein themselves outnumbered five to one, them Georgia boys fell back, tryin to reach a local homestead maybe a mile or so to the south. We could hear the shots three miles away over at Fort Jones where the Hussars was put-up, so we headed off to the rescue. We figured we would soon cover ourselves in glory but it weren't long fore we found ourselves in much the same fix as them we was tryin to rescue. That's when I saw that naked fella (turned out he was one of the Gwinnett boys) runnin like lightnin, tryin to put some distance between hisself and his red pursuers.

I guess the whole thing weren't as funny as I'm makin out, as Coswell Tims and his comrades might have left their bones right there on the battlefield on that very day in the spring of '35 just as easy as not. If that were the case, I would have never met Cynthia, the love of my life, or Sanford for that matter, and Jesse and me would have never owned a successful bloodhound trackin business. As a matter of fact, if it hadn't been for them mounted boys from Steward County under a captain named Jernigan who just happened to pay us a little visit later on in the afternoon, it's a sure thing I wouldn't be pennin this little missive.

Things did turn our way and we learned some valuable lessons that spring day. We learned that Georgia boys can always count on one another when things get tough, but we also learned that sometimes fightin and killin, bad as we might hate to do it, is often a necessary part of life. A man has to do what a man has to do and that might just say it all.

Lookin to the tally, that naked fella was reunited with his clothes and by the time the smoke cleared, we had them Creeks full on the run. I admit to killin three of the enemy in that skirmish, two with my musket and one close up with a sidearm. I don't mind sayin that each one made me feel kinda proud as I knew I was doin right by my family and my community. They was the first two-legged critters I ever tracked and shot but I reasoned it out that each one of them dead savages would make Mrs. Clark's pain all the more bearable.

We fought the Creeks the better part of the spring and summer, trackin em best we could. They would travel single file with the last one brushin out the trail. Sometimes them rascals would lie in the mud of the swamp or hide up in the branches of the trees and lay in wait. You had to track em like you would a wild animal, not a person. I would tell you they were sure hard to find and generally avoided a major battle, settlin for hit-and-run attacks of their own choosin. We lucked up and caught a good number of em late in the summer down in Baker County near a swamp where we killed more than a few and were able to secure a large amount of their food and supplies. We drove em off so quick that many of their babies were found abandoned and dead. We began to see that if we kept em on the move, they had trouble replenishin their supplies and payin us them little surprise visits.

By late August at Cow Creek we pretty much put an end to the Indian uprisin by stoppin em from reachin the Okefenokee Swamp where trackin would have been near impossible. There was quite a bit of hand to hand fightin there as I remember, and I saw for the first time Creek women fightin and firin weapons. I shot several Creeks that day and killed one with my knife, looked him right in the eye when I took him but I'm mighty thankful I didn't kill any of the women. I suspect that I would have had trouble sleepin later on, knowin I had done such a thing. I always was of a mind that a man don't need any stingin memories in his pillowcase when he lays his head down hopin for a good night's rest.

In September of that same year, the Hussars finally returned home to Milledgeville although some Indian fightin did continue on to the south. It felt good to be home, alive and in one piece and to be able to see my family and neighbors once again. I even had a nice sit-down visit with Mrs. Clark and told her all that had happened. To my surprise the woman had a silver plate put in her head to replace the scalp that was taken. I am happy to say that she is still livin to this very day but I still can't for the life of me keep from wonderin how that silver plate was ever fastened on to her skull. As I was always afraid to ask, it remains quite a puzzlement, indeed.

Now there's another part of the story that needs tellin here. You see this war with the Creeks in Georgia was only part of a greater war that continued on in the south, mainly in Florida. The war come to be called the Great Seminole War and as far as I know, it never really ended with a clear-cut victory for either side. The war was some eight years in length with several thousand Americans killed and, by all accounts, some forty million dollars spent by the Federal Government. At least the Baldwin Hussars and our Georgia comrades had kept the Creeks from joinin up with these Seminoles but that didn't stop their chief (a fella named Osceola) from decimatin the entire sugar cane industry down in Florida. Lots of scalpin, lootin, burnin and takin of slaves. Pretty nasty business, made more difficult by the swampy terrain them Seminoles called home.

Basically the army tried to do the same thing that we done in south Georgia, keep the Indians on the move so's they were unable to replenish their food and other resources. They also come to find like we did, that you had to fight like a redtail if you wanted to give yourself half a chance of victory. Truth to tell, the Indians did have superior weapons to ours. Their breech-loadin Spanish rifles was quicker to load and beat hell out of our .69 caliber flintlock muskets. Over time, however, the government gained the advantage if not the victory.

We all continued to follow the war from home in the local newspaper and one thing that really caught me and Jesse's attention late in the conflict was a new strategy that the government attempted. Martin van Buren, our esteemed president, sent officials off to Cuba to inquire bout some bloodhound trackin dogs they had over there. It was reported that them dogs was special and had the reputation of bein the best in the business. Ben Franklin had suggested just such a thing almost one hundred years previous to take care of an earlier Indian problem, but nothin ever come of it. The United States this time, however, bought thirty-three of these hounds. I believe they paid one hundred and fifty dollars for each one, if I remember correctly, with a little extra throwed in for the Cuban handlers. The dogs was expensive, that's for sure, but sometimes I figure quality is much more important than cost.

The dogs was divided up among American navy, marine and infantry units and sent into the swamps and woods after the Seminoles, but the results were not what was expected. The dogs acted confused as the type of trackin they was bein asked to do was not the same as what they had done in the past. The swamps, the Indians, the lack of a scent item all was different than the trackin of negro slaves that had run off the sugar plantations back in their native Cuba. Although newspaper reporters began to sour on the animals, Jesse and me understood and appreciated the different set of circumstances here.

Also, abolitionists up north started in accusin the government of "inhumane behavior," usin dogs to track down human beings. We all knew them abolitionists were really fixin their triggers on the activities of folks in the south regardin the bloodhound's part in the chasin of black slaves much more than they were concerned bout any redtails runnin round down in the swamps of Florida. They made such a fuss of it, though (and with poor results from the government's investment) the idea was finally abandoned.

This noble effort, however, weren't lost on Jesse and me. As we continued to read accounts of the war in the *Southern Recorder*, we began to think more and more of a bloodhound trackin business that might just be a good way for us to earn a livin. We would have the best. It was true that there were other fellas trackin round Milledgeville, but most of em was born tired and raised lazy and only worked at trackin part of the time. Many of their dogs was of equally poor quality too, some just barn-yard mutts probably better suited for chasin rabbits out of the garden if they could even do that. Jesse and me had no doubt if we put our minds to it and invested our money wisely, we could compete and be successful. As we had always been taught in the Tims family, the man who works the hardest, thinks the longest and does his job the best, why that man would be in a good position to be successful. Now we weren't thinkin that our bloodhounds would be runnin after any redtails mind ya, but we could well imagine any number of folks maybe a shade darker in color that might just be on the run up in our neck of the woods, valuable property that owners would pay handsomely to have returned. We made up our minds right then and there that it wouldn't be long fore the Tims boys would have themselves some well-trained-up bloodhound trackin dogs that would soon be nippin right on the heels of any black man or woman that took to fleein their responsibilities or their lot in life.

Chapter 7

"YOU'LL KNOW HER WHEN YOU SEE HER"

Jesse and me built a pen over at his and Becky's place with the whole of the Tims family more than a might excited over our new business venture. Jeremy Prigg was a neighbor who knew a great deal bout the trackin business and said he had the good fortune to have had one of these bloodhound dogs near the end of his trackin days. He told us if he had knowed just how good they was he never would have bothered with any other, but the fact was that J.P.'s legs give out and his back was all a-twist by the time he got one. He said it was a downright pity that he had to up and quit the business when he did. I still get to chucklin from time to time when I think on a comment he once made regardin this amazin animal. "Son," he said, "them dogs could find a flake of flea shit in a pile of pepper." I would have to say that ol Jeremy Prigg was a man of true insight and one you could set stock by. He proved many times over durin the years to be a valuable friend and neighbor to the Tims family.

We got our first two bloodhounds pups from a fella up in Cartersville. He had hisself a fine reputation and had been breedin those animals quite some time and he give us some good advice on how to raise em up to be good trackin dogs. We did make our fair share of early mistakes, but the Tims' name and their fetch hounds come to be known throughout the area fore too much time had passed. After a couple of years our little bloodhound family had growed to four dogs and we was makin nough money to support Jesse, Becky and me with a little left over after all was said and done. I knew I could now support a wife of my own if I had the good fortune to find me the right one.

Life had changed considerable for us with Jesse and me workin every day together. Daddy got along just fine without me down at the shop and Jesse was happy to have quit the mill. Some things never change, though, with the Tims menfolk still elbow to elbow, servin monthly on alarm duty and also takin our regular turn at slave patrol.

Now there really weren't no need to use trackin dogs when we was doin regular patrol duty at night. Mounted horsemen could move about quickly on their own, securin the roads in the community, makin sure the negro curfew of nine o'clock was strictly observed and they all was in their proper place for the evenin. Lastin till maybe three or four in the mornin, slave patrolin could most sure interfere with a man's daily routine, but knowin the necessity of the thing and, course, the chance for some socialization with friends and neighbors more that outweighed the inconvenience. As long as a person owned property in the community, they was obliged to serve on slave patrol. Stead of goin on patrol theirselves, it is true that some of the wealthier citizens and women property owners chose to hire it done and pay the two dollar daily fine. As a general rule there would be a group of five or six patrollers formed up for a month's time, ridin usually three nights a week. Armed with whips, guns and bindin rope, these mounted citizens could keep a pretty watchful eye on the ten or so square miles assigned to em. This was not just the case round Milledgeville mind ya…this here procedure was followed religiously throughout the entire south.

Now the key to bein a successful "pattyroller," as we was often called, always lay with the element of surprise. Change up the hours some, patrol on different nights of the week, visit different plantations or different areas where runaways tend to frequent and you could put uncertainty into the minds of potential fugitives and keep em at bay. Many folks round here have speculated on what would happen if the "contagin" were to start up again and things were to go every which-a-way. No one will soon forget the summer of '31 when that runaway Nat Turner went on the rampage over in Virginia. Claimin that he was a prophet sent by God to destroy slavery, he and other black rebels killed and mutilated some sixty or so innocent white folks, many of em women and children. As I recall, they had moved quickly from plantation to plantation killin and lootin, pickin up guns, horses and more black recruits on the way, tryin to put together a slave army of some sort. It's a true blessin, indeed, that locals was alerted to the danger and with help from surroundin counties and cities, a stop was put to the thing fore it spread too far. Certain people was brought to account for their actions in the matter and Nat Turner hisself, I heard tell, was hung up on the gallows, had his head cut off and then skinned up to boot. There are any number of folks in the south that lay claim to havin handbags or billfolds in their possession made up of the tanned hide of the rebel Nat Turner. Now nobody wanted to see such a thing happen again, so keepin everythin right and proper on the local level with these here patrols was probably the best way of preservin our peculiar institution.

As I remember it was a few years after Jesse and me had started in the trackin business and before Cynthia had come into my life, that we was doin some regular patrolin near our homes in Baldwin County. We had dropped in earlier in the evenin at the McKinley plantation but turned up nothin suspicious down in the quarters. Plantation owners was usually unhappy as all get out for a drop-in visit by the pattyrollers, particularly when disciplinary measures needed to be taken and valuable property compromised. Individual slave owners was grateful that their niggers was bein watched by other whites in authority, but didn't like to suffer any losses themselves. Just like Daddy used to say bout admission into Heaven above…"Folks all want to go there till they find out what is required to make the trip."

At the McKinley place we had been nosin round for the usual things, any tools of insurrection like weapons, poisons, incendiaries and such. Also, any evidence of education like books or writin paper would be a dead giveaway that certain laws was bein ignored. Maybe these visits would turn up a person or persons who did not belong there, or reveal the absence of one who did. Large gatherins of blacks was also unauthorized behavior which needed to be watched closely. We left there certain-sure that any problems we might encounter this evenin would not come from the slave quarters at the McKinley place.

It was well on to midnight when we made the decision to head over to Pleasant Ennis's house for a little fortification gainst the chill of the night. The Ennises were well known for their home-brewed body warmin whisky, in fact, it was often said that three glasses of Ennis whisky could even cause a man to not know his mamma. Pleasant was a good friend and comrade on patrol and a generous man as well. Our group of Patrolmen Ennis, Ben Johnson, Middleton Dawkins, Richard Mayhorn, Jesse and myself reached the Ennis cabin some twenty minutes later.

"There sure be a little nip in the air!" Ben Johnson announced as we dismounted and went inside.

"And a little nip requires a little nip," Ennis interjected in an attempt to add a little humor to the evenin's activities. "Now I ain't holdin any man to a count, but you all know what needs doin tonight and too much of this stuff can cloud a man's judgment. Bein warm ain't no good if this stuff knocks you stupid, right boys?" Ennis added. This remark was followed by a dull murmur, givin at least some acknowledgement of Pleasant Ennis's attempt at fatherly advice.

Excesses by pattyrollers was well known and probably more than a few of these instances was the result of too much "fortification" gainst the night air. Some people in particular were subject to a certain orneriness when drinkin. I had a feelin this last remark may have been directed in particular at Mr. R. Mayhorn who a few years back while on patrol duty, beat a negro named Nathan half to death with his whip. The slave had evaded questions and refused to give what Patrolman Mayhorn thought was a proper account of hisself. The slave did have a lawful ticket signed by his master, but I think the alcohol had somethin to do with the risin demands placed upon the bondsman. As I remember, Mayhorn really got a dressin down in court when Master Carey brought charges agin him. The judge dismissed Mayhorn from patrol duty for one year, sayin he had "acted meaner than a suck-egg dog," but hoped a lesson could be learned from the experience, so's he could return to his civic duties sometime in the future.

But it was chilly that evenin and maybe we did settle in a little more than was usual. Milledgeville politics, local gossip and the ruckus down at the whorehouse the other night all become subjects of conversation, but what I seem to recollect most was a remark that Pleasant made concernin women and the institution of marriage. Pleasant Ennis was a good family man, married to Evelyn with five kids, the whole clan was known for their large, close-knit families. Not bein married myself, I was just lookin for a little advice from some of the older fellas and I remember him tellin me: "Coswell, when the right one comes your way…you take my word on it now…you'll know her when you first lay eyes on her…you'll know her straightaway!" Jesse agreed with that assessment and told everyone how it had been with him and Becky. It was good that my brother opened hisself up a little on this subject. As often as I was with him I could only remember a few times when the pain of that loss was revisited.

An hour or so had gone by when we mounted up and returned to patrol duty. As a general rule we stuck to the main roads as we found we could cover the most ground that way. We knew the roads well on account of slave patrol duty startin off when we was but sixteen years of age. (A man's obligation in this regard did not end until he reached the age of sixty.) Slaves goin from plantation to plantation would use these same roads as they was the easiest way to travel. Even runners would use em at night, but most like as not they would travel in the bushes and swamps durin the daylight hours.

Well, as I remember, we was out on the old Mill Road, near the north road that leads to Eatonton. That was a road that slaves would often use if they was inclined to head in a northerly direction with many of em usin the North Star as a guide to freedom. Of course that star is to be found up in the sky and any walkin or runnin the fugitive had to do was to be done right here on the ground. Nature could sure throw up more that a few obstacles if that was all they had to go by. Most slaves knew very little bout the area outside their own plantation less they had been sold off frequently or had worked as a coachman or traveled with their master as body servants. Word-of-mouth was mostly what they relied on.

As would often be the case, slaves that were up to no good would be quickly intercepted by the pattyrollers, punished with a whippin and brought to the local jail where the owner would be required to pick em up and pay a fine. There would then often be another whippin, if not given by the slave owner, then laid on by the local sheriff for a small fee. Runaways might end out with fifty or sixty lashes before they was returned home to the plantation. Owners of slaves that were killed by pattyrollers in the line of duty was reimbursed by the county.

It was a little after two o'clock in the mornin when we spotted three negroes comin up the road. Now in all honesty we did not expect to see a lot of slaves movin about as it was Tuesday night. Had it been a Saturday night, expectations would have been different. Sunday was a day of rest for the black man as well as the white man and many bondsmen would secure passes from their masters as a reward for good work durin the past week. A male slave might be goin off to see his woman or his broadwife, a wife that lived on a different plantation than his. For that matter, some negroes just felt the need to visit their kin or friends. Lots of slaves would be off the plantation on weekends, but on a Tuesday night we really expected few if any, specially at this late hour.

The three we had our eye on made no attempt to run into the woods as was often the case. I guess men that sit up high on a horse can be a frightful sight indeed, and we have found that even slaves with a lawful ticket might run either from fear or maybe just for the sport of eludin the pattyrollers. When this did happen, it usually went worse for the ones that got caught. These slaves had no such ideas in their heads. They was all from the same place and had been rented out to another plantation to work the later part of the week. Their owner give em a very specific pass with the slaves names, where they had permission to go and for how long. It also included the owner's written signature. The only thing that really bothered us was the lateness of the hour, but they assured us that their master had made arrangements late in the day and it took a while to get this small work party put together.

Specifics like these were much appreciated by patrollers as the general pass that some owners give their slaves often made the job more difficult. A pass that was supposedly good for a whole month or one that lacked other specific documentation was often questioned. One slave owner in our area, I remember, used to complicate things up considerable as he would hang a wooden sign on the neck of his human property that read: "Anyone messin with this here nigger will have to answer to me," with his signature boldly inscribed for all to see. After examinin the tickets for these three and askin a few more questions, these bondsmen were allowed to pass on without incident.

Not much time had passed and it was gettin on time for us to be headin for home, when some movement down the road apiece caught our attention. We had been quietly settin on our horses back off the road some, when a black buck and wench was spotted comin in our direction. Suddenly they took to duckin into the bushes just bout the same time Ben Johnson had lit up his pipe. I thought I also saw each of the travelers carryin a tote sack of some sort, a sure sign that the trip they was plannin might just be a little longer than the next plantation over.

"Let's go!" yelled Ennis as we rode down to the place in the road where they were last seen. It didn't take long, however, fore we found ourselves leadin our horses through some pretty thick underbrush. This continued for some time till finally we emerged from the thicket and mounted up again.

"I think I see em," Ben Johnson yelled as he spurred his horse to get out in front and head em off. As he did this, the male negro turned so's to retreat back into the bush and that's when Mayhorn rode his horse right over the fugitive. As we dismounted to assess the situation, I couldn't help but notice Patrolman Mayhorn's obvious delight over the whole affair. His merry eyes just glistened as he pushed the concerned woman from the injured man's side and roughly put the leg shackles round the ankles of his dark skinned captive...all this despite the moanin and groanin comin from the injured party. I thought to myself at the time that there's some folks who enjoyed this slave-catchin business a heap more than others.

We began to ask some questions, but both seemed quite reluctant at first to speak out. Mayhorn did come up with a right fine idea and said he'd gladly whip the woman if the questions continued to remain unanswered. I got to admit that did make the male negro see the logic of the whole thing.

We soon learned that the buck was named Julius and the wench went by the name of Cordelia. Julius, he admitted that they had been on the run for several weeks now and judgin by their clothin and the condition they was both in, I could see where that might very well have been the case. They said that they had run away from a very cruel master named Walker from down New Orleans way. Now runnin from a cruel master was understandable and quite common, but it was the part about New Orleans we found difficult to swallow. Why that city was several hundred miles away and besides, any slave runnin from such a place would generally follow the Mississippi River north on to Ohio, not head northeast on foot and end out in Baldwin County, Georgia. If what he was sayin was true, then they may just have been following that North Star and seein as though it had been cloudy for the better part of last week, well maybe they sort of up and got theirselves good and lost. If that were the case, they sure was a long way from home. Of course, as pattyrollers we were quite prepared to deal with that. We brought em to a new home that night, one with bars and keys...the Milledgeville jail down on Penitentiary Square. Sheriff Strother said he would soon send word down the old mail road to New Orleans with information for their owner regardin their current place of residence but it would be up to him, this Mr. Walker, to come and claim his lost property.

Several weeks had gone by and one day when I was in town I saw the young sheriff and he give me the latest news on our captives. "Hey, Coswell, we still got them two runaways from New

Orleans locked up over in the jail. Sure would like to get rid of em. Just cause the law allows us to sell off unclaimed human property, by the time we wait a whole year as the law requires, they'd have cost us more for upkeep than we would get for their sale. Your little group might just make a tidy sum, though, if that Walker fella antes up. As soon as he sends word, I'll let you know."

It was true that pattyrollers could be paid if there was a price on the runaway, but most times a slave was caught before the overseer or owner even knew they was gone, so there was usually no postin and no reward.

About a week later a telegraph message reached the sheriff. Mr. Walker sent five hundred dollars for the runaways and money for the fine and upkeep in the local jail. He also requested that someone bring the two back to New Orleans as he said he was too busy to make the trip hisself. He tossed in three hundred dollars travelin expenses and said he would add to that and make it well worth someone's while to do him this favor. We now knew this Walker fella was a real flesh and blood individual, not the product of some slave's active imagination, and by the way he seemed to be throwin his money round, we figured the man to be of considerable standin.

That night Jesse and me discussed all this over supper. I was livin over at his place at the time as Becky had recently passed on and I was concerned that my older brother might be in need of some tendin.

"Jesse, what do you think about me goin down to New Orleans?" I asked. "I'd probably be gone the better part of a month. You think you could handle the trackin business without me?"

Jesse said that any work that required two people, he could call on our neighbor Ben Johnson, or for that matter Jeremy Prigg, who was retired from the trackin business but despite his age, had forgotten more than most people ever knew bout this line of work.

"You go on, Coswell," Jesse concluded. "This Walker fella is obviously pretty well off...might even be the biggest toad in the puddle down there and I think this just might be a good thing for the family business."

With Jesse's blessin I wasted no time the next day bookin passage on the Washington City to New Orleans mail route. This was one of the longest roads in the country and had been operatin through Milledgeville since away back in 1815. It really weren't nothin more than a narrow path cut through the wilderness with ruts from many a vehicle that dared to travel its length. Ol Mr. Bird, the postmaster, warned me that the road was bumpy and swampy in places and that it was uncomfortable with all the mail sacks and such, but they did take passengers providin they was willin to pay the fee. These two niggers, he said, would go as baggage and be assessed as such. By law, they were not allowed to sit with white passengers (as it was with any type of public transportation) less they was special attendants of some kind. I paid the fee and agreed to be back tomorrow at noon with my "baggage" in tow ready to head out for the city of New Orleans.

Chapter 8

A DIFFERENT WORLD

The next day I stopped over at the jail and was put in charge of the two fugitives. “Coswell, you got a long trip ahead,” the sheriff had said. “My thinkin is that you should keep restraints on their ankles but there’s no call to chain em together as I figure neither one really wants to be somewhere where the other ain’t.” I agreed with the sheriff’s assessment and figured the slaves Cordelia and Julius would ride outside in the baggage compartment of the coach and I would ride up top with the driver so’s I could keep a close eye on my human packages. I don’t think either one of them darkies spoke but two words the whole way, kinda downcast and resigned to their fate, they were, certainly not like a person would generally be when they knew they was headed for home.

Six days later, probably twenty horse changes, at least half a dozen times stuck in the mud, and more rattlin round than most bodies could tolerate, our mail coach finally rumbled into the city of New Orleans. We had stopped at travel houses long the way, but the ride was long and most uncomfortable and I was mighty glad to be gettin off the coach and onto some good solid ground. I give a good-bye to the driver, a fella named Artimus Baxter whose hard-luck story he felt the need to share with me over the better part of the previous week. I helped the prisoners out of the baggage compartment, with the rattle of chains causin several bystanders to take notice as the two stepped to the street.

Lookin round, I had to admit I had never seen such a big place in all my born days. Tucked under the arm in a bend of the Mississippi River, this low lyin, crescent shaped area of land was wedged tween the river and a huge lake that emptied out into the Gulf of Mexico. This port city was all a hustle and a bustle with people of all colors and persuasions movin purposefully about. The buildins was large and stately, lookin like those a person might see in a picture book of Europe or someplace like that. Some of the streets was quite wide, while others cozied right up to the many businesses located on either side. Locals, I found, was bent on sayin that some of these streets was haunted with memories of the city's long troublesome past. Yellow fever victims from years ago, I heard tell, still moan and cry in the final throes of their misery as Latin prayers from long dead priests are said to still be heard in the dark hours fore dawn. Down on Congo Square where the city's blacks have met up over the years, they say you can still hear the voodoo drums of jungle days. Truth be known, the whole thing was a little unsettlin for the likes of a small-time Georgia trackin man. Milledgeville was considered a city by Georgia standards but Lawd Almighty, it looked like a tiny little one-horse town compared to this place. I had never been this far from home before, even during the Creek War when I found myself in south Georgia and northern Florida, but at least I did have a fair notion where I was headed so I didn't take to dwellin on the size of things all that much.

The trader yard was my destination and the directions Mr. Walker had give me were adequate for the occasion. I entered a trader yard and, as instructed, located the office of one of Mr. Walker's closest associates, a man named Long. Actually this fella was the owner of the whole shebang and a man Walker frequently done business with.

"Excuse me sir, would you be Major Long," I asked as I entered the office that had his name inscribed above the door. I had both fugitives in tow.

"I am, indeed," he replied. "And you, sir, you must be that Coswell Tims fella. We've been expecting ya'll. We got word from the sheriff and, oh, yes, I recognize these two," he said as he give the two runaways a knowin glare. "Mr. Walker will be quite happy to have you back. I'm afraid there is gonna be some pretty severe punishment to be had seein though you've been gone so long."

I thought it rather unusual that this man carried a bull whip in his right hand, particularly while he was settin here in his office. I never knowed anyone to do this. When he switched it up to the left hand as we commenced shakin, and then returned it to the right when we was done, I figured the man had a powerful need to carry that thing about. Why, it almost seemed as if it had grown attached somehow and was a natural extension of the hand that held it.

"Would Mr. Walker be here, sir?" I inquired.

"Mr. Walker is currently indisposed," Long answered. "I believe he is down at the auctions on the wharf. You can leave these two here if you've a mind to and go down to see him. I'll assure you I will take very good care of his property and see it don't wander off again."

"I think I will do just that," I said, and after another handshake where Long handed me a receipt for the returned property and I watched the whip change hands once more, I set out to find the wealthy and well-known slave trader.

Walker, like so many of his kind, saw tremendous business opportunity in the sale of slaves to meet the risin demand for labor in the deep south and in the newly developin western territories. Despite the fact that the slave trade had been outlawed by Congress, I believe back in 1808, there weren't no law that prohibited the breedin and movement of slaves that was already here. Why, I remember a slave owner in southern Georgia named James Roberts who bragged on the fact that he kept fifty or sixty slave women at his place that were specially good breeders and could tally up some twenty-five negro children each and every year. Of course that would mean that the youngins would be taken away from their mammas as soon as they became sellable. Breakin up black families became more common at this time as able males was often the first to be moved in to clear land and plant cotton, rice or sugar cane for a new plantation. Goin down river in specially designed boats or chained together to make the journey on foot, many of these coffles found their way to New Orleans, which because of its location, became the slave tradin capital of the south. I come to find that fate seemed to favor this Mr. Walker at every turn, always seemin to be in the right place and at the right time to make the greatest profit… which I reckon would be the best description of a good businessman.

I had no trouble at all findin that part of the slave tradin yard where the auctions was bein held. For one thing I noticed quite a smell as there were several hundred negroes crowded into pens that looked like they was made to hold cattle. The other thing I was noticin was the great amount of noise there was. Not only was there many bidders about, but the excitement made em even louder than they might normally have been.

I could hear a shrill voice that rung out over all the others. This voice was cryin off the slaves one at a time, actin much like an auctioneer. I found out later they called this man "Whisperin Joe" which seemed rather odd seein as though people said you could here the fella holler clearly some five miles off.

Before "Whisperin Joe," spoke out, a curtain would come down that had been hidin a group of maybe twenty black men, women and a few children. They was all instructed to come forward and go up a few stairs to a wooden platform for viewin and inspectin. Whisperin Joe Taylor would strut about, whip in his hand, a pepperbox pistol stuck in the front of his checkerboard trousers. He skillfully moved slaves about on the platform, carefully choosin the order of sale and the best positionin of each one. Reminded me how store owners sometimes rearranged their stock in the windows so's to bring in the most business. He then began to announce their names one by one. He also added their ages, their abilities and whether or not they had religion. Havin religion meant that the slave was most likely compliant. Marks on the back might indicate that the slave tended to be troublesome. Potential buyers was very careful as a general rule, wantin to invest their money wisely.

Most of the bidders had on white gloves and I noticed that they would rub their fingers over the slave's teeth and look inside the mouth. They would check their hair with the gloves to make sure it had not been colored so as to make em look younger. Also I noticed some of the bidders took to runnin their hands over the slaves bodies lookin for body paint that might hide some flaws, deformities or whip marks. One naked slave woman, much to her obvious embarrassment and shame, was given a thorough and intimate examination in full view of others by a potential owner who said he was interested in gettin a good breedin wench. All the slaves were asked to hop, trot and jump about to prove that they was fit and also to show that they was good at followin instructions. There was a great deal of biddin and negotiatin, but within a few hours time, most all their number had been sold off and left with their new masters for new homes and a new life.

I did not see Mr. Walker, not that I would have knowed him if I set eyes on him, but I did listen pretty intently when the new owners was announced. Hearing nothin, I finally asked a well-dressed gentleman who stood nearby if he knew this Mr. Walker. He told me that he did know him, in fact, he guessed most folks knew him if they did any slave-tradin business here in New Orleans. The man I was lookin for, he said, was currently aboard the steamship *ENTERPRISE* which was docked down at the end of the wharf. He asked me if I was a buyer or perhaps a driver, but I told him I was only a citizen who was doin his duty and returnin lost property.

After just a short walk, I spotted the *ENTERPRISE* next to maybe a dozen or so other riverboats tied up along this side of the wharf. It was an old but rather noble lookin rear-paddle-wheeler that had obviously traveled the river for many years. It was somewhat in need of a paint job but it looked sturdy enough. My attention was drawed to the lower deck where many blacks was crowded in together, chained in pairs. I reckon that was to prevent some desperate individual from jumpin overboard and killin theirselves in an attempt to end their misery or their uncertainty over a recent sale. It certainly was a poor return on a man's investment if things ended that way. You could hear very little conversin among their number, just some low voices and maybe an occasional wail from one of the womenfolk. The smell was bad too. I guessed that this area of the boat was the most difficult to keep clean.

As I walked further down the wharf, I found myself lookin up at the boat and takin notice of how much larger it was than the ones we have on the Oconee, when I bumped right into a young black boy at work on one of the dock ropes. I sent him a-sprawlin. "Pardon, massa, pardon," he said as he got up. "Sanford terrible clumsy to be in massa's way."

"No harm done, young fella. Did you say your name was Sanford?"

"I did, massa."

"Sanford, you probably know as much as anyone round here. I want to ask you a question. Would you happen to know a man by the name of James Walker?" I asked.

A big smile come to the young boy's face, revealin a space tween his two front teeth. He told me that he knew Walker well, (or as well as any slave would know his own master). He described Walker, with some pride, as a very powerful man and added, as we looked over at the boat again, that all of the slaves on the lower deck were his property. Some still needed to be sold off, he said, and some he was takin back up river to his farm in St. Louis. Sanford added that his master had made a lot of money in the slave tradin business. Abolitionists in the north often referred to these people as "soul drivers" so I guessed our Mr. Walker must have made hisself quite a good livin drivin many a hapless soul up or down this long, wide river.

I inquired as to the current whereabouts of his master and Sanford give his reply. "Massa Walker, well, he be right dare on dat boat, fer certin," he said, pointin towards the upper deck of the craft.

As I looked to where the black finger pointed, I could not see any slave trader but my eyes did come to rest on a woman, a quite handsome woman in fact, who appeared to be all alone and regally surveying the docks and those below her. I remember saying to myself at the time that this might just be the most beautiful woman I had ever in this life laid my eyes on. I could feel myself takin a full step forward.

This lady could not have been much more than twenty or twenty-five years of age and her beauty was absolutely strikin as she began to move slowly back and forth on the upper deck of that boat. She was dressed tolerably well but not in refinement and I guessed just bout every person on the docks must have been strainin their eyes to see her same's I was. She had light colored hair, straight and long, that rose and fell softly with her movements and a slight breeze that I could feel blowin up from the river. She stopped briefly and looked over in my direction. "What a fine lookin example of womankind!" I remembered sayin to myself.

But what I soon come to learn from Sanford on the matter was that this here individual, this beautiful white-lookin female…why she weren't what she looked to be at all. Fact of the matter was, the boy said, this woman was ***one of Walker's slaves!*** Now if'n this boy weren't fablin and takin me for a damn fool, she must be what folks called a quadroon or maybe an octoroon, a white lookin nigger with a passel of black blood that still run through her veins. There is a term used down south : "one drop," which means that if one drop of colored blood be in a body, then as a general rule that whole person would legally be considered black. (Of course there are them folks that like to think that "seven-eighths" would be more fittin so's to accommodate many a proper white family.) Now this here woman looked perfectly white to me and she had a way bout her that looked anythin but servile. Without movin my head from the image that had captivated me, I pressed Sanford for more information.

"Massa Walker jus come by her," Sanford related, now standin more to the rear of me as I had tried to reposition myself yet again for an even clearer view. "She from plantation jus awdside Vicksburg. Massa hep dribe her and maybe thirty utter niggers down to da riber…drove em hard, too! She look dern site worse bowt a week go. Massa took fancy to her, want her powerful bad. Say he gonna make her hed ob his housekeepin up dar in St Louis if'n she willin to do what he want. She gib em da go-by and tell Sanford here dat she would never gib herself to dis evil man, she would up n die fust, she sed. But da clothes she be wearin and da fancified room she be in, say she comin round ter Massa's way of thinkin. You can believe dis chile when he say, Massa give her a couple of younguns and sell the whole lot of em off someday when he take a mind ter."

"Her name, boy…what is her name?" I asked with a risin sense of urgency as I reached back and, without lookin, grabbed at the young informant's shoulder.

"Her name, Massa?" Sanford replied. I could feel him shufflin bout as if in need of more time to review the question. When I took to shakin the boy one last time the answer finally come forth. "Why, why…dat nigger's name be Cynthia!"

Chapter 9

THE FORK IN THE ROAD

I did eventually spy a shadowy figure lurkin like some booger off to the side of that second deck as pointed out by the young slave boy Sanford. That did not, however, cause my eyes to stray too far from the image that had captivated my full attention. I remember that the ship most fell away into the background while I had gazed, full-eyed, on this fetchin young beauty, but now that she and the man with her had passed from my view, I began to take notice of the *ENTERPRISE* once more.

This boat appeared old and weather-beaten, but serviceable. I knew it to be a fact that these here shallow-bottomed, steam-driven paddle-wheelers had been goin up and down this Mississippi River long before my time, pickin up passengers and distributin cargo long the way. From New Orleans to St. Louis (a distance of maybe 1,200 miles) a good steamboat with a decent steam, I heard tell, could most likely make that trip in bout five days' time.

Sanford said in two days' time the *ENTERPRISE* would be

leavin for St. Louis, carryin the beautiful young lady and the other slaves with it, many to start new lives at Walker's farm just outside the city of St. Louis. Sanford also let it be known that the wealthy slave merchant was not married but had a fair number of black housekeepers and a whole passel of mulatter children they had produced on the place. Appears he was one of them fellas that took a strong likin to slave women and preferred their company over women of his own kind. I would say there are more folks than not (both white and black) that look down on such behavior, citin the high moral duty of a slave owner to provide a good example for his slave family and perform his duties towards em in a proper way in the sight of God and all concerned. Most folks I know believe the races should be left separate and not mixed in together as that was thought to defy the natural order of things set up by the good Lord hisself. From what I was startin to piece together here, this Mr. Walker, seemed to be a man who cared little for others or their opinions and had but one way of goin bout his business and most like as not, that way was his own.

Again Sanford proved his worth when he said he would take me to see his master. I did not want to lose track of the reason I had come to this city in the first place...a business venture involvin the Tims Brothers and a wealthy slave owner.

We crossed over on a gangplank to the lower deck and I walked with Sanford close at my heels up a flight of stairs to the second. Anyone with half an eye could plainly see that conditions was more favorable on this deck, what with dinin rooms and state rooms for those people fortunate nough to be able to afford the difference.

As I entered a large stateroom, I quickly spotted a man I knew had to be Walker. He was a-standin there just like he was the big dog with the brass collar, folks all crowded in round him like he come down from the mountain or somethin, maybe carryin a couple of stone tablets in his hands. My first impression was that he was a might taller than most, but then thought that could be due to the large wide-brimmed hat and tall boots that supplied the top and bottom of the man. His clothes was handsome for sure. Dark trousers was neatly tucked inside brown boots and his green frock coat, you could tell straight off, was made of the finest material and done by tailors who knew their craft. His face was long but his jaw was squared and favorable at the end, yet I was quick to notice he had a habit of pushin that jaw out in the direction of any person he happened to be talkin to. Walker had light colored skin like a man whose livin had been made more indoors than out and that was set off by the thick dark mustache that drooped down past both sides of his rather thin lips. All in all, I did have to admit the man had a very impressive and commandin manner.

Walker was holdin a recently poured drink in his hand when he spotted me and announced loudly so's all-around could hear: "Don't tell me…you, sir, are the indefatigable Mr. Tims are you not? Come all the way from Georgia in the name of duty, honor and profit?"

Well, I would have to say that this fancy way of talkin took me back apiece. I have heard folks gassin round, buildin up air castles with their words many times previous, but I reminded myself that me and Jesse have always been quite proud of the time we spent with Mr. Denison down at the Milledgeville Academy gettin us a fine education. We learned readin, writin and cipherin under the direction of this Yankee from Vermont and he even taught us a little poetry which he was partial to. Taught us a lot of fancy words, too, but I had never in all my born days heard anyone use the word "indefatigable" and found myself wonderin silently as to its meanin.

"I am Coswell Tims, sir, and I have done as instructed," I finally replied. "Your two wayward slaves are cozied up with Major Long as we speak." (I notice the man give a slight smile when I said "cozied up" and took it to mean that I was country-folk and perhaps beneath his lofty station.)

"Excellent, then you must have a drink with us, Mr. Tims. Let me introduce you to some of my associates," Walker responded. Some brief introductions followed. I got the impression that all of these people was wealthy slave merchants, all in the slave tradin business for sure. (I couldn't help thinkin that there was one person, a female associate of his, that I would much rather be meetin, but I also knew full well he wouldn't be takin to introducin me to her anytime soon.)

"I have some money here for you, Mr. Tims. Would $1,000 make your long and arduous journey worth the time and effort?" he asked rather loudly as he handed me an envelope he had taken from his coat pocket.

"That would be right fine," I answered, as I put the money in my pocket without makin any attempt to count it. A slight smile come to his face once more but I couldn't figure out why. One of Walker's black servants poured me a drink and I remember thinkin after takin a sip or two, that Pleasant Enniss' whiskey was a damn site better than what this very wealthy slave trader had to offer. Why, you would think a man with Walker's money and connections could afford the very best of everythin. I thought to myself...sometimes money just don't buy quality.

"I am sorry I have to leave you Mr. Tims after so brief a visit, but I have a great deal of business that I must transact before I leave in two days. Please feel free to finish your drink and if you require anything else, you can ask one of my servants," Walker stated as he turned in haste to leave.

Most of Walker's associates began to resume their former conversations, so I put the unfinished glass of whisky down on the counter and headed for the stairs. With the luxury of the second deck left behind, I soon found myself in the roomin house I had rented up for the night. I figured Jesse would be right happy bout the thousand dollars in that envelope and I fully admit I counted it out to my satisfaction a number of times.

The bed in the roomin house weren't much different than others found in places such as these. The bed sheets had not been changed in some time which was pretty much the way it was with most roomin houses and taverns. Changin em maybe once every two weeks or so or maybe after a real good soilin was usually bout all a traveler could come to expect these days. Now an expensive hotel the likes of which a Mr. Walker might fancy would be quite different. I sniffed the sheets some to see if there was any turpentine smell as that would indicate that a sick man had slept there previous. I paid very little attention to the tobacco stains on the walls and floor and the unemptied spit box that lay next to the bed. Blowin out the night light, I found myself thinkin back on the events of the day.

The money that I would be bringin home caused my chest to puff some, but I soon found that overshadowed by the image caught in my mind of a beautiful bird imprisoned inside a floatin cage called the *ENTERPRISE*. I guess it was the unfairness of the whole thing that struck me, this woman lookin white and all yet condemned to live the life of a negro slave. Now there's them that might look to the slave pens and the wailins of black families as they was cried off and separated as much more unfair, but to me, that just seemed like the way things have always been. But how could a man's eyes be so deceived, I thought. Black is black, white is white! Now could there be any two colors that was more different than them two? A negro should look like a negro and a white man should look like a white man if there was to be any good reason for colorin people to begin with. What would be the sense, I wondered to myself, of creatin two creatures that looked different if'n they were hard to tell apart. Was Mother Nature just tryin to confuse people and have herself a little fun at our expense?

Somethin else come to mind as I thought back on what I had observed over the years regardin mulatters and quadroons. I had always heard tell that in places like New Orleans, Charleston, Baltimore, and the like, the white lookin nigger was preferred and often even put on display, kinda like what I saw today with this woman Cynthia. In the country and round Milledgeville, however, bein a high yeller was most near the kiss of death. I always thought that it might be cause the mistress of the plantation wanted no constant reminders of her husband's infidelity, his trips down to the slave quarters on a Friday night totin a jug of stump liquor in hand, lookin to root round with some of his slave stock. That quadroon child who took to lookin more and more like daddy or maybe the oldest son each day, was probably goin to be in for a mighty rough time from the plantation mistress and maybe even from the master or son if guilt got to weighin heavy on em.

I guess the last thing that come to mind fore I fell asleep that night was not so much the fairness or unfairness of it, but more the logic of the whole thing. If some people (like people livin up north) would judge this woman to be white, and other people like people in the cities in the south saw her as black but preferable and the southern countryside folks saw her as black and undesirable, the only thing that seemed to be a- changin here weren't the woman herself but the opinions of them that was around her. What then was the truth on the matter? Mr. Henry Denison would be proud of me usin my head and ponderin such a wonderment, but then again, my teacher and mentor had been dead and in the dirt of Memory Hill since 1819 and if I didn't get me some sleep pretty soon, I thought that fella just might be havin hisself some company there on the other side.

I was well aware as I drifted off to sleep that night of the unseemly reputation the city of New Orleans enjoyed. Outside the door to my room I conjured up any number of activities goin on that most respectable citizens of Milledgeville would never be a party to. Pirates, prostitutes, pickpockets and other people of lowly purpose were afoot for sure, but when I placed my revolver under my pillow, I figured that whatever dangers might lurk in this strange city, Coswell Tims could probably give a good enough account of hisself to get back home and in good workin order.

One danger, however, I had not counted on…one bit of illegal activity that I really gave no mind to and didn't find out bout till some time later, was happenin at the very moment ol Coswell's head was a-restin right there on that dirty pillow. I reckon ol Jeff Davis had it right when as a United States senator he earlier spoke to Congress bout hidden dangers and treachery that his home state of Mississippi was subject to. Despite bein in the deep south like her sister state Louisiana, Mississippi Senator Davis complained to Congress his state was awash with abolitionists who used that "highway to the Ohio," the great Mississippi River, to snatch and carry off the rightful property of its citizenry. Dr. Alexander Ross, Gerrit Smith and a fella named Tappan were examples of these scalawags who would ignore the law to suit their own purpose. I was unaware at the time but all three was busy at work in New Orleans this night.

I come to find out later that this Ross fella had a little touch of the confidence man in him, as early on up in Vicksburg he had been makin negro contacts on the plantations there by claimin to be some kinda bird expert. (I believe "ornithologist" to be the proper word here.) He had been collectin bird samples from the local plantations and those owners believed this clever abolitionist and consented to help him with his work, all in the name of science. Authorities found out only later that the good doctor would instead select key negroes, indoctrinate em with stories of Canada and freedom, supply em with fire arms, compasses and contacts and then encourage em to separate from their lawful masters. I guess I never could understand why a man would go to these lengths and risk hangin just to meddle in someone else's business affairs. Now these here abolitionists were not suggestin that these slaves become northern citizens or compete against whites there for jobs, mind ya, or for that matter marry up with their sons or daughters. No sir, they just didn't want these niggers to be owned by southern whites as far as I can see. Never could understand the logic of it! My daddy used to say that a man would do well to keep his nose at home and in his own affairs.

I found out in drips and dribbles from a couple of different quarters later on, that these three abolitionists reaped the reward of the many contacts they had made during the previous several weeks. Puttin their plans into motion, six slaves from the city of New Orleans were to meet up in an old livery stable down by the wharf in the early mornin hours. For whatever reason only three made the rendezvous, and after waitin only a short time, I guess them abolitionists decided they could wait no longer. Headin out of the shop in an old wagon with horses shod with pieces of carpet, Smith, Ross and three black fugitives found themselves headed for Baton Rouge on the first leg of their journey northward.

A hard knock at the door woke me with a start but I was somewhat relieved to find that my hand had already wrapped itself round the worn handle of my Colt. I opened the door to see none other than the grand Mr. Walker standin right there before me. It struck me that it would be more proper that he should be standin in the doorway of the St. Charles Hotel which was probably the most luxurious hotel in the city. I had noticed that elegant building yesterday on the way back to the roomin house, and when I commented on it to a fella in the street he said it took up a whole city block with its restaurants, shops and rooms that could sleep and accommodate over a thousand people. It was so large sometimes even slave auctions was held inside, he had said. Somehow seein Walker in the dingy, worn-down place where his Georgia-cracker bounty hunter and other undesirables were holed up (and it was so early in the morning, too) must mean somethin well out of the ordinary had taken place.

"Mr. Tims, I need your help," were the first words out of his mouth. "You have been kind enough and expert enough to have restored my lost property to me in the most recent past. I would ask that you do that for me once again!"

"Excuse me, just for a moment, Mr. Walker, while I put on my boots and get tidied up some," I replied, busy-like, admittin to myself a certain pleasure respondin in somewhat the same high-handed dismissive manner as he had done me board the *ENTERPRISE*.

"What seems to be the problem?" I finally asked as I strapped on my trusty sidearm.

"Captain Reynolds has informed me that several of my slaves have run off last night and he does not feel that as captain of the *ENTERPRISE* he should be held responsible for their recovery. I, of course, disagree but I don't want to debate that now. I need to use all my resources to have my lost property returned as soon as possible. That is where you come in Mr. Tims," Walker stated.

"Surely, Mr. Walker you have your own people down here who know a heap more that I do and could carry out such a task!" I countered.

"Remember, Mr. Tims, I make my home in St. Louis. I must admit this has never happened to me before here in New Orleans. I am convinced this is the work of a well-organized and well-financed band of northern abolitionists. Seeing them hang and my property restored would make me a very happy man indeed and I assure you that my happiness would equate to a handsome reward for you, sir," he added.

"I am in business to make money, Mr. Walker, but I am at a

disadvantage here and feel I might just be stumblin round somethin awful if I was to take on this job. It is true that I am a trackin man by trade, but I find myself without my trackin hounds. I am not familiar with this here neck of the woods, nor do I have any local folks on whose observations I can rely. I'm sure there's better people suited for the job," I concluded.

"Mr. Tims," he answered, "One thing I know for sure. I am a very good reader of people and I know competence when I see it. I can instinctively detect confidence or lack of it in a man, something about the way he carries himself and the look in his eyes. You are a man, comfortable with yourself and your talents, Mr. Tims. Now I wish I had that same ability with my darkies. They always seem to be "puttin on the Massa" if you know what I mean. They'll say one thing and yet they'll do another. They'll play stupid when you know they know better. They would tell you it was raining when the sun was shining if they thought they could get away with it. I guess I may have put a little too much trust in certain black folks over the years and now I am paying the price."

"Well, Mr. Walker, I guess I would be willin to give it a try. Sides, I do have to wait several days for an available mail coach returnin to Milledgeville. I'll start straightaway," I responded, as I picked up a few more of my belongins and walked with the slave trader to the door.

Before Walker and I parted ways I felt the need to ask him two questions. Would he give me permission to use the whip on his slaves, includin the ones still aboard the *ENTERPRISE* and was the original timetable to leave for St. Louis still bein considered?

"We are not going to leave for a few more days," he replied. "As for the use of the whip, feel free to apply it where necessary to gain information or force compliance. I would ask, however, that you not use the whip on one of the three fugitives when you catch them. I have never whipped this one in particular as I have developed a special fondness for her despite her arrogance and her recent betrayal. She is a quadroon named Cynthia. All efforts must be made to bring her back unharmed. As for the others, I suppose that if they were both killed or damaged in an attempt to return them, their loss could be absorbed. Obviously, Mr. Tims, as a man of business, I would prefer that you make every effort to minimize my losses and maximize my investments!"

With mention of the name Cynthia, I felt most like a bolt of lightnin from Heaven above had shot right through the whole of me, suddenly leavin air trapped inside my goozle. Why it felt most like I had to gasp for breath to restore the balance. I could feel my heart start in racin fast and hoped Walker was ignorant of my reaction. I stared at him blankly and must admit at the time to seein only the woman he spoke of whose image would be forever fixed in the back of my mind. I could still see her standin there on the deck of the steamship, her long straight hair reachin down most to the middle of her back. I could still see her turn and continue to pace back and forth. I could still hear Sanford tellin me for the first time that she was the property of a rich white man. I remember it was at that very moment she took to throwin her shoulders back in a proud, almost defiant manner, and then she placed her hands firmly on the railin of that run-down old slave ship as she looked out at a world of freedom and privilege that circumstance had denied her.

It also suddenly come to my mind that she must have knowed bout the escape bein planned for that very night, yet there weren't the slightest hint of impendin flight. No sir, not only beautiful, I thought to myself, but brave and strong in character and will. I reckon I would need to see all them things close up for myself to know the truth of the matter, but as for now, I tried to set my mind straight and think on Mr. Walker's business proposition as I suddenly become aware he was quietly standin there awaitin a reply.

"I will do everythin I can to return your lost property," I remember hearin myself weakly say as Walker and I shook hands fore partin.

Takin stock of my circumstance, I realized my contacts in this city, outside of Walker, was limited to two others...Mr. Long and the young negro boy, Sanford. At the very least they could be a place to start, I reasoned, maybe they would even figure in more prominent.

Within an hour or so I returned to the trader yard where I found it much different than I remembered it the day before. It was quiet, and bein as it was early mornin, no auctions was bein held and none of the slaves was anywhere to be found. I suspected that any of em still unsold was bein kept in an old warehouse out behind the yard, but then I did not know that to be a fact.

One thing that was the same, however, was that Major Long was in his office pourin over his business affairs. As I walked through the door I wondered if he held that whip in his left hand, seein as though he was now so busy writin in his ledger with his right.

"Good mornin, Major Long," I said in greetin. "I find myself still in the employment of your associate, Mr. Walker, and have come to ask a favor of you, sir." Long nodded in my direction.

"It seems as if three of Mr. Walker's bondsmen up and left the *ENTERPRISE* last night for parts unknown and Mr. Walker believes I can be of value returnin em to his service."

"Why that is most unfortunate," Long stated, as he got up from his chair and put the whip he held in his left hand down on the table between us. "Not that you are again gainfully employed, sir, but that our Mr. Walker has had more than his fair share of business reversals of late, has he not? What specifically do you require of me, Mr. Tims?"

"Maybe some information first," I answered. "As owner of these yards you see and hear many things. Are you aware of any abolitionist threats or have you noticed any potential customers who have been conversin with the slaves and not buyin? Maybe noticed a change in attitude on the part of some of your stock?"

"I have noticed no difference in the attitude of the slaves, Mr. Tims, but then of course they do not stay here very long as a general rule," Long answered. "I did hear tell of an abolitionist named Ross been working some of the plantations to the north and maybe might be up to no good right here in New Orleans. Just rumors, though, I figure."

"I see. Well, I also could use the services of a couple of armed men and a wagon," I added. "I am unsure of how many slaves actually escaped last night and, if abolitionists are to blame, or how many of em were involved. Can you make these arrangements for me, Mr. Long?" I asked.

"I can indeed, Mr. Tims. They can be ready in less than a half hours' time. I'll be sure to put their fees on Mr. Walker's account... business, you know," Long explained.

"Why of course, Major Long. Now one more request if I may. I would also like to ask for the use of a whip. I felt no need to bring mine all the way from Milledgeville, Georgia and I believe circumstances may now require its use."

"I would be happy to oblige, Mr. Tims. Of course I could never part with this one," he said, pointin to the leather object that lay fully independent of his hand on his desk in front of him. "I assure you that this whip has great sentimental value," he said as his voice trailed off most like the object lyin there had taken on a certain reverence or brought back a sudden flood of fond memories.

Regainin the moment, he reached into one of his desk drawers and rather abruptly announced: "This one may suit your purpose, sir." He handed me an old, well-worn tool of the trade, tellin me to consider it a gift. The whip was as limber as an old rattlesnake and looked to be every bit as dangerous.

Now there are many people in the south that use and carry bullwhips...pattyrollers, overseers, plantation owners, local sheriffs, slave traders and professional trackin men like myself. Although I learned to handle a whip from ol Jeremy Prigg who bragged he could snap a fly off a fence if he'd a mind to, I seldom would use it on the back of a slave. Used it more for intimidatin than for the destruction of valuable property I felt obliged to return. Jesse and me both regularly refused the five dollar bonus that owners often give slavetakers to administer a professional whippin as a lesson for misbehavior. Any whippins, we always believed should come from the rightful owner or his overseer or for that matter the local sheriff who could legally lay on a beatin. Bein good citizens, me and Jesse always felt that the letter of the law should be observed.

After tellin Long that I would return shortly to meet with his people, I left his office with whip in hand and headed over to the *ENTERPRISE* to interrogate young Sanford. I found him there, workin on the lower deck of the steamboat, tryin to tidy up some.

"Good mornin, Massa Tims," were the first words out of his mouth upon seein me.

Lookin him sternly in the eye, I began my interrogation. "Sanford, I need to speak with you bout a very serious matter. Do you see this whip I have here in my hand?" His eyes grew wide. "Has your master ever beat you before?" I asked.

"O Lordy, massa. Massa Walker be very free with da whip and has done whipt me to his sabisfaktion many a time. Please don't beat dis nigger, Massa Tims!" he replied.

I got to chuckling later on when Sanford hisself told me how he come to avoid an earlier encounter with the whip. He told me bout when one of Walker's associates Sanford had been servin spilled a drink on hisself. Walker then sent the young negro to the local jail with a dollar and a note with instructions, on the pretext of pickin up a trunk that was to be delivered to a steamboat. I guess Sanford suspected the worst and got a sailor down at the docks to read him the note. After findin out that the message was for the sheriff to administer a beatin for the dollar fee, Sanford engaged nother young negro to retrieve the trunk and give him a dollar to do it. Twenty lashes later, the unsuspectin victim come out of jail with a note for Mr. Walker which he give back to Sanford, the intended victim. It indicated that the boy was not only saucy but a liar as well and the twenty lashes he give him was to set him straight. Returnin to Walker, Sanford later told me he wet and reddened-up his cheeks some and told his master when he give him the note that he had had the worst beatin of his young life and that he was thankful to have learned such a valuable lesson.

"Sanford, I do not want to use this whip on you but I have your master's permission to beat you into next Tuesday if I've a mind to. What do you know bout the woman Cynthia and the other two slaves that escaped last night?"

"Massa, Massa, de be no need for a whippin. If I come wid you, mebe I could hep!" he pleaded.

I got the feelin that the young slave boy was lookin for an opportunity to change his circumstance. Mr. Walker was a tough taskmaster and probably most anythin was preferable to continued service under this soul driver, but I could ill afford any distractions or added responsibilities if things got interestin on the trail ahead. I told him he would be stayin right here and repeated my demands.

"Massa Tims," he replied…"Hep me…I needs to have me nother massa! You good man, not like Massa Walker. Mebe yuz buy dis child to takes home wid ya?"

"Do you know what I do for a livin, boy?" I interrupted, grabbing him by the collar. "I hunt down people like you who illegally run from their masters with dogs and return em for money. Why would you think I would do anythin to help you?"

I could see that Sanford was hesitatin, thinkin real careful like bout what he was gonna say. Maybe weighin the risks, with downcast eyes he began to offer up a soft reply. "Pardon, Massa, pardon…but Sanford here see da way yuz looks at dat woman. Yuz wants her powerful bad, but not like Massa Walker. Sanford know dese things. If you heps me, I can tell ya bowt dat slavewoman and dem niggers dat run off last night," the young slave boy concluded with his voice gainin confidence with his answer.

I paused for a minute. That information sounded promisin and I really was not at all anxious to use the whip on that boy. One other thing I needed to add into the mix…despite his years, this young slave boy Sanford was also square on the money in his assessment of the young woman.

"I ain't promisin nothin," I said finally as I let go of his collar and dropped the menacin whip down to my side. "But if you give me the information I need, I will do what I can to alter your situation."

I soon found out that Sanford did know quite a bit bout the fugitives as he was supposed to be included in their number, but a last minute task Walker had assigned him had disrupted the plan and caused the young boy to be left behind. Despite Major Long's incorrect assumption about Ross, Sanford said it was him that headed the whole thing up. He described Ross as a big burly man with a heavy beard and said there were two other white men whose names he was unsure of. They was to meet up in an old livery stable on the wharf and were goin to go by wagon out of the city, north to Baton Rouge on their way to freedom. They figured to stop at places sympathetic to their cause on the way. When I asked if he remembered any names or places, he said he thought he remembered Ross sayin they was goin to a far-off place called "Kenida, The Promised Land," and he had said something bout first stoppin at the house of a man named "Tappan" or "Tippin" or somethin akin to that along their way.

Leavin Sanford and meetin up with the two men down at Longs, I rented up a horse from the livery and with the two armed men in the wagon, the three of us headed out on the road. I knew I would have felt a darn sight more comfortable with my trackin dogs and Jesse watchin my backside, but this was all new territory for sure, and I had to make do.

I figured that the fugitives in question had bout a five hour head start as they probably did not start runnin till after the city slave patrols changed shifts round one in the mornin. Most major cities like New Orleans had night watchmen to check the wanderin and unruly tendencies of their blacks. Cities could be problem areas with the large congregations of negroes. Vandalism, theft and arson was major concerns long with the sale of alcohol and other illegal trade goods. Usually patrollin on foot from the ring of the bell at nine o'clock, right through a change of shifts at one, and then on through to daylight, these patrollers kept a very tight rein on nighttime activity. Most of these here city patrols was also paid, unlike what we had in Baldwin County. Truth to tell, many were really professionals, hired and paid for through city taxes, fines and money granted by the state legislatures.

Assumin the fugitives was able to avoid the city night police, they would then need to avoid the usual mounted pattyrollers out on the country roads. With all the swamps there was round New Orleans there weren't many roads runnin north to Baton Rouge so I come to figure we had a fair chance of bein on the right one. We stopped a number of times to ask folks if they knew the home of a man named Tippin or Tappan, but never got the answer we was lookin for till bout noon of that day. We had been ridin nigh on two hours when a woman we run across informed us that a man named Tappan did indeed own a house in the area. She did, however, say he had a funny way of talkin and was seldom to home.

As we left the main road headin down the smaller dirt road which led to the house, I noticed somethin that sparked my interest. I could see that there was recent wagon wheel tracks plain as the day was long, but there did not appear to be any horses' footprints mixed in with em, or at least they was not well defined like one would come to expect. Now the way I come to figure, either them horses was ridin up inside the wagon with the passengers or some fool had invented a strange type of horseless carriage. These horses, from my experience must have been shod with carpet most likely to keep things quiet. I believed us to be on the right trail and said as much to the two hired men in the wagon.

The Tappan house was back off the dirt road some. It had a white picket fence round much of it, but it looked to be in need of a little whitewash. There did not appear to be anyone bout when we reached it, but I figured that wagon just might be hid up inside the barn. Walkin up towards the door, all three of us drew our revolvers at the same time and got ready for any resistance that might come our way.

What happened next seemed to happen so fast the whole thing is still fairly blurred in my memory. I do remember comin through the door hard with pistol in hand and seein two abolitionists in the room turn tail and most stumblin over one nother in a foot race for the back door. The two male fugitives that was also in the room froze right there in their tracks.

"Get these two niggers tied up and into the wagon," I ordered, pointin to the two slaves who both wore the look of absolute terror on their faces. "And then get after them two white scalawags. Walker will be real happy if we bring em back for a proper hangin!"

The two male runaways were quickly tied up with some bindin rope we had brought from the livery. They was then led out and tied securely in the wagon so's their captors could concern themselves with the kidnappers that had managed to run from the house into the thick woods out back. I began to search the rest of the house on my own, goin from room to room. There was only one fugitive that remained at large now, but that one I knew was HER, that woman I had seen on the deck of the steamboat, the quadroon named Cynthia. My heart beat a little faster in anticipation as I slowly went on about my business.

After searchin several rooms with not the slightest thing to show for it, I finally come upon a closed door to one of the upstairs back bedrooms. With gun in hand I opened it and stepped inside and hearin nothin, waited for my eyes to get theirselves adjusted to the somewhat darker quarters. It was right then and there that I began to make out a shadowy shape of a human figure off in the far corner of the room. Standin just as still as a statue and quiet as a grave, this dark form must have suddenly been overcome by the terrifyin figure silhouetted against the light of the hallway and took to runnin for an open window maybe three full steps away. Perhaps thinkin better on the idea or maybe realizin that escape was near impossible, this form all of a sudden come to a dead-full stop. Turnin slowly and takin several small steps in my direction, a woman's form inched its way into the light. When she finally come out to where I could get a good look-see at her, she had taken to foldin her hands one on the other in front of herself and stood there just as calm as you please. I saw her look down only briefly maybe so's to gather up her thoughts and courage. She was now close enough to invite conversation. This woman's eyes, I could now tell were light in color and her face, why it was even more beautiful than I had remembered it from a distance back at the dock. We stared at each other for quite some time without a single word passin tween the two of us, my gun remainin in my hand but now hangin limply by my side.

Finally it was her that broke the silence. "My name is Cynthia," she offered. "Are you here to take me back to a lifetime of bondage?" Before I could give a proper answer, she quickly added: "Would you take me back to...to live with that evil man as his property?"

I was speechless, dumfounded to be more clear on the matter. The sound of her voice and what she had said echoed round and round inside my head. It was the first time I had added hearin to seein and my first impression was that it all seemed to fit with what I knew of the woman up to this time. It was so effortless and so natural and said so direct but not without a hint of pleadin in it. I knew full well before I ever opened my mouth to speak that I had reached a fork in the road. The time for decidin was now at hand. The Coswell Tims who got off that mail coach just a few days back, would not be the same fella that would be leavin this small upstairs room. No sir! Not by a longshot. Givin the whole matter just a little more digestion, I figure maybe I must have knowed all of that when I first looked up and saw her standin there on the deck of that steamboat. Maybe, just like Pleasant Ennis had offered up just a short time back while we was all out on patrol duty, "You'll know the woman when you first see her, Coswell, you will know her straightaway!"

Chapter 10

NO TURNIN BACK

Hearin the sound of voices and the door openin at the end of the hallway shook me to my senses.

"Quick, under the bed!" I instructed.

Cynthia complied, movin most quick as a cat towards the bed and droppin face down on the floor, she slid herself sideways till her form completely disappeared from view. The whole thing was accomplished with such speed and such grace that I still think on how it was done to this very day. I turned round just as both of Long's men come through the open bedroom door.

Out of breath the tall one announced: "We done lost em, Mr. Tims…sorry bout that.That swamp back there ain't no place a body would want to spend much time in that's for sure. By the sights and sounds of it all I'll wager there's more snakes and gators to be had in there than there would be places to hide. Anythin turn up here in the house?"

"Not a thing and I give the house a good look-see too," I answered. "I'm afraid all we got for Walker are them two runaways tied up out there in the wagon. Now I want you boys to get em back to the *ENTERPRISE* straightaway. I'll be stayin on for a spell to see to the tracks out back. You be sure to tell Walker that I'm checkin on the last of his fugitives and will be on my way directly."

With that, Walker's bondsmen were driven back to their master to face their punishment. My guess would be that the slave owner's frustration for not gettin his prize quadroon back might just go all the worse for them. Tryin to take in the whole of what just happened and givin some thought as to the future, I knew I needed more time to think and plan. Any missteps here I knew could prove more than a might costly.

The message I sent back to Walker would buy me some time, that's all. When I did get back to the *ENTERPRISE*, I figured I would tell him that the woman's footprints just plain disappeared along with those of the abolitionists into the mud of the dark swamp. I'd offer up that she was gone and never to be seen or heard from again, with either the kidnappers or the swamp to blame. Hopefully I could convince the man of the reality of his loss and he would accept this unfortunate turn of events.

I heard a voice from somewhere ringin in my head.

"Why did you do that?" it asked.

Coswell Tims had never done anythin like this in all his life. Lyin, stealin…never lied to Mamma or Daddy or deceived anyone in a business deal, never broke a law that I can recollect. The sons of Obadiah and Hattie Tims was lawbidin, upstandin people for sure, but to deprive a man of his lawful property was surely to the left of bein right. I had always prided myself on bein a law and order fella. Why, as I thought more on the subject, I did bout everythin but wear a badge over the years. Always did my civic duty, like servin on slave patrol, alarm duty, workin for the sheriff's office and the state prison from time to time chasin escapees. Anyone who knew ol Coswell knew him to be a public servant, always tryin to do right. Folks knew I respected the law and wanted to see justice done. I certainly never figured myself to be a man who would ever in this life go back on his raisin.

A conversation come to mind that I had one night years ago

down at the Big Indian Saloon with owner Gus Randolph. Despite the fact that innkeepers and saloon owners often required the use of more slaves than many farms, ol Gus was of a mind that some of the strict Georgia slave codes did nothin to help his business. I thought I was right smart to be tellin him that a law was a law and it didn't matter a lick whether a person approved of it or not. If this was a nation of laws, I remember arguin, a man could not just pick out the ones he fancied and disregard the ones that he don't. Made a heap of sense when I said it, but at the present time I knew I had my reasons for breakin the law and I guess I also knew that the law might just suffer further casualties in the days ahead.

"Why did you do that?" that same voice come again, this time louder and more insistent. It come, not from within my head where I had first imagined it to be, but directly behind where I stood. Cynthia had emerged from under the bed and was standin there, waitin for my response.

I turned round and said nothin at first, but finally managed to mumble something bout how I couldn't stand the thought of her bein a slave and all.

"But I have always been a slave," she calmly answered.

"Not any more!" I shot back. "I want you to go back to Georgia with me," and as I said that I reached out rather sudden like, grabbin for her arm. She pulled back, sendin me a look that said she was unsure of my intentions.

"Coswell Tims, you are this side of a fool," I thought to myself. I should have knowed better than to have done such a thing and if I had been thinkin clear on the matter I probably could have predicted that very response. What made me any different in this woman's eyes than all the men she had ever come across, black ones or white ones, young or old, that her beauty had attracted since she was a young girl of maybe eleven or twelve? It was a well-known fact in the slave community that the beauty of their women was often considered a curse. An attractive slave girl that might catch the eye of an owner or one of his relatives or friends could find herself very quickly in a compromisin situation where she was powerless to protect herself from their advances. Slave mothers, knowin full well they could do nothin to defend their attractive daughters, often tried to protect em by makin em look a sight worse than they actually was. I never really thought much on the matter before, but I'm thinkin now this kind of thing must have just bout broke a mother's heart!

"I'm sorry I startled you like that," I offered up, tryin to recover from my earlier offence, "but there's somethin bout you, somethin that makes for different feelins inside me. Can't say as I can really put a finger on it at the moment," I added.

Now I was seldom at a loss for words, but here I was stumbling round like a founderin mule, maybe even one that's got hisself a bad case of the blind staggers. I always felt pretty good regardin my vocabulary. Most people in my profession (and probably most of the folks I know) couldn't write a lick or speak very well neither, but me and Jesse was a little higher up the totem pole. This type of speakin, however, I come to believe don't come from the head but from the heart. It don't come from no book-learnin, no matter how much a person has. It comes from feelins and that was a different bucket of possums altogether. I had to admit this was a language that was new to the likes of Coswell Tims.

We just stood there for a moment lookin into each other's eyes and finally I regained enough sense to slowly reach out my hand once more. After introducin myself real proper like and apologizin once again for my earlier behavior, I calmly spoke up. "I'm sorry, but we need to skedaddle now if your answer is yes. Or if you are of a mind, you can stay here or follow them abolitionist friends of yours and try to strike out for freedom. Either way, I never want you to be a slave again!"

She paused momentarily and I could see she was workin over all I had said in her mind. After a spell, Cynthia, the slave property of Massa James Walker, slowly raised up her hand, makin it available to my grasp. As we touched for the first time, I took notice of how small that hand was compared to mine and how warm it was to the touch. Why it fit inside mine just like it was always meant to be there, I remember thinkin to myself.

"I'll go with you," she said softly.

Returnin to the city had a different feel to it than earlier when

I had been goin the other way. I was headed in a different direction for sure, as much had happened on this trackin job that needed proper digestion. The addition of the passenger that now sat up close behind me on the horse was makin my compass needle point in a direction that was unfamiliar. Her arms was wrapped round my waist and I thought I took notice of Cynthia clingin more tightly to me the further on we traveled. Of course that might have been due to her gettin tired and tryin to keep from fallin off the horse, but it suited my fancy to think she was gettin more comfortable with the decision she had made back there in that small upstairs room. Maybe it was that she saw this as her only option at the time, but I know for a fact that I felt her head sorta press sideways into the center of my back a few times. It felt good and caused me to sit up even straighter in that saddle, it did.

With every step the horse took back to New Orleans, I knew I needed to be one step closer to formulatin a plan to get us out of this here situation. Time was a-growin short and my mind was goin to and fro like a fiddler's elbow, jumpin from one thing on to the next. Cynthia and I spoke very little. I kinda got the feelin that she knew I was in a difficult place and needed some time to think my way out of it. I needed to use my head again, not think with my heart as I had done back there at the house. (Sure God, if I spent much time thinkin bout that emotional decision I just made back down the road apiece and changes sure to come, I'd most likely be tremblin like an ol quiver bug.) As I stared blankly at the trail ahead, however, I began to put some of the pieces into place.

One thing that favored us was the time of day. It was late afternoon and I knew that night would find itself before we entered New Orleans proper. Hopefully, fewer people would be about and we could return to my room at the boardin house without rousin too much attention. I was not worried bout the slave patrols stoppin two white folk, but we would look kinda suspicious, a man ridin with a woman up close behind him, especially one...my goodness...one that had no shoes!

Well I'll be black dogged!I had not taken notice of that little detail till that very moment in time when I happened to glance down to see Cynthia's bare-naked feet just kinda danglin off the sides of the horse. Now it's a fact that most slaves generally went shoeless in the summer months but was given a pair of shoes for use in winter and on dress-up occasions, usually one pair a year. I do not remember if she had shoes or not when I first saw her walkin that steamboat deck or if she had lost em when she took flight that night, but I figured either way, that would be the first thing this woman would be needin when we returned to New Orleans. I also began thinkin to myself that while we was at it, maybe we should get a few other things as well. She would need a dress, but not one made out of negro cloth like the two given most slave women every year, often done up by their mistress. No sir, this should be a more fancy dress. Hellfire, I concluded, it should be somethin right smart and befittin the fine lookin woman she really was. Why the more I thought on things, the more high-falutin it all become. A hat, a fancy hat, maybe with a plume stuck in it would set the whole affair off just right, I added, as these ramblins finally give way to a blankness of mind and a view of the trail ahead.

I remember everythin was quiet, very quiet with my mind most completely at rest when suddenly, like a man converted on a Sabbath mornin, an idea come flashin cross my brain! In short order, I could feel a broad smile begin to take up residence on my face. I was startin to see a way out of our predicament, a way to get past the powerful Walker, a way out of New Orleans and back to Milledgeville. It could be done, I concluded. My mind was goin full chisel as I started puttin all the pieces of the plan together. It was only after I had ruminated on it all for quite some time that I calmly turned my head to the side to share my thoughts on the matter with the passenger close behind me.

"You ever hear of William and Ellen Kraft?" I asked.

Now I knowed full well Cynthia had to remember these two. Why in the slave quarters information travels faster than it does with the new-fangled telegraph that went through these parts in '48. Not only did slaves regularly and eagerly pass on information to each other as they worked other plantations, but white folks often talked round their black staff as if they was invisible so they unknowingly give em all the latest news. I remember that some white families wised up to this and started lowerin their voices and watchin what was said when their servants were nearby. On a plantation in Milledgeville, I recall an owner and his wife started speakin French in front of their bondsmen so's to keep the conversation to themselves.

Blacks knew the story and whites, both in the north and in the south, were familiar with it as well, maybe for different reasons. It had been in all the newspapers.

The Krafts had been slaves over in Macon, just a stone's throw from Milledgeville. Ellen Kraft was a fair-skinned and kinda white-featured woman. Her husband, William, was as black as the darkest night. A couple of years back they come up with a plan that would take em from slavery, out of the south, up to Philadelphia, on to Boston and eventually to England. Without the aid of abolitionists, the use of the North Star or attempin any of the usual escape routes, their plan succeeded. It was the boldness of the thing that done it. Why, they stayed in public hotels in Charleston and Raleigh and rode public transportation like trains, ferries and steamers. It all had to do with the disguise, not William's, mind ya, but Ellen's. That woman, you see, dressed up like a wealthy, white MALE slave owner! Now if she had been a woman of means, she could never have been seen with a male servant alone in public, so out of necessity she transformed herself into a man dressed in a black suit, cape, high-heeled boots, green spectacles and a dandy top hat. She added a muffler, as I recall, hidin her lack of whiskers and pretended to be hard of hearin so's her female voice wouldn't give her away. She also put her right arm in a sling so's she would have a readied up excuse for not signin papers as she had never learned to read or write. I guess "he" was a sight to behold. "An elegant gentleman very much indisposed," I believe was how the newspapers later spoke on it. I guess William Kraft would explain to folks that inquired how his master was in frail health and was seekin medical attention up in Philadelphia. And so, the sickly slave owner and the dutiful servant who saw to his master's every need, made their way to freedom with the blessins and well-wishes of the many white folk they had met up with along the way. An elegant and respected individual with a loyal attendant...hmmm...what could be less suspicious than that, I thought to myself before sharin my plan with the woman fugitive ridin up so close behind me. This woman, this woman named Cynthia, formerly the property of Mr. James Walker of St. Louis, Missouri would soon undergo a right smart transformation, I began to figure, and if all went well, this young, attractive and shoeless slave girl might soon come to share more with Coswell Elias Tims than just this old broken down rented horse that was carryin us back to the city of New Orleans.

Nobody seemed to pay much attention as we reached the city and quickly passed to the temporary safety of the room I had rented up at the boardin house. As we come inside, I told Cynthia that I would be leavin but would return directly as I needed to see Walker, close accounts and get the horse returned to the livery.

"But what if you don't come back?" was her response. That would not be the last time I would hear that same concern, but I convinced her that I would be just fine and would be back in short order.

When I arrived back at the livery, one of Long's men took care of everythin, assurin me that all expenses was goin on Mr. Walker's account. It made me think for a moment bout one little item in our business dealins that was unaccounted for. I do believe that any feelins of guilt I may have had on the matter stood bout as much a chance as a pig in a dog race when compared to my feelins bout this woman that had just taken up residence in my life.

It was only a quick walk to the *ENTERPRISE*. Up the gang-plank and then up the stairs to the second deck, I entered that same large room where the slave trader and I had first met. No one was to be seen, but soon Walker did suddenly appear with hand out-stretched in greetin.

"Mr. Tims, I have been expecting you. Did you bring home the last of my little flock?"

"I'm sorry to say, Mr. Walker, that the quadroon in question disappeared into the swamp with her kidnappers. My feelin is that unless they was well acquainted with the area, they're goners....all of em," I answered.

"I am extremely disappointed, Mr. Tims. I put a great deal of faith in you, and," lowerin his voice some he added, "and I had plans for that girl, I surely did!"

"I did my best Mr. Walker. Maybe if I had my dogs..."

Walker interrupted. "Well I guess it's no fault of yours. Here's $200.00 for returning the other two. Thank you for your time and effort, Mr. Tims. Good night!"

Walker turned and walked away without a final handshake. My mind turned back to Cynthia alone over at the boardin house. We would need to get another place to stay if we was to remain in the city for the next couple of days, I reasoned. Women were actually not allowed in the boardin house, leastways not respectable women, and Walker certainly knew where I was stayin and I didn't need him changin his mind and wantin to review the situation any time in the near future. Also, his influence in the city was great. There was many eyes and ears that would be eager to report any suspicious activity on the chance that the wealthy slave owner would financially acknowledge it. We needed a place to lay low while gettin ready to leave the city. The St. Charles Hotel, I thought. Just like the Krafts…bigger would be better and more public would draw less suspicion.

Just as I was bout to step off the boat I heard a voice call to me in a half-whisper from behind several cotton bales that stood stacked on the dock. "Massa Tims…Did yuz find what yuz lookin fer?"

Turnin round I saw a grinnin Sanford standin there and thought once more on the part I had imagined he would soon play in our escape. I responded in the same low voice that I had indeed found what I had been lookin for. In fact, I felt the need to add that I had been lookin for this very thing most all my life and I had no intention now of ever lettin it go.

"Sanford, as to your situation," I added, "Cynthia and me need your help to get us all out of this city. You come over to the St. Charles Hotel round midday tomorrow and you tell the clerk there that you are deliverin an important message to a Mrs. Alexander Sills. Tell em it's very important and you must deliver it personal like. You find out what room she be in and go to that room, you hear?"

"I hear, Massa Tims," was his quick reply.

"We both will be in that room and you make no plans to return to the *ENTERPRISE*, you know what I be sayin?" I added.

"Bless you, Massa Tims," was the last thing he uttered as I reached my hand out to feel his smooth chin and jaw.

"Sanford, it will still be some time fore any stubble grow on that young face of yours and I believe that to be a good thing. Oh, and let me take a good look at you so's I can figure all the sizes right. We ain't home free, but if the three of us do what needs doin, I think we can all better our circumstance. Remember, now…Mrs. Alexander Sills!"

Leavin the young negro, I turned and headed over to the St. Charles Hotel. It was a good thing that I had a fair amount of financial resources at my disposal thanks to Mr. James Walker. I had no trouble securin a room in the name of Mrs. Sills. I told the clerk that she would be accompanied by a negro attendant, a young girl who saw to her mistress' every need. With key in hand I checked the room on the second floor and left by means of the back staircase. I could see no problem returnin that same way.

I got back to the roomin house and I could tell by the way her face lit up that Cynthia was more than a might glad to see me. I suggested that we leave immediately for better quarters and within 20 minutes or so we had exchanged our dingy, tobacco stained room for a room in the finest hotel in the city of New Orleans. And if we didn't look a sight...a man with more trail dirt on him than a rented mule, a woman who didn't even own herself a pair of shoes and a soon to be arrivin young slave boy yet to be converted for the occasion. All this would change in a blink of an eye.

Chapter 11

PLAYIN THE PART

"Now sit upright and keep them shoulders square," I instructed, as Cynthia took the pen in hand, attemptin her first few letters. I remembered those were Mr. Denison's first instructions when Jesse and me was learnin to write. I remember full well his insistence that we do the job right and proper. That's what had made him the fine teacher that he was.

"Now, keep that wrist above the paper, boys, and rest the hand lightly on the nails of the third and fourth fingers, which should touch the paper directly under your palm," I could still hear him a-sayin.

"Hold that pen lightly now, and let's form this here "S", risin up from the base line, up to the top line, twistin back home and runnin over a little to connect to that little "i", and follow up with two big loop letters called "L's", I said to Cynthia as she worked to form up her letters for the very first time. I half chuckled to myself as I thought back to Denison's insistence that we keep all letters on a fifty-two degree slant. "Fifty-two degrees gentlemen," he would say. "Unless you be writin to yourself, all folks' letters and words need to look alike. Communication, gentlemen, communication. Yes sir, that's what good writin is all about!"

Cynthia was tired and so was I from the events of the day, but this lesson had to be learned now as her signature would be required in the days ahead. No puttin her arm in a sling as that had already been done by that Krafty woman. Cynthia was a willin student for sure, but experienced some difficulty in the shape and size of the letters. I guided her hand as I stood in close behind her at the small desk, formin up them five little letters that would make her passage into white society possible. S-I-L-L-S…(I had written em out above to make her attempt at copyin em a-might easier.)

"Now the 'I' and then the..." Cynthia stopped just short of the "L" and turned slowly in my direction. Our eyes met much like they had done at the Tappan house, but the short time the two of us had spent together had shrunk the distance between this slave woman and this slave catcher considerable. She caught my look direct and began a silent exploration of the man who had so recently come into her life. Thinkin back on that moment, it seemed as if I was powerless to prevent this invasion, maybe even welcomed it, as she took to lookin deeper and deeper into the likes of Coswell Tims.

Cynthia's eyes, I could not help but notice once more, was a beautiful blue-green color which stood out in lively contrast to a small circle of black that lay in the very center. Why anyone definin them eyes as black, I thought to myself, just cause there was that tiny speck of black to be had there in the middle would have to be this side of a fool. But then again, if a person was to use the center of the eye to judge, why they would have to conclude that all folks was made pretty much the same, wouldn't they?

Now there was more that lay behind and beyond the color. Maybe I imagined it or maybe I saw it clear as day, I do not know, but I swear I caught a glimpse of the pain, fear, maybe shame and even anger that she had been forced as a slave woman to carry. Later on, Big Sandy's eyes would tell much the same story. How many people really look into the eyes of another, I wondered, specially if they are of from another race or place? Just keep em at a distance I suspect would be the general rule. I would have to say I saw kindness and gentleness in them eyes as well. She held me with em, held me just as sure as shackles and bindin rope would hold a fugitive that was bein escorted back to his plantation home.

I noticed too, those eyes seemed also to hold more of a knowin or trustin look than they had previous. They soon glanced slightly downward and I took Cynthia's meanin as our lips come to touch for the very first time.

It was true that it was the eyes that sparked this conversation, but I will admit there was soon other parts of our bodies that got involved. After a long and tender kiss where we held each other close for some time, we come to find ourselves cozied up on the bed that stood to the far side of the room. It was there that this whole thing seemed to progress just as natural as the letters we had been shapin up, which when strung together, went on to form words. I would have to say that I can't recall a single word that was passed tween the two of us durin this time, but despite that fact the next hour or so was spent doin some of the most honest and meaningful communicatin a person in this here life can be a party to.

Now this weren't my first time bein with a woman, and I knew full well it weren't her first time bein with a man, but I would wager that it was the first time that she did this of her own free will and I know for a fact, that this was the first time for me when there was any real meanin to be had in it. Now this lovemaking thing… when it's right, I'm of the opinion a person just sorta naturally falls square into the arms of their lover as a simple matter of trust and surrender. Folks at this time then get all tangled up with arms, legs, emotions and such, and course bein naked as the day you was born, why it's most like one says to another: "I have taken down all my defenses now and can show you no greater love than this. You are with me at this most intimate time and I am vulnerable here, so I trust you'll do right by me," or maybe words to that effect. Certainly any words formed up with loop letters, tail letters, capital letters or the like would fall well short of the mark here and I expect as a general thing most people would dispense with em altogether when they find theirselves in this particular type of situation.

I would have to admit it was Phoebe Brown that was the first woman I had ever been with. She and Mary Baily had a place down there on the west end of Franklin Street in Milledgeville, not two blocks from the Governor's Mansion. This was sort of a right of passage for many young men, and that's where me and Jesse got our indoctrination into this type of activity. As I remember it cost us each a dollar but most like as not we got our money's worth more on the retellin end than the actual bein there. This "bordello", as some of the uppity people liked to call it, was the very place that Lem Smith was killed a few years later by that fella Flournoy, the man that fell victim to the scalper's knife and was skinned alive down there in Columbus by the Creeks in '35. Parents used to warn their sons to stay out of places like this and I guess as a general rule that would be advice worth takin.

As tired as we both was we continued to spend the better part of our first night together explorin each other in other ways, mostly through conversation. You learn a great deal bout a person by watchin em, that's a fact, but you can also learn much by just listenin to what they have to say. It's a certain-sure shame that some people do so much talkin on their end that they run out of time and can't do justice to any serious listenin on the other.

Cynthia told me she was born some 24 summers ago on a plantation up in *Huntsville*, over in northern Alabama. It weren't no secret, she said, that the plantation master had fathered both her and her younger sister Penia (or "Little Peeney" as she was called) but Cynthia said she could never quite figure out why her white lookin mother and her two daughters was treated so poorly seein as though mama passed so much time away with massa in his private quarters. Cynthia said that although she grew up with the rest of the plantation negroes, she did not feel much in the way of kinship. She said she felt like she and her sister was different, but maybe even superior in a funny sort of way. Bein singled out for harsh treatment by both blacks and whites give her a strong sense of who she was as an individual and that was most likely responsible, I reasoned, for that defiant and almost regal manner she showed back there on the deck of the *ENTERPRISE.*

She told me somethin bout her name that has always stuck with me. She said her master fancied hisself a scholar of sorts and took to givin out fancy Greek and Roman names to all the slaves on the planation. "Cynthia," she told me, was the Greek goddess of the moon who was born out of wedlock when her daddy—none other than the great and powerful Zeus—lay with a woman of lowly station and of little or no consequence. When Zeus's wife Hera heard of such goin's on, I reckon she liked to take to highsterics right off and proclaimed loud and clear that this new woman weren't fit to roll with the hogs and if she was to have any briarpatch child it could not be on land or sea. I guess the queen figured she had just bout covered the whole of it and could soon wash her hands clean of the entire affair, but then fate stepped in and the mother-to-be lucked up, discoverin herself a floatin island of some sort which did not fit either description the angry queen had decreed. So, Cynthia said, she was born like this goddess of long ago, somewhere in between, a little of this and a little of that, not really belongin to anyone, anywhere or anythin in particular.

"Well, that's quite a tale," I felt the need to say. "Whatever become of this young goddess?"

"Well the way I heard it told she became a great hunter, had her own lop-eared hounds and rode a golden chariot pulled by white horses across the sky every night. I guess she may have looked quite a sight, but then I also heard she was bout as lonely as a body could be."

"Is that what you are, Cynthia…lonely, I mean?"

"I guess maybe, but in the story she did have one lover. His name was Orion, but their time together was short," Cynthia concluded, droppin her eyes down to the bed where we now sat.

I turned her face to me and kissed her once again. "Maybe if this Cynthia and this Orion had tried a might harder, their time would have been considerably longer," I whispered in her ear.

The room got very quiet after that as we both looked long and hard in each other's direction. It was a plain hard fact that the light in the room that night was quite dim which left a great deal unseen, but thinkin back, maybe that was all the light that was needed at this particular time.

It was clear to me that we had been drawed together for a

number of reasons. The fact that she was an absolutely strikin woman weren't no small matter, but the confident way she carried herself despite what society said had special meanin for me. Even as a young boy on Mamma's knee, I had struggled with the idea of the negroes' basic inferiority to the white man, wonderin whether it was real or conveniently imagined. I guess there was no doubt I hid behind the law some considerin my present occupation, but there was also no doubt in my mind as to the resourceful nature and great potential there was in the black community despite their humble circumstance. Sometimes, I reckon, it's just easier to accept what others say rather that swim upstream agin it all. And now for a black woman to be with me in this way, well it might just give a thinkin man pause. I would have to say for sure that there was many things swirlin round in both our heads that night as we finally fell asleep in each other's arms in the finest hotel the city of New Orleans had to offer.

Wakin up early the next morning, Cynthia practiced that signature till it looked quite tolerable while I got ready to go out to do a little store tradin.

Back in Milledgeville, store-boughten clothes was hard to come by. Maybe the only thing a person could buy from the store already readied-up was a hat or maybe a pair of shoes or boots that had been worked up previous. Most women's clothin was made by the woman doin the buyin, fall and winter bein the best times to purchase new broadcloths, flannels, linens and cashmere and the like which would come in just in time for the fall legislative session and the expected increase in the population.

New Orleans, however, bein a large seaport city had many of the already made-up clothes that were all a fashion in Europe and other places. I went down the back stairs and out into the street. It was early but there were a fair number of folks already stirrin bout. It didn't take me long to find a shop that sold some of the finer women's clothin, and I bought me some of the necessary undergarments and attachments that went with a proper travelin dress befittin a woman of Mrs. Sills lofty station. A wide-brimmed hat with a plume looked just dandy and I didn't forget them high top shoes that she so desperately needed. With her physical form pretty well etched into my mind from personal exploration the night before, I thought I had done more than a respectable job of findin things that would smart her up just right. I even added a parasol and a travelin bag to the mix, a nice touch I thought, givin my lady that look that men fancied and women would admire. She would cut a fine image, she would, travelin by coach up that Federal Road to the new life that awaited her in Milledgeville. Why she and her servant, "Lizzy," would…"Coswell!" I said to myself. "Now you keep your mind right son, you hear." Why I had most forgotten bout Sanford and his part in this little play as I had been so intent on spendin Walker's money on Cynthia.

I knew that there were two ways of thinkin regardin Cynthia's female attendant. Most slaves wore homespun, negro cloth as it was called, and maybe a turban-like coverin for their hair, usually made up by the mistress of the plantation. But some slave owners dressed their favorite slaves, particularly those that accompanied em when they traveled, in their own cast-off clothes or special clothes that showed off the owner's influence and wealth. Actually, the choice was easy as any slave cotton would need to be hand-worked and there was no time for that. Of course we did need that head-kerchief thing to hide the young boy's gender. Yes sir, I would have to spend just a little more of Walker's money to do this whole thing up right and proper.

Finally satisfied that I had both the main players in this little drama properly fitted out, I headed back to the St. Charles with packages in hand. Throwin her arms round me when I come through the door become a tradition with us that started this very day. She was glad to see me and I was glad to see her and I have to admit a fair amount of time passed fore we ever took to openin the packages that contained her fine new wardrobe.

Well, it was nigh on to midday when we heard a knock at the door. It weren't a real powerful knock like someone in authority was checkin the premises, but more of an apologetic kind of knock, the kind a servant might use. Sure enough, Sanford was a-standin there when Cynthia opened the door. A smile come to his face when he laid eyes on her and when he stepped in and saw me, why I believe that smile of his growed even wider.

I always thought that the smile of a negro was somethin special. That dark skin and all them pearly white teeth in lively contrast and with Sanford, that rather wide space tween the two of the front ones give that boy a special look. Despite the newness of his surroundins, I think he knew straightaway he was in friendly territory.

As folks often like to say, we needed to "absquatuate, skedaddle and vamoose" as soon as possible. By not returnin to the *ENTERPRISE*, Sanford's absence would soon draw suspicion. He did admit to bein a might skeptical at first as to the role he was asked to play for the next week or so, but the boy was bright as a steel trap and understood the necessity of it all. Puttin on his new clothes, I complimented him on his transformation, but lookin was one thing and bein was somethin else again. I cautioned him on some of the things he should remember, but much of what he would need to do, we all realized, would have to be made up on the fly as new circumstances come his way.

Dressed in her new clothes Cynthia looked like she was born of high society. The woman was beautiful to say the least, and I have to admit the clothes fit her tolerably well, too. Mrs. Sills and her new faithful servant Lizzy practiced their roles, walkin round the room and talkin to one another for the better part of the afternoon. The whole thing beat a circus, it did. Why, I was startin to half believe all this myself!

"Now remember," I said to Cynthia the next mornin as the two were bout ready to take their leave. "You will be needin to sign your name over at the stage-line depot when you pay for the trip and when you change lines. Here is some cash money now for you and Lizzy. You'll also be payin for food and lodgin when you stop to change horses and such." I knew that the coach lines was more expensive than ridin on the mail stage. At ten cents a mile and a dollar with each stop for food and lodgin, which generally happened every 16 miles or so, I give Cynthia two hundred dollars for her and her young female travelin companion. I was unsure how they would charge for a colored servant, but my guess was that she would not be considered baggage under these circumstances and could ride in the coach as an attendant right up near her mistress.

I put my hands on Cynthia's shoulders and assured her that everythin was gonna work out just fine. She had about a 400 mile trip ahead of her which would take up the better part of a week. I cautioned her bout other passengers and folks in the taverns pryin into her affairs, and advised her to think on her circumstance so's to have ready made-up answers for any questions might come her way. A kiss goodbye...

"You are only goin as far as Macon," I revealed. "I'll send off a telegraph message to my brother Jesse up in Milledgeville. He'll meet the two of you there with our wagon and take you the rest of the way, so's to break up the trail case anyone takes a mind to follow. I'll be comin long directly, don't you worry none. You two be careful now, you hear!" Those were my last words as I looked square into her eyes once again, kissed her, this time up on the forehead, and give her one last quick squeeze for good luck.

With that, the two of em left the room and headed over to the stage line depot which was just across the broad street from the St. Charles. I watched until they disappeared from view.

Cynthia told me bout a week later what she and her young friend had been through. I guess when I first saw that woman standin on the deck of that boat, givin not the slightest hint of her impendin flight, I sensed this here was an individual with very special abilities, one who was at her best when times got the toughest.

Cynthia related that the depot was a fine lookin buildin with carriages aback all painted either yellow or red. Turns out her coach was yellow, pulled by four horses and could hold a total of nine passengers in three rows of seats. Women, she said, set in the middle where it was most comfortable as a broad leather strap for leanin back had been thoughtfully provided there. With one door only and cramped quarters for sure, things got even tighter she told me when passengers had to shift together to the high side of the coach from time to time to keep the whole affair from tumblin over. She and Lizzy was most relieved, however, that there was to be only three other passengers that had signed on and was leavin New Orleans with em. That early enthusiasm come to be somewhat dampened, however, when they discovered that two of em was slave traders and the other was a nosey reporter for a Charleston, South Carolina newspaper. That reporter was writin on the difficulties of travelin the almost 1,000 miles of the Federal Road from New Orleans to Washington City, the country's capitol.

The reporter's name was William Gilmore Simms and this was his second trip over the road in the last seven years and I guess he told everyone that his readership desired an accurate assessment of all the improvements and conditions on the road as well as any other stories he might became a party to on the way. It didn't take that curious fella any time t'all to start pokin around.

"Mrs. Sills," he inquired. "Is this your first time traveling this wretched road?"

"It is, sir," she answered.

"And what has occasioned this most unfortunate decision, Madame? I assure you the trip, unless it has changed greatly from my first time, offers up little more than bumpy roads, dangerous swamps, overpriced lodging with disgusting food and uncomfortable beds. Sometimes immoral and insulting drivers are a problem, hostilities with Indians could still occur even though most were moved out in '36. Snakes! Mosquitoes! You name it. If it's unpleasant, why you can probably find it on the Federal Road."

He rambled on. "Did you notice that no one wishes you a pleasant journey, just a safe one? As a man told me when I first rode the line, only if a person keeps his spirits up, does he even begin to have a chance of getting through," Mr. Simms said as he finally concluded his longwinded, round-about inquiry.

It was a good thing that Cynthia had taken my advice to heart as she answered back. "I am on my way to join my husband in Macon, sir. He is of English descent and travels a great deal. We will not be staying there long, I'm sure."

"Well, perhaps I will get a chance to meet him," Simms replied. "There was an English woman writer that I did get to meet a few years back when I rode the line for the first time. I believe her name was Harriet Martineau. As I remember, she was more interested in the flowers and trees along the way than anything else. I also remember that she took great interest in the negroes that she saw occasionally out the window of the coach. She wrote an article about how downtrodden, how low and lost they all looked. Funny thing is, though, when she asked them directly where they were headed they all said: "into Yellibama", so I guess they knew just where they were after all! Can't say this woman did much in her writing to advertise our peculiar institution, however," he concluded.

With that, one of the two men who appeared to be associates, chimed in with his thoughts on the matter. "These folks that come in here from other countries or from the north, which I personally consider to be another country, come down here and always seem to be shootin their mouths off bout things they just don't know nothin about. Why look at this young wench here," as he pointed to Lizzy sittin alone on the front seat. "She don't appear any the worse for wear, bein a slave and all. Let's ask her what she thinks of the institution."

"What is your name, girl?" the other slave trader asked.

"My name be Lizzy, Massa," Sanford replied.

"Well you are a fine lookin little nig, for sure. Now you tell us all here what your feelins are bout this enslaved condition of yours.

"Don't know much bowt slavery, massa, but my mistress treat me well when I behave proper, but when I misbehave, oh Lordy, she corrects me with a good switchin." All three men smiled at the answer. Now that's Sanford for sure, I thought, when Cynthia told me this story later on. That boy is clever and just plain good at dodgin around!

That seemed to satisfy the men who later admitted to being very active in the slave tradin business. Cynthia said she felt her heart just bout drop from her chest when one of em mentioned some business dealins he had had in New Orleans recently with a Mr. Walker. She must have recovered quickly, however, as she related this amusin part of the story.

Seems as though they had been travelin for some time and as night come on, the driver stopped to light off the pine-knot torches that was set to either side of the front of the coach so's he could better see where he was headed. The lamps was round and made of iron, formed up to hold lightwood tightly as it burned. As there was no windows on either side of the coach (only openins where windows would be) black smoke from the lamps found its way inside and covered all the passengers. When they finally stopped for breakfast, Cynthia told me, everyone got a good laugh as it seemed the soot from the lightwood had converted all four of the white passengers into negroes!

"Why Mrs. Sills," said one of the slave traders, "I do believe you are as much a nigger as that young servant of yours over there."

"Why it appears I am, sir. It appears, I am," Cynthia replied, quietly chucklin to herself over this strange new turn of events.

After washin away their blackness and settin down to a tolerable meal of boiled pork, corn bread and some rather rancid butter supplied by the tavern owners, the horses was changed, the axle greased and the passengers soon found themselves back on the road once again.

After a half a day's journey, they reached the old site of Ft. Mims at Murder Creek. That would be the very place Daddy told me about many years ago where them murderin savages under Red Eagle killed some 500 or so white settlers that was inside the fort. Always lookin to teach his sons a lesson, I recall him sayin that the soldiers responsible for protectin the place had paid no nevermind to some sand that had formed up from a recent rainstorm, makin the gate impossible to close. Guess they figured they would tend to it in their own sweet time and paid the price for their negligence. "It's a dangerous world out there, son, and a man don't need to make things any worse through his own efforts," I remember Daddy a-sayin. There was over three hundred scalps taken that day and I guess the only ones spared was the slaves the Creeks took for themselves. I doubt if anyone on board the yellow coach knew any of this, maybe exceptin the driver (or possibly the reporter, Mr. Simms) as this was way back in 1813 and things had changed considerable over the years. Mrs. Longmyre's Tavern stood nearby and that is where Cynthia told me they stopped and spent the second night.

Now many of the early taverns that had dotted the Federal Road had been owned by Indians, half-breeds, or whites that was in partnership with one or the other. Nowadays, the majority of the taverns was owned by mostly respectable white folks. Mrs. Longmyre was well thought of by travelers for her fair prices, her more than passable meals and relatively clean beds. She was also respected by her neighbors for her knowledge of medicine as she had once nursed one of the stage drivers who was down sick with a bad case of bilious fever, back to health.

"Good afternoon, folks!" was her enthusiastic welcome. "Come on in and get the trail dust off ya! We'll have tea and supper shortly," she concluded.

Cynthia said that after a surprisingly good supper of rice and chicken, communication round the table picked up considerable. As Sanford had been banished to the kitchen as was only right and proper, the white folks began to engage in some lively conversation.

Mr. Simms, of course, started the whole thing off, inquirin into the affairs of the tavern owner, a woman seemingly alone for the most part and operatin her tavern in a fairly remote area. Mrs. Longmyre answered the inquiries of the persistent reporter.

"Things ain't as bad as you might think," she said. "Fact is, the Alabama River runs just north of here and a lot of the world comes a-callin from just that place. Why most of my supplies come right up that river, as well as many of my guests."

One of the slave traders mentioned that in the mornin, the two of em was headed for that very place to do some business. That would make the coach a little more comfortable, Cynthia thought to herself, but then again it might also make Mr. Simms's questions all the more frequent.

"And you, my dear," the innkeeper said to Mrs. Alexander Sills, "What brings you through these parts?"

"I am meeting my husband in Macon," Cynthia repeated, "where we will be staying for only a short time. I do not know what his plans are beyond that," she added.

"What does your husband do, Mrs. Sills?" she further inquired.

"My husband is a man of means, Madame. Neither he nor I invite questions of a personal nature regarding our affairs," Cynthia responded, quite proud of herself for her rather high-handed defense regardin her imaginary life. She told me once how it was growin up on the plantation when she would often be mistaken for a white child. She said she would pretend and go on and on whenever a white visitor made that mistake and would only stop when someone pointed out that she weren't white after all. I guess life in many ways had prepared this woman for the part she now needed to play.

"Forgive me, my dear, I meant nothing by it. I just hope you are married to a good and honorable man who does right by you and your neighbors, that's all. My Efram was such a man. It was such the pity to lose him a few years back. I was unable to save him when he took sick and I suppose that's why I've learned so much bout medicine and always try to help those in need," Mrs. Longmyre concluded.

Cynthia told me that she got real quiet after that, thinkin bout me, the kind of work that I do and our future together. She knew that my business mainly involved huntin down escaped slaves and despite the lovin nature of our relationship to this point, she admitted to herself that she had only known me a short time and there was many questions that remained unanswered in her mind.

I wish I had been there to reassure that woman of my honorable intentions regardin her and defend my reputation as an honest and upright individual. At that very moment, however, I was purchasin a horse and saddle for two hundred dollars more of Walker's money and was startin my journey up the old mail line some two days behind the yellow coach. If Walker's spies saw any of these departures, I figured it would be hard to connect a disguised quadroon, a young black boy dressed as a slave girl, and a lone horseman by the name of Coswell Tims.

Chapter 12

DODGIN ROUND

Cynthia told me that the next day the three remainin passengers, along with their driver, crossed over the Alabama River on a ferry. That ferry was large enough, she said, to accommodate six horses attached to a wagon or carriage, maybe twenty or so people and a fair amount of supplies that someone might be carryin or tradin. The land for some time after that was very swampy with bugs and snakes to spare, but them sturdy corduroy roads held together and so did the stagecoach and its passengers. I had never thought much on it before, but back home in Milledgeville, where the Federal Road goes by the Lafayette Hotel at the corner of Hancock and Jefferson Streets, that stretch of road is often referred to as "Shakegut Road." I imagined that just bout described what the two fugitives in the stagecoach had experienced on this unpleasant leg of their journey.

Travelin at maybe five miles an hour, the yellow coach stopped a number of times to change horses, make repairs and accommodate the passengers with such natural urges as eatin and relievin themselves. Travelin most of the next night, Mr. Simms and Cynthia made it a point to sit in the seats facin backwards so's to avoid another skin color change once the coachman lit up them lightwood torches. Simms told Cynthia that bein black for one day was about the limit of his endurance and he said he felt he spoke for her as well. She told me she smiled, nodded and thanked him for his kindness and consideration.

It was early mornin when the ground become more passable and all three was able to fall asleep. Cynthia told me that it was a good thing that women sleep lightly by nature, as she was quick to notice that the little head-kerchief Sanford was wearin had slid off during his slumber, revealin a hair style no young lady, white or black, would ever be a party to. Luckily, the reporter slept most soundly of all, and any story that might have delighted his readers, was lost, or at least lost for the moment.

Late afternoon, Cynthia said they reached Lucas's Tavern, near Montgomery. This was the end of the line for the little yellow coach as it would soon be rerouted back to New Orleans. A new signature, another payment and another somewhat older lookin stage, a Cumberland model, would replace the one that had brought em this far.

Now this Lucas Tavern was one of the best known stops long the road and had been since the early 1820's when Walter B. Lucas and his wife Eliza bought the place, fixed it up and ran it for many years. In 1825, the famous revolutionary war hero Lafayette, his son George Washington Lafayette and his secretary, a man named Levasseur, come down that very road from Milledgeville, stoppin at this same tavern for a one night stay on their way to New Orleans.

I still remember the famous Frenchman's visit to Milledgeville in the fall of '25. All of the Tims family and what seemed like the entire town turned out to see him. There was parades and speeches, toastin and the like, but what I remember most was that one of the cannons used for the occasion accidentally lit off, killin one of the local artillerymen who was in charge. I heard tell he caught his sleeve afire tryin to reach into an artillery box, which took to settin off all the charges at one time. Poor fella was burnt horrible and died the next day. No such tragedies later at Lucas's Tavern, Cynthia was told. The fact that the famous general and his little group had once passed the night there was enough excitement for Mr. and Mrs. Lucas and a few of their neighbors for many years to come.

When Cynthia was tellin me the story later on, she said she had very unpleasant memories of their one night stay at the place. She said as they was all settin up on the front piazza three men rode up on horseback accompanied by what she guessed were twenty or more trackin dogs. They come into the yard next to the tavern which had a fence around the side of it and they proceeded to kennel their dogs there. Mr. Lucas seemed to know the men and brought out somethin to feed their animals. The men, Cynthia said, were quite proud of their hounds and asked the travelers and the innkeepers to come over to the fence and get a good admirin look at em. Cynthia said they was ferociously thin and looked to be bout as savage as a meat ax, kind of a cross between a bloodhound and a fox hound. The dogs, she said, had short, sleek hair colored yellow and brown. They had short ears and long noses and were built for scentin, quick action and speed. Their masters said they fed em only on Indian corn bread as that made em eager and lively for their business, the business of trackin and catchin slaves. One of the men bragged that sometimes it did his heart good to let the dogs have at their quarry just for the sport of it. Both Sanford and Cynthia had seen the kind of damage some dogs can do when their owners let em loose on those they be trackin. Cynthia told me that she once saw an old black woman torn to shreds by the dogs as her master considered her too old to work and reportedly told the trackers they would be doin him a favor by lettin the dogs finish the job. She said that Sanford's eyes growed big as saucers as he listened to the stories and although she managed to force a false smile of appreciation for the men and their work, Cynthia told me the whole thing made her sick to her stomach.

When Cynthia was a-standin next to the fence, she said, several of them dogs come by to give her the once-over, sniffin up a storm. Now it is said that the nigger dog knows that kind by smell as they are bred just for that purpose, but I found no truth to the matter. People that live in the same places, eat the same foods and have many of the same habits may have somewhat similar scents, but Jeremy Prigg assured me that every individual person has his own particular scent and that a dog will follow it providin the proper scent item is introduced. "A nigger dog will follow a white man sure as he'll follow a black man," he had once told me. Despite that fact, Cynthia said she felt them dogs was lookin right through her white disguise! One dog in particular, she said, kept lookin into her eyes and did not look away for the longest time. "I know who you are," it seemed to be sayin. "I know who you are and others will know soon!"

The slave trackers stayed for supper, eatin in the long central hall which was located in the front of the tavern, forward of the three boardin rooms to the rear. They left soon after eatin. These men, Cynthia said, were crude, uneducated, looked a sight and smelled even worse. She got the feelin that even ol Mr. Lucas and his wife were glad when they finished their meals, gathered up their dogs and rode off to do their grisly work. I could almost hear Cynthia askin: "Is this what you do, Coswell? Is this who you are, Coswell Tims?"

S-I-L-L-S, Cynthia wrote on the travel log as she and Sanford got ready to depart in the mornin on the last three-day leg of their journey. A new passenger had been added, an ol country doctor named Elroy Stanton. He was a smallish man with a fair size belly and armed with an oversized leather doctorin bag. He signed on for Macon, sayin he was checkin in on a dear aunt who had done the better part of raisin him. He wrote his name right under Mrs. Sills in the log book and the woman in charge took his bag, as she had done with the other passengers. Cynthia said the woman was efficient but disagreeable, not at all like Mrs. Lucas. Her name was Mrs. Bonham. Heard tell she once had her own tavern maybe ten miles south of Montgomery, but got a reputation of bein so ornery that after a while folks kinda avoided her place if they could. She now stayed in a small cabin off to the side and slightly behind the main buildin where she appeared from time to time to take care of the business at hand.

She worked for Mr. Hugh Knox who owned and operated the

stage line between Montgomery and Milledgeville. This arrangement allowed Mrs. Bonham's abrasive but efficient manner to sorta keep balance with Knox's outgoin personality but his fondness for whisky and attractive passengers. Evidently Knox had owned the line for a number of years and had done well despite an occasional complaint from passengers, usually womenfolk. Cynthia said that Dr. Stanton recalled hearin bout a lady traveler named Anne Royall who described Knox as "an insolent ruffian who was given to takin liberties," but as there was no man with her at the time to defend her honor, nothin ever come of the complaint.

Knox had definitely made a good livin operatin three lines from Montgomery to Milledgeville. He boasted of ownin "199 good horses, three commodious coaches driven by sober, skillful drivers, convenient stands and excellent road conditions," or so it said on the waybill. Evidently this advertisement went a long way in coverin up some of the more unpleasant experiences people could have along the way.

The next stop would take Cynthia, Sanford, Mr. Simms and the doctor to the very house of Hugh Knox, which was located, Cynthia recalled, near the Flint River. Evidently he had used his influence to reroute the road makin his house the best place for meal stops and a change of horses.

Two other passengers joined in at the last minute, just before the stage left the Lucas Tavern, with Mrs. Bonham stringin together a series of oaths Cynthia said she never heard the lowest gutter-man utter. After signin in and payin their fee, the late arrivals timidly walked past Mrs. Bonham and put their baggage in the storage boot in the back of the coach and got in. They acknowledged all the passengers (cept'n Lizzy, of course) with a nod or a tip of the hat. Both were planters and Cynthia later described both of em as "cotton worshippers and the talkenest people she ever met." After all the proper introductions, she said all they conversed on for the better part of the day was cotton…long or short staple…twenty cents a pound and such. They also talked bout some of the problems of bein a planter.

"Biggest problem," one of em said as the stage rumbled towards Macon, "is the folks in the field. Them shiftless, no-a-count niggers is what's killin the business. Why they cost a man a fortune. You pay maybe fifteen hundred dollars for a good strong field hand and most as much for a good breedin wench and what do they do? Why they run off the first chance they get. There is no loyalty, no appreciation, no, none at all," he concluded.

"And they are clever, too, I'll tell you that for sure," the other added in. "There was one I heard tell over Virginy way, had hisself nailed up in a box and mailed to some abolitionist up in Philadelphia. Got away with it too, he did!"

"I remember 'Box Brown' and don't forget those Krafts up there in Macon," the other offered. "Everybody has heard of them. I'll tell you one thing…If I had me a high yeller that I thought would pass for white, I would do what Elijah Stubbs up in Milledgeville done with his mulatter, the one had the blue eyes, the white skin and the straight light colored hair and looked like any of us a-sittin right here. Ol Stubbs got hisself a hot branding iron and burned a big letter "S" right into that boy's cheek! Yes sir, that's what a fella needs to do with these white-lookin niggers that can disappear into proper society."

As a man who was well acquainted with words, Mr. Simms, thinkin he would use his vast knowledge from all the years in the newspaper business, put what he thought would be the finishin touches on the conversation. "The nigger is born to run," he added. "It's a scientific fact! Dr. Sam Cartwright back there in New Orleans is said to know more about darkies than anyone else. He's studied them, treated them, and observed them. He says they suffer from a condition called drapetomania, which manifests itself in the almost uncontrollable urge to run away. Has something to do with too much carbon in the lungs. He says the only cure for this condition is a proper whipping. Something about crying out and the lungs finally getting in the proper air. It's all very scientific. What do you think, Doctor, you being in the medical field and all?" Simms asked, as all eyes turned towards Dr. Stanton.

"Negroes will run that's a fact," said the doctor, "but maybe they run because they're unhappy where they are and hope to get to a better place. Can't say as I think they have any special medical condition."

Cynthia began to feel uncomfortable as the conversation seemed to invite the opinions of all the white passengers gathered in close proximity. Sensin that she would soon be asked her opinion, or asked to answer specific questions, Cynthia spoke up. "I can't say I know as much about darkies as you all do, but my husband and I have had Lizzy here since she was a young child. Why she's like a member of our family and I know she would never run away from us, but then we treat her well too."

"That don't matter a lick," one of the planters countered. "Sometimes the better you treat em, the more they take advantage. Just don't do any travelin up north, or that young servant of yours will disappear right quick and you won't have any way of gettin her back, despite what the law says. Folks up there are hostile to slavery and will break the law to suit themselves. You keep a good eye on your property, Madam, or it will soon go missin, you mark my words," he concluded.

Cynthia told me that she thought she should not pursue the conversation any further at the risk of sayin somethin revealin. Lizzy sat quietly in the front seat on the side away from the other passengers, her hands folded in the lap of her dress. The others in the coach faced each other which, of course, made conversation easier and more intimate. Things got very quiet for a spell, Cynthia said, when right out the clear blue sky come a question from the newspaper reporter that Cynthia said just bout knocked her clear off her seat. As Simms leaned forward and looked her full in the face he inquired: "Mrs. Sills, you said that husband of yours is a man of means. Why is it that fella has not seen fit to put a proper wedding ring on that pretty finger of yours?"

Chapter 13

SLIPPIN THE NOOSE

A weddin ring! My God, why it appeared we had disremembered that tiny little detail. Of course a married woman of her station would be havin a weddin ring on her finger. Been the very thing for high society folk the last ten years or so. But what kind of gentleman would ever ask a proper lady such a question? Not a gentleman, Cynthia later reasoned, but a nosey reporter just might. Cynthia told me she become somewhat swimmy-headed at this time and could feel things start to swirl about. She said she could feel all eyes lookin in her direction in the close confinement of the coach as all anxiously awaited her reply. She had not prepared herself for this question, but she knew an answer had to be delivered up and soon, lest the passengers see right through this whole disguise that up till this time had appeared so convincin. She said she steadied her mind, thought for a spell and clearin her throat, she said she give out an answer in as forceful a manner as she could muster. "Robbers, sir, robbers!" she announced.

Gatherin some confidence from her first statement she began to add on to it. "With what my rings are worth, do you think I would put temptation in the way of the ruffians one might encounter along this road?" I guess bein an expert at dodgin round weren't just confined to the young negro servant, but was true of the mistress as well, I thought to myself when Cynthia told me later on what had happened.

Heads nodded, Cynthia said, in silent agreement with the logic of the answer and Dr. Stanton even added his testimony to the story with a recountin of a famous robber named Hare several decades earlier who had robbed many a traveler on just this section of road. I guess this fella, Joseph Thompson Hare, and his gang of thieves and cutthroats lived in a large cave a few miles off the road in Conecuh County, Alabama. Dr. Stanton explained how they would dress in disguise and paint their faces red or black so's to draw suspicion on to Indians or niggers, but I guess after a number of successful robberies, it become their undoin when one of the victims noticed that the thieves failed to paint their hands the same color as their faces and were caught "white-handed" as the newspaper article said recountin their capture and eventual hangin.

"Disguises never fool anybody for very long," the good doctor added.

Again everyone nodded their agreement. Cynthia thought on the frightful truth of that last statement and seein a chance to set the issue to rest, took to flatterin the gentlemen in the coach.

"I would like to say that if I had known that I would be surrounded by such honorable and as upstanding gentlemen as yourselves, I might not have felt the need to keep hidden from you those things I value!" Now there was a lie that had several shades of color runnin through it, I thought to myself when Cynthia later related her story.

The stage rumbled on, headed for the last tavern stop before reachin the town of Macon. Hugh Knox's place was now not more than a few miles away. Lookin out the open windows, the travelers took notice of the rutted, red sandy soil that slowed the coach considerable but was balanced off somewhat by the beautiful green piney woods with trees packed in tight together and those colorful

Cherokee roses that Cynthia favored and often mentioned to me that grew rampant by the roadside.

The stagecoach arrived at the Knox place just after dark and the tired travelers filed out one by one from their cramped and uncomfortable quarters. Their host, Hugh Knox, was standin there just as big as life on the raised and lit-up porch…just like a plantation master overlookin his lordly estate. His hands was on his hips and he was smilin broadly. He instructed everyone to tidy up and make ready for supper. As the only two females in the group, Cynthia and her faithful servant were given a separate cabin next to the tavern. The others would have to share one room with several beds and would have to endure each other's snorin and other nightly noises.

After this short opportunity to clean up some, the tired and hungry band of passengers were summoned by Knox to the dinin room where a blazin fire and a meal of pork and sweet taters greeted em. Cynthia took note of the cook who was a very attractive young quadroon who she learned had worked for Knox for some time. Dark skinned with dark eyes but white features like many quadroons, she was accomodatin as well as good at preparin meals, but Cynthia said she noticed that Knox's critical stare often forced the servant girl to lower her head and quiet her ways.

Cynthia described Knox as a rather large and muscular man, not unattractive at first sight. Rather talkative and somewhat charmin, he could be both amusin and somewhat threatenin all at the same time. He had a need to hog the conversation as well as those things and people around him. That decisive and confident air he had was probably what had made Hugh Knox the successful businessman folks knew him to be.

The meal was well received by the guests, but soon the conversation began to get heated. "I'm tired of hearin you planters complainin about the workforce," Knox replied in response to the comments made by the two planters who continued to offer up that same opinion they had expressed back in the coach.

"If you done things proper-like with a good overseer, maybe one from the north—they're known for their calculatin ways and freedom with the whip—you wouldn't be losin so much of your two-legged property! It's mismanagement, more than anythin else," he added.

Unwillin to antagonize their host any further, the two busied themselves with the drinkin of spirits that was provided. A fair tastin beer made from fermented molasses was bein liberally consumed round the table and Knox's flask of cognac whiskey was findin its way into the hands of several of the assembled guests. Simms and Dr. Stanton began discussin travelin conditions long the Federal Road and the two planters soon resumed their familiar conversation regardin the worthless negro.

Knox, holdin his flask of cognac, approached Cynthia who had earlier declined the spirits that had been offered. "Mrs. Sills," Knox inquired, "would you care to share in a little friendly socialization?" he offered, raising both the cognac and a couple of drinkin glasses suggestively.

"I am extremely tired, Mr. Knox, but I thank you kindly. I do believe that my servant and I will retire for the night," Cynthia responded.

Hugh Knox glared at the beautiful young traveler and puffed up some by the whisky, asked if she might reconsider. Again lackin a positive response, he then asked if perhaps she considered herself different or maybe better than everyone else in the tavern. Before she could respond he added: "And, by the way, where is that husband of yours, madam? I can't say I think much of a man who would allow his woman to travel such great distances with only a young nigger wench for protection!"

Cynthia knew a response was needed here. Refusin to drop her gaze, she squared her shoulders as she had done many times in the past and lookin her host straight in the eye, responded: "Your comment sir, is improper, as is your question. I will not dignify either with a reply. Good night, sir!" Cynthia told me later that experience had taught her when to be compliant and when to be more assertive. As she walked away she hoped she had made the right decision, although the alcohol that had been added to the mix, give her more than a little cause for concern.

Back in their cabin, the two disguised fugitives began to ready themselves up for bed. Sanford desperately wanted to shed his head-kerchief, as he complained that he was not used to wearin such a restrictive thing and it was makin his scalp itch somethin fierce. Slave women and even young girls generally wore a similar bandana with the color white bein reserved for the highest of house servants. Lizzy's was red which was probably the most popular color worn by the majority of black servants, but it was decided that it was to be left on as one last call to the johnny house out behind the cabin was suddenly thought necessary.

A few minutes after the young servant left to answer nature's call, a rather large, shadowy figure appeared in the cabin doorway. Cynthia had removed part of her travelin clothes and had her back to the door, facin the bed. As she removed one more part of her dress over her head, she told me later she felt the presence of someone in the room and knew instinctively it was not her familiar young travelin companion. She turned quickly, almost half expectin to see the very visitor who stood there, and asked quite forcefully: "Mr. Knox…What is the meaning of this intrusion?"

He answered not with words but with action. Several quick steps brought the intruder within reach of his half-dressed house guest. Grabbin her by the arm as she attempted to flee, he tossed her backwards onto the bed. Cynthia attempted to voice her objections when a large hand covered her mouth and she heard her attacker's deep voice. "You are in my house now, my dear…your uppity ways and your missin husband ain't gonna save you now."

She could feel the weight of his body and smell the alcohol on his breath that he had liberally consumed as he began to grope at her body. Cynthia told me later that the strangest thought passed through her mind at the time. She wondered if this was the fate of all women, not just slaves who was forced to endure the physical attention of their masters. Here she was, white and all, wealthy as well, and yet she was in a compromised position once again. As she struggled to mount some kind of defense, she said she heard a sound like someone had dropped a heavy object to the ground from some high place above. She could feel the shock of it as well, as the human form above her suddenly went limp. As she lay there momentarily, tryin to determine what change had taken place, she said she suddenly become aware of a warm liquid that began to trickle down her cheek and on to the bed sheets beneath her. Musterin all the strength she could, she shoved the body of her attacker from her, lookin backward quickly at a large red stain that had formed on the linens. She pushed again and Knox's unconscious body fell in a heap to the floor.

"Yuz be alright?" Sanford asked, standin there with the heavy wooden crossbar from the door held firmly in his hands. Evidently Sanford had entered the room and had witnessed the attack in progress. Lookin round the room, he had spotted the crossbar leanin up against the wall by the door and had enlisted its aid as he introduced that heavy object to the head of the attacker.

Dr. Stanton, who had been out on the porch smokin his pipe, was immediately drawn to the scene. "What's going on here?" Stanton declared upon enterin the room. The other travelers, alerted by the commotion, soon crowded in behind him. Knox lay on the floor with a sizable gash in the back of his head. Dr. Stanton bent over the injured party and give instructions to fetch his medical bag. Knox was alive but was injured pretty good, the doc reported, as he began to administer aid to his patient.

The reporter, Mr. Simms, eagerly began a series of questions. "What happened here, Mrs. Sills?"

Cynthia, hurriedly attempted to put on enough clothin to be presentable, forcefully stated her case. "Mr. Knox entered my quarters unannounced with the intention of doing me harm," Cynthia responded. "Lizzy, my ever faithful servant, came to my rescue with this crossbar here."

"That is most interesting, Mrs. Sills, that a young female would have the strength to carry out such a task," Simms added, lookin somewhat disbelievin at the heavy oak crossbar and then back at the young servant girl in a turban and dress who stood near the end of the bed with her hands timidly folded in front of her.

"You know as well as I do, Mr. Simms, that individuals are capable of great things when they are in stressful situations," said Cynthia, hopin to head off any further inquiries regardin Lizzy's new-found strength.

Questionin in this area stopped when one of the planters brought up another point. He turned to Lizzy and said: "Do you know it is against the law for a nigger to strike a white man?"

The Georgia Slave Code, passed in '48 was generally known by most folks. The death penalty was considered appropriate if slaves was found guilty of insurrection, arson, poisonin, rapin or murderin of whites and also "assaultin a white person with the intent to murder, or with a weapon likely to produce death," I think was the exact words as I remember them. Certainly the heavy wooden crossbar would qualify as a potential lethal weapon that was likely to produce death.

"If I am not mistaken," the doctor offered as he continued to work on the injured tavern owner, "there are certain circumstances in which such behavior is warranted. It seems to me that protecting one's master or mistress from an attacker is allowed, providing the attack can be substantiated ...no colored testimony is admissible though, if I remember the law correctly."

Knox began to stir. Dr. Stanton had stopped the bleedin by wrappin a bandage full round his head. The innkeeper was slowly regainin his senses.

"What happened?" Knox asked, more to himself than to any individual person standin in the room.

"Mrs. Sills says you attacked her and her servant here came to her aid," Dr. Stanton offered.

"Why that is a dog-faced lie!" Knox replied. "I went to the good lady's cabin to see if there was anythin more I could do for her and I was rewarded with this," he said, reachin back to feel the still risin bump on the back of his head.

"Well, I guess one thing we can all agree on here," Simms added. "The damage was done by the young nigger wench, not Mrs. Sills."

"And that's against the law!" Knox offered loudly. "Any slave that strikes a white man will hang for sure. We have no sheriff here, but I know the sheriff over in Macon and he'll want to see you arrested and properly dealt with," he said, pointin an accusin finger at the young servant.

"This is an outrage!" Cynthia remembered sayin. "I can tell you all for a fact that this man here came into my quarters with the intention of doing me harm and my servant, bless her young heart, came..."

"That is for the law to decide," Knox interrupted, "and it will be my word against yours. I'm sure a jury would see the need for you lyin to protect your property, Mrs. Sills. That servant of yours has a violent nature, for sure. Best to be done with her before she poisons some fine citizen, maybe lights their house on fire or murders em in their sleep!"

Cynthia told me later on that it seemed odd how Sanford had been so invisible to her white travelin companions for most of the trip, but now seemed to be the very center of everyone's attention. Dr. Stanton told Lizzy and her mistress that they would have to answer the charges brought by Mr. Knox when they got to Macon and that their stay there might be a little longer than she had originally planned. Stanton and the other whites in the party would assume responsibility for the accused in the absences of proper authorities.

"Maybe that English husband of yours can hire some fancy, high price lawyer and get your property back, but I wouldn't want to take bet on it, no sir," Knox said, as he reached up yet again to feel the substantial bump that had risen to new heights on the rear of his head.

The excitement of the evenin kept most everyone from any type of restful sleep, and things was pretty quiet when all the travelers boarded the stage for Macon the next mornin.

"Tell the sheriff that I will be along in a day or two," Knox stated as the coach made ready to leave. "Soon as my head clears up some and I get my business affairs in order, I'll be there to press charges. Give the sheriff my warm regards."

Very little was said as the stage lurched forward on the last leg of its journey. After a while, Mr. William Gilmore Simms broke the silence as he suddenly announced: "I think your young servant is innocent, Mrs. Sills, and should properly be acquitted of this crime." Cynthia said that this statement at first give her some hope that sympathy and support were to be found among her fellow travelers.

"Not very likely," one of the planters contested, "Hugh Knox is a very influential man. I'm sure there's lots of folks owe him favors. That little wench sittin right here is headed for the gallows, mark my words."

"Here's what I think we should do, Mrs. Sills," Simms continued. "I will do a story about our little misadventure here. Yes sir, a story about a beautiful young traveler and her faithful servant and a violent encounter with a backwoods ruffian and bully. My readership would love it. Besides I have drawn these sketches here of both of you. A tolerably good likeness, don't you think? Did them when you slept on the stage. That story will get such sympathy for you that no jury would dare convict young Lizzy here." Cynthia looked down at the quite remarkable pictures the reporter had drawn.

"Please don't write anything, Mr. Simms," Cynthia pleaded. "I just want this whole thing over and done with as soon as possible."

"I'm sorry, my dear, but people have a right to know the news," he replied. "I will assure you, however, the world will know of your heroics and those of your faithful attendant. I will promise you that!"

Cynthia saw no need to further argue the point. She knew that the last thing that she and Sanford needed was exposure, but Simms had made up his mind. With their likenesses soon to be spread all over the newspaper and a trial which was sure to reveal their true identities, Cynthia told me later that she thought that perhaps the only way out of this mess lay with someone she had never met…a man by the name of Jesse Tims. She hoped my brother had gotten my message and could spirit her and Sanford away fore everythin began to unravel.

I had told her that once in Macon she and Sanford was to check into the Lanier Hotel, a two-story new, but poorly constructed affair, that was bout the best the town had to offer. She was to check in under the name of Mrs. Alexander Sills and Jesse, posin as her husband, would soon be there to gather em both up.

There was very little conversation when the travelers reached Macon around noon and began to disperse. The doctor wished Cynthia well, but said that he was on his way to see the sheriff, somethin he had promised Knox he would take care of and was legally bound to do. Cynthia told him to tell the sheriff that she and Lizzy would be at the Lanier Hotel but that common decency should allow some rest and refreshment fore any legal proceedins started in commencin.

One of the planters did give Cynthia a less-than-sincere wish for the best and the reporter Simms said that he would stop by tomorrow for some more information he needed for his story. Lizzy took their two travelin bags out of the boot of the stagecoach, fumblin round for some time in the process.

The two female fugitives checked into their new quarters with Lizzy carryin the bags. Their room was on the first floor, facin the back of the buildin. Both collapsed on the bed, exhausted from the events of the last twenty four hours. Both quickly drifted off to sleep but it weren't too long after when a knock was heard at the door. A black hotel servant announced that a man was in the lobby named Alexander Sills who was inquirin bout his wife. That was the name Jesse was told to use, so as not to draw suspicion on to the Tims brothers.

Cynthia acknowledged the message and dismissed the servant and then turned to Sanford. "It's Jesse Tims, Sanford, come from Milledgeville to fetch us. Go down there and play like you were from the hotel here and tell him to drive the wagon round back. You tell him that his party will be down shortly."

When Sanford returned to the room, the two fugitives moved quickly to ready themselves up for the trip to Milledgeville. I guess clothes flew every which-a-way and when all was said and done, Sanford opened the window to the back alley and the two of em slipped out just as slick as you please. Closin the window behind em, they walked over with their baggage in hand to the back street that would soon bring their rescuer.

Jessie told me later on when he come round that corner with our wagon and saw Cynthia for the first time, he said she was a-standin there with baggage at her feet and he was struck by her appearance. Here was a young woman, he thought, not much more than twenty or twenty-five years of age, with long light colored hair and flashin blue-green eyes, dressed not in refinement but dressed tolerably well. She was beautiful for sure, he told me, but she also had a certain confident way bout her. Jesse said that the woman was an absolute sight to behold.

There was a black boy there too, my brother said, dressed in homespun, standin right next to her and smilin broadly. Jesse got out of the wagon to meet the two for the first time. He told me his first impression of the boy was that he was bright and cheerful and bore a strong resemblance to the black slave girl (right down to the space between the two front teeth) who worked in the hotel and had just recently instructed him where to go with the wagon.

Stretchin out her hand the young woman offered: "Good day, Mr. Tims. My name is Cynthia and this young boy here is Sanford. I guess we just might be your house guests for a spell."

After the brief introduction, the wagon headed northeast towards Milledgeville. Jesse told me later that he had his fair share of questions, but figured he would get answers in due time. Jesse drove and Cynthia sat up front with him, lookin for all the world to see like man and wife as they headed for home. Sanford, he sat in the back of the wagon atop the travelin bags. People would probably never imagine for a minute that in them bags was the evidence of their illegal flight, disguises that had masked their true identities and hidden em from sight during the better part of the past week. The only thing missin in them bags was a pair of high topped shoes that Cynthia had become quite partial to and happened to have on her feet at that very moment. They went tolerable well with her old clothes, she remembered thinkin, blendin both the old in with the new. She had hopes that maybe this new life she was to start in Milledgeville would work out in much the same manner.

People seekin Mrs. Sills and her faithful and protective servant in the early mornin hours back at the hotel would soon be disappointed to find their room deserted. Any inquiries would reveal that the woman's husband had come askin for her and no one had seen neither hide nor hair of any of em since that time.

Cynthia told me that it was the oddest thing as she had just been thinkin bout them likenesses that the nosey reporter had drawed up and how troublesome they might become in the future, when Sanford tapped Miss Cynthia on the shoulder and, with a big smile on that face of his, showed her the two sketches which he had miraculously secreted out of the reporter's travelin bag. That boy was more than a might resourceful, Cynthia remembered thinkin at the time. I guess William Gilmore Simms would have to draw up the two heroines' faces from memory sometime in the future if he was still inclined in that general direction.

Chapter 14

TRAILIN BEHIND

I reckoned to be only but a day or so behind the yellow coach as I had made up some valuable time on horseback. When Lafayette and his party come down this same road back in '25, I heard tell they were smart enough to have switched from the coach to ridin horses. Faster and, truth to tell, much more comfortable.

Talkin to Cynthia and Sanford later on, I found we did share some of the same stops long the way, but because I was able to move a might faster, arrivin later or earlier in the day at places they had visited, my journey was a little different. I did stay one night at Longmyre's…wonderful woman, very accomodatin. I did inquire bout recent guests and she told me of a group from down New Orleans way who come by and stayed the night. "Lovely young lady," Mrs. Longmyre had said. "And that attendant of hers, why she was everything a person would want in a young servant girl." Obviously the two escaped fugitives were playin their parts well, I thought. I did have concerns, however, when she told me that they shared the coach with two slave traders and a nosy reporter but further descriptions of Cynthia and Sanford made me think that at least to this point they were in no danger of revealin who they really was.

I crossed the Alabama River on that same ferry earlier used by Mrs. Sills and her party at the cost of seventy-five cents for me and my horse. The boat was just a flat-bottom affair with no real sides to speak of. Two pulley ropes allowed the ferry to be moved from one side of the river to the other, and the two fellas that owned the ferry worked the lines themselves. I crossed with two slave drivers, their horses, and a group of six or eight slaves chained together that was bein driven up to Macon for sale. Their chains made quite a bit of noise when they shuffled on past me to get aboard, but they soon stood quiet-like with their heads lowered as we crossed the river. Negroes always spoke joyously bout "crossin dat river," but I guess this one was not the one they was always speakin on as there seemed to be little joy among any of em that I could see.

When night closed in and there was no tavern close by, I simply stopped by the side of the road, tied the horse to a nearby tree and slept the night away right there on the ground. Me and Jesse had spent our fair share of days out on the trail, nights too, so makin do with what we had weren't nothin new for either one of the Tims boys.

One particular night, though, a strange thing did happen. I was lyin by the side of the road, just this side of fallin asleep, when I saw somethin that give me quite a start. I heard it first, then saw the thing, uncertain as to its true nature. Whatever it was it was comin down the road at a fair rate of speed, headed right in my direction. All I could make out was the ghostly outline of a fiery apparition of some sort. The thing seemed to be glowin all over, as it was lit up on both its sides. That light cast an eerie shadow over the whole of it. I couldn't help but remember back to ghost stories me and Jesse was told as young'uns of wangdoodles, catawampus and boogers of all shapes and sizes that would come up from the underworld at night to snatch the souls of all they could catch. Old negroes in particular had a knack for tellin them kind of scary tales and young white boys like me and Jesse, with all the curiosity of youth, proved to be willin listeners. They would tell em with such conviction, with their eyes gettin great big, and the emphasis of voice and gestures in all the right places, why we believed every single word of it. I also remember that I was glad to have an older brother who would later sleep in the same bed as me and would at the very least, share the same fate. Upon closer scrutiny, however, this here weren't no apparition but only a stagecoach that was simply burnin lightwood in gratins mounted on arms on its sides as it moved along, tryin to make the sixty mile a day minimum that coach operators and owners demanded. It passed by so quickly I'm sure there weren't a soul aboard ever took notice of a horse and a lone traveler who had taken up temporary residence by the side of the road.

With sunrise, I mounted up and continued on. I began thinkin bout Jesse and how he had always been someone I could count on when I was scared or in trouble. I knew if he got that telegraph message I had sent, he would be at the hotel up in Macon for sure and bring my Cynthia and young Sanford back home to Milledgeville. I thought bout what I would tell him regardin em and our "situation." I thought bout what maybe I shouldn't tell him, given the feelins most people, includin the Tims family, had towards the negro and his legal standin in the community. I hated to keep anythin from Jesse, it just didn't feel right, but I held out hope that everythin would work itself out in proper fashion.

There was maybe an hour or so of daylight left when I finally dismounted at the Knox place on the Flint River. It had been a day's ride out of Montgomery, and after this stop there would be maybe a half day's ride on to Macon. Another half day if all went accordin to plan, I might just find myself back at Jesse's home again, hopefully with a new family right there to greet me.

As I looked around I noticed several buildings on the property, a stable for horses and wagons, a small cabin somewhat off to the side and the tavern itself with a large front porch and smoke risin up from the chimney. It was all a welcome sight but I thought it was odd that no one was anywhere to be seen.

Soon a young female attendant did come from out behind the tavern and without speakin a word, took the reins of my horse and motioned with her head for me to go on into the tavern. She soon quietly disappeared into the stable as I walked up the porch stairs alone, across the piazza, to a closed wooden door that brought tired travelers into the world of owner Hugh Knox. Openin it, the weight of the door I noticed was considerable and the heavy oak crossbar propped up against the wall behind it brought to mind the dangers many of these taverns had to face over the years with the red man and with white ruffians that had frequented the area. People would be glad to have reached the safety of such a place as this, I thought to myself.

As I closed the door behind me and walked across the dinin hall towards a fireplace that was set to blazin in the far corner of the room, I couldn't help but take notice of the sound my boots was makin, creekin up a storm and fallin heavy on the wide-planked pineywood floor beneath my feet. It was a lonely sound, for sure, but it did have its own echo for comfort. This had been a lonely journey and I was missin certain folks even more as nighttime come on. The emptiness of the tavern did nothing to change that feelin. Maybe some decent food, a reasonably comfortable bed and what I probably needed most of all...a good night's sleep, would do much, I figured, to improve on the situation.

I warmed myself at the hearth, rubbin my hands together and blowin on em for good measure. I shuddered as I felt a slight chill take leave of me and the coolness of the trail give way to the warmth of the fire. I sat down at a nearby table and lit up my pipe, enjoyin the moment, full expectin someone to soon appear. This would be a dollar well spent, I thought, as this place had a comfortable feel to it and I sure was tired of sleepin out there on the trail and eatin the few things that I had brought with me from New Orleans or taken from places I had stopped along the way. As I looked round the room I imagined Cynthia's stay here and hoped she had pleasant memories of the place.

Pretty soon a big fella come in. He had a bandage of some sort wrapped round his head. I got the feelin he was the owner or at least someone who was in authority as he welcomed me and asked if I be wantin any supper. "Why that would suit me just fine," I had replied.

"You want anythin to drink while we wait?" he added. "We have some excellent beer and also some fine brandy. Might even be able to rustle up some cognac whisky if that would suit your fancy," he offered.

"Why that brandy sounds like somethin a tired traveler could really take a likin to," I answered. "Thank you most kindly."

The innkeeper seemed like a friendly sort of fella, certainly accommodatin, but I did think he seemed somewhat out of sorts. He snapped sharply at the attractive female attendant who had appeared suddenly but then retreated quickly into the back to prepare the food. I suspected that the bandage he wore round his head had more than a little to do with his current disposition.

After about two (or maybe it was three) very tolerable glasses of brandy, that same girl come out with a supper of venison and rice and a bowl of turnip soup. The innkeeper sat down at my table and as we was the only people to be found in the place at the time, we began to have us a little conversation as I eagerly began to consume what the woman had set before me.

I found the man was indeed Hugh Knox and that he was not only the owner of the tavern but also owned the stage line from Montgomery all the rest of the way to Milledgeville. I also found the man to have a rather high opinion of hisself and in some ways I think that was good, lookin back, as he was so busy braggin on himself that he never even asked me my name or anythin bout what I do or why I was on the trail. One of the talkenest men I had ever met, he did go on and on. In fact, the more he spoke the less I come to like the fella as his braggin was startin to distress my ears and interfere with proper digestion. Maybe it was cause he made everythin sound so good or maybe it was that high-handed tone of his that made me finally inquire into the recent misfortune that surrounded his head.

"Damn nigger wench did it. Snuck up behind me and hit me with the crossbar of a door. I'm goin to Macon tomorrow to press charges. She and that uppity mistress of hers are goin to get a dressin down from the law, I will assure you that," Knox said forcefully.

With that, my interest in the conversation picked up considerable as I had a strong suspicion just who he might be referin to. I began to think bout the incident and what must have happened if, in fact, it was Sanford who had taken such drastic measures. There was no way that boy was goin to strike a white man and call any special attention on to hisself or Cynthia under normal circumstance. It only made sense to me that he must have been tryin to protect his mistress from harm and had no other choice or he wouldn't have risked doin such a thing.

"What did the woman's husband have to say on the matter," I asked, tryin to determine if the parties in question were the ones I suspected.

"Oh, there weren't no husband to be had," Knox replied, "but she did say she was meetin him up in Macon. Damn fool of a man, I would say, to let a lady like that travel alone."

"What was so special bout this woman?" I inquired, takin another bite of the welcome vittles laid out before me.

"Oh, she was a real beauty, a real looker, all dressed up real fancy-like," Knox added.

"Were you preparin dinner when the attack occurred?" I asked somewhat jokinly, tryin to draw out more information surroundin the attack.

"Can't say as I was," Knox answered. "I was actually over at her cabin tryin to see to the needs of the young lady…beautiful young thing, deserved all the attention a real man could give her."

Knox took another sip of that cognac that I noticed he seemed quite partial to and with a slight smile startin to creep cross his face and lowerin his voice some so's to appear to speak man to man, he added in: "To tell the absolute truth here…that woman was enticin me somethin fierce and when things just got to commencin, why it was at that very time the little nigger wench snuck up behind me and…"

I barely remember comin up out of my chair! What I do remember, though, is hittin this Knox fella hard with my right hand, full on the chin. (This would be that same chin he had been stickin out for the better part of the last half hour or so with all his braggin.) Food that was left over went a-flyin and so did he, as he fell backwards onto the floor. I pushed the table out of the way and picked the innkeeper up by the shirt. Standin him up straight as he would go, I let fly nother blow right into the man's belly. I had learned early on that the best way to make a man quit a fight is to take the starch right out of him with a well placed blow to that very area. Knox crumpled to the floor in a heap, the bandage fallin from his head. Misfortune seemed to have taken to followin this Knox fella around for a time, I concluded.

The young servant girl come rushin in and couldn't quite believe her eyes when she saw what had happened. Her boss man, or maybe it was her master, lay there on the floor, all quiet for a change. I stood over him as I spoke.

"I'll be leavin now. Here's a dollar for the meal and you tell this fella lyin here on the floor when he wakes up not to bother with any legal proceedins over there in Macon tomorrow as he is a liar and I would be willin to say as much. Also you tell him he needs to mind his manners with guests, specially the ladies. You tell em that, you hear!" She nodded as I stepped over Knox, picked up my hat, and walked out the door.

As I rode away from the tavern, I reflected some on what had just happened. Now I know that losin your temper can prove mighty costly to a man, but it was most like I had no control over what I had just done. Emotions just boiled up inside me, I reckoned, and I guess that led me to thinkin with my heart rather than with my head. Luckily, Knox did not know my name or where I lived and he probably would think that that beatin I just give him had more to do with the treatment of ladies in general, rather that the treatment of one in particular. In any case, I reasoned, Hugh Knox was a bully, and bullies was always cowards when you take a good close look at em. I figured he would lick his wounds some, reconsider his legal case against Sanford and probably stay right there at the tavern and go right on tendin to his business and bein the same person he always was. My daddy used to say that a man don't throw off his habits as easily as he does his coat. No amount of beatins would most likely change the nature of a man. I suppose it could happen, but such a conversion, I have found, ain't to be expected, and if it does occur, it don't figure to last all that long.

It had just been gettin dark when that incident had occurred at the Knox place and I rode steady, reachin Macon round midnight. With the lateness of the hour and the lack of moonlight, the dim outline of old Ft. Hawkins was barely visible as I approached the town.

The rottin wooden walls and the long abandoned blockhouses give some richness to the history of the area, as did the Old Creek Burial Mounds that surrounded the better part of the city. Macon was another river city like Milledgeville, this one built up on the banks of the Ocmulgee River. Although settled later than Milledgeville, it had growed rapidly over the years on account of its location as a trade center. Cotton was king in Macon as it was in many part of Georgia, but my one reason for visiting was not business. It was just hopefully the last stop on my journey fore reachin the Tims' homestead.

Buildins, some with lights still a-burnin, drew me as I rode into town. I stopped a fella in a wagon who seemed to be on some late-night errand and asked him the best place a visitor could bed down for the night. He said that the Lanier Hotel was the best the town had to offer and it was open all night, but I hesitated at first thinkin bout what may have happened there recently. The sheriff and the hotel people and maybe others were most likely lookin for clues to the disappearance of a fine young lady and her attendant from New Orleans. Of course that was if Jesse had done his job proper like. However, if he had not for some reason then the two fugitives would still be there, makin it great to see em earelier than expected. I decided either way that the Lanier was the place I would spend my last night on the Federal Road and at best our reunion might be commencin sooner rather than later as I had planned.

Walkin into the lobby of the hotel, I strolled right up to the main desk and asked for a room. The man there had me sign my name to the register and when I did I got a good look-see at some of the guests who stopped by recently. Sure nough, there was the name S-I-L-L-S down the list a-ways, with a little notation sayin that she was accompanied by a negro attendant and that they had two travelin bags. I also noticed that she was no longer here, as a mark that had been put next to her name was the same one that appeared on all the people's names furthest up the list. Jesse had done his job. I would sleep well tonight, I figured, as the three were most likely headed back to the safety of Milledgeville at this very moment, or maybe cozied up back at Jesse's place already.

I had my saddlebags throwed over my shoulder and was bout

to head to my room with key in hand, when two men come into the lobby and walked up to the desk. The taller one wore a badge, the other one, more fancified and fleshy, was dressed in a business type suit with one of them fancy new bowler style hats.

The taller one spoke up. "You say this woman was married to a wealthy Englishman, Mr. Simms?"

"That's a fact, Sheriff," he replied. "I think they were traveling about. She said they were only going to be in Macon for a short time. My guess is that he came to get her and they couldn't wait... maybe they had to catch a riverboat or something."

"That's possible," the sheriff said. "Let's ask this clerk here what he remembers."Turnin to the clerk behind the desk, the sheriff inquired bout what he had seen and his impressions of the missing guests. I heard him say that he remembered the lady as she was a fine lookin woman and also said that a man come a-callin not too much later who called himself Alexander Sills.

"Do you remember what this Mr. Sills looked like?" the sheriff asked.

"Yes I do," the clerk replied. "He was a tall, kind of a scruffy fella, had his fair share of trail dirt on him, he did. Didn't speak with no English accent, I can tell you that for sure."

"Very interesting," the sheriff said as he turned to leave with the other fella following along right on his heels.

I did more than a little turnin and twistin that night thinkin back on the conversation I had overheard. Maybe the sheriff would reason that Jesse worked for Sills and had been sent to pick up his wife and servant. Maybe the clerk misinterpreted what he had said. I finally settled my mind down some when I thought that either way, the sheriff lacked any trackin dogs like the ones the Tims boys had that could light out after a missin party and follow their trail to Milledgeville.

I admit that the next day I pushed that horse a might harder than was normal the last thirty miles or so. I was anxious to see Cynthia once more and hear bout what had happened since she and Sanford had left New Orleans. I also had not seen Jesse and my hound dogs for several weeks. It would be good to be home. It would be good to be back at Jesse's place with Cynthia and Sanford hopefully right there with him.

The last of this little journey seemed to take forever, but finally a familiar house did come into view. I had always known that place to be a welcome sight. Jesse and Becky had built it with help from the entire Tims family on the outskirts of Milledgeville right after they was married. They were happy there (as brief as their union was) and I remember visitin em quite regular, but also remembered tryin not to make too much of a pest of myself. I would take Daddy's horse from our place in town and ride out to see the two of em. Often times they would just be settin out there on the piazza. Jesse, he'd be smokin his pipe and Becky would be workin on her knittin. They just seemed so happy and content just bein with each other. Someday Cynthia and me would have a house of our own and be just as happy, I thought to myself.

As I approached the house and the end of the journey, I heard the dogs start in a-wailin as they recognized my scent and I soon spotted a familiar dark figure scurryin bout the yard. Sanford had a load of firewood in his arms and was headed inside. He let all the wood drop to the ground in a heap when he saw me and come runnin over my way.

"Massa Tims, Massa Tims!" he shouted excitedly. "We made it through, we surely did!"

After dismountin, I put a hand on the boy's shoulder. "I knew you two was equal to the task," I said. "Now where is that beautiful and resourceful mistress of yours?" I inquired.

"She inside wid Massa Jesse," Sanford reported. "She been missin you sumpin awful!"

I must have looked quite a sight when I come through the door as travelin will sure take its toll on a man, but Cynthia didn't seem to mind in the least. As soon as she saw me, she come rushin over and throwed her arms full round my neck. Her feet come clean off the floor, they did, revealin those black high-topped shoes for all the world to see. Probably not very dignified for a lady of Mrs. Sills lofty station, someone might have argued, but an honest emotion nonetheless. We spent a little time in silent greetin, unmindful of the two others that was in the room. When we did turn to acknowledge em, they both had wide grins on their faces. I guess they was both happy that I had finally found the woman I had looked for all my life.

"Did you know her straightaway?" Jesse asked in obvious reference to Pleasant Enis' comment made just a few weeks back when we was all out on patrol duty. My God, I thought to myself, it seemed like a year since we was out there chasin down them two runaways that needed bringin back to New Orleans. Long, Walker, the *ENTERPRISE*, the Federal Road, Cynthia, Sanford, Knox, the fancy clothes, all had come into my life in such a short period of time.

"I knew when I first saw her, Jesse, standin there on the deck of that boat. Yes sir, she was standin there so proud like..." I stopped short. My brother probably figured my emotions was gettin in the way of my tellin, but I stopped short for a different reason. I did not know how much Cynthia or Sanford had revealed bout our circumstance and I still hadn't thought on exactly what I was gonna tell my brother.

Chapter 15

BUSINESS AS USUAL

"I think he's on the river!" Jesse yelled back to me, as he led the way followin the tracks to the banks of the Oconee. "I think this may be a pretty slick one, Coswell, must come with age. See them marks over there where a small boat was hid up in the bushes and dragged down here to the water?"

I nodded. The tracks and footprints was as plain as the nose on a man's face.

It felt good to be back out on the trail, it truly did. Bein back longside my brother, back to where I was bout as comfortable as a broke-in old pair of shoes, back to doin what we both done best. Jesse was a sight for sore eyes, after all the new faces that come my way durin the past few weeks. He said nothin had changed much hereabouts as he told me that chasin runaways hadn't stopped with my goin to New Orleans. Fact was, he said, he had lit out after two durin that time. One of em, he said, he tracked usin Moses, who was now older and wiser than that time previous when his legs shook with excitement down there at the prison. Two hours later, Jesse said, the fugitive was up a tree and an hour or so after that he had the cash money for his return in his billfold. The other fugitive, he said, was a young negro woman he tracked for the better part of the day but never caught. She was picked up by the patrollers, however, later that night. No money for the Tims brothers, but justice done nonetheless, Jesse noted. "We know that there be many of em that try, but thank the Good Lord, few make it," he added. I found that bein reminded of that reality did not have quite the same effect it might have had a short time back. Maybe Coswell Tims was slowly slidin down to the little end of the horn, I remembered thinkin to myself…that would be the end where all the misery and the pain lies.

I had brought back a little less than four hundred dollars for my work in New Orleans, after deductin travelin expenses for Cynthia, Sanford and myself, the clothes and horse that I bought, and all the incidentals on the way. I would have to say that financially the Tims boys maybe weren't doin as good as some, but they was probably fairin a darn site better than most. That decision we had made back in '40 to follow the government's example and go into the bloodhound trackin business proved out to be a good one...better for us than for them, that's sure. We caught more than our fair share of runners over the years and had the cash money to show for it, but I'm not sure the government ever caught any of them redtails down Florida way with the dogs they had. Maybe the fact that the Cuban handlers was sent home early might have figured in, but me and Jesse think it must have been the dogs themselves. Any dog that "seems indifferent to the blood-stained garments and weapons left by the fleeing Seminoles," as one of their local papers put it, I believe cannot be a true bloodhound. In fact, a reporter who was sent to the scene once described these dogs as bein "a variety of colors, with erect ears that were cropped at the bend and loins, haunches and tail like a greyhound." Now there ain't one of them features match up with the bloodhound breed, no sir, not by a jugfull! Sometimes Jesse and me have found that people often get to callin any trackin dog a "bloodhound" whether they is or whether they ain't. Seems to me there was so many stories bout people who was chased by bloodhounds, it would be hard to believe there were enough of those fine critters livin in the south to even make that possible. Maybe it was that the government was careless in mislabelin their sizable investment. Don't know that for sure, but then not bein of a political mind, I guess I really shouldn't be weighin in on the matter t'all.

"Look here, Jesse," I added. "There's other tracks round here as well. Some barefoot, some with shoes, some large and some small. Don't look to be any boots or fancy footwear, though. All slaves most like as not, but from different places I'd suspect. By my count there's five of em all tole up. Must have met right here at this spot. Probably had a plan, too, less they was just plain lucky to find this here boat. I am of the opinion they didn't just run off like a lot of em do and if that be the case, I reckon they didn't just row off haphazard-like to see whatever fine sights there was to see."

Jesse nodded his agreement. We had brought Molly with us that day, a fine lookin red female with a black muzzle that we had been usin the better part of three years. She was rarin to go, sniffin the ground like an excited bull bout to surprise an unfortunate intruder who had just wandered into his pasture. I have to admit to bein pretty excited bout the chase myself, despite recent events that was startin to cast their shadow on to this type of activity. I knew I had to separate out my personal life from my business life as a trackin man. After all, I reasoned, the money I would make would help support the folks I cared most bout and also draw less attention to our rather unusual circumstance. Daddy used to say that a man shouldn't worry on things he couldn't help. I remember him sayin to me one day: "A man would often be better off if he charged the whole thing up to the dust and let the rain settle it." I suspected there could be problems as time went on, but as for the moment I simply needed to set my mind on the trail left by an old negro runaway named Abraham and bring the ol boy back to his legal master, Colonel John McKinley.

In her eagerness Miss Molly was blowin scent off the ground, alternatin sniffin and blowin in an attempt to get as much information as possible up into that large black nose of hers. I remember a line from a poem I had read somewhere regardin bloodhound noses that reported they was so effective that this dog could "sniff the guilty at a distance and the fugitive would then lead a doomed existence," or somethin akin to that. Pretty much true, I suspect. The clothin that the bondsman Abraham had left behind at the plantation that we had taken with us would soon put that dog's compass needle straight on that slave's brown backside. Molly would find this Abraham, of that there was little doubt.

The dog moved back and forth, pausin on occasion to shake her head violently from side to side. Ears went a-flyin too, makin a funny sound, it did, most like a woodpecker tappin out a tune on a holler log. We knew this gesture, as the slobber from earlier sniffin went off in every direction. I come to spy some drool that got hung up on Jesse's trousers, but if he saw it he paid it no nevermind.

It is our thinkin that the slobber mixes up with pieces of scent and that gives the dog the best taste of a man. If a dog with a dry nose cannot smell, then maybe the moisture does just bout the same as for folks when, for example, they take to addin water to dry corn meal to make some fine smellin and tastin pone. It's the water in the mix that gives flavor to things and starts a hungry fella to droolin. After all that head-shakin business the bloodhound's watery nose could now begin to trap more delicious clues as to the identity and whereabouts of the person in question.

Now this particular slave had run from the McKinley place sometime early in the mornin. By the time one of McKinley's men took to rousin me and Jesse, we figured that the negro Abraham had at least a four hour head start. Sanford was the first one to hear the knock at the door, but Cynthia, who slept lightly anyway, was first to investigate the early mornin visitor.

Takin off his hat as a sign of respect for the white mistress of the house, the visitor had announced: "I'm here from the McKinley place, ma'am. One of our slaves done run off last night and Colonel McKinley is mighty upset about it. We got dogs over there but they ain't worth a damn...pardon my language, ma'am," the white messenger again added respectfully. "Is your husband about?" When Cynthia told me of this conversation I couldn't help but wonder what that fella would have said or done if he knowed that fine lookin lady of the house he was addressin weren't exactly white in color.

Jesse and me was told that this Abraham was one of the slaves that had run off back in '35. By all counts there may have been as many as a thousand escaped the plantations at that time, although as I remember, less than half that number was actually reported missin by their owners which I always found quite curious. Many of em had come from the rice plantations in South Carolina, but some had come from Georgia. Most all of em had headed south and liked to join up with the Creek and Seminole Indians down in northern Florida. People had a special name for this type of runaway, they was called "maroons." These maroons mixed in with the Indians and become their allies agin the white man. I'm supposin that it was cause the black man knew the white man's language and his habits, that the Indians found em so useful. Together they did a heap of damage too, wipin out the sugar cane industry down long the St John's River, just west of St. Augustine. They burned over 20 sugar plantations in the area, they did, killin many of the owners and their families. Reports said that these negro maroons was more fierce fighters than the redtails themselves, but that's a might hard to swallow. Some called it the largest slave revolt in the country's history. Most of the runaway slaves were eventually killed or recaptured and returned to their masters, but the problem was that many of em got a good taste of freedom while they was away from the plantation. Also there was some that had become expert in the use of firearms and military tactics and others that had become successful farmers durin that time. One thing sure, many showed themselves to be downright hostile when returned to the confinements of slavery, and this Abraham fella, we were made well aware had been a problem ever since he was brought back.

It made sense that Abraham would fancy a boat for his escape as it was the waterways, the swamps, rivers, and creeks that were the "roads" into the remote homeland of the maroons. The Oconee River runs through Milledgeville and joins up with the Altamaha to the south. It then knocks along on its merry way to the sea. Now there were many branches off them rivers, to be sure, and who's to say if it weren't possible for someone intent on returnin to the wilds of northern Florida to make that trip entirely by water in a small boat. I would not be willin to wager a day's pay that journey was impossible.

"This may be a little longer trip than we were figurin," Jesse announced. "Our hound's got her nose up in the air so she got that driftin scent. Let's follow down river apiece."

Miss Molly had indeed picked up the scent that had come off the water and fetched up on some of the vegetation long the banks. Sometimes when the river is slow movin or if the water is standin still as it would be in a lake or swamp, the scent will hang right there on the surface. We have tracked people that have drowned with the dog leanin one way or the other in the front of the boat and Jessie or me on the oars followin its lead. When the dog starts in bayin and wants to take to the water, that's the very spot where the person most likely up and drowned.

We walked along the banks, followin the river south for a couple of miles till we reached Ben Johnson's place which was set back off the river some. We knew he had a boat tied up at a small dock that we thought might prove useful so we stopped to have a little quick conversation with our fellow pattyroller and neighbor.

"Hey, Ben!" I said, as I spotted him out in the yard tendin to some of his animals. "We're trackin several fugitives that run off last night. Mind if we use that boat of yours?"

Ben was agreeable and said he would get a message back to our place sayin that we might be a little later than we had expected. He also told me he was surprised to hear of my meetin up with a fine woman who had come complete with a black servant of her own. "You are a lucky man, Coswell," I remember him sayin as we all headed down towards the river. "How was it you come by such a woman?" he asked.

"A man don't need to look too far when he has his eyes full open," I replied quickly, realizin I was gonna have to do much better than this with future inquiries.

"I'm happy fer ya," Ben answered in return. Poor Ben had never been married and as far as I know never even had a woman. He used to say that he didn't need all the bother, but I always thought that deep down he wished he had a wife to call his own.

A red bloodhound trackin dog soon stood in the front of the

boat, nose full up in the air, leadin this little party down river. We had taken off the leather trackin harness as we was most certain that we would be in the boat for some time. Now it has been our experience that a bloodhound can catch an airborne scent that don't come from the ground or other vegetation for probably up to a mile if conditions be right. Not too hot, not too cool, and not a lot of moisture in the air neither, which of course will tend to drive the scent to the ground. The reason we know this to be a fact is that a bloodhound will leave a trail that even a handler can see with tracks and all, and suddenly head right off in a different direction where a fugitive is soon found...and all that after catchin a wind-blown scent. As for now, it looked like Molly was usin the scent deposited by the runaways along the watery trail.

"You want me to row for awhile, Coswell?" my brother asked. I told him I was agreeable as I had been fatigin myself pretty good, tryin to make up some of the distance between us and our quarry. We figured that the five slaves in the boat ahead would weigh it down considerable and also, takin mind of the tracks back there on the riverbank, we knew that two of the fugitives was most likely women and they would probably not be sharin in the workload. Jesse took the oars.

I found it quite interestin that this slave we was trackin, this Abraham, had the same name as the famous maroon who had once advised and counseled the Seminoles back in '35. Everyone knowed who he was. Many said that "Negro Abraham," as he was called by whites, was more important than the Indian chiefs themselves. He had been described as intelligent, well-mannered and calculatin, always had a smile on his face and his words were said to "flow like oil." Physically, this Abraham was strong built, with a high forehead, broad face and the thick lips befittin a full-blooded African. The only other identifyin feature was the distorted right eye which some say gave him a slightly cross-eyed appearance. He also had a thin mustache and always took to dressin in Indian fashion. The "Abraham" we was lookin for didn't look much like that, lackin the cross-eyed look, had no hair on his face to speak of and what little he had on his head had turned gray. Now sometimes a slave owner will turn out an old bondsman to rid hisself of future responsibility despite laws to the contrary. Colonel McKinley must have been quite partial to this fella to spend good money to get him back. We didn't think we would have any trouble identifyin the old negro when we caught him, but then Molly, as always, could be relied upon to be the final judge.

For us to recapture this Abraham and return him to Colonel McKinley, we needed to catch him before he and his little group reached the safety of the swamps. Once there, the geography would favor the fugitive and could also increase his chances of findin friends. Tanglin with Seminoles or Creeks or whatever you want to call them red savages, was not somethin that the Tims boys was set on doin. I had my fill of em back in '35, and bein maroons made the prospect of meetin up with em even less attractive.

It's a fact that our grandfather, Benjamin Tims had been killed by Creeks way back in the spring of 1798. Indian agent Ben Hawkins, workin for President Washington at the time had reported that our granddaddy had been killed in the area that would later become Macon, but it was unclear what he was doin on Indian land at the time. The fact that he most likely was trespassin did not make our family feel any more kindly toward his killers. These Indians, as far as we was concerned, had always been a dangerous nuisance and it eased our minds some to know that most of em had been run off and moved to reservations out west. These maroons, though, they was the last dangerous holdouts.

We had enough food for a couple of days, that was all. We had brought our usual supplies…shotgun, bindin rope, shackles, our sidearms, of course- but we was not equipped for any long journey and we were for certain not armed well enough to be fightin off any large number of murderin savages, that's for sure. Jesse was pullin hard on the oars.

It was late afternoon when we switched up once again, continuin the routine we had started early on with each one of us tuggin on the oars for bout an hour's time. The only one not changin places was the hound dog. Molly just stood up there with her front paws on the bow of the boat, kinda proud like, with her nose up in the air, movin her head slowly from one side of the river to the other. I couldn't help but revisit an image I had fixed in my mind of a proud and defiant two-legged critter standin in much the same fashion on the deck of a New Orleans steamboat just a short time back. "Now your mind don't need to be wanderin away from this here river," I found myself quietly whisperin under my breath.

All three of us in the boat was pretty quiet, intent on what we was doin. All that could be heard was the steady creakin of the oars and the splash that come when both hit the water at the same time. I knew that at some point I needed to confide in Jesse bout Cynthia and Sanford and the events of the past several weeks, but I guess I would know when the time was right. I hoped he would full understand and keep by me as he always done. Keepin this whole thing under lock and key was wearin me down considerable.

"Somethin's changin here," Jesse shouted, as the dog made her way quickly to the left side of the boat. I remember once someone tellin me that that was called the port side of any vessel.

"There's a small river runnin off after them bushes there," I observed as I stopped rowin momentarily. "This hound dog is tellin us we need to head off in that direction!"

I pulled on the oars as we headed down a much smaller waterway on our port side and it weren't more than a half hour later when all the evidence of a swamp began to rise up before us. Green lily pads with their white and yellow flowers was to be found on the water and we began to see more of them tupelo trees and more and more cyprus trees with their lower branches hangin down, seekin water. Black moss (or Spanish moss as some folks call it) hung down from most of the branches. You kinda got the feelin that you was slowly bein closed off from the outside world and that you were enterin some primitive place that time had just plain forgot.

I took notice that the water had changed color too. It had turned brown, kinda like the color of tea that one might brew up on a chilly frosty mornin. I knew from my military days down in the Okefenokee that this was from the peat that had formed-up at the bottom of the swamp and that bordered it on all sides. Kind of surprisin, the water was always good to drink despite the unwholesome look it had. I remembered in that swamp that layers of peat might be five to ten feet thick in places and you could feel it shake when you took a step, which give you a funny feelin inside. The Indian word "Okefenokee" meant "land of the tremblin earth," a fella once told me, which I figure matched pretty well with my experience there. I figured this here swamp to be pretty much the same kind of institution. I knowed full well me and Jesse trembled some as we took stock of the new world we had just entered.

Sounds had changed too. Startled birds flapped their wings to get into the air and gators could be heard bellowin and hissin off toward the marshy shore. Only once in a while would a person see a gator on the Oconee but just like here, it didn't take long once you got into the remote areas off the river that they would begin to appear. At night their eyes would glow red if a man was to shine a light on a large one and their eyes would give off a green light if they was young'uns. Never really understood why there was a difference but I never cared much for the creature myself, old or young, as they could cause real problems with the dogs. Bloodhounds are careless when it comes to dangers like these as all they think on is the fugitive they be followin.

I remember a sad story of a slave named Octave Johnson down Louisiana way that stole a gun from his master and took to a nearby swamp much like this one. A professional tracker named Eugene Jardine come after him with all twenty of his bloodhounds only to lose eight of their number to the slave's good aim. As if that weren't enough of a tragedy right there, the gators took to feedin on the other twelve and Johnson done said in one of them slave narratives the abolitionists were always fond of publishin that the gators relished the flesh cause they preferred the meat of dog to that of the black man. When I heard the story I wondered if it were true or just another made-up heart-tuggin story regardin the poor unfortunate slaves down in the south. "The land of Legree and the home of the slave," as one clever abolitionist once put it, without tossin in any of the details that would allow a man to properly decide the truth of the matter for hisself.

Any number of other sounds…insects, reptiles, animal life all added to the mix, but suddenly, out of nowhere come a sound that overtopped all others. It was not somethin that Dame Nature sent our way, but in many ways it more dangerous and terrifyin than any of the ones that we had heard up to this point. It was a gunshot!

Loud and clear and life threatnin for sure, fired from somewhere on the left bank of the marsh. It had been intended to end the life of my brother who had been standin up momentarily as he had taken to releavin hisself off the back of the boat. The bullet struck the port side of the vessel and stopped my brother in mid-stream.

Instinctively, both of us ducked below the low sides of the rowboat, drawin our pistols in the process. Jesse grabbed the dog by the loose skin that formed up the cape round her neck and shoulders and pulled the exposed manhunter down with him. We waited.

As we peeked out over the side of the boat, you could see smoke risin from a stand of bushes and swamp grass not fifty yards from where we was at. Another shot rung out!

It's most like Jesse and me thought with the same brain sometimes, as we both come out of the crouchin position, Jesse firin off a couple of shots in the general direction of the attackers with his pistol, as I started rowin furiously, headin for that very spot on the river bank. Jesse turned to put the harness back on the dog. We had both figured that given the amount of time between shots that there was only one gunman or at least only one gun to be had, and we could not afford to just sit dead in the water waitin for Abraham's aim to improve. We knew we had to act and act quickly.

We come ashore with Molly full in the lead. She was pullin somethin fierce, newly left scent must have been drivin her half crazy. We could see the tracks clear in the mud....several people, deep imprints, evidence of a hasty retreat. We knew they was armed (or at least one of em) and they was dangerous, but we had firearms and knew full well how to use em, and besides, they was on the run so we figured we had em spooked with the advantage swingin over to our side. We also figured that unless they ran into some friendly faces, why they didn't know this swamp any better than the two of us did. I did, however, take to wonderin if what they said bout these darkies and this kind of swampy terrain was true...that the African jungle they all sprung from never left em despite bein raised up on southern plantations. We would have to risk that, I reckoned. Miss Molly led us deeper into the dark swamp.

We was losin daylight and that become a concern. It made no nevermind to Molly, of course. I remember an old hound that Jeremy Prigg had that was most totally blind and still give a good account of hisself on the trail. The nose was in many ways the bloodhounds' eyes. Of course Jesse and me needed the light, but then again so did the fugitives. We figured we had bout a half hour or so before evenin would fully find itself and the darkness would put a halt to our little operation, that is, less we lucked up with a moonlit night. We continued on the trail.

"Look over there, Coswell," Jesse said some time later, pointin up to the moon which had commenced to risin up behind me. Daylight was most nearly gone, but it looked like the chase was goin to continue as fate seemed to favor the Tims brothers this night. As daylight give way to moonlight, we got our eyes accustomed to this new way of seein. I remember from possum huntin that the best thing was not to look directly at somethin when tryin to see it in the dark or near dark. Best to look to the side some, if the plan was to see an object more clearly.

A full moon was on the increase and comin up fast, makin it even easier for us to see where we was goin. Molly paid it no nevermind and just went bout her business as most animals do. People? Now they're different. I've come to believe that moonlight affects folks in many ways. The Lunatic Asylum in Milledgeville is filled with the strangest noises on moonlit nights. Farmers I know won't plant or harvest durin certain moon cycles. I remember Mama said that bacon or any other meat that was killed when the moon was on the wane, would shrink in the pan for sure.

The agitated behavior that Molly began to show let us know that we was gettin close. "We better put a muzzle on that hound fore she starts in a-bayin," I offered up.

Jesse quickly complied, takin the muzzle out of the leather satchel, the strap of which hung from his tall, narrow shoulders. We wanted to come on the little party unannounced if possible to have the best chance of gettin our fugitives back, especially seein as though they had that stolen rifle with them. Maybe they was a might rusty with that thing, but we did not want to take any unnecessary chances.

The dog kept goin, tail a-waggin and pausin on occasion to shake her head and let the slobber fly through the muzzle. As we entered a less marshy hammock area with its small trees and underbrush, we saw the first traces of human habitation. We began to make out the shapes and sizes of planked-sided cabins with thatched roofs, maybe five of em at first count, and well cultivated fields with fences all around. I recognized corn stalks growin, and I could even make out some cattle standin quietly in a fenced-in area to the side. Some raised-up, high pitched roofed structures, curiously open at the sides were also to be found.

"Well," Jesse said, "Looks like they found themselves a few friends. What do you think now, little brother?"

This changed things considerable. How many Indians or maroons was held up there we had no way of knowin. We also had no idea what these folks had for weapons. As the two of us knelt down behind a small stand of trees to ponder the situation, the deadly hiss of an Indian arrow captured our full attention as it lodged itself in the very tree where I had just been restin my hand!

"Well, I guess that answers the question!" I shouted, as we spun round to face the on- rushin attackers. I made out one with a turban of some sort on his head, a bunch of feathers stickin out atop it. The fella was knotchin his next arrow as he run towards us. I fired and he fell in a heap.

"Let's get the hell out of here!" Jesse yelled, as we pulled hard on the dog's lead and started in runnin back towards the boat. Now I'm sure Molly must have been wonderin what kind of new game these foolish people was a-playin, as we were now, in her estimation, headed in the wrong direction.

The dog could not help us here. We was movin quickly, usin the moon and our memory as a guide. The hunters had become the hunted. We knew we was headed in the general direction of the boat, but if we missed our mark by more than a little, we knew this business venture probably would not end well for the Tims brothers.

Several arrows flew through the air, missin their mark, but the evil sound they give off scared hell out of the two fleein bounty hunters I would tell ya for sure. Several pursuers, we figured, no firearms was probably most likely. Back in '35, Seminoles and Creeks was armed with Spanish rifles as I remember, probably better than the muskets we had used. To continue to use em over the years, however, would have required mixin in with some element of white society and this remote settlement probably figured it best to avoid any sort of contact at all, seein as though most Indians that whites knew of (even the good ones) had been run off and resettled elsewhere. Bow and arrow were a renewable resource and history had showed em to be more than a might lethal.

As we hastily retraced our steps, we both offered suggestions on what we remembered. Human trackers learn from their hounds over the years, so we were both quite good at recognizin tell-tale signs of the trail. The moon was now full-up, givin us a reasonable chance, we thought, of reachin the safety of our rowboat. A broken branch here, leaves turned up there, a footprint in the wet ground, we were movin fast in what we thought was the proper direction. Molly was enjoyin the run, thinkin this must be some new kind of game we must be playin. (If people only knew that this supposedly vicious "negro dog" was more playful, affectionate and fun-lovin than it was threatnin, why bloodhound trackin men like us would most like as not be out of a job.)

The boat! There it was just as we left it with its bow resting on the marshy bank. Pushin the thing into the water, all three of us jumped in. Our pursuers was comin up fast, we could feel it. Jesse fired off the shotgun into the rustlin bushes and a black maroon fell forward, his bow fallin from his hands. He lay silent on the ground. More like as not he was not one of the more recent arrivals, but a maroon that was well acquainted with the Indian ways judgin by the way he was dressed. Several others soon appeared by his side and sent their arrows in anger our way. I was rowin hard, tryin to put some distance tween us and our pursuers when suddenly I heard Jesse cry out. Stickin out of the upper part of his right leg was a colorful Seminole arrow!

"Damn!" I heard my brother say. "That fella just lucked up at our expense." Jesse fired two shots back in the general direction of the bank, more in frustration than anythin else. Both missed their mark.

"Don't pull it out Jesse, I'll tend to it soon as I can," I added, redoublin my efforts on the oars.

I don't know how long I rowed that little boat, but fear or anger can sure change the way a man goes bout his business. Back on that Federal Road, I got to thinkin that my Cynthia weren't lyin when she explained her female servant's sudden new-found strength with the heavy crossbar to her fellow travelers with Knox a-lyin there on the floor. Well, at least she weren't lyin all together, I thought, with just a momentary smile comin to my face.

We reached the Oconee as the moon dropped behind the clouds for a spell. It seemed most as if someone had blown out the night lamp, half expectin all to retire for the evenin. I rowed cross the river and brought the little craft safely up on the opposite shore.

"How you feelin, Jesse?" I asked, knowin full well what his answer would be.

"I've been better," was the predictable response. I proceeded to take out my knife to tend to the business at hand. Figurin I lucked up some with the moon beginning to reappear, I cut away part of Jesse's trousers so's I could have a better look-see at what I was doin. I remember ol Doc Fort sayin that you should never pull an arrow straight out of a man as most times you will leave the head inside and that would require some pretty messy and painful investigation. Indians fasten the head to the shaft with sinew which loosens quickly when blood and body fluids get to it. Now that shaft does point directly to just where that head is at, so there ain't no question as to where a man needs to look. With knife in hand, I made the reddened area round the wound a little larger. I saw Jesse roll his eyes back some, but he didn't complain one lick. I was gonna use my fingers to grab the head when I happened to look down at my knife. I always carried that thing ever since Daddy made it for me in the blacksmith shop many years ago. Knowin how useful it could be, he had fashioned up one for both his boys. The handle had a wire wrap on it and I recalled ol Doc sayin that wire was just the very thing needed to extract an arrowhead from a wound. "Ain't it true that a fella never knows when he might need to be rememberin somethin he is told early on?" I thought to myself.

I was able to unwrap it with a little effort, and usin the wire, I pushed it down into the wound long side the arrow shaft. Finally feelin the head of the arrow, I looped it round the potential lethal object and slowly drew it to the surface. I quick looked up to notice that Jesse had throwed his head back and had clenched his teeth tight together. It was a good thing that arrowhead had not lodged in the bone as that would have made the whole affair even more difficult and also a great deal more painful.

"Maybe you should have been a doctor stead of a trackin man," Jesse managed to offer up as I wiped my blood-stained hands on my trousers.

We both knew we had to be gettin back to Ben Johnson's place, borrow his wagon and return to Milledgeville as soon as possible. Jesse would probably again be needin some of that special red bark concoction that Doc Fort was always brewin up. This would be a long night for sure.

Jesse was settin in the backseat of the rowboat. Molly was up front but looked to now be more out for a little sight seein than doin any serious trackin business. I grabbed up the oars once again and started to row back up the river. My brother was facin me, and after I saw him wince a time or two and he saw me take notice, we now found ourselves in full view of each other. It just hit me that the time was right.

Bringin the oars to a sudden stop in the moonlight and leavin em both extended full up in the air, I blurted out: "Jesse?"

"Yes, Dr. Coswell Tims," he replied, half mockingly, half in appreciation for services recently rendered.

"Jesse, I've been meanin to tell you this for some time now. It's...it's...bout Cynthia."

"What you be sayin Coswell?" he replied.

"Well Jesse, you know this is the woman I love more than anything else in this world. Now, you know I feel the same way bout this woman as you did your Becky..."

My brother looked at me with a puzzled look on his face, like he was confused as to my meanin.

I continued on. "I need to tell ya straight out somethin I ain't never told no one before. My Cynthia's black, Jesse. She's a nigger, just as sure as you and me was born in Georgia, Mamma and Daddy was born white, and their two sons are a-settin here by the side of the river in this God damned rowboat!"

Chapter 16

SETTLIN IN

Now it ain't as if Jesse suddenly come into possession of some kind of incriminatin evidence and turned us out that caused Cynthia, Sanford and me to move into a place of our own. Fact is, my brother told me he had his suspicions all along regardin our situation but felt that my passion was more important than any concerns he might have had. We all did agree, however, to tell no one else. In addition to bein agin the law for a white man and a black woman to live as man and wife, neighbors certainly would have had none of it and livin in a community such as Milledgeville would have just been near impossible. Also, the fact that she and Sanford was stolen property might have just landed ol Coswell in that prison Charles Nelson tended to down on Penitentiary Square. Me and Cynthia did speak on the wisdom of our union from time to time, but our feelins for each other overtopped any good sense for sure. As we faced the future we was unafraid, but vowed to go cautious and not let our little secret leak out.

We spent a great deal of time over on our new property. Twelve hundred dollars had bought us ten acres and a run-down house with a few out-buildins, not a mile from Jesse's place on the outskirts of town. Not much to look at that's for sure, but it was our own nonetheless. Maybe the real joy was workin it together. Jesse helped out too. It seemed most like if we weren't out on the trail, we was all clearin the overgrown land, replacin rotten timbers or crumblin down old chimneys.

Sanford was a tireless worker, he was. Despite his youth (we figured the boy to be bout thirteen years of age at the time) he throwed hisself into the effort like it was gonna be his very own place. It's kind of funny as I think on it, how slave owners was always complainin bout the shiftless nature of the nigger and their tendency for dodgin around, but I'll be dogged if it weren't a fact that if one of em got to feelin like they was gettin somethin out of the deal, why their "basic nature" seemed to change considerable.

Now free negroes was discouraged in Milledgeville as they drew a lot of suspicion from home folks. There was only nigh on twenty or thirty of em that fit this here description out of the maybe 4,000 darkies in Baldwin County…and they was closely watched and regulated. After all, people feared they just might be the spark that could set the local bondsmen to revoltin as slaves made up half the total population of the entire county.

I wanted good things for Sanford, I surely did, and although we never talked on it exactly, it was probably best that he legally remain a slave with Cynthia and me protectin him while he was in our care. I reckon our relationship was somewhat similar to that of Wilkes Flagg who was bondsman to the good Dr. Fort. The doc and his family taught Wilkes how to read, taught him blacksmithin and give him the use of the shop after hours to make some extra money for hisself. Some folks suspected that he had bought his freedom and that the house he lived in with his family was his very own, but Wilkes Flagg legally remained a slave rather than draw any suspicion as a free man. It was rumored at one point that he had his own bank account of some $25,000, but most folks knew him simply as a servant who was the best and most sought after waiter in all of

Milledgeville. Didn't seem like there was a social function of any real importance hereabouts where Wilkes weren't to be found scurryin round providin service for those in attendance. Just like Sanford, Wilkes Flagg always went bout his business in a positive way with a big bright smile to be found on that black face of his.

There was someone else besides Sanford that I was determined would draw no suspicion from townsfolk and that was my Cynthia. We set our weddin date for October after talkin some to Father Johnson down at St. Stephen's church. That Episcopal Church was small, both in the size of the buildin and the number of folks that was to be found in the congregation. I reckon it may have been the smallest of all the churches in Milledgeville. The Methodists, course, they was the most numerous of all the local organized religions, followed up by the Baptists and then there was the Presbyterians. But this little church was friendly and welcomed us warmly. We was goin to be respectable for sure, as we decided to continue that public boldness that took us out of the city of New Orleans. The Krafts were the ones that proved the point...the more out in the light things was the less suspicion was left to grow in the dark.

As far as the city of Milledgeville goes, I guess you could say that there was more than a few of the townspeople who was "unchurched," to use a word I heard not long ago. There was many people outside our town who held a strong suspicion that Milledgeville might even be the center for depravity and crime, probably due more to the presence of prostitution, the riffraff that followed the penitentiary inmates, and the flood of outsiders that come to the capital for the annual fall meetin of the legislature. But I would have to say that we did have our fair share of Godly folks, too, to toss into the general mix. Why them prayer meetins that was held out in the open fields round town was lively affairs indeed with lots of gyratin and shoutin, groanin and weepin. To prove the point, Dr. Fort's daddy, Arthur Fort, come to Jesus in just such a place. When he had his conversion down there in the field by Fishin Creek, he said he felt hisself raised up several inches off the ground and felt he could see clear as day the smallest object even at a great distance. He said his hands become transparent and were as smooth as ivory. Well, I don't know how I feel regardin such things as a general rule, but Arthur Fort was a fine man and maybe this incident had more than a little to do with that bein the case.

Now religion weren't somethin I ever spent too much time ruminatin about. Mamma always did have a Bible right by her bedside and read from it from time to time, even read stories to Jesse and me when we was little ankle-biters. Can't say as though we ever heard a real heartfelt prayer in our house though, till Mamma took sick in '42 when the smallpox come back. Daddy prayed up a storm but it didn't do no good. In fact, that disease took him as well, just like it done with Jesse's wife Becky a year earlier. Slave girl down at the Carnes place off Jefferson Street started the whole affair and despite the guards and patrols that was posted to keep people from comin and goin, a fair number of local people died. Don't know how much prayin was actually goin on, but I suspect that if folks had taken the vaccine that the state government had offered up at the time, maybe them prayers would have stood a better chance of bein answered. It's a sad thing but when Jesse and me got ourselves inoculated, we just couldn't convince the older folks this was the proper thing to do.

October 23, 1850 was a red-letter day for sure. Father Johnson, who had been the priest at that little church for the better part of four years, was in good voice. Sanford was allowed in but had to sit to the side where the church's colored brothers and sisters regularly attended services. We invited Ben Johnson and some of our friends and Jesse, of course, he stood up for the two of us. A few folks that Daddy had knowed down at the blacksmith shop and ol William Rockwell, one of the long-time vestrymen of the church, who I'd been knowin all my life, added to our little weddin party.

Cynthia looked beautiful that day and had made her own marryin dress from that very fabric we had purchased down in New Orleans. We both got to chucklin bout that from time to time. The whiteness of her skin and the whiteness of that dyed dress fit right in with the white pews that took up the better part of the sanctuary of that little church. We was white and pure for sure, and as such, why we received the blessin of the entire white congregation and community as well. We was serious bout our vows and our commitment to each other and wanted all to know that we was officially, legally and spiritually fastened together. No jumpin the broom or other ceremonies blacks would concoct so's to feel joined. Negroes was not allowed to legally wed, of course, as they was considered property that could be separated at the master's whim. Many plantation owners, however, did realize the importance of a stable and happy work force and often made a big thing out of their servants' weddins, so called. Some even recited the traditional white marriage vows, but they often ended em with "till death or 'distance' do we part," givin a little hint of a most uncertain future.

The house was ready a couple of weeks after the ceremony and the three of us finally moved into a place of our own. We called it "Briarwood" and although there was more than a few of them catbriers to be found on the property, we probably named it more for the struggles we had all gone through, rather than a description of the actual place the house was nestled in.

It was a different feelin, it was, bein family and all. We considered growin some cotton to sell but then decided agin it. The trackin business would make our livin, despite Cynthia's occasional protests as to its basic unsavory nature. She knew, like I did, that no one was gonna change the law or people's minds on the matter, leastways not any time soon. Things was the way they was and that was the way it was. Sanford would work the vegetable garden to help put food on the table. Cynthia would manage the house. Daddy used to say that it was only right and proper that a woman should have great power inside the family and although a man might officially be the head of that institution, he would say, in reality a man was most often a lot closer to the feet. He said women had them smiles and encouragin ways that give em great power over a man and could make em do most anythin. To get right down to the heart of the matter, I remember him sayin, women were just born better than a man if they had half the chance. You could see it early on as girls never went around causin mischief and tryin to kill things like boys done. I remember Daddy sayin he thought it was a wonderful thing indeed, that these kind, tenderhearted creatures would have anythin to do with men at all, but they did, and he figured that was one of the great mysteries of life. I agree with Daddy on the power and purpose of womenfolk. Runnin the house and seein to the people that made it up was hard and important work. Cynthia was in her proper place, for sure, doin right by nature and society. In my mind runnin Walker's slave household up there in St. Louis and bein subject to his constant demands and abuse weren't what the Good Lord had intended for such a fine example of womankind.

Cynthia and Sanford offered up many things bout their earlier lives when we all moved in together at Briarwood. Cynthia told me her life of bondage before bein sold to Walker had been spent mainly on the Fitzsimmons plantation over in Huntsville, Alabama. It was a cotton plantation with 50 or so field hands and five or six servants that worked in the Big House. She said there was always problems there between the house niggers and the field niggers which she said she could never quite understand. The field niggers resented the better clothes, food and living condition of the Big House servants, specially if they took to bein the least bit uppity. Cynthia did say her own mother was somewhat guilty of that as she wanted her two daughters to associate more with the Massa's family and not with blacks down in the quarters. But Cynthia said the house servants often took to bein envious of those in the field as them folks had their own living quarters away from the whites, regular workin hours with Sundays off, more time for their families and were not on constant call to do the white mans' biddin. Every house servant, Cynthia said, had the same exact prayer: "Oh Lord, let heaven be a place where a body can be left alone and to finally set down and rest a spell!"

Cynthia said that with very little support or friendship comin from the fields, it was also hard to count on anything but trouble from the Fitzimmons family. It was a well-known fact that James Fitzsimmons had fathered her and her sister, Little Peeney, and that made for problems with Mrs. Fitzsimmons. The woman was a constant scold, Cynthia related, and she carried a little switch with her wherever she went. She would find fault with the cleaning of the clothes or the settin of the table, maybe even somethin you said or forgot to say to a guest. And if you was one of the two white nigger girls in the household, well, there weren't no pleasin the woman t'all. Gettin a switchin or a hard knock to the head was somthin that happened most every day...and it was the Mistus, herself, Cynthia said, who finally got her way and sold off her mother.

"We cried when Mamma walked out the door with her new owner. We knew we would never see her again. She told us to be strong and to be smart as well.

"After Massa died things got even worse," Cynthia continued. "At first I was almost glad when the Mistus told me I had been sold to a man named Walker even though I knew I had to leave my sister. In the short time I was with that man, however, I come to think on Massa Fitzsimmons most like a saint," Cynthia concluded. "Even the Mistus don't seem all that bad any more compared to him. Oh well, I reckon all these things are long past now."

Life was good, business was good. We seemed to enjoy the blessins we had been given by our friends and neighbors that very day in October. The loneliness I had felt much of my life, the whippins that young Sanford had to endure, the compromisin situations Cynthia's beauty had once forced upon her, seemed to slowly fade from our collective memories. We was all settlin in for sure, with no reason to believe life would ever change and certainly no way things would ever go back to the way they once was. But then again, ain't it also a fact that no one knows for certain what any new day might bring along with it.

That dog pen aback our home that Sanford and me built up for the hounds, we figured, would hold the financial future of our family. Them bloodhounds was smart and of course if I were to liken any of them critters to a man like James Walker, well, I know that would be an insult the dogs would not take lightly.

Events were soon to unfold, however, that would show this slave trader from St. Louis, Missouri to be more like my bloodhounds than I ever could have imagined...capable of stayin on a scent much longer than I would have ever dreamed possible.

Now several years had passed since Cynthia and Sanford had escaped Walker's control and I had temporarily been in his employ. Except for that set-to with Big Sandy and the loss of our Beauregard awhile back, things was good as we had regained our footin with a prize hound by the name of Moses and had several other dogs we had trained up as well. Big Sandy even stopped payin me them nightly visits and I felt any nightmares I might have had at long last had come to an end.

Any fair-minded individual would have thought that by this time any trail back to Walker would be bout as cold as the "Billie Blue Flugins," which was an expression old timers used that I never quite understood, only that I took it to mean it was as cold as cold could ever get. You would have thought that rich slave trader would have found other things to set his mind and money on other than to root round in the past. But truth to tell here, James Walker must have caught the scent again when he heard that Dr. Alexander Milton Ross, the famous Canadian abolitionist, was intendin to give a lecture just over the border in Alton, Illinois, just a stone's throw from Walker's farm in St. Louis. Alton was generally considered to be the center for abolitionist activities for the entire state, and most everybody, proslavery people as well as abolitionists, knew bout this little get-together to be held there for folks dedicated to destroyin the institution of slavery. I figure it must have been just too temptin for Walker to resist.

Now Walker weren't no abolitionist, that's for sure, but the name of Alexander Ross was not to be disremembered and my guess is that he wanted to meet the man who he believed had so successfully spirited away his prize quadroon down in New Orleans a few years back. There was no doubt in the slave trader's mind that it was Ross that headed up their escape. The two slaves that was returned to Walker the night in question said as much under the threat of torture. Eyewitnesses also put Ross in the general area only a few days before.

Walker had turned the city of New Orleans upside down he had, hirin slave hunters and detectives, payin informers and interviewin any and all that might provide some information as to the whereabouts of his lost property. By all accounts that come our way later on he was most frantic, but not one trace of Cynthia or his trusted (or so he thought) servant, Sanford, could be found. Maybe that swamp did swaller her up, as was suggested by that Tims fella he had hired, but it sure didn't get Ross or Tappan as accounts of both of em and their abolitionist activities (including an accountin of this run-in with Walker) surfaced later on in the newspapers. And Sanford...well, he had been quite friendly with the lovely young slave woman and it may have seemed more than a coincidence to the slave trader that the boy would go missin at the same time.

Walker weren't no fool, so I know he must have hid a pistol in his belt as he headed his wagon out the front gate, headin northwest for the lecture which was to start at seven o'clock that night. Normally, one of his black servants would drive, but it was common knowledge that violence often accompanied these meetins so the gun in his belt and the absence of a black driver might provide some protection from the often emotional outbursts that occasioned activities such as these.

It would have been some thirty minutes later when the armed slave trader arrived in Alton and entered the spacious home of John and Mary Jones, two free negroes whose prosperous tailorin business in Chicago put em at the very center of abolitionist activity. Rumor had it that scores of escaped slaves had been secreted in their home from time to time and it was a well-known fact that their house often served as a meetin place for local and national abolitionist leaders, as was the case this very night.

Dr. Ross took the floor shortly after the meetin got under way in the largest of the rooms, kind of a combination livin room and study. Many chairs had been brought in for the large group that was expected. The heavy set, full-bearded doctor spoke for over an hour on the evils of slavery and the need for it to end here in America, the land of the free, he had said. He boasted of some five trips he had made into the southland and the several score of black men and women that he had helped escape to Canada and freedom. For the most part the applause was loud despite some of the protestin by those partial to slavery that could be heard comin from outside the buildin.

I can well imagine Walker sittin very still, tryin to get a full understandin of the man he knew to be his political enemy. When Ross finished speakin, folks crowded in round him for handshakin and conversation. As the crowd finally began to file out, Walker saw his opportunity and approached the doctor as he was puttin on his coat gettin ready to leave.

"Dr. Ross, I wonder if I might have a word with you." Walker asked.

"Why yes, of course sir…to whom do I have the honor of speaking?" Ross inquired.

"My name is James Walker, sir. I believe you and I had some dealings about two years ago down in New Orleans. I never actually met you as I was aboard the steamboat *ENTERPRISE* when you came unannounced like a thief in the night and ferreted away some of my personal property!"

"Would you be talking about human property, sir?" the abolitionist countered. "If you are, then you should know that no one can own human property. It is abhorrent in the eyes of God and is only acceptable to those who subscribe to the most base nature of mankind," Ross concluded forcefully.

"Be that as it may, Dr. Ross, do you admit to being their 'deliverer' then?" Walker asked as he moved menacingly towards and in front of the accused, placin his hands upon his hips and exposin the firearm he had placed in his belt earlier. "What say you, sir?" he added.

As Ross later related this event to his abolitionist readers, he said the gun and the aggressive nature of the slave dealer give him pause, but he counseled his followers that rootin slavery from our country after all these years weren't goin to be easy and a certain amount of courage was necessary if the job was to get done.

Equal to the task and the accusation, Ross responded: "I do remember those slaves of yours that came off that filthy boat. Let me say it would have been a great privilege to have assisted in their successful escape, sir, and I would be proud to say that I was their "deliverer," but as I recall, all three were recaptured by your reprehensible henchmen and returned to your evil grasp! I am glad to find out they were somehow able to make their escape, even if it was without my efforts."

Walker's mind whirled at that one word Ross had uttered. It was not the word "reprehensible", nor the word "base". It weren't the word "filthy" or even the word "evil". Puttin his face within inches of the doctor's, Walker most hissed out the question: "Did you say ***three***, sir…Did I hear you say ***all three***?"

"Tims, Coswell Tims...it had to be him!" I can almost hear him a-sayin when I gave the matter a little more thought. Course I don't know every bit of this for a certain sure fact as I was not there at the time, but Dr. Ross's written recollection of this run-in with an angry and frustrated slave dealer and Walker's later behavior told most of the story. Yes sir, I'm sure most of what I'm sayin here has to be true cause this slave trader we thought we had left behind would soon come a-callin up our way and it would not be for a friendly visit like when a neighbor would drop by your place and put his feet up alongside of yours on the front porch railin.

The fella must have realized that I was the last one to have seen or been close to his prize quadroon, that I was the one who reported the footprints in the swamp, that I had sent Long's men back early and remained alone in the house. Walker probably also had information that tied me to Sanford while I was doin business aboard the *ENTERPRISE* and may have figured I was involved in his flight as well. I'm sure his spies reported that I had left the city two days later, alone and on horseback, but the slave trader most like as not figured that I could very well have met up with the two fugitives somewhere out on the road back to Milledgeville.

Yes sir, James Walker was a man who was used to havin his own way. This deception, if his suspicions were to prove correct, must have stuck in his craw somethin awful. It must have been right then and there, I figure, that he set his mind to visitin the capital of the great state of Georgia, and it wouldn't be to see the workins of the state government or any of the fine sights! No sir, it wouldn't be that by a longshot!

Chapter 17

AN EVIL WIND COME BLOWIN

I guess no man can tell the future despite the claims of some to be able to do so. I suspect that all a man can do is add up the days gone by and then draw up a little guess as to what might be layin in wait down the road. An unusual day and one I found myself unprepared for despite some earlier thoughts on the matter, would start out with one of the oddest trackin jobs I ever took on.

The dogs started in barkin when they heard the horses early that mornin. Sheriff John Strother and three others that was servin as deputies dismounted and come up to the front door. Sanford greeted em with his customary smile and roused me and Cynthia.

"Mornin Coswell," the sheriff began. "How bout bringin some of them fine trackin dogs of yours down to the jail and do us a little favor. We got us a killer on the loose and I think we will all rest a little easier when he is back behind bars. This is an odd one, for sure," he added. "I'll give ya all the particulars on the way back into town."

I put on my boots, strapped on my pistol and reached for the sawed-off scattergun that rested gainst the wall. I put the shackles and leg irons into the saddlebags like I always done and grabbed my coat and hat. Of course the last thing I grabbed was my wife, Cynthia…grabbed her round the waist and said what I usually said most days while starin into them blue-green eyes of hers. "Now you be sure to miss me, you hear?" She smiled. Sanford smiled. I turned to him as I was goin out the door. "You tend to your mistress," I added.

I tried not to make too much of a thing out of it, but I always worried each and every time I walked out that door. I knew the woman would never leave me of her own free will, but then Becky didn't want to leave Jesse neither. Sometimes, I reckon, things just happen the way they do in life. I had never been able to shake the feelin that someday I would come back home and Cynthia would be nowhere to be found.

I took Daisy Mae out of the pen and put the long leather lead around her neck. She was a good dog, a good tracker despite her rather diminutive appearance. She was a black and tan, not a red like Molly, Moses and Beauregard. She weighed maybe 85 pounds but made up for the lack of size with intelligence and determination. The sheriff and his boys waited on their horses while I saddled up my horse and tossed some bindin rope cross the front of the saddle.

We was headin towards Jesse's place which was on the way to town and the sheriff started fillin me in on the runaway. Seems the fella in question was a white man named Bonner, James Bonner to be exact. He was accused of murderin an entire family…all eleven of em was either dead or at the point of death. I asked Sheriff Strother how this all could have happened and bout fell off my horse when I heard his answer. "Voodoo, Coswell, it was voodoo that done it," the sheriff had offered somberly.

I found that most curious. I do believe Voodoo or Hoodoo as slaves call it, was found in some form on the majority of plantations in the south but was practiced strictly by the black folks there. Of course New Orleans and the areas along the southern coast seem to have the most of it, but black conjurers could be found most everywhere, includin Milledgeville. The Lamar place had African Peter who the slaves said was born with the caul and bein packaged up in such a manner had the gift and could fix people when they was sick, put a spell on someone if they was deservin or give slaves protection from evil spirits. I remember sittin back and readin an article in the *Southern Recorder* which I read to Cynthia and Sanford not long ago, by a Reverend C.C Jones, who said that the niggers of Georgia typically believe in "second sight, apparitions, charms, witchcraft and in a kind of irresistible Satanic influence," despite their claims of bein Christian. White people usually discouraged this type of thinkin as they knowed very little bout these here beliefs and the secrecy of the ceremonies that was part of it. It weren't hard to imagine that they just might be rebellious in nature and could even produce potions or poisons that could be used against authority. Most hoodoo believers must have realized that this mumbo-jumbo might work on plantation society but it definitely had no place with the white folk.

Big Sal over at the McKinley place was supposed to be a conjurer and I heard tell she once worked up a spell to help a young field hand so's she would never be whipped again. At first it appeared to work real good but when others tried it and wore their charm bags filled with that goofer dust round their necks and took to sassin back their master, why they was beat somethin awful. I reckon this must have pushed the magic a bit too far and broke the spell somehow. Boiled cockroaches, cat soup or chicken blood mixed with green frogs and plant roots...I always thought it all to be a foolish waste of time and effort and figured the only reason black folks even believed in this stuff t'all was on account they wanted to feel that there was powers at work in this world higher than those of their white masters.

Despite bein white, the sheriff said Bonner claimed to have the gift of voodoo and when a relative, John Harris disputed that claim, why Bonner he took offense and threatened him by sayin that he and his entire family would be dead within a month. Appears as though this prediction had come true, too. Harris, his wife and their nine children had sat down to dinner one night and directly after took sick, becomin violently ill and were startin to die off. The doctor could not for the life of him figure out the cause of it, but when the ailin Harris told authorities bout the threat, Bonner was arrested on suspicion of murder, either by poisonin or by some other unknown means. The stomachs of them folks that had died were examined by medical people but no signs of poisonin had been found. While waitin trial Bonner had somehow managed to escape, the deputy in charge admittin that for some unexplained reason he had dropped his guard and allowed the suspect to flee. Sheriff Strother had no doubt that we was trackin a very dangerous and most unusual fugitive.

When we come on Jesse's place, things looked kind of quiet and serene and when I knocked on the door my brother yelled out from his bedroom that he was feelin a might poorly this day and as bad as he hated to do it, told me I'd better go on without him. As much as I hated to work without Jesse watchin my backside, the sheriff and his posse, I figured, should provide enough protection for me and the dog.

When we got back to town and went inside the sheriff's office, Strother produced a bed sheet from inside the jail cell where Bonner had spent the better part of the night. Daisy was takin notice and once she give that bed sheet a good and proper sniffin and I yelled out the command, why she took to runnin out the door all by herself like she had been shot out of a cannon.

Now Daisy Mae was an unusual dog in ways other than color and size. She was the only bloodhound we ever had that could track off lead. She would go a ways and stop and wait for us to catch up fore continuin on. None of our other dogs could do this, despite occasional efforts to train em up that way. It was just somethin she had always done from the time she was a pup. It was a great benefit to have your hands free, or for that matter to be trailin behind on a horse instead of walkin. The problem was, of course, that the hound could get in harm's way without the handler's protective care.

The five of us mounted up and the hunt began, man chasin man, somethin that had probably been goin on since the beginnin of time. How long these bloodhound dogs have been part of the story is hard to tell. I remember one of my frequent visits to the Milledgeville Readin Room when I was a young fella, where I read accounts of ancient Romans who had trackin dogs that was called "sanguinarii" which I remembered come from the Latin word for "blood." I would have to say that this readin room was a God-send for a young fella like myself who fancied book learnin. It's kind of odd that no one ever knew who the benefactor was…who paid for the buildin, the books, magazines, and newspapers and such that were to be found inside. Whoever was responsible was a wise and good person indeed, and I always vowed if I ever discovered the man's identity, I'd walk right up to him, say howdy, shake his hand and thank him for all the priceless hours of learnin pleasure he made possible for a few dollars a month.

Now thinkin back on them Romans, I figure when a man is excited and runnin, the excitement gets in the blood somehow and he gives off even more scent than normal. Of course it ain't the blood the hounds be a sniffin, but what leaks to the outside of a man and falls off to the ground. Little particles of skin, I would say, hard to see for sure, but there nonetheless, is what a bloodhound would be interested in. If a man was to scratch up his scalp when it's good and dry, he might get a look at a little larger version of what a trackin dog takes up his nose. If the man is scared and he be runnin with the sweat comin from him, why them little flakes are gonna tell that hound just bout everythin he needs to know on the subject.

Now this Bonner fella, bein a white man and all, had a few more choices than some of the others we had followed over the years. We could see that he used the roads some, went into the bushes on occasion. He seemed to be goin due north as if he was headed for some special place. When I asked the sheriff if this made any sense to him he said Bonner and his wife did live just north of town up in Putnam County. Daisy was trackin quickly and I knew we was makin up ground as I'm sure Bonner would not have been runnin as he would have drawed more suspicion that way. We did find some tracks in a marshy area and by the depth of the heels and the toes and the distance of one from the other, they give us what we needed to know here…that Bonner was walkin just as we suspected.

Now it's mighty important when trackin that the handler be aware of clues and not rely on the dog altogether. Trackin dog and handler are a team, each with their own special skills. A tracker needs to look to the bushes and such for broken branches or pieces of clothin, check all visible footprints and the ground for any discarded items that the fugitive might have dropped or left behind. As a general thing, the dog and the handler are never more than twenty feet apart, separated only by a thin leather or rope lead. Each could feel the tug of the other, each comin to trust the one at the other end. This was a little different here with Daisy runnin out in front, stoppin on occasion, and us followin up on horseback from behind, but we was makin very good time.

We reached the Bonner house after a couple of hours on the trail. Daisy was to be found a-settin right up there on the porch waitin for us. The sheriff knocked on the door. Peekin out from inside, Mrs. Bonner stared out at the little group rather suspiciously.

"What do you boys want?" she inquired.

"We want your husband, ma'am," the sheriff replied. "I'm sure you are aware that he has been charged with the murder of the Harris family. We know he's in the house. We tracked him here with the dog. You tell him to come out peaceful like, or there are gonna to be some real problems…more than we already have."

"He ain't here, Sheriff, I'll tell ya for sure," Mrs. Bonner answered. "Haven't seen neither hide nor hair of him since you took him off a couple days ago. You can check the house if you're a mind to."

We accepted the invitation, all five of us goin in for a little look-see. Daisy continued to stand guard right there on the porch while we went inside. After a pretty thorough search of the place, we had to agree that Mrs. Bonner had been tellin the truth. Her husband was nowhere to be found. But things in the house were kind of all in a jumble, particularly in the kitchen where dishes and pans was found layin every which a-way. Quite curious, I thought to myself, less this woman's housekeepin skills just needed a little refining.

Sheriff Strother asked the woman if they owned a horse. She said they didn't, but a quick look in the barn behind the house proved otherwise. Not only did they have a horse, but a wagon as well….both were missin, but recent tracks in the red dirt testified to their existence. The sheriff shot the woman a stern look and pointed a finger in her direction. "You should know, madam, that aidin and abettin a criminal makes you just as guilty as them. You had better hope that nothin happens here that you are gonna share responsibility for. I'll tell ya, we can accommodate a man and his wife down in the state penitentiary, maybe on different floors, but we certainly have plenty of room for both." Turnin quickly to leave, he glanced in our direction and added: "Let's go boys, time's a wastin."

By all of us ridin and the dog runnin free and in the lead, we felt we had a pretty fair chance of soon overtakin the fugitive. Bonner would be ridin the wagon pretty hard, we figured, but we would be movin quickly as well. The chase would be a fast-paced affair, unlike many trackin jobs we had taken on.

Now as far as speed goes, by far the fastest means of transportation available to a man runnin or just travelin round for that matter, would be by railcar. I remember the first train I ever saw when I was trackin down Savannah way nigh on ten years ago. That train, as I recall, went all the way up to Macon. I'd never seen the like of it. I wondered what pulled or pushed that heavy metal contraption along. It was loud for sure, hissin and spittin, it smelled like fire and brimstone and the ground shook when it rumbled down the track. There were those people who feared it and called it the "Devil's Coach," but I knew then and there that I was lookin at the future... lookin at somethin good. Why, by the 1850's railroad tracks would be run all over the south and a lot of blessins would be visited upon the fine folks who lived there. But I guess it would be a foolish thing for a man to think that only blessins would come. Daddy used to say that a blessin, so called, could really be a curse in disguise and a man always had to keep his eyes skinned in order to dodge that kind of thing. Shakin loose of that memory, I shook my head and listened, but the only sound I could hear at that moment was the steady hoof beats of our horses in pursuit of a fleein wagon.

At the city of Memphis, the wealthy slave trader, Mr. James Walker emerged from the lower deck of the steamboat *ENTERPRISE* and descended the gangplank that led down to the dock. Puttin the pieces together later on, I could see in my minds eye the two black servants that accompanied him and followed him onto Memphis soil. Ol Andy Jackson had christened that Tennessee city on the Mississippi River awhile back, namin it after the ancient capital of Egypt and in just a few short decades, why, it had growed to rival New Orleans and St. Louis as the river's finest port. Not only did the city have excellent harbor and anchorage for steamboats travelin the river, more importantly, it had a railroad that wound its way through parts of Mississippi, Alabama, Georgia, all the way to the Atlantic Ocean at Charleston, South Carolina. Walker was lookin to travel east and to make up for lost time. The iron horse would carry him to Milledgeville, Georgia, home of Coswell Tims and, if his suspicions was correct, reveal at last, the hidin place of a valuable possession that he felt fate had so cruelly taken from his grasp.

Walker and the two black shadows that followed behind walked purposely and briskly by the Gayoso House, the finest and most luxurious hotel in the city. A wealthy local planter had spared no expense providen some 150 rooms, lavish facilities throughout and wrought iron balconies that looked out over the river. It was a frequent stop for the slave trader as it suited his taste well, but there would be no time for that now as the three headed for the train depot.

"You boys need to pick up the pace some," I could hear Walker sayin. "We have a train to catch and there have already been enough delays. Step it up now, you hear!"

The two negroes complied and shortly after they reached the train station where Walker paid the fare at the M&C depot for three. At five cents a mile for one person and a distance of some 400 miles to the Georgia city of Gordon which was as close to Milledgeville as that line would go, that fee could add up. The comfort and speed at which they would be travelin, however, would more than outweigh the expense. The two servants sat next to their master in the comfort of the passenger section. Usually slaves would be sent to the baggage car where there would be no seatin or maybe long, uncomfortable wooden benches might be found. It's kind of funny, but whites often sought refuge in those same baggage cars to drink, smoke or gamble, which obviously added to the discomfort of the negroes who were still happy to be travelin by rail and more than happy to smile away these frequent invasions. It is true, I guess, that everthin in this world is a mixed blessin of sorts.

As Walker took his seat I'm sure he was glad he had that shoulder holster made up back in St. Louis. This pistol holster also had a knife sheath stitched to the other side of the thing which held a vicious lookin bone-handled dagger. He knew the necessity of bein armed. He also knew the discomfort of a long journey where a pistol in his belt, or even hangin at his side, would prove bothersome. Better the gun be concealed, he must have thought, rather than out in clear view or on his lap where even those trusted servants of his might be tempted. One should never tempt a slave, no matter how loyal, with a firearm. The days of negroes bein allowed to hunt and have access to guns on the plantation were long gone.

The train rumbled on. Walker had used these iron horses before. The railroad at Vicksburg was one of the oldest lines in the south, comin all the way through Jackson and on to Brandon, some sixty or so miles of track that had allowed Walker to expand his slave empire and his evil grasp eastward. Cynthia, in fact, had come from a plantation just outside that city but she and about thirty others had been driven back on foot to the waitin steamboat at Vicksburg, a choice I'm sure Walker did not regret. The time he spent observin this woman was well worth it, he may have reasoned. Despite her somewhat ragged appearance at the time, her natural beauty and her proud, almost regal manner must have made a deep impression on the slave trader.

Walker had made a strong impression on Cynthia as well. One night at Briarwood not long ago, Cynthia, Sanford and myself was settin down to supper, when my wife took to tellin me a story bout that first day she had met the man. She said there had been a young mother in the coffle that was bein driven back to Vicksburg with her and the woman's baby had become a might tearful. Walker told the young mother to quiet that child, but when it continued to cry, he grabbed it by its legs like you would some barnyard animal and after shakin it some, took it to a nearby house by the side of the road. Despite the wailin and screamin of the hysterical mother, Walker give it to the white mistress of the house. "I am going to make a present to you of this little nigger baby as I can no longer bear its wailings," he had said. The cries of "Please, Massa, please, let me have my child!" went unheeded, in fact, Walker took to beatin the woman when her protests continued. "I now know where that child gets its inclinations," he had said as he proceeded to whip the young woman into silence. After bearin witness, Cynthia told me she knew right then and there that Walker was truly an evil man and vowed if she ever had the chance to see justice done in this world, it would be a chance she personally would be willin to take. "If I had a knife in my hand and was close enough I would have slit his throat," she had said with a look in her eyes I had never seen before.

I have no doubt the image of the slave Cynthia had never left the slave speculator's mind neither. The way she looked, the way she carried herself…he had not seen her in a couple of years now, but she was etched in his memory for sure. He would have her yet, he must have imagined. I can picture Walker settin in his seat, leanin back, crossin his arms and maybe restin his eyes. He could probably feel the security and comfort of the gun under his coat. A black leather travelin bag containin the restraints that would soon bind her to him lay at his feet. I can also imagine his two attendants maybe noticin a slight smile come to their master's thin lips. "Milledgeville is where she's at, I'm sure of it," he must have been a-thinkin to hisself, as the train hissed its way east, closer and closer to the home of Coswell and Cynthia Tims.

I could tell by the look on Sheriff Strother's face that he was somewhere between confused and amazed. "Maybe this damn fool dog knows what she is doin after all," I remember him mutterin. Often times people just didn't understand the abilities of these animals and really just couldn't believe that some old flop-eared hound could do what they could do. Me and Jesse knowed better. I swear someday if one of our dogs opened their mouth and started in talkin just like a human person does, why we wouldn't have no trouble believing it could be so and would enter straightaway into a proper conversation.

We had been travelin several hours, stoppin at each intersection where Daisy Mae would give a little extra sniff to make sure Bonner stayed to the main road. Each time she did this she would turn round to make sure we was right behind her and then continue on with her nose returnin to the ground.

We had been travelin east for several hours. The number of houses we were seein was on the increase and we soon found ourselves on the outskirts of a town called Warrenton, over in Warren County. Funny little town it was. Came up exactly one mile short of the railroad and had to have a mule car carry people back and forth to the rail line so that folks started callin it "Muletown." Watchin Daisy Mae out in front of us, I noticed that exaggerated behavior with head shakin, quicker movements and all, and knew that the end of the chase was near. Mr. James Bonner was in Muletown for sure.

Daisy began to run, head now up in the air, her urgency revealin the certainty of her quarry's whereabouts. We urged our horses forward and shortly come upon the dog, sittin right in the road next to Bonner's horse and wagon tied out in front of a roomin house. As soon as I reached the dog and dismounted, she bolted and headed round to the back of the buildin. The sheriff and his deputies dismounted as well and, after a short discussion, it was decided that two of em was to be sent through the front door, with the remainin three of us drawin pistols and cautiously headin round to the back.

I don't remember that it took very long to reach the back door and I don't know how much time it would have taken to make what I saw possible, but when I got there I saw my dog, layin still as death on the ground. There was a contorted look on her face and her tongue hung from the side of her mouth where some saliva had formed up on the lips. I could not believe my eyes.

"Bonner done used some kind of witchcraft on your animal!" I remember the sheriff sayin.

I bent over the lifeless body of one of my favorite hounds, thinkin how only a short time ago she was playin her favorite bloodhound game and was settin right out there next to that horse and wagon waitin, proud like, showin me what she had found.

"Ain't no witchcraft bout it," I answered, pickin up what was left of a corndodger that was lyin nearby. I give it a little sniff. "That son-of-a-bitch poisoned my dog!"

I took to rememberin a story of a Christian minister who once claimed to have invented the sayin "hush puppies." Named em after the corndodgers he cooked up and give to bloodhounds that was trackin negro slaves he was bent on savin. Put strychnine in the mix, he did. He bragged that it worked fast and, after all, the "only good bloodhound was a dead bloodhound" as that would be one more negro who would have a chance for freedom. I knew Bonner weren't no abolitionist, but Daisy Mae was dead and gone just the same.

The sheriff and his deputies combed that roomin house but did not locate the elusive Mr. Bonner. In fact, no one even reported ever havin seen the man inside. Why it was as if he had just sort of up and vanished into thin air, most like magic.

"Sheriff," I said. "This man ain't no wizard. He's flesh and blood and leaves a scent just like the lot of us. I will find em, you mark my words, but it's gonna take one of my hounds to do it. I'll ride back and start again on this trail by tomorrow mornin at the latest. In the meantime, you fellas might just luck-up and run cross him. I would ask you a favor…please do somethin with my dog here."

I give Daisy a last look and put my hand on her still warm lifeless body for the last time as I readied myself to leave. "You were a good and faithful friend, Daisy Mae, and I will miss ya for sure," I remember sayin out loud. Leavin somethin behind that you have loved in this life ain't never easy and I would tell you it don't get a powerful much better as time goes on.

I rode hard, some thirty miles or so back to Milledgeville… give me some time to think on things. I got to thinkin on the condition of the Bonner kitchen with everythin throwed this way and that. I should have realized that the fugitive was cookin up more than just a plan to escape. I blamed myself for letting Daisy track off lead. I had always had the feelin that somethin bad might happen to her without my protection. I got to thinkin too bout all them little voices that a man sometimes hears comin from inside his head.

"A man should pay close attention to them voices," I heard myself actually sayin out loud as the horse galloped for all he was worth in the direction of Briarwood. I made a solemn promise to myself to listen even more carefully and to go more cautious in the days ahead.

Finally reachin the house, I dismounted, comin through the door a might quicker than I would most times. "Cynthia?" I hollered upon enterin our home. "Cynthia, where are you at girl?" I repeated, "I got somethin to tell ya! Cynthia?" I shouted once more as I went down the hall and into the back bedroom yellin again even louder.

"Sanford, where are ya boy?" I added to my growin list of unanswered questions. There was an eerie silence that followed each inquiry. My heart began to drop through my chest. Somethin was wrong here, I could feel it, not just inside my head but throughout the whole of me. Any good thoughts I had in me were fast dryin up like hot iron throwed into a slack tub. Voices that had been whisperin in my ears for the longest time now seemed to be screamin out for all they was worth. *"When you return home one day, Coswell Tims, the woman you love will no longer be there. She will be gone from your life just bout as quick as a hungry dog can lick a dish!"*

My God, that prophesy had finally come to pass. I smelled smoke comin from the barn!

Chapter 18

DARK DAYS FOR SURE

I smelled no smoke t'all when I had first come into the house, but sure as there's fire in hell, I could certain-sure smell it now. With no answer comin from Cynthia or Sanford inside, I run out back to the barn to find dark smoke risin from up underneath the barn doors and out the openin to the hay loft above. Throwin open the large doors, I took a quick look-see inside.

Merciful Heavens! What greeted my eyes was the familiar form of none other than our own Sanford, danglin from a rope which had been tied firmly to a beam over the boy's head. His hands was bound together and stretched skyward. His head hung down kinda limp like. His chin was restin on his chest and the toes of both his feet was barely touchin the ground. Why I coulda cried right out loud, it was such a pitiful sight to behold!

An image of a wealthy slave dealer I wished I could disremember suddenly flashed through my mind. I had no doubt Sanford had been left hangin somewhere between heaven and earth and somewhere between life and death by none other than his former master, Mr. James Walker. I could not imagine anyone else who would do such a thing.

The poor boy was naked from head to toe with whip marks coverin pretty much the whole of him. That slave trader certainly had left his signature there for all to see. The raw flesh was caked and coated with dried blood, the whip marks was deep and many. Strainin my ears, I thought I heard a faint moan and then a slight cough come from the mangled body which hung there like a side of beef in a butcher shop. Good Lord! Sanford was still among the livin! I spread my coat out on the dirt floor of the barn and took out my knife. Cuttin the young boy loose, I carefully laid him down.

"Massa Tims," he groaned with great effort. "Massa Tims," he coughed. "Massa Walker done got Miss Cynthia. I tried…"

"Don't you talk now, you hear," I instructed. "We'll take care of one thing at a time and get you tended to first. Maybe we better get you outside where there's a little less smoke and you can breathe a might easier."

I bundled the young negro up and carried him out the barn, layin his tore-up body down once more.

"I'm goin to fetch some fresh water from over by the dogs' pen, you hold tight now Sanford."

I headed for the pen only to soon realize that this nightmare had taken on a life all its own. I suddenly remembered that I had not heard the dogs barkin when I rode up to the house. Normally they'd have a powerful need to give ol Coswell a proper greetin and let me know they was glad I was home. I guess I was doin too much ruminatin on the voodoo murderer and hopin to see Cynthia again to take proper notice. A look in the pen confirmed my worse fears…I would be buryin more than one hound dog this day.

"You son-of-a-bitch!" I muttered to myself. I yelled the same thing again, this time as loud as I could muster: "Walker, you are a dead man, for sure!" I added. Molly had been shot. Lady Bess lay next to her, a contorted look upon her face. Lancelot, my big, beautiful black and tan, he lay off to the side. Not a sign of life anywhere. They had all been cruelly executed as they had stood helpless in the close confines of the pen. Why them dogs never had a fightin chance, no sir! But wait...Moses. Now where was that big red hound?

Before I could give the matter much extra thought, I took sudden notice of a familiar voice back in the direction of the house. "Coswell, where you be at?"

"Back here, Jesse," I answered.

My brother come round the corner in short order and took stock of the situation. I was kneelin next to the pen tryin to make sense of it all. As he rushed over to my side and took a look at the dogs, I told him bout Cynthia gone missin and Sanford hurt and lyin out in front of the barn. I drew a bucket of water from the well and the two of us run back to help the young victim.

I couldn't help but think on the way back to the barn how me and Cynthia had really growed attached to this boy. Why he was everythin you would ever want in a friend, a neighbor, or even a son for that matter. Loyal, honest, hard workin, he was family for sure. Jesse fetched some cloth from inside the house that Cynthia had stored up in anticipation of better days.

"He's in pretty bad shape," my brother observed as we started to tend to the young man. Sanford suddenly took to shiverin somethin fierce. We cleaned things up as best we could. "We got to get Doc Fort up here and we got to get him here straightaway," Jesse concluded.

We decided that Jesse would ride and I would do my best to take care of Sanford in the meantime. We brought him inside and covered him up with a sheet after tendin to his wounds, addin in a blanket for good measure to try and help with all that shiverin.

As we was goin bout our business, I couldn't help but remember a story Sanford had once shared with me regardin his former master. He said the slave trader's daddy up Virginia way used to "smoke" his negroes whenever they misbehaved. He would tie em up in the smoke house, whip em good and then take old tobacco stems and light em on fire. Once that slave was "well smoked" with enough "coughin, wheezin and sneezin to be pleasin" as he liked to say, that slave would finally be let go, hopefully havin learned a valuable lesson. Walker's daddy called the whole affair "Virginia Play." Now that tobacco I had in the barn we had growed ourselves like most folks do hereabouts. Almost made me wish we had had the money to buy that fine readied-up Virginia tobacco for sale down at Wiley's grocery. That way there would have been no temptin stems left about to be used in such a devilish manner. I remember Daddy growed up his own tobacco years back which he would chew down at the blacksmith shop, and his mamma, years before him, why she'd put snuff up her nose on occasion. I guess we all learn a great deal from those who come before us. The treatment of Sanford by James Walker showed that apples don't as a general rule fall too far away from any family tree.

After Jesse rode off, I started in cleanin the boy's face again with a cool wet cloth when suddenly I heard a scratchin noise at the door. I opened it and do believe I stared in disbelief at the welcome sight that greeted my eyes. It was bloodhound Moses! He was just a-settin there on the porch, lookin up at me with them big, sad and red eyes. The dog still had on his leather trackin harness and the leather lead could be seen trailin off behind him. Except for the sad expression he wore on his face, he didn't look none the worse for wear.

I found out later that Jesse had taken Moses on a job later that same day when my brother was feelin a might better. He had tracked his quarry all of some one or two hundred feet, he said, from a slave cabin to under the floor of the overseer's place. Like most slave escape attempts, it was done on the fly and poorly thought out. Most like as not the slave in question figured on layin out for a few days rest with others of his kind feedin him, which was often the case. After Jesse got the individual brought back to face his punishment, he told me he thought he had tied Moses up to the hitchin post along with his horse when he reached Briarwood but was unsure in all the confusion. Moses must have sensed that the pen out back needed some tendin and pulled loose of the post.

Now a person don't know how a dog really feels concernin such things as death, love, hate or other human emotions. I suspect they understand a heap more than most folks are willin to give em credit for. I believe you could see it right there in those eyes if you were to look real close. Moses licked Sanford's face and then give a quick look over in my direction. That dog definitely knew somethin bad awful had happened here but probably weren't sure what his part in all this was gonna be. I reckon I had the advantage over my sole-survivin four-legged friend. I fought the urge to grab the leather lead and light out after the one responsible for all this but as I thought through the thing, I knowed full well me and Moses had to wait till my brother got back from town with Doc Fort fore any plans of that nature was to be put in motion.

Walker had left Memphis on that iron horse earlier in the week and rode that line as it dipped down into Mississippi and cross to Alabama where it tied in with the old Decatur-Tuscumbia Railroad that had been operatin since the early 30's. Back into Tennessee and up to Memphis, that line ended at Chattanooga, just north of the Georgia border. It then connected to the Western and Atlantic Railroad which run southeast on to Atlanta, a distance of some 138 miles. I remember readin somewhere that even though it cost the good people of Georgia some five million dollars to complete that part of the line, many folks complained that it was "the crookedest road under the sun." I guess crooked was far better than goin straight and bearin the cost of bridgin rivers and tunnelin through mountains. Just before Dalton, however, there was a thousand-foot tunnel that had been cut right through Chetoogetta Mountain. One thing Walker and his henchmen did not have to contend with was havin to walk over that mountain with baggage in hand to catch another train that waited for them on the other side to take em the rest of the way—like people had to do up till a couple of years ago before that tunnel got dug. I reckon that way the three of em had more time to sit there in their train seats and plot and plan any devilment they was gonna do when they finally reached Milledgeville.

Now when that railroad reached Atlanta, there was two ways a traveler could go. They could travel east to Augusta and then on to Charleston, or south towards Macon and then on to Savannah. Walker chose the latter as that was the only way that would allow him to get to Milledgeville entirely by rail. After reachin Macon, he could continue on a piece, reachin Gordon (it read Stop#17 on his map) where he would change lines to the Gordon-Milledgeville

Railway which would take the soul driver north the last seventeen miles to his final destination.

Talkin to folks later on, several people did remember seein a well-dressed, wealthy-lookin businessman arrivin in town with two black attendants. Zeke Chandler, the postmaster, said he recollect seein em get off the train and Jacob Daniels down at the livery said he even rented em up a horse and wagon and give em directions to the home of Coswell and Cynthia Tims on the outskirts of town. He remembered that this here business fella had said he was quite interested in employin Mr. Tims in a business venture and was most anxious to meet his, by all accounts, lovely wife whose name he said sounded somewhat familiar. It was a cryin shame none of these people could see Walker for the low-life scoundrel he really was. My daddy used to say that a man who brings no sorrow to his friends and neighbors lives to a higher purpose than one who does. Yet despite his money and power, Walker lived only to his own selfish purpose, and folks that's inclined that way, I believe, have more than a fair chance of endin their days alone and in the bottom of the barrel after all is said and done. The only trouble here is that this particular process may take a fair amount of time to sort itself out and a great deal can happen in the meantime.

Doc Fort and Jesse arrived several hours later, Jesse on horseback and the Doc in his familiar top buggy, the one that had the cloth roof that kept the sun from his head. He always drove himself even though he could afford a driver. The doc never did abide slavery much, sides, gettin to a place in a hurry was better done alone without complications involvin other people, slave or otherwise.

Doctor Tomlinson Fort placed his medical bag down on the table next to the bed. Examinin the young boy, he confirmed Jesse's earlier opinion that Sanford was bad hurt and went to work closin some of the deeper wounds, usin that red bark solution on much of the rest.

After slaves was whipped it was often the case that they was given salt baths, vinegar baths or maybe even given a good cleanin with turpentine. I knew much of that was designed to inflict even more sufferin on the victim, but strangely enough all did seem to have some medical healin qualities. As I watched the doc work, I realized how much we all owed this very gifted man who walked with a limp caused by a musket ball still lodged in his leg, all from doin his duty back in 1812. He was a wealthy man and that was quite somethin seein as though he tended the prisoners at the state penitentiary, the folks at the lunatic asylum and slaves…all for free. Guess it was them governors, legislators and wealthy planters he tended to on other occasions that made all the money possible. After listenin in all the right places and checkin all the vitals the doc gave his assessment of the current situation.

"I think he'll make it. Be a little while healin, but I think we can expect Sanford here to make a complete recovery."

With a welcome sigh of relief, I give Sanford a gentle pat on the arm and headed out in the direction of the barn. Partway there, I turned back and returned to Sanford's bedside. Bendin down over the boy, I felt the need to ask him a few questions.

"Sanford, can you hear me?

With some effort he nodded.

"Was Walker alone when he came-a-callin?"

Sanford's eyes twitched open and I repeated the question.

"No," Sanford painfully and slowly answered. "Bacchus and Gabriel…two niggers from de plantation, de was wid em…Walker, he done the whippin…I member…I member he done say dis child was, was…a ungrateful nigger…say I deserve all I waz gettin…dem utter two was busy hangin me up...knows they didn't wants to do it…but I knows they couldn't be goin agin Massa Walker," Sanford concluded, chokin and nearly out of breath.

I admit to bein more than a might crosslegged at the time as I again headed back out to the barn with only one thing now on my mind. I had tended to the burnin tobacco stems when Jesse had gone for the doc, and most of the smoke had cleared out as I walked through the open doors and looked round for that one item that a trackin man needs to have in his possession. Walker's black accomplices would have left their scent on the rope for sure, but I wanted Walker's scent just in case the three of em parted company. I could see Walker's boot print in the ground but maybe somethin better, I thought. Ahhhh!

There it was, tossed like a worthless rag over in the corner of the barn…the bloodstained whip Walker had used on his former bondsman. Bad as I hate to say it, that familiar instrument belonged to none other than Coswell Elias Tims. Lord God Almighty if it weren't my whip for sure! It was the same one Major Long give me down in New Orleans, the same one I had threatened Sanford with on the boat. Now I would like to think I would have never used it on that boy, even though I said I might. At that moment I wished I had left that infernal object down there in Louisiana in a world we thought we had left behind. That whip, when I thought on it, was a real reminder of how I still made my livin and maybe how little I had changed despite the circumstances. Feelin my fair share of guilt at the moment and addin in Cynthia's concerns, I vowed to give even more serious thought in the future as to my present line of work.

As for now, I found myself just starin at the leather object that I had earlier hung up on the wall of the barn but now lay carelessly tossed to the barn floor. Before I picked it up, I took notice (not for the first time) of the long, tightly woven leather thong, some seven feet in length, taperin wickedly down to an attached leather fall. That thin strip of leather gave way after about a foot or so to a cracker or "popper", as it was sometimes called, which had tassels all sprangled out at the end. I knew from experience it was them tassels that cut the skin and did all the damage. They was soaked in the young negro's blood as was much of the lower thong. There was no blood on the handle, however. I thought it likely that Walker's hand may have protected this part of the whip from the blood splatter, and felt a little smile come to my face when I realized by him holdin the whip tightly in his evil hand, he had left his scent and now had no way to protect hisself from the inquirin nature of a curious scent hound.

I returned to the house. After talkin to Jesse a short time bout him takin care of some things over in Warrenton with the elusive Mr. Bonner and thankin the doc yet again for what he had done, I bent over the bed and spoke to Sanford with full intention for all in the room to hear.

"You rest and get well, Sanford? There's a passel of things that need tendin to fore I see y'all again. There's a serious debt that needs payin here and Walker, why that man needs to pony up on his end. He will get his just comins for sure and I will bring Miss Cynthia back home. I will make that promise to all of you right now," I concluded as I put my hat on my head and made ready to leave.

When I stood up, Moses rose to his feet as well. Maybe he took stock of what I had just said or maybe it was his nature to know we was soon goin someplace special. Either way, he perked up his floppy ears as best any bloodhound could possibly do and come over and set down on his haunches right in front of me like he was half expectin that trackin harness to suddenly be gathered up from the table where I had throwed it early on.

I soon stood with whip in hand, Moses beside me out in the yard. As I often did in my trackin business, I began to read the ground and imagine Walker's time spent at the Tims homestead. Tracks in the soft red earth indicated a wagon of some kind had stopped by with three sets of footprints gettin out and goin off in the direction of the house, but it was obvious only two of those people made the return trip to the vehicle. The man who wore the boots was the odd man out, and that man by all accounts must have been Walker. Somehow he must have become separated from his servants only to find hisself abandoned, his wagon and his two slave attendants gone. Accordin to Sanford's account they had been willin accomplices when they had strung him up as ordered and stood by while the lashes was laid on, but maybe the slave trader wanted to be alone in the house for some reason and was willin to risk losin his two unguarded servants for the prize that lay inside. Now I wonder what or who that prize could have possibly been?

Later we would learn from the two slaves who was apprehended on the old North Road by pattyrollers the next night that Walker did indeed want to go into the house alone to "tend to business" (as they said) with a young lady. They said they heard screams and a great deal of commotion comin from inside the bedroom of our home and knew right away what was happenin and saw this as their chance to escape. They did say the young lady in question must have put up quite a fight, but there was no doubt in either of their minds as to how the whole thing must have turned out.

As I took a good look at the ground outside the barn, I could read the signs of earlier activity…it was written clear for an experienced trackin eye. Walker had come out of the house after the wagon had left, draggin a woman with him. Their tracks then went south while the wagon went off in a northerly direction. As I followed the tracks of the slave trader and his captive, I saw where they had started out, but after just a short time returned to the dogs' pen where Walker had shot the helpless animals so's not to be followed.

Oh, how I wish I'd been there to protect my family and my hounds. I remembered how helpless I felt when I learned from a loud-mouthed tavern owner Hugh Knox what had happened on the Federal Road when I was not there to make things right. This was worse, much worse, as this man had come into my home, invaded my life and took from me the things I held most dear. I wanted Walker, wanted him real bad, maybe even worse than the four-legged critter who now sat patiently by my side awaitin my command.

Finally, I presented the offendin evidence to Moses. "See this here whip, Moses? I want you to lead me to the Promised Land, boy!" I said, as I give him a fair sniff of the handle. I was rememberin the promise I had just made inside and also thinkin back to that famous Bible story of that Hebrew fella and his legendary journey from Egypt to Israel.

"You find, Moses, find!" I said, as I tossed the now useless bullwhip again to the side. I vowed never to touch that thing or any other of its kind ever again. Fully trustin now in the dog Moses, I turned my attention to the white man's trail ahead and let the "negro dog" pull me in the direction of his choosin.

Walker's earlier plans to bring his prize quadroon back to Gordon by wagon had to be abandoned. He had to know that bringin Cynthia back to the Milledgeville station could be troublesome, as local friends of the Tims family might want to know the circumstances (despite the fact that he had brought the original bill of sale for both her and the boy.) Also, given Cynthia's boldness, she certainly could not be counted on to keep quiet bout her abduction. He had earlier decided that it would be best to take the slave woman further from home where the situation could better be managed. Walker had counted on his two trusted servants to be with her in the baggage car where her protests would go unheeded by white passengers, but then the black scoundrels had run off, forcin him to change plans yet again. One more time, Walker must have felt, he had been deceived by the black man. Never again, he vowed, would he put any faith whatsoever in them connivin, ungrateful people. If you treat a horse well, Walker must have reasoned, it would work hard for you. The nigger was not even far enough advanced to be equal to a horse. They needed to be treated harshly and that was all there was to it. Walker believed the whip was the only thing they really understood. I got to thinkin if that was true, why Sanford must have got a heap smarter thanks to Walker's recent efforts on his behalf.

I learned later that Walker decided to pull Cynthia down a long wooded trail, away from our house and towards the nearby town of Gordon, out of sight of pryin eyes. She told me he had violently led her by a rope tied to her hands which he had bound together in front. He would have preferred the main road, she said, but fear of exposure forced him to quit that option in favor of a more difficult path. Walker knew he needed to move south as quick as possible just in case they was bein followed, and catch the train at Gordon which would then carry em both back to the port at Memphis.

"You are trying to slow me up," Cynthia remembered Walker sayin. "If I have to stop and beat you again, I'll do it. If I have to shoot you and leave that fine womanly body of yours lyin here on this trail, I will do that too," he added.

Cynthia said she was draggin for sure. She had bruises and cuts from the harsh treatment she had received both in the bedroom and earlier on the trail. The anger and frustration that had built up inside the slave speculator over the last two years had spilled out in violence and rage as well as passion. They had walked the better part of the day and in her weakened condition Cynthia finally dropped to her knees.

"I can't go no further," she said she remembered sayin mostly to herself. "If I gotta die here, then that's the way it's gotta be."

Walker took a final step, pullin the woman forward. Cynthia fell, face first to the ground. Dirt, mixed in with sweat and blood had to make her somewhat less attractive than Walker had remembered her to be, but then that was before she had deceived him and run off with that damn slave catcher from Milledgeville. She told me Walker took out a knife whose sheath shared the backside of his shoulder holster and had come toward her with it tightly held in his hand. The knife and the angry look in his eyes, Cynthia said, made her think he was gonna cut her throat for sure.

"You are what you are," she remembered him sayin with his lips pulled back tight gainst his teeth, and that jaw of his juttin out in that all too familiar way. He bent down on one knee, wavin the knife menacingly close to her throat.

"You left New Orleans a lady. Oh yes, I know the story now. People I hired finally put the pieces together talking to folks along the Federal Road. You left a lady, but you will return a slave, which is what you always were and always will be."

With that he grabbed her and his knife began to do its work… cuttin and slashin…but…it was the woman's hair that was the strange object of his rage. Most of its long lengths soon lay on the ground at her feet. Out of breath with the excitement of the moment, Walker added: "I swear, woman, if I had a branding iron with me at this very moment I would put my initials right there on your forehead, I would. There be no mistaking you for any fine white lady then, would there?"

Pullin her to her feet, the two continued on for nother hour or so till darkness finally halted their progress. With the ground now uncertain under their feet and branches and undergrowth threatnin to put an eye out, Walker stopped after reachin a grove of trees. "We'll stay here the night and head out at first light," he announced.

The rope that connected the slave speculator to his property was now undone, soon to be rewound tightly around the captive's ankles.

"And these, they'll have to go," he said as he untied a pair of high top shoes that his money had unknowingly paid for back in the city of New Orleans. Tossin em to the bushes, he felt give any story Cynthia might concoct at the train station bout bein any fancy white lady, one less chance of success.

"You can walk the rest of the way barefoot like a proper nigger wench should," Walker added, as he bound her hands behind her back, attachin that rope to her ankles, hobblin her up for good measure.

Formin several rocks that was still visible on the ground into a small circle, Walker took some lucifers from his pants pocket and lit a fire to counter the chill of the night air. There was no food to cook, no tea or coffee to offer any further comfort as they had left the house of the Tims family in quite a hurry and had failed to take anythin with em. The distance back to Gordon and the railroad was less than twenty miles, a distance that should have easily been walked in a day. However, unfamiliarity with the territory and the obvious attempts on the part of the quadroon to slow things down, had added time to the journey. Walker must have reasoned that they had to be quite close to their destination with the comin of mornin provin him right.

Moses was not happy when I finally forced him to quit the trail. A bloodhound needs no eyes to follow a scent that's for sure, but the terrain could provide hazards that could prove costly to either dog or handler. We stopped for the night. I lit a fire and Moses settled down some, knowin that the fire meant we was goin to rest there for a spell. When the dog finally put his head on my lap, I was careful not to spill my hot coffee as I run my hand over his wrinkled up head and began to think back to his comrades who had been so cruelly shot back there in the pen.

"You're all I got now, Moses," I said to him. He let out a loud grunt as I stroked him, tellin me that at this moment things was all right, even if the past and the future might prove otherwise.

Dogs, or most animals for that matter, seem to have the ability to live in the moment, a trait I sometimes wish I had. I spent the whole of the night worryin bout the past as well as the future. I thought back to Bonner, the voodoo practitioner, still on the loose up there in Warren County. I thought bout Sanford, lyin there sufferin from an attack no one should have to endure, let alone a young boy. Cynthia, the love of my life, why she was still in the clutches of this evil soul driver, now weren't she? What would tomorrow bring? While the dog slept soundly lyin next to me gatherin up his strength for the comin day, his master (a creature of supposed higher intelligence) stared blankly into the fire, eyes wide open and blinkin only on occasion.

Mornin come and I rotated the cylinder of my revolver, checkin to see if all was in workin order fore grabbin the leather trackin lead and headin out. The scent was still fresh for Moses as we took to the trail before the dawn's earliest light. There was a renewed eagerness on his part that maybe a restful night's sleep made possible. I was tired from lack of sleep but was anxious to make up ground.

It was only a short time later when the manhunter stopped dead in his tracks, shook his long floppy ears from side to side and returned his head and nose to the ground. Hair, human hair was strewn all about! Long and light in color, I recognized it straightaway as my Cynthia's and could not imagine for the life of me what had happened earlier on this very spot. There were signs of two people scufflin, but there was no blood (only hair) and it looked like the two continued on even if the way they were walkin seem to change some. Moses and I both knew the necessity of improvin our efforts, so we stepped up the pace considerable.

With the comin of dawn, Walker had surveyed the situation. The slave woman lay secure next to the fire, sleep had overcome her. As he looked round, I imagine he saw the wisdom of stoppin when they did. That grove of trees was quite close to a bluff that dropped off rather sharply. Had they continued to travel south, all plans to reach any westbound train might have been permanently cancelled. I know a smile must have come to the man's face, though, when he heard the sound of a train whistle off in the distance. What Walker could not hear, however, not far off in the opposite direction was the bay of a bloodhound…fainter to be sure, but closin quickly. It was mournful as well as forbodin. Cynthia said she heard both, one filled her with worry while the other give her hope.

"It won't be long now," Walker said out loud, more to hisself than to the woman who lay on the ground awake with eyes closed.

Walker turned to look down at Cynthia. She was still beautiful, he thought, despite her compromised condition at the moment. Her hair was cut in jagged patches, mud covered much of her face and arms and scratches with dried blood were abundant wherever her skin was exposed. Her clothin was ripped and shredded in places. Her bare feet looked to be bout the only part of the woman that had avoided any recent damage thanks to them high topped shoes she had been so partial to over the better part of the last two years.

When I first saw her feet a-danglin off to the side of the horse on the way back to New Orleans, I guess I already knew this woman was a lady regardless of what she was or weren't wearin on her feet. Walker must have thought much the same as he began to untie her ankle restraints. Cynthia stirred, grateful that her cramped condition would soon be relieved. She said she soon thought different on the matter, however, when she felt the weight of the soul driver's body on her own. Walker would have her again, for whatever reason she knew not. Was it just to show her he was master and she was slave? Was it to show some twisted form of affection that only he understood? She told me later that the man groped at her under what remained of her clothin, but this time she figured she might just as well return the favor. She reached inside his coat, she told me, searchin for relief that come but seconds later when her hand grabbed the handle of the knife that only the night before had come to take much of her beautiful hair. As she slowly withdrew it from the sheath, Walker suddenly was diverted from his risin passions to the danger that now presented itself. He reached in on the other side of the holster for the handle of his gun, but Cynthia told me her hand had already reached that bone-handled dagger. In her weakened condition, but with all the strength she could muster, she drove the sharp point of the knife hard into the right side of the man's chest, missin the ribs, but findin suitable flesh in between.

"Ahhhh!" Walker gasped as the knife sunk deep. He sat up and took notice as the sharp instrument was withdrawn from his body, remainin in the hand of the formidable quadroon. Grabbin that hand by the wrist, Walker proceeded to draw back the hammer of his gun, pointin it square in Cynthia's face. Again, she told me, she thought her life was over, but before the slave trader from St. Louis could put an end to this saga of rebellion and disloyalty, a loud sound caught his full attention. It was a bloodhound, a large bloodhound by all accounts, and it was alarmingly close. Must have brought on them chills that the pursued over the years had come to know only too well. Ignorin the pain he must have felt, Walker rose to his feet, bringin the quadroon up with him.

Seein yet another opportunity, Cynthia said she struck upwards with the knife that had remained in her hand, barely missin the man's vitals. Reactin instinctively, Walker hit her hard over the head with the barrel of his gun, knockin the slave woman senseless to the ground. "You stupid bitch!" he said lookin down at the now motionless and barely conscious form lyin still at his feet. His anger, however, subsided some when he turned to flee.

"I loved you, you know!" Cynthia seemed to remember him sayin as he picked up the knife, grabbed his injured side and disappeared into the bushes.

Moses was most uncontrollable when we finally come on the fugitive's campfire. Bein twenty feet ahead of me, the big dog got to Cynthia first, sniffin her still form and lickin her face. Pausin for only a moment, the dog wanted to continue on to finish the chase. I held tight to the lead as I knelt down to take Cynthia in my arms. Raisin her up some, I found she was still breathin. She even opened up her eyes when the dog tugged on the lead I still held in my hand, which shook her slightly.

"Coswell," she said. "Is that you?" she asked as she reached up and run her hand slowly over my face. "I can't see too well and my head be swimmin somethin awful," she admitted.

"I'm right here darlin," I replied. "I'm so sorry I weren't there for ya, causin all this to happen," I added, as I squeezed her and kissed her bruised, battered and beautiful hands and face.

She winced, but managed a response: "It ain't your fault, Coswell, and sides, I'm still alive, ain't I?" she said, even managin a slight smile.

I found myself suddenly caught half-aways twinx laughin and cryin here. I guess that was her way of sayin things was tolerable, despite how bad it all looked at the time. Got me to thinkin that my whole life I had always felt the need to be in control of things for em to turn out in proper fashion, and that could be the way it is with men in general, but then here was this woman who had lived through two decades of slavery, made it up the Old Federal Road usin her own resources, and now had survived a deadly encounter with a powerful white man, all without any real help from the likes of Coswell Tims. With those things in mind, I give her another squeeze for good measure, but was mindful of her present condition. Moses continued to tug on the lead in a futile attempt to regain my attention.

Walker needed chasin, that was for sure, but my injured wife was more important than anythin else. I would love that woman till death took one or both of us and I reckon she knew that full well, but I believe Cynthia also knew in her heart the deep respect I had for her. When she later told me Walker had said he loved her, I knew a man like him could never understand that part of the institution. Love ain't really an emotion, I reasoned out, but a way of livin. Folks who love one another treat each other with honor and cherish em just like it says right there in them marriage vows. Just sayin you love someone don't make it so. She mustered yet another smile and kissed me with some effort on her part square on the lips, finally sayin: "Coswell, would you mind fetchin my shoes somewhere over there in the bushes?"

Now that was a job I figured I could manage successfully and maybe even without the help of my trackin dog. I found em straightaway, lyin there in the leaves and put em back on her somewhat swollen feet.

"Let's see if we can get you up now, darlin. We won't have to walk far. We'll be takin the railcar back to Milledgeville."

Chapter 19

"JESSE, THAT MAN NEEDS KILLIN"

I could see it all clear as day – Walker crashin blindly through the underbrush, one hand shieldin his eyes from thorns and bushes, the other pressin tightly gainst his bloodied side. The bay of the bloodhound that sent him scurryin off must have put a fair-sized knot in the man's tail. After what he done to Sanford, Cynthia and the dogs back there, he knew full well that if Coswell Tims was to be the man found at the other end of that dog's trackin lead there was gonna be hell to pay if we crossed paths again. He rightfully figured to have bought some time what with Cynthia in need of some tendin, but he had to know it weren't gonna be too long a time fore a certain slave catcher from Milledgeville, Georgia would be comin up the road in his direction.

After a short spell the slave trader from St. Louis, Missouri must have slowed to a walk and then to a dead stop. In the early mornin hours, despite the coolness of the day, I figured Walker to have been lightheaded, out of breath and close to exhaustion. He would have been holdin his side since he took to runnin and my guess is the amount of blood that he had lost was more than a passel, drainin his energies and stainin both his clothin and the palm of his right hand...the very hand that had been protected from blood splatter earlier on when he was doin some pretty serious overhaulin on poor Sanford. It was bloody now for sure, but leastways this time it weren't the blood of an innocent individual. I could picture the man in my mind's eye, unbuttonin his vest and pullin his shirt out of his trousers to investigate the extent of his injury. Cynthia knew she had stuck him pretty good, but also knew she had missed the vital organs. Walker weren't no fool. He had to realize he needed medical attention as well as some rest to rebuild his strength if he had any chance to make it back to the safety of his St. Louis farm.

Near as I could reconstruct afterwards, the fugitive must have takin stock of his situation, realizin he had nothin to treat the wound with and no food or water to sustain hisself on the trail. He did have a gun which was secured in his shoulder holster along with the offendin knife he had picked up from where it had fallen from the grasp of the treacherous quadroon. He had four hundred dollars cash-money in his billfold which also contained the original bill of sale for his human property and three returnin train tickets to Memphis, all fairly worthless at the present time. The wealthy slave merchant must have realized that he had few resources to draw upon and was faced with a most difficult situation. Despite that, I figure the man's pride and arrogance, which had contributed mightily to his lofty station in life, might be the very thing to come to his aid again. He weren't gonna let circumstance dictate his fate. No sir... this fella could be more stubborn than a cross-eyed mule, was a heap smarter and, I'm afraid, a great deal more dangerous. I believe that James Walker must have at this very time reached down deep inside hisself and gathered up all the strength he could muster to continue on.

The walk to Gordon weren't long under most circumstances, but with Cynthia leanin on me heavy and the dog still pullin mightily, why it seemed "to take forever and maybe a day or two more," as Mamma used to say. Cynthia apologized repeatedly for bein a burden. She was havin real difficulty seein as that heavy blow to her head had loosened up her legs some and made standin on her own no easy matter. Despite that fact, she excitedly told me several times bout havin stabbed Walker good enough to have certainly slowed him down.

"All that matters right now is you, darlin," I remember sayin several times. "You lean on me and we'll make it back home together, we surely will."

This little walk did give me some time to clear my head on the matter, and as I did, I began to question the wisdom of takin the train back to Milledgeville. Although it was the fastest way to travel, things could complicate up if folks began askin questions concernin Cynthia's appearance. There really weren't no good way of me explainin things, her hair bein cut the way it was, her visible wounds as well as the compromised nature of her clothin. A nosey, but well-meanin neighbor ridin that train could become a problem. They might take to wonderin how all this could possibly have happened, who might have done such a terrible thing to her and why. And of course there I'd be with my trackin hound in hand…all quite a puzzlement indeed. We really didn't need to invite any suspicion or start any gossip that would unravel our little secret or jeopardize our hard-won standin in the Milledgeville community.

Now I did have a fair knowledge of the neighborin town of Gordon, and knew more than a few people who lived there. My trackin business had brought me to that town on occasion and the railroad that connected it to Milledgeville shrunk the seventeen miles that separated the two towns considerable. I remembered that ol man Gibson, a fella I had done business with in the past, had a livery there and I began to think that might provide a less public option for our return home.

It was still early in the mornin when the two of us stumbled into Gibson's Livery. You could hear the sound of horses in their stalls as ol man Gibson had already commenced to workin in a large open space in the center of the shop. I figured that man to be the better part of eighty years old if a day, but he could still tap out a pretty good rhythm on the anvil and could still handle most daily activities of the business. Gibson was bent over a wagon wheel, his bald head reflectin what little there was of the early mornin sun that had taken to comin through the open door. He was coolin off the rim of a wagon tire he had just forged up and placed on the outer part of the wheel. Smoke rizzed up from the rim as the coolin steel shrunk to fit the wooden form. Uninterested in the process, Moses helped hisself to a drink of water from the slack tub. That caught the old man's attention and he stood up straight as his old body would go and took stock of the situation. His eyes went from the dog, to me and then to the woman leanin on my side.

"Looks like you got your hands full here, young fella," was all he said.

On my end I offered up little in the way of explanation other than to say I was workin on an important trackin job and needed a wagon straightaway. The wrinkles in the old man's forehead and the looks he give Cynthia and me said he felt he was on the short end of the information equation, but I told him it was important that things needed to be kept kinda quiet-like for now. Cynthia moaned softly and leaned on me maybe a little more than previous, addin a little more urgency to the matter. Mumblin somethin neither of us could understand appeared to cap the climax, as we both now felt the need to put the unidentified injured woman up into the rented wagon. He suggested it might be wise for her to get some immediate medical attention and that if I didn't mind goin out of my way some, he had his firstborn son outside town who was a right fine doctor and would certainly see to the woman's present condition.

Dr. Thomas Gibson did, in fact, live on a farm on the west side of town and despite my obvious desire to go north towards Milledgeville as soon as possible, I knew the farrier's suggestion to be a good one. I paid him for the loan of the wagon and headed west with Cynthia lyin in the back, covered with a blanket. I would tell you that was one anxious driver that took the reins that day, despite the large hound dog whose look of quiet assurance seemed to preside over the whole affair.

Lookin at the position of the sun overhead, James Walker plotted his course of action. He knew he wanted to go west to try and catch a train at the town of Griswoldville. He had remembered earlier, when he'd first arrived in these backroad towns on his way to Milledgeville, that stop #18 at Griswoldville on his map had come before the one at Gordon where a change of trains had taken place. If only he could physically make it, he must have thought. It certainly hadn't seemed that long by railcar.

After another half hour or so of staggerin west, James Walker fell to his knees and finally, face first to the ground. His energies used up, he found hisself lyin on a deserted dirt road that connected Gordon to Griswoldville. Despite the open road that lay before him, this spot looked to be the end of the line for the wealthy slave merchant. He may have only partially heard the whistle and the noise of the train as passengers headin west passed not a quarter mile from the spot where he had fallen. I'm sure from what the two who found him said that he had no recollection whatsoever of the wagon that stopped to give him a look-see.

When Walker finally opened up his eyes sometime later, he found hisself lyin on a table with the face of an older man with eyeglasses intently peerin down at him. He may have sensed that several other people was in the room as well.

"Where am I?" the slave trader asked.

"You are at the home of Dr. Thomas Gibson," the tall man standin over him answered. "You have these two people here to thank for bringin you here," he said, glancin off to the side of the room.

"Another hour or so lyin there on that road and what life was left would have drained right out of you. These folks would have taken you off to the morgue instead of a doctor's office. I have closed and dressed the wound. You should be all right, providin you get some much needed rest."

"I've got to be going!" Walker shot back as he attempted to rise from the table.

"If you do, you won't be goin for long," the doctor replied, as he put his hand out to halt any efforts in that direction. "Now you just lay back a bit." Motionin off to the side, he continued. "These are the two folks you have to thank for savin your life. They are from the Thompson place and were bringin some fresh vittles into town from the plantation when they spotted you lyin there doin your best to depart these coasts for the great beyond." Two black forms stepped forward.

"This here is Achilles and the big one over there is named Darius." The two negroes stood silently with hats in their hands. Now I am sure it never crossed Walker's mind, or if it did, I'm sure he wouldn't give a lick to know that the purpose behind givin grand names like these to slaves often lay in the subtle humiliation of that individual. It was purposely devised so's to make the difference between great and small all the wider, leastways that's the way I always looked on it. The negro needed to be constantly reminded of his inferiority whether it be with the whip, his marital status or even the name he was given. One name was most often the case for slaves, unlike the two reserved for their white masters...sorta like a fella would name a dog or a horse or some other critter that was to be found out in the barnyard. With Achilles and Darius standin before white authority and introductions a necessity, the difference between the two groups needed to be kept clear and consistent.

The two black men dropped their gaze as they met that of their superior who lay on the table before them. "We knowed yuz was bad hurt, Massa," Darius offered almost apologetically."We knowed yuz needed hep an needed it right quick!"

"Your master will be very proud," Walker answered. "Yes sir, very proud, indeed. Why I just might have to say that if I had the services of two fine servants such as yourselves, I might not have had the misfortune to be lyin here on this table. I will thank your master personally when I get the chance."

With that the slaves was dismissed and Walker lay back on the table. Movin only his head, he began to look round the room as the doc had begun to busy hisself, writin down some things in a ledger as he sat at his large, oversized wooden desk. His black leather bag rested on the floor beside him. It was open with one of them listenin scopes partially hangin out over the edge. Shelves seemed to be everywhere, containin medical bottles and ointment pots. A human skull sat on a shelf on the far wall. Various surgical instruments, some used just recently to patch up a nasty knife wound were to be found on a small, portable table next to where Walker lay. A fair amount of bloody cotton gauze lay in a heap next to the instruments.

"Doctor Gibson?" Walker blurted out. "I do believe you are probably right about my condition. I can barely lift my arms here and I'm clear out of breath from just talking to those two niggers. Is there a place where I can kinda lay low for a couple of days?"

"I might be able to arrange that," Gibson replied, gettin up from his chair and removin his glasses. "Now I noticed your shoulder holster when I undressed you to patch you up...you some kind of law and order fella?" the doctor inquired.

Walker had to think quick on the matter. He knew full well that he was in territory that could prove unfriendly. "My name is, ah, Smith, sir, Samuel Smith," Walker announced. "I...I work for the Pinkerton Detective agency based up there in Chicago. Formed up back in '50, we were. We are doing some work here for the railroad. I really can't disclose the nature of that work but I would sure be obliged if you could get me back on my feet so I can get back to doing my job."

With that, Walker stopped to await a response, quite proud that he remembered the name of a long-dead relative from up New England way and a story he had recently read on the train in a local newspaper bout the creation of that rather new Chicago agency. It had interested him because he thought it had great law and order potential. But what had bothered him were rumors the article had mentioned regardin its founder, Allan Pinkerton, and his association with abolitionists. Either way, that agency would serve the slave trader's purpose this day.

"I really do not have room for you here but I know a place nearby where you can get proper care," the doctor answered. "The Thompson place has a fine sick house on their grounds used mostly for the slaves there, but also used by family and employees. Several plantations in the area joined in to contract the services of their very own white physician who makes the rounds when needed. It's a small but well-kept brick buildin, staffed by darkies who really know their business."

With that, Darius and Achilles were again summoned and after carefully loadin the injured Walker back into the wagon and placin a thin grey blanket over him, the three men set out for the Thompson plantation. As they started on their way, the wind began to pick up some, gently depositin the scent of all three individuals on the ground below.

Another injured party moaned slightly as their wagon hit yet another bump in the road. Cynthia had complained of a terrible headache when ol man Gibson and I had laid her up in the back of the wagon down at the livery and she had soon become unconscious, stirrin round only slightly when the wagon shook. I was terrible worried bout her condition and jumped right out of the wagon without even tyin up the horses when we finally reached the home of Dr. Gibson less than a half hour later. I went in directly, seekin the good doctor's aid and to tell him of his daddy's recommendation to get some immediate medical attention for the injured woman in my care.

Dr. Gibson come rushin out to the wagon with me as we picked up Cynthia and brought her into his office. I held on to her as he pulled off a bloody white sheet that had been draped over what looked to be an operatin table of some sort and, after wipin up some blood that had seeped through to the table with a cloth towel in one hand, he quickly reached into a drawer with the other grabbin a new sheet to take its place. This doctor must be a very busy man, I thought to myself.

"Put her down on the table, son, and let me have a look at her," he instructed. It was probably best that Cynthia remained unconscious as the doctor went to work. After checkin all her vitals and feelin round in all the right places, the doc turned his attention to the nasty gash Walker's pistol had inflicted on her head. With a pearl-handled straight razor, he carefully shaved a little pathway through what remained of her once beautiful long hair, and after dabbin it with some kind of ointment, commenced to sewin. I would have to admit that it made me a might sick and even a little weak in the knees to see that curved needle plungin in and out of Cynthia's flesh. I suspect it had a heap more to do with my feelins for the patient than it did the actual medical procedure, seein as how I had doctored Jesse some time back and experienced no such problems.

"This your wife, son?" the doctor asked, as he continued to work.

Thinkin on the confidential and professional nature of a physician, I replied truthfully. "Proud to say she is Doc. Ain't nothin more important to me in the world than this woman lyin right here." I reached out to touch the side of Cynthia's battered face. "She's been through a lot more than you know Doc," I added.

Doc Gibson nodded as he finished closin the wound and began to peel back her clothin to treat the many other cuts and scratches she had sustained throughout the ordeal. I noticed a heap of bruises over much of her still beautiful and now unclothed body. After cleanin everything up best he could and puttin back on what remained of her clothin, the doc give her some smellin salts which finally brought her head up off the table.

"Coswell, we got to get goin if we're gonna catch him!" Cynthia suddenly blurted out.

"Whooooh! Hold on there, young lady," the doctor responded, as he gently pushed her head and shoulders back on to the table. "I just had a fella in here a little while ago that needed tendin. He was a Pinkerton agent from up Chicago way and he was just about as anxious to leave as you are. Nature needs time to take its course, it does. Wounds to the head or puncture wounds to the chest need some time to heal," he added.

"Who are you?" she responded. Where is my husband? I can't see nothin here in the dark."

"I'm right here, darlin," I said as I reached for her hand. "You mean you can't see me or Doc Gibson here?"

"Oh, Coswell, I think I've gone blind...I know I have my eyes full open but I can't see a thing," she announced with a slight tremble to her usual confident voice.

"Doc, is she gonna be alright?" I asked.

"Blows to the head can have this effect," he answered. "Guess time will tell. My thinking is..."

Suddenly diverted from his medical explanation, Dr. Gibson took notice of a noise outside his office that we both could not help but hear. "What in tarnation is all that commotion out there?" he asked loudly, as he promptly went over to the window to get a better look-see.

I had tied the dog to the front part of the wagon for the trip here, but Moses had twisted hisself up somethin fierce in his attempt to get to the ground. I had heard him stirrin bout for some time, but when the doc and I reached the wagon, Moses was howlin as if he was possessed by the devil hisself. I could not imagine what had sparked his interest like this, but I made numerous attempts to quiet him down, knowin we soon needed to leave for Milledgeville and could not afford any distractions.

"Your dog always this excitable?" Gibson asked, as I untwisted the lead and tried to distract Moses with reassurin words and soft strokes to the head.

"Usually the only time he acts like this is when he's real close to someone he's lookin for…can't really account for this," I added.

I paid the bill and thanked the doc for all he had done. He helped me put the patient back up into the wagon. I would tell ya that dog howled the better part of an hour after we left his office, but finally calmed down as Cynthia and I got closer to home.

Cynthia complained of bein sick to her stomach most of the way and tried to sit up with me on the seat to slow down the dizziness she felt. She said she could make out some light and shade but for the most part was still unable to see. She put her head on my shoulder as we traveled the last few miles back to Briarwood. Made me think of an earlier time when her arms was wrapped tight round my waist as we rode back to New Orleans. There was much unknown then and it appeared there was much unknown this time as well, but in both cases, we did have each other and that was no small matter.

It was late in the day when the wagon finally reached our home on the outskirts of Milledgeville. Although Cynthia could not see the place, she said it had all the feel and smell of home despite the recent invasion and the painful memories it conjured up.

Hearin the approach of the wagon, Jesse come out the door to meet us, happy to find I had brought the mistress of the place home, but I could see by the look on his face that he was more than a might concerned bout her present condition. She did look a sight.

When we got Cynthia inside and laid her down on our bed, Jesse started in askin questions as I went to the back bedroom to check in on Sanford. He smiled broadly when he saw me, reassurin me he was on the mend, and after tellin him bout Cynthia's return, he ignored his own wounds and come right out of his bed to see to the latest casualty in the Tims household.

"Miss Cynthia, Massa Tims done bring you home jus like he promise," Sanford said, as he knelt by her bedside. But as Sanford looked more closely at the woman who lay before him an honest reaction was offered…"Lord in heaven, Miss Cynthia, what has Massa Walker done to ya?"

Feelin for Sanford's arm in the direction of his voice, Cynthia grabbed hold but seemed to look right through him as she responded. "Oh, I probably look a darn site worse than I am, Sanford. Why, once these eyes open up, I'm gonna be just fine."

Sanford took notice of the vacant open-eyed stare and looked over at me for an explanation. I hunched up my shoulders some but said nothin, not really knowin what we could all expect.

We sat and talked for some time, the three of us crowded round Cynthia's bed. One small oil lamp dimly lit up the room. There was much I needed to say and many questions that needed to be asked. Cynthia joined in when she was able.

Finally sleep overtook her and Sanford retired for some needed rest as well. "Jesse," I announced as the two of us walked together into the parlor, "this man Walker needs killin. Now you know I ain't a violent man by nature, but I'm gonna unbutton the man's collar for sure!"

Jesse nodded his full agreement.

"Can you tend to everythin here if I was to leave early in the mornin?"

Jesse assured me that everythin would be taken care of, but thought I should take a quick look at somethin the sheriff had dropped by yesterday.

"The sheriff said it come from the wagon Walker's two darkies was drivin when they was picked up by the pattyrollers," Jesse offered, as he handed me a small leather travelin bag.

I was struck by the weight of it. Openin the thing up, I found two sets of chains…hand and leg irons with keys stuck in em that obviously were to be used to package up Walker's personal property for the return trip to St. Louis. Also, there was some receipts for steamboat and train fares recently purchased and a copy of a local newspaper, the *Federal Union*. Takin a quick glance at it, I was ready to hand the seemingly worthless paper back to my brother when I looked one more time at the page it happened to be opened to and took notice of the headline at the top of the page. It read: *"PINKERTON DETECTIVE AGENCY SUSPECTED OF ABOLITIONIST ACTIVITIES!"*

Now in all my born days I had never heard of that organization till earlier this very day when Dr. Gibson first made mention of it, and now, why here it was again in the newspaper...and a newspaper that belonged to James Walter, nonetheless! I began to think back to what Gibson had said regardin the man claimin to be a Pinkerton agent with a puncture wound that he had fixed up. Did he say that wound was to the chest? My God! My mouth must have dropped most clear to the floor when I finally made the connection. There was more than a little wool pullin goin on here. "***Walker***!" I said out loud. "***It had to be you***!"

My mind began to race. The man must have been there just fore we arrived and concocted this here story to avoid possible detection. Maybe that might have even been his blood the doc had cleaned up from the table. Now I knew what Moses was tryin to tell me. "How could I have been such a fool?" I said again out loud, as I let the paper drop to the floor. "I'm sorry, Moses," I added, turnin towards the dog who sat all by his lonesome over in the corner of the room.

"What's all this bout Walker and what are you sorry for Coswell ...and why are you talkin to that dog?" Jesse added, tryin to make some sense out of all my ramblins.

"Give me a hand puttin a few things up in the wagon for tomorrow, Jesse, and I'll tell you everythin I know," I replied.

Chapter 20

"OVER HELL AND HALF OF GEORGIA"

As mornin managed to find itself yet again, I found myself helpin Cynthia manage the johnny house out back for a necessary early mornin visit. She was apologetic for the inconvenience and felt that she could certainly navigate on her own in the future once she measured out the proper steps in her mind, she had said. Still very much a lady, once she was inside that small buildin, she started in givin instructions not to stand too close to the door and maybe a little hummin or whistlin on my part just might be in order. I have to admit, I didn't feel much like doin any whistlin or hummin at that particular moment. What if the rest of her life had to be spent in this condition, I began to wonder to myself. All the other injuries Walker had inflicted on her would heal right quick and that beautiful hair of hers would soon grow out, but this…why this might just prove to be the permanent signature he had threatened to brand her with back on the trail.

I was not concerned for myself. For my part, if I had to spoon feed the woman or carry her round the house in my arms I would do it for sure. No, I was more worried bout what it might do to her, what it might do to her spirit, maybe wearin her down over time. Bein a slave once more, this time to the darkness, might just prove to be more of a burden than this strong woman could bear.

When we got back to the house, the two of us set down at the kitchen table for some much needed conversation. I told her what I thought needed doin with Walker and how Moses and I needed to be out on the trail real soon if we had any real chance of catchin up with him. As much as she wanted her former master "tended to," as she said, she seemed more concerned bout what might happen to me.

"Oh Coswell, if anythin bad happened to you, I don't think I could live another day," she said. "I know Sanford or your brother would see to my needs even if I was to remain blind, but I don't think life would be worth livin anymore. I just couldn't bear it, that's all."

I told Cynthia how much I loved her and how I felt life without her would affect me much the same way, but I felt the need to say that there was things beyond us (maybe a fair-minded individual would call it justice) that needed to be figured into the mix. Walker needed to get his just comins. I also reminded her that we didn't want him ever comin back into our lives again. The whole thing with this man needed to be settled once and for all. The only way I figured that to be possible, I told her, would be to see him lyin lifeless on the ground before me, his body as cold as an old wagon tire. Cynthia offered nothin further and sat quietly on the other side of the table. I took her silence as agreement for what I had in mind as my hand sought out hers across the table.

A short time later this same woman would manage to stand in the doorway of our home, actin much like she always done when I left to go out on the trail. "Now you be sure to miss me, you here!" I shouted from the wagon, as Moses and I turned the horse and headed back south for the town of Gordon. She waved in the direction of my voice.

"I'll be seein ya real soon," she said. I smiled back as I took her meanin, but I also caught notice of the need for Jesse to help her as she staggered back inside the small farmhouse.

Now I do not believe that Sanford or Cynthia was fablin when they offered up that they was feelin a might better with the comin of this new day. I was encouraged, also, knowin I could count on my brother once again to take care of things while I was gone. How many times over the years had Jesse come to the rescue of his little brother? Too many to count I guess would be a fair answer.

After deliverin up all my heartfelt good-byes, I could now concentrate my efforts on Mr. James Walker of St. Louis, Missouri. As the wagon rolled further and further from the house, any good feelins I may have had regardin my wife, my home, or my brother, began to pass from me. I did not need a mirror to tell me my face was beginin to wear the wrinkles of anger and hatred that were workin their way up from the inside. I could feel the blood risin, my stomach tighten and could sense my eyes squint out and my jaw start to become taut. Now I know anger can be a terrible and destructive thing when it takes hold of a man, but I felt at this moment like standin up before God and all the angels in heaven and proclaimin loud as could be that I craved human blood on my hands… Walker's blood! I wanted to draw the very life from his body. Never in all my trackin days had I ever felt this way. I could almost hear Daddy say: "Son, when a man gets as wrathy as you, why it would be fit cause for even the most well-intentioned Georgia preacher to lay his Bible down!" Daddy would certainly understand my anger and I believe he would be right beside me at this time if'n it was in his power to make that return trip from the grave.

Walker was prey and I was now predator, and his image, why it was fixed right there in back of my head much like I knew his scent was still workin in the nose and brain of my now quiet bloodhound. Moses just set there in the back of the wagon, head a-restin on the front seat next to me, lookin straight ahead. I knew somewhere in that red, wrinkled, beetle-domed head of his was Walker's image. I believe I could even tell what this dog was a-thinkin. "You get me back on that trail, Coswell, and I'll do right by ya," or somethin akin to that. I entered into this imaginary conversation with an out-loud comment of my own. "You're right, Moses, we got some unfinished business to tend to, just you and me!" That large red hound give me a look and a yawn, but then commenced to puttin his chin back on the seat, starin down the road once more, knowin the time for chasin was not yet at hand. A trail of drool on the seat next to me traced his recent head movements.

I took to wonderin if this bloodhound, with worried eyes starin down the road, knew the evil that was in this particular fugitive. I wondered if Moses sensed Walker's part in Cynthia and Sanford's painful situation or took notice of my desperation when we was connected by the thin leather trackin lead. He had to feel somethin different was a-happenin here. He must have felt the emotion or the sense of urgency when we was on Walker's trail. This weren't no "business as usual" trackin job and I'm sure the dog was somehow mindful of that fact.

I thought back to Walker and how I never took a shine to him from the get go. I have come to believe that first impressions are often the most reliable and I knew straightaway that I didn't like the man the moment I met him aboard the *ENTERPRISE*. Now when a bloodhound gets a scent for the first time, he don't go to changin his tune at some future date as to the smell of the individual. No sir... that first impression the dog got was always a lastin one. Walker had left his stench on my life, my home and my family and should pay in proportion to the offences committed, I figured. I had made that promise back at the house and fully intended to keep it. We would start at Doc Gibson's office. He might have a fair idea where his patient was at and if he didn't, well, at the very least Moses could pick up the trail from there and commence to doin what a bloodhound trackin dog was born and bred to do.

As the wagon continued south, I found myself starin out at the trail ahead much like my four-legged companion next to me. I let my mind wander back to the story of another Moses, a man in the Bible that Mamma had told me bout as a child. I guess this Hebrew trailblazer was set on bringin his people out of slavery to some place special, a land of "milk and honey" that God had promised. The journey, however, had its fair share of problems as I recollect. For one thing, his people often did not believe Moses when he instructed em on the proper path to follow. I got to rememberin back to Moses' behavior at Doc Gibson's place earlier on and my failure to recognize its meanin. I figured there was a lesson in that story for me as well.

I also remembered this journey to the Promised Land took some 40 years. Now somebody was either walkin round in circles or back-trackin considerable for that to have ever been the case. I suspect Moses' leadership skills might have been the problem as God had to tell the man he would be denied entrance to that special place even though He said He'd give him a little look-see fore he died. Seemed a pity after all that work and effort, this Moses fella would be brought up short. I fully expected my Moses to finish the job and be able to enjoy the fruits of his labors. I would never allow this bloodhound that final kiss, however, not after the run-in with Big Sandy. No sir, I would not make that same mistake twice.

It had been the better part of two days and Walker could feel his strength returnin. Despite bein in rather close, cramped quarters with some of them shiftless, black no-accounts he often said made up the plantation workforce, an older negro woman had tended to his every need, makin his stay not an unpleasant one. The doctor had put in an appearance on the mornin of the second day as did the master of the plantation, Colonel William Thompson shortly after. All were glad to see he was makin such fine progress. Despite that, I knowed that slave merchant might just have got hisself a bad case of the bum fidgets whenever the plantation dogs would start in a-barkin. Large plantations like the Thompson place often had their own kennels, tended to by the slaves themselves. Dependin on the number of runaways a plantation might experience in the course of a year, havin their own dogs could prove a financial advantage. Can't say that I knowed of a plantation or farm, large or small, that didn't have problems with runaways at one time or nother. That's just one of the facts of life in the south that made pattyrollers necessary and kept private contractors like the Tims brothers in business.

Now everyone knows that a bloodhound takes to makin a sound like no other dog. It ain't really a howl like a wolf or a bark like a dog, but it would be more of a mournful, drawn out wail made with the thick lips of the hound set in almost a perfect circle. As a neighbor of mine once said bout his bloodhound he called Big

Red..."His voice maybe weren't on the perfect 'C', but more like a deep basso profundo," which, if I catch his meanin clearly, must've referred to opera singers or folks that take to the stage for a livin. With the dog's large, deep chest and long and wide snout, I figure them things all combine to make this very distinctive bell, or bay as it's sometimes called. I have often thought it was most as if nature had conjured up some kind of furried four-legged wind instrument. During his stay Walker must have spent some time intently listenin for this music, and when he finally did hear Moses' familiar song comin up the road, I'd be willin to wager it sent shivers down the whole of his spine, maybe even forcin the man from his sick bed to the window for a proper investigation.

If that was the case, I reckon he would have spied one large, tawny colored bloodhound in the back of a wagon, sniffin the air, howlin on occasion, and a man next to him holdin tight to the reins, shotgun laid up against the front seat. If he saw all that—the wagon, the dog, and this trackin man—then he full well knew their intended purpose. I believe it was at this time the fella started to run.

Doc Gibson's directions had led us to the Thompson place, savin us valuable time. I guess Moses and I may have looked a formidable sight as Walker hastily dressed, put on his shoulder holster and hat, and quickly exited the buildin. In a panic, he headed for the stable where one of the black attendants greeted him.

"Mornin, Massa Smith," the attendant said. "It is fine to see yuz up and bowt dis mornin."

"I need a horse!" the slave trader shot back.

"Massa Thompson don't say nothing bowt no hoss, Massa."

"Do not argue with me, boy," Walker said as he drew his pistol from the holster and ordered the bondsman to saddle up a horse for his immediate departure.

The negro's eyes growed wide with fear but he did take notice of a slight tremble in the hand of the still recoverin white man makin the demand. The negro began to weigh his chances of overtakin this Mr. Smith and possibly gainin some favor with his master. Stealin a horse from Massa Thompson, Pinkerton agent or not, was not somethin that would be tolerated. Horse stealin, the negro knew, was akin to stealin other valuable property, two-legged included, and the punishment would be very severe. However, given the uncertainty of things and lackin the resolve needed to accomplish such a task, the black servant relented. Walker soon found hisself on horseback headed for the Griswoldville train station and the safety of the iron horse that he hoped would begin his successful return to his St. Louis farm.

"Why, yes, we do have a gentleman here…recoverin from a knife wound, he is. Been here a couple of days," Colonel Thompson replied when asked bout any recent visitors.

"I'm doin Doc Gibson a favor by housin him. The doc's done right by me and my people and I didn't figure this here would be any problem. You say he ain't a Pinkerton, but a fugitive with a price on his head?"

"That's a fact!" I responded, despite the fact that I had muddied up the truth some. "I can think of three or four people that would give all they have in this world to bring this low-life scoundrel to account and one of em would surely be me."

Just as I was bout to have the colonel show me where Walker was put up, a tall negro rushed hurriedly into the house. "Pardon, Massa, pardon, but Massa Smith done took one da hosses from da stable and lit out!"

With that, the three of us rushed over to the stable which was just a stone's throw from the sick house where Walker had spent his last two days. Moses had become quite interested in all that was goin on and asked to be let down from the wagon to get reacquainted with the fleein quarry. The wag of the tail and the lowerin of the body as he frantically searched the ground told me there was no doubt the scent remained all too familiar. On command the big hound dog jumped back up in the wagon, but he stretched his neck out and put his nose up in the air as far as it would go so's the fugitive could get further review. Colonel Thompson asked if there was anythin he could do but admitted that most of his men were in the fields with the workers and they could not be organized any time soon.

"I'll add you to the list of folks that want to see this fella get what he deserves, Colonel," I offered as I got up in the wagon. The plantation master nodded in agreement and wished me well as Moses and I drove out the front gate, in a race to catch a rider and a stolen horse I knew full well was headed for the Griswoldville train depot.

Now that town of Griswoldville is small for sure, but was once described by a railroad traveler as "the prettiest town on the Central line and a handsome and thrifty little village." I guess that would sort of match the personality of its founder, one Samuel Griswold, a Yankee from Connecticut who sold his cotton gins in town. Bein an ambitious man of business, Griswold expanded things to eventually include a foundry, smithy, a gristmill and a soap factory. Houses was built up for family and workers, slave quarters was in abundance long a stream at the southern edge of town. Griswold hisself lived in a fine home just south of the tracks and, make no mistake about it, it was them tracks, this railroad, that give life to this little factory village.

As Moses and I reached the Griswoldville depot, I could see the large water tank and the huge piles of wood that lay in readiness for use on the line. A pile of rail sidin lay off near the track. The stolen horse stood alone, hitched to a post outside the depot office. I was not surprised as there had been little doubt in my mind this was just where Walker had been headed.

Leavin the dog tied up in the wagon for the moment, I took my pistol from its holster and cocked back the hammer as I walked the short distance towards the depot office. Walker's horse whinnied as I brushed by him, alertin the ticket master inside. Unarmed, the man put his hands to the air and felt the need to yell out: "I will tell ya mister there ain't nothin worth stealin in this here office!"

"I'm sorry to give you such a start," I answered in reply, holsterin my Colt as I come through the door. "I'm lookin for a man recently rode in here and left that horse that's hitched up outside."

"The man your talkin bout left on the train for Atlanta maybe twenty minutes ago," the ticket master answered. "Said a man would come by later for the horse. Maybe you're the man he was talkin bout."

"Well I might be the man he figured would show up here, but

I don't believe it would be for that reason," I answered back.

"He sure was a nervous fella. Seemed to be in a real hurry and was powerful glad when I told him the train stop was a short one… had a return ticket, he did."

"I would ask if the man favored his right side some?"

"I believe he did. He seemed most out of breath when we was conversin and I saw him fairly collapse in the seat when he finally got aboard. I figured something weren't right with the man."

"Oh, I will tell ya for a fact that there's somethin ain't right with the man. From my experience, I can tell ya that for sure," I added in, reviewin a list I kept updated in the back of my head. "When is the next train makin this same journey?" I inquired.

"Oh, be along in bout two hours time," the ticket master answered.

I bought a ticket and walked back to the wagon. We had no other choice but to wait. Gave me some time to hire a man to take Colonel Thompson's horse and my wagon back to the plantation. I figured that was best as I had no way of knowin how long Moses and I would be out on the trail.

I sat down on a wooden bench next to the tracks and got to thinkin on bloodhounds and how one had once followed a cold scent after some two weeks and another that had stayed on a trail for some 150 miles, both with good results. Yes sir, these dogs were the stuff of legends and I was confident I had me one that was as good as any of the best that ever was. I knew Moses was equal to the task as he lay quietly beside me as we both waited patiently for the next train.

I also at this time got to thinkin bout that scent Moses still had up his nose. It crossed my mind that it would have made more sense back at the house when Cynthia was stolen away, to give the dog her familiar scent instead of the stench of the slave merchant. I began to wonder bout that. Could I take that to mean that at the time I was more intent on revenge than I was in gettin my wife back safe and sound? If I had me a clear-cut choice at the time twinxt gettin Cynthia back unharmed with no Walker to be brought to account, would I have wished for that over me havin the satisfaction of killin this man but maybe have my woman bad-hurt in the process? Of course my wife's safety was the most important thing, I come to figure, but it was a fact that Walker's image never left my mind. I knew Moses weren't concerned bout such things as I reached down to stroke the big red hound. I also knew he weren't, any time soon, gonna turn loose of that scent he had up his nose neither.

I could the well imagine Walker at this very time on the iron horse, settin all by his lonesome maybe near an open window. As the train rumbled on, I'm sure he barely took notice of the towns of Macon and Griffin passin by as he most likely was deep in thought. He knew I would be comin after him, but by the time I caught up, he must have figured all his resources could be turned out to meet any threat that might be comin his way from just one man walkin behind a single flop-eared hound. Yes sir, he had to believe things was turnin his way once again. It was true that he would not be returnin with his stolen property as he had originally hoped, but Walker must have felt pretty fortunate to be returnin at all, given all that had happened. I could see him clearly, leanin back and maybe closin his eyes, confident he could now rest easy while the train carried him west towards the Mississippi port of Memphis. The *ENTERPRISE* would be waitin there and would take him home at last. As he set in his seat, I could imagine Walker resistin the urge to put his hands up behind his head to stretch out. A painful reminder in his right side told him not to get too comfortable.

Two hours later, a north-west bound train arrived at the depot right on schedule. Moses and I boarded that train, only to have the conductor threaten to banish the dog to the baggage car. I insisted the bloodhound would have to stay by his handler.

"This here dog is goin bout lawful and official business," I had said rather forcefully. "He needs to be right here with his master for justice to be done," I added. Moses was allowed to stay, but I don't think there was a passenger in that car besides me that was happy bout the situation as the slobber and stink of the hound moved a boodle of folks from offen their seats.

That dog spent a good deal of time at open windows, reviewin the air on both sides of the railcar. He would put his large paws right up on the window ledge and then stick his quiverin nose out to get the latest report on the fugitive. Now I don't believe there is anyone alive who knows how a bloodhound could detect a person under these here conditions, but they can and I would not be afraid to swear in a proper court of law that I have witnessed it myself.

I leaned back in my seat. Walker had a little more than a two hour head start on us and we needed to make up the difference. Fate may have favored the slave trader up to this point, but I really felt in my heart that his luck was goin south despite the northerly direction of his train. I started thinkin back to all I had known regardin this man, with none of it bein good. What I had seen with my own eyes and what Cynthia had told me would often set my teeth to grindin. Somethin Sanford told me some time back regardin Walker also come to mind which did nothin to improve on his reputation.

While workin for the man down in New Orleans, the *ENTERPRISE* had just recently docked and Sanford said he was tyin a rope line round a post on the wharf when a darkey come runnin by with several white folks close at his heels. They was all yellin "Stop the nigger! Stop that nigger, he done stole the meat!" Most out of breath the slave answered back. "I never stole nothin!" as he plunged head first into the water to avoid his pursuers. Sanford said he disappeared into the muddy water but soon come up under the bow of the *ENTERPRISE*. Walker, Sanford said, was standin on deck, lookin out over the whole affair, most likely wonderin what all the commotion was about.

"Get a pike-pole from the railins there and fish him out," Walker finally ordered after assessin the situation. "And if he don't come out, then drown him right were he is." Several attempts was made, Sanford said, to grab on to the slave's clothin with the hook at the end of the pole, but when that proved too difficult, the young negro, despite his protests of innocence and his pleadins to let him talk to his master, was pushed under and hit on the head repeatedly whenever he attempted to rise. Finally, a lifeless body was brought up from the water onto the deck where a few of the white folks kicked it some to see if the slave was playin possum. Finally satisfied that he was dead, Walker ordered the body to be tossed over onto the dock where he said it would be picked up by the mornin trash wagon. Sanford told me that body laid there the rest of the afternoon and throughout the night with nobody cept the flies payin much attention to it. Round nine o'clock the next mornin the body was picked up, throwed in with the trash and in short order was covered with dirt and other debris that had been cleaned off the streets.

"Don't this just say what James Walker is all about?" I asked myself as I reflected on that story. This is the way he treats people, all people and it really don't matter what color they be. Why he stole a horse just a while back from a white man that had shown him nothin but kindness and helped him to get back on his feet. I'm of a mind that Walker must have cheated his business partners whenever he had the chance. No sir, there was no honor in him t'all...he was as crooked as a barrel of snakes. I felt deep down inside that fate must soon abandon this evil man.

Atlanta, Allatoona and Dalton was all short stops on the way, but Chattanooga was where Walker had to change trains, fore goin down into the Tennessee River Valley west toward the Mississippi River. He didn't see this as much of a problem as he knew his pursuer would have to do the same. There was one thing, however, that Walker had not considered, not bein from these parts, and that was the spring rains. They could be a real problem this time of year as much of the area was quite low in nature and floodin often resulted. Although the weather was clear as the train come to a stop at the Chattanooga station, passengers was told the bad news...the typical April floodin had indeed occurred, threatenin some of the tracks on the way to Decatur. Passengers was advised to find an alternative route if they wanted to pick up the train again on dry ground west of that town. A riverboat would be the best way to go, they were told, as the risin waters made their passage all the easier. As luck would have it, Captain Charles Pell stood ready to ferry train passengers down the waterway on the newly launched sidewheeler the *HUNTSVILLE*, a vessel of some 500 tons. Captain Pell must have run out the gangway and I can't imagine it was very long fore most of the newly arrived railroad passengers had exchanged their seats on the train for ones on board the paddle-wheeler.

Now these here steamboats are an interestin thing to consider.

Not particularly well-built, they most likely wouldn't last ten minutes on the open sea, but served folks well on rivers, movin large amounts of both cargo and passengers from place to place. They come in many sizes, some with as many as three or four decks, some with stern paddles and others that was paddled from the side, but generally they all tended to be flat-bottomed, shallow-draft affairs with a pilot house lookin down over the whole of it. All had a pair of tall smokestacks to keep the sparks away from passengers and cargo. Now I could not say how long these ships stayed afloat, but my guess is that most did not fare very well. Newspapers always seemed to be filled with horrible stories bout steamboat tragedies. Aside from their poor construction and the great weight of the boiler and the wheel causin problems, they had to navigate rock reefs, gravel bars, log snags and rapids in the rivers, avoid collisions with the shore and other boats, and watch that the boiler don't explode when the engineer tried to balance off the steam. Then again, there was also the ever-present danger of flyin sparks from the smokestacks which could start the whole thing ablaze. I figure it is no wonder that riverboat people are the most superstitious folks I've ever met up with.

Now I always believed that superstition had a lot to do with how much you felt you could count on the way things would turn out. If a man was pretty sure how things were progressin, he wouldn't be doin any of that fancy mumbo-jumbo stuff. But you put someone into a position where the outcome was uncertain, why he'll be throwin salt over his shoulder and carryin rabbit feet round in both his pockets for good measure. Maybe that is why I seen entire steamboat crews suddenly turn their backs to the shore when settin out so's to keep the good luck inside the boat. Why, old riverboat people have been known to search for hours lookin for an unlucky cat that someone thought they saw come aboard. Of course everyone knew the worst and most unlucky thing you could ever have on board a steamboat would be a red-headed woman...or a preacher ...or for that matter, a white horse. I guess all was equally offensive and potentially dangerous. I heard tell of one sternwheeler a few years back that had an unfortunate accident where they found afterwards that all three of them highly offendin parties had been aboard. I guess they all had to agree that with that much bad luck on board the outcome was never in doubt, but then they started up a fiery debate as to which of the offendin parties was MOST responsible!

I wondered what effect an evil slave trader from St. Louis would have on things when we got the news in Atlanta bout passengers switchin to riverboats after the train reached Chattanooga. That telegraph sure could come in handy as some folks got off at Atlanta and went their own separate ways. It didn't change my plans none. Be it train or boat, I would stay right behind the fleein slave speculator.

Comin aboard the *HUNTSVILLE*, I can't imagine it took long for the white fugitive to settle in. After payin the eight dollars for cabin fare, Walker would have retired to his private cabin to rest for a spell, most likely still feelin the ill effects from the stabbin. As I imagined him gently rubbin his injured side he must have thought hisself lucky to not be below in steerage with the cargo. Despite the reduced fee totalin but two dollars, them folks down there had to supply their own meals and beddin and deal with the crowded conditions. Slaves in makeshift pens would also add to a person's discomfort. I figure Walker would have thought hisself above all of that, in more ways than one. Things would and should be provided for him. Life had taught him it was only natural and right for it to be that way.

I know James Walker's main concern at the moment must have been any lengthy delay the boat might encounter which would bring his pursuer ever closer. As he looked out the cabin window, he most likely could see that most of the train passengers had already come aboard on the moveable landin stage, his best guess bein that the last of the cargo would soon be put on the main deck. After only what seemed like a few minutes, he would have heard the throaty, long sound of the boat's steam whistle, knowin they would soon be makin nough steam to be gettin underway. I could just see Walker noddin his head and smilin over the whole of it.

Moses put his nose to the ground as soon as we got off the train at the Chattanooga depot. The large animal began to pull hard on the leather lead, givin every indication he had more than a fair idea where he was goin. We did receive more than a few stares from curious people as we headed in the direction of the docks. I knew my pistol was visible despite the long coat I wore, and with the shotgun that rested on my shoulder, well, I reckon folks must have rightly figured we was lookin for someone on the run. I'm sure they probably assumed it was a nigger we was after. I can't imagine anyone would be guessin the fugitive to be a wealthy white man who had legally tried to get back his stolen property.

I give very little thought to the matter, as crowds of people mingled bout. Passengers comin and goin, porters movin cargo and baggage. Freight lay all about on the docks. Moses paid no attention to the lot of it.

I had hoped that Walker could be within our grasp if his ship had been delayed here for some reason, but Moses soon come to the edge of an empty wharf and looked dejectedly out over the river. Realizin the inevitable truth of the situation, he sat right down and cried he did. His mournful howl carried out over the water, knowin full well our quarry at the moment was beyond his reach. I certainly shared his feelin of disappointment and thought I'd like to join in the cry myself, but instead I took to questionin a young man movin freight about the dock.

"Excuse me, young fella. Could you tell me the name of the steamboat was just docked up here?'

"It was the *HUNTSVILLE*, mister, left a few minutes ago. If you were supposed to be on it, you didn't miss it by more than a whisker, if that makes you feel any better," he reported

"Don't make me feel any better t'all," I replied, "but thank ya kindly for your concern."

Large steamboats like the ones you would see on the Mississippi River found it most difficult to operate on rivers like the Tennessee, but packet ships of some 500 tons or less like the *HUNTSVILLE* could navigate from Chattanooga all the way down to Muscle Shoals near Decatur, exceptin maybe durin the driest months of the summer. One thing this river did have in common with most rivers, even the larger ones, was a fair number of other types of craft also found on its waters.

Boats called "lighters" were to be seen in abundance. They was flat-bottomed pole-pushed affairs that was used to lighten a load when steamboats run aground, somethin that happened quite frequently. "Rafters," now there's another type of river craft, steam driven they was, and small, usually under 100 tons. They could be used as tow boats or do the job the larger steamboats could do only carryin limited amounts of passengers and goods. What I thought was important to my circumstance was that these here rafters was often faster than regular steamers and might be just the very thing to help us overtake Walker. I spotted just such a vessel not two hundred yards from where Moses and I presently stood on the wharf.

The rafter *ANNIE B.* was piloted by a man named Harrington. In fact, he and his brother, I found, had earned a right fair livin since comin down from the Ohio, ferryin people and cargo along this waterway. The boat was white in color, light and small, but you could tell right off it was of sturdy construction. Been round awhile, I figured, but looked to be agile and fast. Moses and I come aboard.

"Well now, that's a mighty big dog you got there," Captain Harrington said as we crossed over the gangplank. "My guess is he's lookin for somebody and I hope it ain't either one of us!" he said, smilin and lookin off in the direction of his older brother who stood nearby.

"You got nothin to worry bout if you're law-bidin people," I said.

"My brother and I are honest businessmen and I would challenge any man that said otherwise," the older one replied rather aggressively as he stepped forward to head up negotiations.

I explained that I would like to enlist their services, trailin and overtakin a boat that recently left this very dock. They knew the *HUNTSVILLE* and her schedule and felt they could be of service but the older Harrington who looked to be rather slippery, said the price could become a might high. I told him I'd give a hundred dollars that I had with me and another hundred which I could get to him after we had intercepted the *HUNTSVILLE* and I took care of some unfinished business on board. I told him I didn't think the whole thing would take up much of their time.

Now I know that people that are in the bargainin business often look for desperation on the face of a man, so I guess this older Harrington fella read me pretty good and thought he could press his advantage here. "Five hundred dollars," he shot back, "or this boat ain't leavin the dock!"

"I made you a fair offer," I countered. "I expect that it will be honored."

"Five hundred dollars and that's right now," he answered back. "And if we keep on arguin, that price is goin up for sure."

Now I had never done nothin like this in all my born days, but with all the purpose and passion of a desperate man bout to lose his elusive quarry once more and maybe for the last time, I pulled my knife from its sheath and with my other hand quickly reached between the legs of this man's loose fittin trousers, grabbin on to what I knew he would consider precious cargo. Holdin the sharp knife to his manhood, I continued negotiations.

"Now that was a fair offer I made and I expect it will be suitable. Otherwise we are all goin to be takin bets as to whether or not these things presently hangin here will float atop the water. Do you take my meanin?" I added, as I gave the whole affair a little tug.

I guess it's true what folks say that when a man is led by his ballocks, his heart and his mind will be sure to follow. I could see his brother off to the side squirmin round some and I knew as a more fair-minded individual he was on board with the proposition. The older brother needed very little further persuadin to see the logic of the matter and the lines was soon cast off and the paddles set in motion. The knife was returned to its sheath, the hundred dollars passed from my billfold to his and the paddlewheels, turnin slowly at first, began to turn faster and faster as the ship left the dock and headed out into the river. The *ANNIE B.* was soon steamin at top speed with its two officers, a single passenger and one big hound dog standin full on his hind legs with paws on the railin...all four of em with the wind in their faces and breathin in the late afternoon air.

Chapter 21

"THE COST OF DOIN BUSINESS"

It had to be gettin on supper time when we first caught sight of the *HUNTSVILLE* shortly after a sharp bend in the river. Captain Harrington said the steward would have most likely called supper by now on the second deck and the first class passengers would probably be settin down in the elegant white dinin room with long tables and fancy furnishins to a right fine meal of wild turkey or venison. After supper, he said, the tables would be cleared and dancin and other merriment would take place. I could not picture Walker takin part in such festivities, but I knew when we did eventually come up alongside, any information regardin his possible whereabouts might prove helpful.

James Walker must have felt much better after the hearty turkey dinner with all the fixins…so good, in fact, that he decided against restin in his cabin and took to the lounge instead. The lounge was above the dinin hall with a great view out over the bow of the boat. Drinkin, smokin, gamblin, and for some folks just plain socializin was all in order.

Walker soon set down at a table with several other men after askin in to a poker game. He fancied hisself a fair player but one did have to be real careful on riverboats as professional gamblers were common and could honey-fuggle a man out of his boots and gallowses in the wink of an eye. Yes sir, a man could soon find hisself walkin round with bare feet and nothing to hold up his britches in pretty short order if the cards didn't turn his way. As was often the case, watches and jewelry was soon throwed into the pot by others and, sure enough, after several hands Walker's unexpected run of bad luck made it necessary to go into his coat pocket for the funds needed to continue.

"These are two of the finest niggers I have ever had and I would use them as collateral," he said as he tossed down a bill of sale for a quadroon named Cynthia and another for a young boy named Sanford. "She's a fine looking wench and would make a good breeder and the young boy is smart as a hooty owl. Yes sir, I would be willing to wager them against their cost, and they didn't come cheap, I will tell you that." I guess Walker figured he could still get some service from those two renegade slaves with the other players at the table bein none the wiser.

"Keep the dog with ya and don't stray too far," I shouted to Captain Harrington as we come up long side the *HUNTSVILLE* and I mounted the railin, readyin myself up to jump aboard. Some of the passengers on the packet had taken a keen interest in the fast-closin rafter and had moved to the side of the upper deck to get a better view. They hadn't seemed too alarmed at the chase as captains on the river often made a pastime out of racin and showin off their navigational skills, but they thought different, I guess, when it looked like I was fixin to leap from one ship to the other. I could see em pointin excitedly and talkin to one another.

I knew Moses wanted to go with me, but I turned to him and offered up a little apology. "I'm sorry, Moses, but I guess this be bout as far as you go." With that, I readied myself to jump from the railin of Harrington's craft which they had so expertly positioned next to the packet. I figured the Harringtons had now taken a keen interest in my little mission here and the older one bore me no further grudge. Course, the hundred dollars they was still owed give some assurance that my dog would not be harmed and I would have a place to return. I knew full well leavin him there just bout broke his heart and it did momentarily put me in mind of that fella in the Bible. Maybe God didn't intend it to be that way, either. Could be it was just circumstances that was the cause. As I leaped to the other vessel, Moses took to registerin his protest with a sorrowful howl that made me wonder if Walker just got some early notification of the Algerine who had just stolen aboard.

I landed on the deck, jarred me some it did, but got my feet up under me and went on to investigate the new vessel. It was quite fancy, much smaller and much cleaner than the one that had once held Cynthia and Sanford, but I did notice a slave pen that had been set up on the lowest deck, much like it was on the *ENTERPRISE*. There was maybe ten or twelve darkies huddled inside that pen, most likely recently sold off to new owners whose plantations or farms must have been located down river. No one was tendin em at the moment but they showed no signs of goin anywhere. I also took notice of a long black bullwhip, coiled up and hangin on the outer side of the wooden gate to the pen. Made me shudder as I thought back to the whip I had tossed aside just a short time ago, swearin an oath to never to hold one of its kind in my hands ever again. It also brought to mind that fella Long down in New Orleans with his strange need to have a whip in his hand at all times. "Major Long would have never left his whip like this," I said out loud to myself. Whoever the owner or slave driver was, I figured he must have had a strong need for whiskey or maybe he was lonely and required some company up on one of the upper decks and just left the whip in the area where it most likely would be needed at some time in the future. I would soon come to realize that this man's opinion on the matter was much more practical than either Long's or mine.

I ascended the stairs, guesssin that Walker and probably a fair number of passengers would be somewhere in the upper levels of that boat. I give the dinin room a quick look-see, but there were only a few passengers there, not what Harrington had led me to expect. I continued on up to the third deck lounge, figurin the man I sought would either be in that room or off in one of the first-class cabins which flanked its three sides.

I could hear someone playin a piano as I brushed myself off and lowered the brim of my hat some, slowly enterin the smoke-filled room. It was a large room for sure, quite elegant, most like I would imagine a palace to be. The floor was carpeted with a fancy velvet pile and gold-colored draperies hung down on the walls over the doors to many of the first-class cabins. Them cabins had fine doors made of rich polished woods and they surrounded every wall of that deck cept'n the windowed one towards the bow. What was left of the day's sun poured through those windows, illuminatin the activities of all who was gathered about. I was struck by the large number of people in this room…must have been all of two hundred or so passengers this packet boat could carry. Some people was movin bout with drinks in their hands, smilin and talkin to one nother, while other folks was sittin in lounge seats and chairs listened intently to the music bein played out on the piano. Everyone looked to be havin quite a time of it. Riverboat companies, I am told, count on the passengers passin their time away nightly in just this fashion and often figure to make more money in the lounge than in collectin fares or haulin cargo. With whiskey at twenty cents a drink and a five course meal to be had for a dollar, the five or six hundred passengers on a large steamboat could certainly ante up quite a sum in just this area alone.

My eyes scanned the room lookin for Walker. Despite the fact that many of the people watchin the piano man had their backs to me, I figured Walker's form or maybe his familiar movements might catch my eye, but I saw nothin. I listened to bits and pieces of many of the conversations that swirled around me, but I did not hear his lofty, high-handed voice anywhere in the crowd. I began to think that if I had only brought my dog aboard, Moses would just ignore the smoke, the noise and the other distractions and walk right up and introduce hisself to the man in question. I had made that earlier decision, however, and knew at least for the moment I had to abide by it.

Uncertainty began to creep into my mind again as I began to imagine that Walker just might be nursin his injured side in one of the many cabins whose doors was visible but remained shut insurin the privacy of the occupants. Investigatin each and every one could prove to be rather bothersome and certainly a time-consumin task which might just require the use of the dog after all. But, before I went too far off in that direction, I began to take stock of a fair number of small round tables that was set up in the middle of the room. Folks was playin cards there, maybe four or a half dozen to a table. I come to imagine Walker's arrogance leadin him to believe fortune might just favor him at such an activity and I thought there might be a fair chance he could be seated in that area.

Excited that the odds of findin him might fast be improvin, my eyes began to wander purposefully back and forth over the card-playin passengers. For some unknown reason I stopped when I saw a puff of cigar smoke that rose heavy over the head of one man facin in my direction, whose face remained partially hidden by the playin cards he held in front of him. Even though I could not make him out, there was somethin quite familiar in the way he moved his head and hands. He appeared to intently study his cards, as I did him, only to at last lay em down on the table before him. I could sense that my eyes must have widened and then started to squint out when I recognized the face. He pushed some of the money he had piled up in front of him towards the center of the table and then sat back puffin one more time on that cigar of his. There was a satisfied smile upon his face. The man had all the look and confidence of a winner. I knew him all too well. He was James Walker of St. Louis, Missouri.

After havin lost four hundred dollars early on and usin the only resource he had left which was two worthless bills of sale for two slaves he no longer owned, Walker had managed to get back on his feet and then some. My guess was that he may have even been feelin a might better bout the unfortunate knife wound he had received as well. Walker most surely had the uncanny ability to recover from misfortune and always end out on his feet despite the height of the buildin he was throwed from. Now generally speakin, I would admire that in a man, but I knew Walker and knew full well the lowly purposes to which he was so inclined.

I set my mind to reviewin the last few days. I had trailed this fella through the woods, chased him with a wagon, followed his train from Griswoldville to Chattanooga and jumped aboard a movin steamboat goin down the Tennessee River, all in an attempt for the two of us to get reacquainted. Up till this very moment he had managed to stay safely out of my reach, but there was a long overdue conversation that needed to soon begin. We would have to discuss the dogs I found shot dead out behind my home and his part in it. We would have to discuss why he took no pity on a young boy, whippin poor Sanford within an inch of his life. An explanation was in order as to why this man felt he had the right to take my wife from my side, takin her to hisself, so to speak, an accountin in any man's book that would go way beyond explanation or apologies. And, of course, the injury he had inflicted on Cynthia that might just doom her to a life of darkness, needed to be tossed into the general mix as well. No sir, this here discussion weren't likely to be had with many words, I thought to myself, but I had no doubt Walker would soon come to know my meanin.

It had been a long trail for sure, and there he sat at last, not twenty feet in front of me, unaware of the danger that had stolen aboard. He was quiet at the moment and so was I, maybe it was the calm before a storm as someone might have said. As I reviewed in my mind the items for discussion one last time, I could feel the blood rise up again inside me, causin me finally to reach for the pistol holstered at my side. That long overdue conversation was about to start.

"James Walker, you are a dead man for sure!" I shouted out, as chairs and tables went a-flyin and people began to scatter. I had left the scattergun back on the rafter as I thought carryin it might make it more difficult to jump aboard the larger vessel. I fired my Colt twice at Walker at point blank range, but I'll be black dogged if he didn't turn the table over in front of him quick as a cat with them bullets wedgin deep into the wood, sendin splinters off in all directions. I caught a look at his backside as he turned and run passed the frightened piano man, who sat dumfounded on his little stool, unsure of what had just happened. I do believe I would have shot Walker right in the back at that very moment with but little twinge of conscience. Of course I can't be completely sure on that point as I had never shot a man in the back before and then tried to sleep peaceful later on. I was certain-sure that I did not want any of the folks that had taken to runnin back and forth shot accidentally… there was enough innocent people, black and white, been hurt already, I noted.

He reached the grand staircase and I took to followin him up the carpeted stairs to the hurricane deck above. He fired his pistol off as he reached the top step, but it was shot in haste, and was well wide the mark. He continued to run out on to the open deck as people sought cover. When I reached the top of the stairs I saw Walker briefly and fired at him but heard the bullet ricochet harmlessly off the side of the pilot house, that structure that looked protectively out over this little island that seemed to float free from the rest of the world. It got the captain's attention for sure and I saw the uniformed man duck down below the open windows for protection. I could sense Walker was hidin in that general area, and as I was bent over and goin cautious, Walker fired again, this time bout endin the earthly days of Coswell Tims. I would have to say that the lead object that I heard pass by my head was so close, why someone from the lounge would have had a hard time puttin one of them playin cards sideways into the space between.

Walker fired again and run, this time for the back staircase with me closin quickly. As he begun to descend, (probably to the main deck where cargo and clutter would aid his cause) I heard him yell: "Get out of the way!" to a passenger who had the misfortune of bein in the stairway same time as him. Pushin the man violently aside, as Walker so often done with people who got in his way, the fella took to rollin down a flight of stairs, comin to rest at the bottom of the second deck. Following with gun in hand, I stepped round the poor fella as I descended.

Walker ran out on to the main deck. I saw him maybe thirty feet ahead and shot once more but the slave trader's luck held as he ducked behind several bales of cotton he had found just in time. Them 500 pound bales made for a fine defense as Walker peeked out from behind and returned fire. I found one of them massive smokestacks just in time, usin the thing as a shield as the bullet ricocheted angrily off the plate metal. I fired back and Walker took to runnin once again, this time towards the bow of the boat, after dischargin his pistol in my direction one last time.

As I continued the chase, I started in thinkin bout the gun the man had. The sound of it and the fact that Cynthia said he had it in a shoulder holster made me think it was a small affair, most likely a five shot. If that was true and my cipherin was correct on the number of times Walker had fired it, he might just be out of ammunition at the present time. There would be no opportunity for puttin in new powder, seatin the lead balls and addin on the explosive caps to the nipples round the cylinder. I had fired five times by my calculations and my .36 caliber Colt would have one more shot left which I figured would be reserved for a very special occasion. Normally folks will put in five instead of six shots into a pistol such as mine for safety reasons, but somethin told me that day to fill all six chambers just for good measure. I have come to learn from sad experience that a man needs to listen to any voices in his head if and when they make the effort to speak up.

People had made every effort to clear out of the way as the chase had continued throughout the boat. No one, not even the captain, had made any attempt to interfere. I did get the feelin, however, that the steamboat was comin to a stop, probably so's the captain and crew could determine the full extent of the commotion.

As I closed the gap between us, Walker turned suddenly as he reached the bow, aimin his pistol again in my direction. He pulled the trigger only to find that his gun had indeed been fully emptied as I suspected. I slowed to a walk and then finally to a full stop as the space between us had now, after all this time, shrunk to just a few feet. The chase was over and this conversation now needed to end. Face to face, with the two of us still breathin hard, Walker stood up straight and dropped the empty pistol to the deck, seemingly resigned to his fate, knowin what the consequences of that empty gun would be. I raised up my arm, aimin my revolver directly at his head but lowered it to his chest as thoughts of Big Sandy mangled skull crossed my mind. I chose my last words to Walker carefully.

"This is for all the misery you brought me and my people and for all the pain and sufferin you caused so many others that had the misfortune to cross your miserable path in this here life," I said in bout as high a moral a tone as I could muster. Doin what I thought was God's work, I drew back the hammer and quickly pulled the trigger before thinkin any further on the matter. I could not believe it! Instead of the loud detonation of powder and shot and the recoil of the pistol to boot, an empty sound, a mere click was heard. This here gun had never misfired in all the years I had owned it! Why in God's name would it not fire now, I wondered, as I pulled the trigger once more which met with the same result.

One thing about this man Walker...he certainly knew an opportunity when it come his way. Quickly, he reached inside his coat and brought forth the knife that had shared a place next to the now worthless pistol that lay at his feet. He started in towards me, well aware that the odds had now swung from the slave taker to the slave trader.

"I am sick and tired of bein chased like some nigger by you and your dog, Tims. I'm gonna carve you up like I should have done to that little bitch of yours when I had the chance back out on the trail," he said as he held the knife menacingly, movin it around in small circles. I backed off, tryin to think on some way to counter the attack I knew was soon to come.

That knife was certainly a devilish lookin affair. It drew to mind what Cynthia's thoughts were when it lay close to her throat that day on the trail, and I certainly knew what it had done to Walker when my woman drove it deep into his side. Suddenly the slave trader thrust that same knife in my direction. I stepped to the side, hopin it had missed its mark. A quick look down told me my coat and shirt was torn some, but I could feel no pain. Blood, however, did start to come from my side but I still felt nothin...had to be just a scratch, was my early thought on the matter. I took off my coat and wrapped it round my left arm, hopin to ward off any further blows to vital areas. Walker swung the knife wildly at my face so's to bring my now protected arm up and when I did, he dropped down and drove the point of that dagger right up between my ribs. I felt every inch of that cold steel enter my body. I knew for a fact this time it weren't no scratch!

Walker stood over me as I fell to one knee. To say I was feelin a might poorly would, I suppose, be more than a little shy of an understatement. I looked up to see a triumphant gleam in the man's eye. He began to circle round me like a bandy rooster, ready to finish off what was left of the likes of Coswell Tims. I did not know how much strength I still had left inside me, but as I rose to my feet to meet this one last challenge, I figured the best thing to do was to skedaddle off as best I could. Stumblin along, I headed for the darker quarters of the lower deck. As I looked quick over my shoulder I could see Walker slowly trailin behind, brimmin with confidence as he stalked his wounded quarry. He knew full well that both advantage and time was on his side.

Without a weapon or somethin to defend myself with, I knew I had very little chance to survive this day. It almost seemed funny or odd in a way that I now shared the same wound as Walker (and from the same knife as well), and was runnin from a determined pursuer just as he had done a short time ago. Life sure can take its share of strange twists and turns, it can. An odd thought crossed my mind that maybe I weren't much different from this man I hated when all was said and done, and, as I staggered by the slave pen I caught sight of that whip that hung on the gate. I got to figurin that if that were so, then I certainly could be every bit as resourceful as the man behind me.

Now I know I said after seein the condition poor Sanford had been left in that I would never touch a whip again, but I have to admit that object looked to be quite invitin, just a-hangin there on that nail the way it was. As I grabbed hold of it, the object uncoiled like a deadly snake in my hand. I give some thought as I looked at it that it may have been a little premature on my part to have taken that earlier oath. Maybe it really weren't the whip itself that was evil, I began to think, but the intention of the man who held it. I was different than Walker, for sure. I had no doubt I was made of better stuff. This whip could be used for good, I concluded, kinda like a school master might use such an instrument on an unruly child in an effort to learn him up a valuable life-lesson or two.

To tell the truth and shame the devil here, it ain't braggin to say ol Coswell was quite good with a whip despite my reluctance to use it in my chosen line of work. Jesse and me used to practice out back of his house when we first went into the business. We would take to hittin cans and bottles, sometimes tearin up a bedsheet or a bale of hay. I never got as good as ol Jeremy Prigg who could take an object clear out of your hand without so much as leavin a scratch, but I knew if I had the strength to lift it up and let it fly, I stood a pretty fair chance of doin some serious damage.

"Where are you, Tims?" come a voice I could sense comin closer and closer. "You are a poltroon and nothing more than a briar-hoppin cracker that don't know his proper place in this world... and you're a nigger-lover to boot. You come out here like a man so I can remind you of some things you seem to have forgot or maybe your daddy never bothered to teach you."

All was quiet for a spell when out from the shadows the long black whip snapped angrily, catchin Walker full on the shoulder, bitin through his clothin. The surprise caused him to drop down slightly most as if he was tryin to gather time to review the situation in his mind and determine what had just attacked him so's he could give a proper response. It took some effort on my part, but I brought the whip back again and sent it off in his direction once more, this time catchin the man full up behind the neck. Walker now knew his enemy to be a bullwhip...an instrument he knew only too well. After all, this was somethin he had held in his white hand many a time as a slave speculator and slave master. I'm sure Walker never imagined for one minute the amount of pain that could be inflicted by the lash, havin never enjoyed the opportunity of bein on the business end before.

The whip from the *HUNTSVILLE* slave pen cracked once again and this time it brought the white man straight up as it tore into his face. He let out a gasp as the pain of this blow seemed to take all the air clear out of him. As his eyes and mine were now adjusted to the dimmed light of the lower deck, he looked at me in disbelief, the knife still in his hand. His coat and the cloth that lay beneath were now shredded from the blows, his hat lyin on the deck where it had fallen from his head. Blood was comin from his neck, stainin his white shirt and fancy tie which had come undone. I took great delight when I noticed the man's collar was unbuttoned. The negroes in the pen had all gathered round and were all quietly standin, shackled together right up close to the pen railin lookin on with eyes full of wonder, most likely tryin to figure out what further devilment was to be found in the world of the white man.

Walker began to measure his chances and took suddenly to runnin the very way we had come, back towards the bow of the steamboat. I began to follow him slowly, not so much out of confidence as he had done just moments before, but more on account of my recent injury. I hoped I had enough strength left in me to finish the job.

We both were able to reach the bow of the boat. I noticed the steamboat now lay completely still in the calm waters. Once there Walker began to move back and forth like a caged animal. He was trapped and he knew it. This conversation was movin right along, I thought to myself, but he said nothin to me and I returned the favor.

Now it's a fact that when a man raises up a whip and sends it off in the direction of the intended target, the loop gets smaller and smaller, increasin the speed at which the end is travelin. Why, by the time it hits its mark, I suspect it is movin hundreds and hundreds of miles an hour. I guess the thought of bein struck one more time with that painful, fast-movin thing was more than the slave trader could bear so when I raised up my arm to strike, Walker took to the water, surfacin almost immediately directly under the bow of the *HUNTSVILLE*.

I stepped forward to the very edge of the bow and saw him there beneath me. He bobbed round some fore I come to realize the strangest thing. Despite his many talents for survival, why my God, this man had never mastered the fine art of swimmin!

Walker was flounderin and sputterin, reachin out for help. He knew he was in death's watery clutches, I could see it in his eyes. Sometimes, maybe most times, a man can sense when his life is near an end. "Maybe your daddy should have taught you how to swim," I muttered at last, admittin to takin a certain delight in the remark.

"Help me, Tims," he sputtered, tryin to stay afloat. "You gonna…you gonna…let me…drown right before your eyes…when you know as a fellow human being you could have helped?" he managed to say between the coughin, sputterin and tryin to take in air. For an instant our eyes met once more. Maybe this man knew me...

knew the decency to which I was inclined, or maybe he was just hopin to luck up with the request. I remembered back to lookin into Big Sandy eyes and how I went on to regret my part in his death. I knew what I had to do. I knelt down on the deck and holdin the railin with my left hand, I held out the handle of the whip with the other near the water as far as it would go. "Grab it, man," I yelled. "Take hold!"

Not questionin, Walker eagerly took up the offer. As the slave trader pulled the leather object tight, I could sense him measurin his newly improved chances. I could see his eyes reflectin a new-found glimmer of hope. One more time he might beat the odds and rise to the top. I pulled him partways out of the water and up towards the safety of the deck but then found myself givin out, and at the end of my strength, I felt the whip begin to slip from my grasp.

"You son-of-a-bitch, Tims!" he sputtered as his head momentarily dropped below the surface of the water only to reappear briefly. His eyes had growed fearful once more, somethin I had seen many times with runaways or animals that was backed into a corner and knew they were soon to breathe their last. His arms began a-flailin in final desperation and I found it quite interestin that the whip he had so eagerly sought still remained tightly in his pleadin hand. Exhausted and breathin hard myself, this time I made no attempt to interfere.

Maybe this last minute flounderin with the whip was his attempt to beat the water into submission and get it to relinquish its claim on his miserable life. After all, that approach had always served the man well before. But nature is nature and water, after all, ain't no peculiar institution. Heavy objects just tend to sink less there be a persuadin argument to the contrary. I guess my adversary here just hadn't stated his case forceful enough, I concluded, as the man slipped beneath the watery surface for the last time.

I noticed it got real quiet all of a sudden. It come to my mind that the devil just may have slipped in and silently claimed hisself another prize.

After all that had happened tween James Walker and Coswell Tims, I half expected the man to suddenly rise up to the surface and once more renew our epic struggle, but at the present time I could see only bubbles comin from below. Tiny and too numerous to count, they was the last of the air or anythin else this slave trader would take from this world. I admit to givin a sigh of relief when I realized this man's takin days had finally reached an end.

As the last of the bubbles burst on the surface, I looked into the now clear, calm water of the river and got quite a start when I happened upon my own reflection. Why there he was, none other than Coswell Elias Tims of Milledgeville, Georgia and that ol slave catcher was starin right back at me! There was the fella I had to live with when all was said and done. At the end of the day I had to fit inside that very man's skin. The reflection seemed to be awaitin an answer to one important question. "Was your strength really all used up, Coswell, or did you just use that as an excuse to drown your fellow man like a farmer might drown a litter of unwanted critters he found hid up in his barn?"

I had no honest answer at that moment, but knew I would be givin it further review at a later time. When I did that I would toss into the mix that whatever might be the case, it was Walker's doin and no one else's (with my injury and all) that caused my strength to be unequal to the task.

Finally, when I regained the moment I glanced over my shoulder only to realize that many of the passengers had gathered around who had witnessed part or all of the entertainment Walker and I had provided. Violence aboard riverboats was commonplace and was often overlooked by local officials. But then there was the first-class passengers lookin down from the lounge, crew members standin bout, and passengers that had been in steerage on the main deck, all lookin to me, I figured, for at least some kind of explanation as to what they had just seen. I stood up good and straight, wincin some, and took off my hat so's they all could get a good look at me. With hat in one hand and the other at my injured side, I cleared my throat so's to be able to speak up loud and clear. "I would tell you all that I am a trackin man by trade and have chased this individual for longer than I care to remember," I said as I lowered my head to take in a much needed breath of fresh air. "He was slippery as he was evil and I would also tell you what a fine preacher back home once proclaimed from high atop his pulpit. He told his congregation that

"***The Wages Of Sin Is Death***" and I don't believe truer words was ever spoken. I want you to know that what you just witnessed here was as natural as the sun risin up in the mornin. Folks always get what they deserve, sometimes sooner, sometimes later, but a day of reckonin awaits us all and you can make book on that."

The passengers remained silent with some heads noddin in slight agreement as I put my hat back on my head, and with more than a little effort bent over to pick up my pistol from the deck. I staggered towards the side railin where a boat with an anxious hound dog awaited my return. I looked back at the passengers one last time fore crossin over and thought back to that big set-to I had with Big Sandy some time back. I had learned a valuable and painful lesson that day.

"This Here's The Cost Of Doin Business," I blurted out loudly. A few murmurs was all I heard in reply. Probably most folks never took my meanin, but the lesson weren't lost on the likes of ol Coswell. Just as Daddy used to do once a week down there with his ledger in the blacksmith shop…life's really all bout balancin up accounts, ain't it?

Moses licked my hand when I crossed over to the *Annie B.* "We got em, boy, we finally got that son-of-a-bitch," I said, as both my hands worked over that large wrinkled-up head of his. That dog was powerful happy to see me and he did forgive me for leavin him behind back there on the boat. Now if a man was to press me on how I come to know such a thing, I would have to say that I have learned over the years that there ain't nothin more honest in this entire world than the wag of a hound dog's tail. That's a fact. There is just no way a man can ever mistake the meanin.

"What do you say we go home for our milk and honey, Moses," I asked, as I felt the *ANNIE B.* began to pick up steam. "We got family waitin on us."

Moses, he didn't answer me straightaway, but soon took to waggin that big red tail of his one more time which told me he was on board with the proposition.

AFTERWORD

Some three days later, Walker's body floated to the surface of the Tennessee River just south of the city of Chattanooga. I remember readin a newspaper account of the event one evenin to Cynthia as the lot of us…ol Jesse, young Sanford and even our prize hound dog Moses (who had temporarily been liberated from his pen out back cause of his recent heroic deeds) had all taken to settin round a comfortable warmin fire that was set to blazin on the hearth.

Life had seen fit to grant us a little reprieve and we was all startin to nestle in once more, glad after what we had been through to still be alive and fortunate nough to be back together in the relative comforts of our home. Despite recent injuries that had surely left their mark, we was all more than a might grateful for the many blessins that had come our way. There was no doubt many dangers still lurked bout Briarwood what with the constant worry over our little secret leakin out and the changin political climate that saw the risin threat of civil war, but we hoped with Walker's death to have maybe gained some much needed space to take in a welcomed breath or two.

Walker's demise and his soon to be forgotten earthly remains spoke to us loud and clear on the changin nature of life itself. It all seems to dangle by a tiny, fragile thread which fate might see fit to pull apart at a moment's notice. I reckon a man does need to worry about how he lives his life as it was pretty obvious here that he could be taken away suddenly and maybe leave things undone. I knew there was a lesson in here for me as well, and further review of my current line of work might just be required in the very near future.

I read the article in the newspaper out loud with great conviction, with even the dog showin more than a passin interest.

"An unidentified white man was found yesterday by two negro boys playing along the river. The body was bloated, making the individual hard to recognize. The person in question could only be identified as a middle-aged man of some means, well-dressed, who was wearing an odd shoulder holster under his coat. No weapons were found. His billfold was empty but multiple train tickets, impossible to read, were found inside. A leather whip was partially tangled about his right arm. With the swelling of the body and the shrinkage to the leather whip, it became impossible to pull one from the other without great difficulty and authorities said they will not attempt to separate the two.

"It is thought the man in question may be a riverboat gambler down on his luck or a transient of some kind. The individual may have been a victim of foul play if the whip was not his own and authorities said damage to his clothing was done before the river claimed his life. Due to lack of identification, the body will be buried in an unmarked grave in the old pest house cemetery on the outskirts of the city unless someone can come forward to identify it."

As I finished readin the piece, I looked up to see unashamed grins on the faces of all assembled…not exactly what you would generally come to expect when hearin news of a man's earthly demise. I will have to admit a little smile come to my face as well. That whip that Walker wanted so bad there at the end…why, wasn't it a fact that the man got his wish just like my daddy said a fella might? Also, ain't it quite something, when a body thinks on it, how that bill of sale Walker had for his human property (listin him as owner and that he'd been so quick to give up in the poker game) might just have been the very thing that give him a fair chance at a proper burial?

It seemed somehow fittin that Walker should lie in relative obscurity like so many of the nameless and unfortunate souls he had trampled over durin his lifetime. One thing for sure, none of us here would be rushin back to Chattanooga any time soon to help solve this mystery and give James Walker any proper or decent send off.

Cynthia looked over in my general direction. "Coswell, what do you suppose will happen to Walker's farm up there in St. Louis?

"Don't know, darlin. Why do you ask?"

"Well, I'm thinkin that with all the whiteness Walker felt so free to spread around, it might just end out with someone other than a white man runnin the place. Wouldn't that beat all to think that if all hands could keep quiet bout their peculiar circumstance and the property be properly tended to, why there would not be a soul any the wiser, would there?" she concluded.

All heads nodded in agreement.

I reached over and took Cynthia by the hand. It was small and warm to the touch and fit perfectly in mine just like when I come to first hold it. "I'm glad you ain't up there in St. Louis, whether Walker's dead or livin," I felt the need to say.

"I'm right where I'm supposed to be, Coswell," she said lookin off in the direction of my voice. "Ain't nothin Walker or anyone else could ever do could change that," she stated firmly with a smile comin to her still bruised and battered face.

Now I reckon this little tale would be somewhat unfinished if I failed to mention what exactly had happened to Cynthia upon my return. I was not sure if that blow Walker had inflicted would leave her blind till the end of her days and if that was so, maybe destroy the woman's will to live. She may have had it in her to overcome such a thing. I ain't sayin she didn't, but I have to admit to bein worried, worried sick in fact, bout her condition when me and Moses headed back home after my set-to with Walker.

The Harringtons had done a respectable job of doctorin me up with bandages round my chest to stop the infernal bleedin, but I did notice the older one give me a painful little tug as they was finishin up, maybe in payment for an earlier tug I done give him. I did get the feelin we was all square after that and didn't bear the man any further grudge. Life, after all, is all bout balancin accounts, even if it was me at the moment happened to be down on the narrow end of the horn.

To finish the story here, I remember I had took what remained of my worthless coat and throwed the tattered, bloody thing into the river as I boarded the *ANNIE B.* and set out for home. I must have looked quite a sight what with the bandages and all, but I never got a single complaint from my four-legged companion who never strayed from my side.

We took the train the rest of the way and I found myself thinkin of little else but Cynthia and givin her the good news on Walker. I hoped and prayed she had some good news for me as well. Nevertheless and notwithstandin, I admit to bein fully prepared for the worst when Moses and me finally come on Briarwood.

Tyin up the horse I had rented down at the train station livery, I couldn't help but notice the smoke comin from our chimney stack and this time it give out that same comfortin smell it most always done. It seemed to be sayin whatever waited for me inside would be somethin all in this house would be able to find the strength to abide.

I remember as I come through that familiar door, I give out with a holler. "Cynthia, where are you girl?" I paused briefly.

"Now where you at, I got somethin right fine to tell ya?" I added.

There was still no answer. I can't say that was very reassurin thinkin back to recent events. I called out yet again, but this time in a much calmer voice.

To be truthful it was Moses, settin right there next to me that laid eyes on her first. The dog's tail told me she was now to be found right there in the room as it took to waggin back and forth and then slappin hard against the wooden floor. I saw Cynthia's form slowly emerge from the dark back hallway. Oh, I had come to know that form only too well over the years. The former slave and now wife of Coswell Tims walked purposefully forward into the light where I got a good look-see at her once more. Why any plain-thinkin individual could see she still had all the grace and dignity of a person born of high station, despite any and all attempts made over the years by certain folks to claim otherwise.

Now had this woman "measured out all the proper steps" I thought to myself, or had those eyes of hers finally opened up?

"Coswell," she blurted out. "What in God's name has happened to ya and why are ya'll bandaged up like that?" she shouted out as what looked to be tears began to swell up in those blue-green eyes of hers and she hurriedly rushed the last few steps into my arms.

ACKNOWLEDGMENTS

This book is the result of circumstances and situations, chance meetings and purposeful encounters. Numerous people along the way deserve credit, adding their pieces in making *The Slave Catcher's Woman* a reality. The bloodhound that my wife Georgia Lee and I bought back in 2004 started it all, initiating research into the breed which resulted in the discovery of the bloodhound's significant role in the antebellum slave catching business. Thank you, Molly, for leading us down this trail.

My many friends and colleagues in the "hobby" of Civil War re-enacting, particularly fellow re-enactor John Callahan gave me early encouragement to develop a unique character that no one else to our knowledge had ever attempted to create...a southern slave catcher, complete with bloodhound tracking dog. With that idea in mind I began to build the persona of Coswell Tims, checking historic accounts and seeking advice from John's wide range of expertise regarding clothing and accoutrements of the time. Pat Caudle, another Connecticut friend of mine who originally hailed from North Carolina, helped me with a workable southern accent. After almost two years of study and practice, my first public performance as Coswell Tims, Georgia slave catcher extraordinaire, took place on September 30, 2006.

It was apparent from my early research (even before the positive feedback from public appearances began to make it quite apparent) that I was on to something quite remarkable with Mr. Tims' story. I remember saying to myself many times over as I uncovered more and more interesting historical information for use in the program... "My God, I never knew that," or "this is great stuff, I wish I could fit it all into a one hour presentation." Eventually I concluded there was a book here that just had to be written.

The person I am most indebted to is historian Hugh T. Harrington of Milledgeville, Georgia. Our encounter started innocently enough as I realized that the character of Coswell Tims had to reside in an appropriate location around which the story could be realistically developed. Milledgeville had been the early capitol of the state of Georgia right up through the Civil War, so I decided it would be a good setting. Mr. Harrington had written several historical books about the city and I was happy to find he was quite approachable as a historic resource. We remain good friends to this very day.

Hugh helped me immensely, making suggestions on the storyline as well as commenting on the geographical and historical elements it contained. The anecdotal stories of local Milledgeville residents he had featured in his own books quite naturally began to find new homes in this one. Hugh also enlisted the aid of a well-known historic re-enactor from the area, Ms. Anne Burgamy, who supplied further credibility to the authenticity of the story. Hugh, his wife Susan, and Anne, were gracious hosts on a trip I made to Milledgeville in the recent past to complete the work. Thank you for opening up your homes and hearts to this inquiring and needy Connecticut Yankee.

Mark Hogan, a high school English teacher with whom I taught for many years, did much of the editing of the early draft. John Geida, a talented editor, put the final touches in place. Richard LaPorta and his staff at Husky Trail Press thought enough of the story's educational and historical message to embrace the manuscript and transform it into the book you have before you. I will always be indebted to them.

Erin Doherty, a High School student in Connecticut (where I still teach after 47 years) also needs to be thanked for adding her artistic skill and imagination to the numerous illustrations that are sprinkled throughout the book. The cover is also her work.

I also want to credit the following non-fictional sources as they added greatly to this effort. Hugh Harrington's three books...*Remembering Milledgeville, More Milledgeville Memories* and *Civil War Milledgeville* were very valuable sources as was *Milledgeville: Georgia's Antebellum Capitol* by James Bonner. *Everyday Life in the 1800's* by Marc McCutcheon and *Whistlin' Dixie: A Diary of Southern Expressions* by Robert Hendrickson helped give the work its flavor. *The New Complete Bloodhound* by Catherine Brey and Lena Reed and *Bloodhounds* by Kim Thornton, along with *Hunting and Home in the Southern Heartland* by Archibald Rutledge (edited by Jim Casada) provided some of the bloodhound and tracking details. *The Very Worst Road* by Jeffrey Benton and *The Federal Road* by Henry Southerland Jr. and Jerry Brown gave a great deal of insight into the journey over that early mail route that both main characters traversed in the book. *Beautiful Crescent: A History of New Orleans* by Joan Garvey and Mary Lou Widmer provided valuable information on that city. *Slave Patrols* by Sally Hadden, *The Slave Catchers* by Stanley Campbell, and *Runaway Slaves* by John Franklin and Loren Schweninger offered insight into the flight of slaves with *The Slave Community* by John Blassingame, *Within the Plantation Household* by Elizabeth Fox-Genovese, *The Peculiar Institution* by Kenneth Stampp and *Roll, Jordan, Roll* by Eugene Genovese contributed a great deal of information on the institution of slavery itself. *Bullwhip Days: The Slaves Remember* edited by James Mellon and *Voices from Slavery* edited by Norman Yetman, along with *The Slave Narrative of William Wells Brown* were also very helpful in understanding the victims of this American tragedy. *Defending Slavery: Proslavery Thought in the Old South* by Paul Finkelman and *Myths and Realities of American Slavery* by John C. Perry allowed this writer to better comprehend the thinking of those who upheld this most egregious institution. My goal from the beginning was to understand all those involved in order to provide a balanced and honest account in the telling of a story which took place at that time and in that place. I would like to believe the voice of slave catcher Coswell Tims provided me that opportunity.

ABOUT THE AUTHOR

James N. Littlefield has taught history in Connecticut schools for 47 years. In addition he writes a monthly history column entitled "History Matters," which captures the importance history has played over the years in family life. Jim and his wife, Georgia Lee, have restored two homes from the pre-Civil War period, each with an accompanying blacksmith shop where Jim has worked at the trade. He is a member of the Connecticut Blacksmithing Guild. This is Jim's first novel.

The Littlefields participate in Civil War reenactments where Jim has portrayed a blacksmith and a disabled Civil War veteran. Most of his presentations now center on Coswell Tims, who inspired the writing of *The Slave Catcher's Woman*.

ALSO AVAILABLE

A list of questions that can be used for discussion, dialogue and debate is available at the following website:
www.JimLittlefield.com/questions

The author is available for organizational and school presentations and may also be contacted at his website:
www.JimLittlefield.com

Comments regarding the book are most welcome.

CPSIA information can be obtained at www.ICGtesting.com
Printed in the USA
BVOW01s0519171013

333982BV00003B/9/P

9 781935 258155